SHERLOCK BONES AND THE SEA-CREATURE FEATURE

SHERLOCK BONES

AND THE

SEA-CREATURE FEATURE

RENÉE TREML

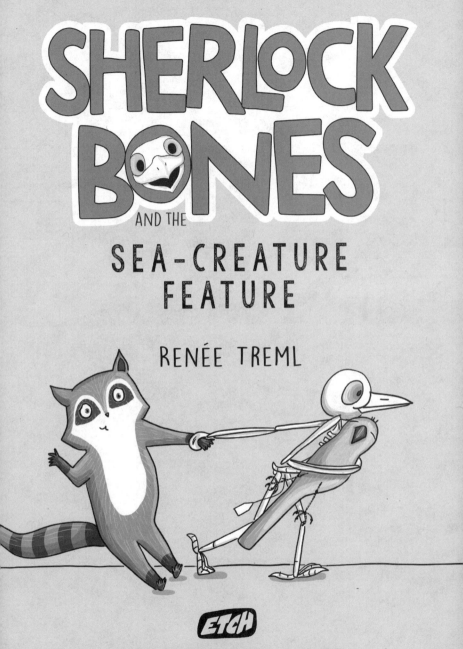

ETCH

HOUGHTON MIFFLIN HARCOURT

Boston   New York

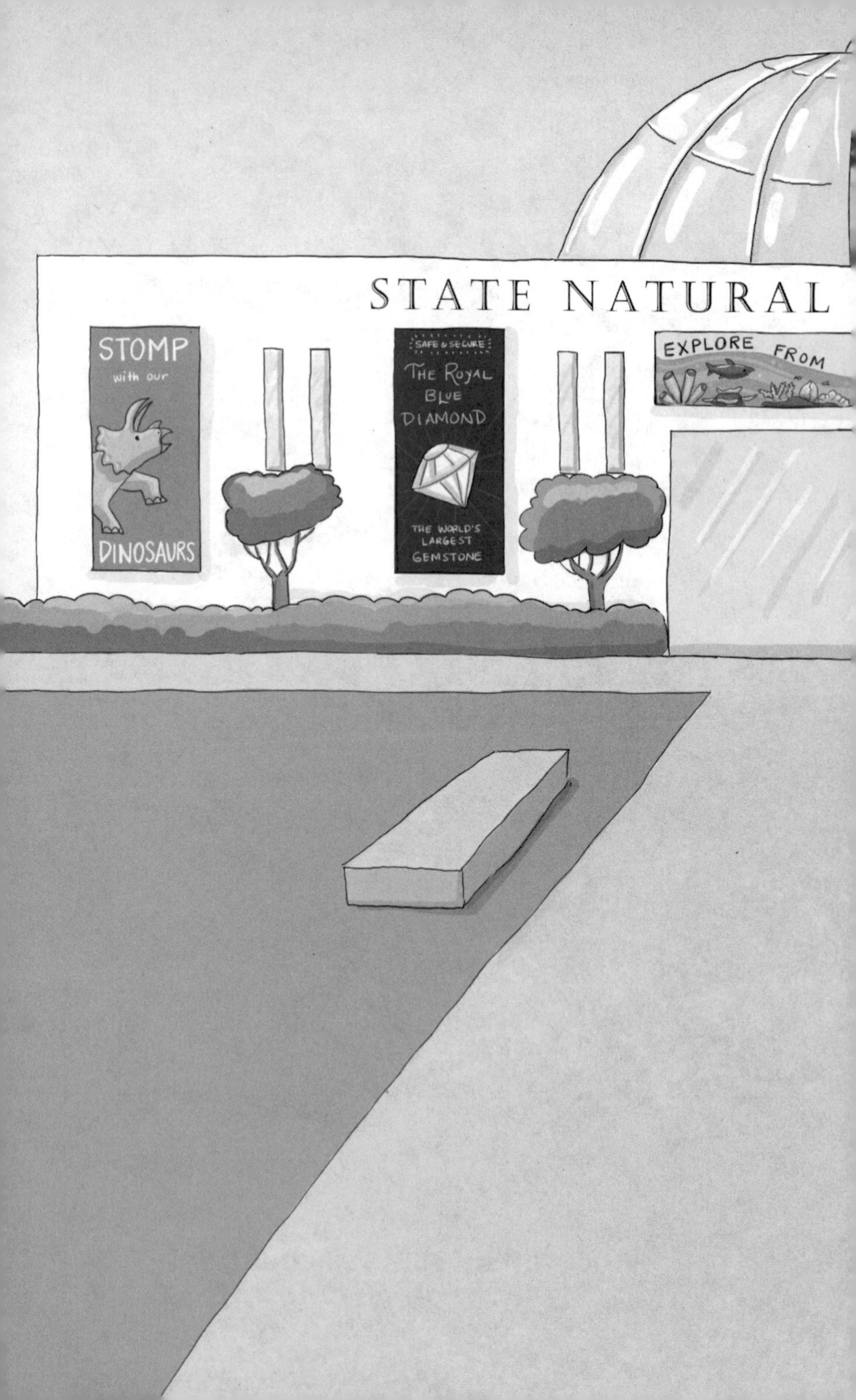
STATE NATURAL
STOMP
with our
DINOSAURS
SAFE & SECURE
THE ROYAL
BLUE
DIAMOND
THE WORLD'S
LARGEST
GEMSTONE
EXPLORE
FROM

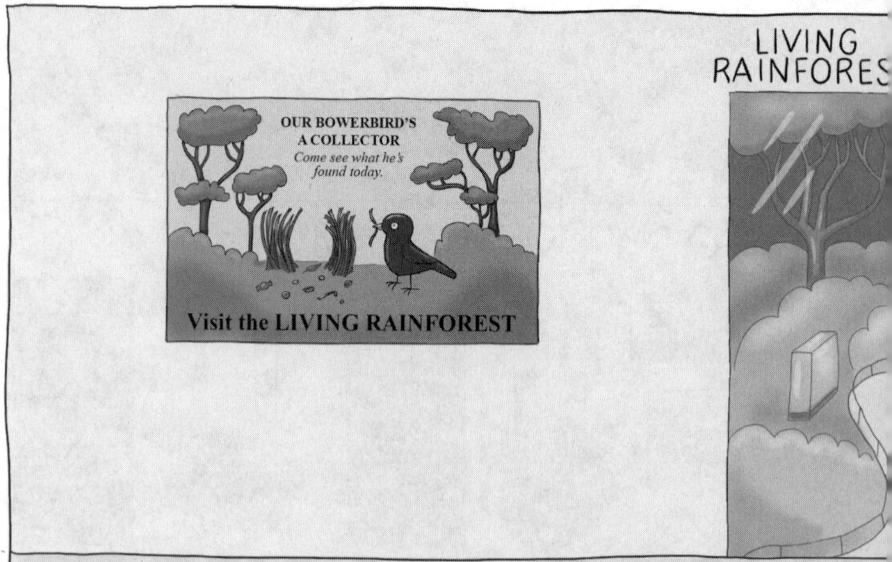
OUR BOWERBIRD'S
A COLLECTOR
Come see what he's
found today.
Visit the LIVING RAINFOREST
LIVING
RAINFORES

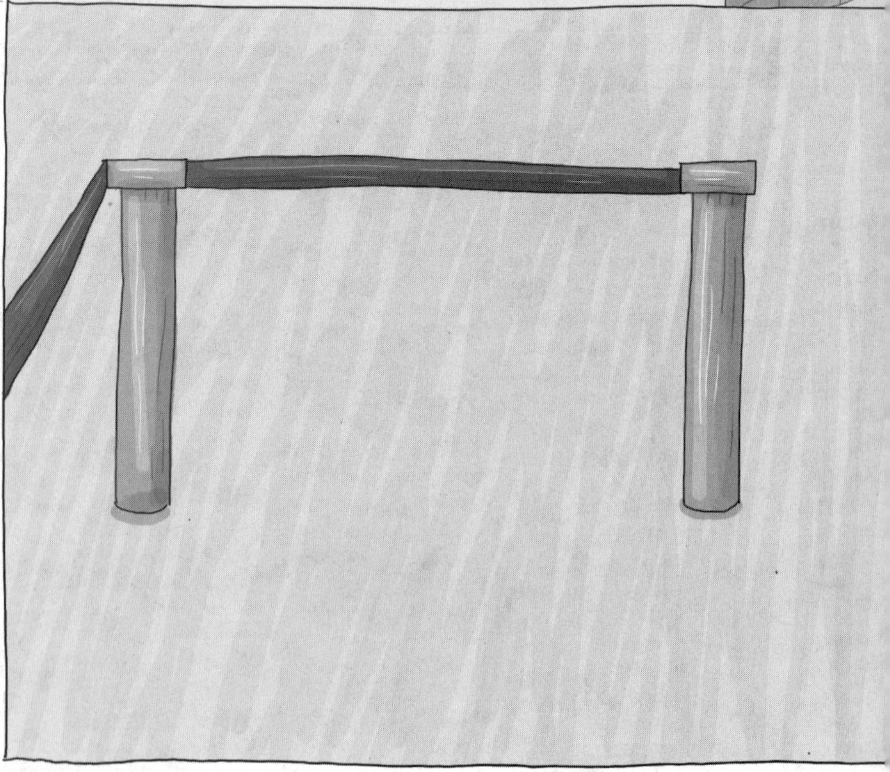

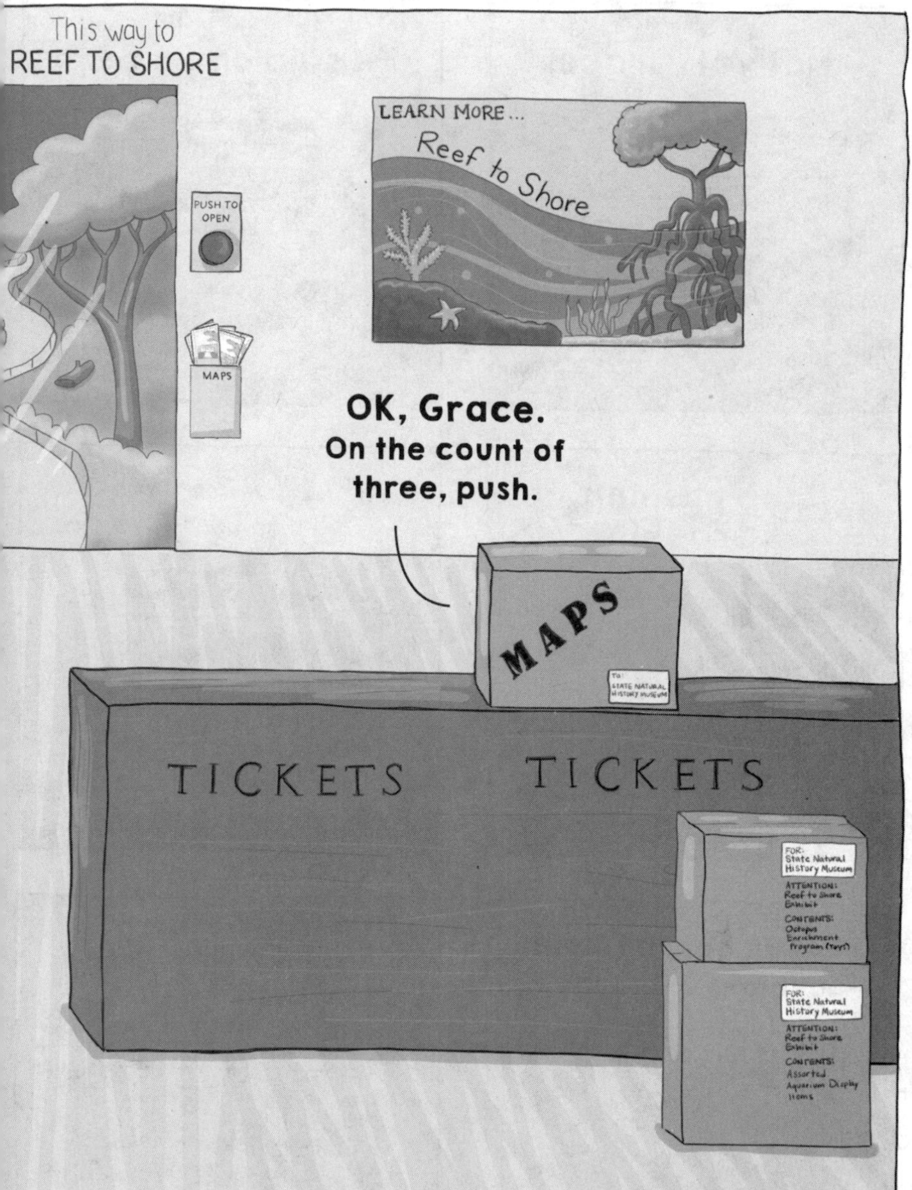
This way to
REEF TO SHORE
PUSH TO OPEN
MAPS
LEARN MORE...
Reef to Shore
OK, Grace.
On the count of three, push.
MAPS
TO:
STATE NATURAL HISTORY MUSEUM
TICKETS
TICKETS
FOR: State Natural History Museum
ATTENTION: Reef to Shore Exhibit
CONTENTS: Octopus Enrichment Program (Toys)
FOR: State Natural History Museum
ATTENTION: Reef to Shore Exhibit
CONTENTS: Assorted Aquarium Display Items

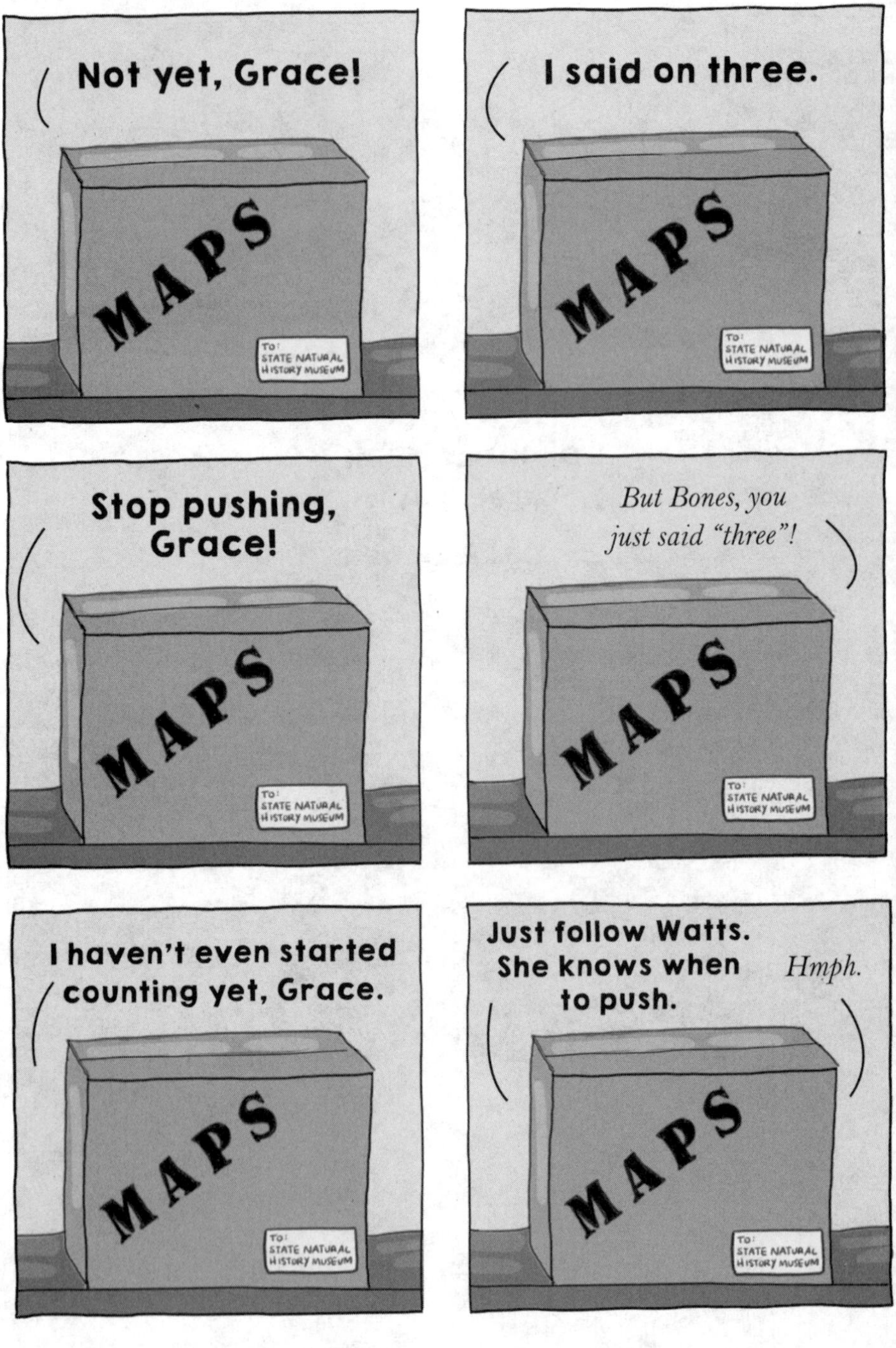
Not yet, Grace!
MAPS
TO: STATE NATURAL HISTORY MUSEUM
I said on three.
MAPS
TO: STATE NATURAL HISTORY MUSEUM
Stop pushing, Grace!
MAPS
TO: STATE NATURAL HISTORY MUSEUM
But Bones, you just said "three"!
MAPS
TO: STATE NATURAL HISTORY MUSEUM
I haven't even started counting yet, Grace.
MAPS
TO: STATE NATURAL HISTORY MUSEUM
Just follow Watts. She knows when to push.
Hmph.
MAPS
TO: STATE NATURAL HISTORY MUSEUM

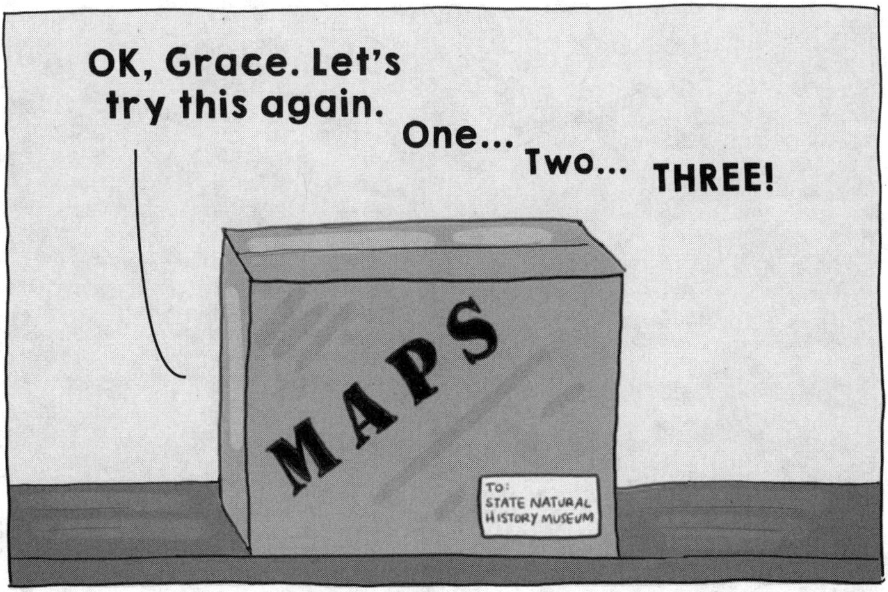
OK, Grace. Let's try this again.
One...
Two...
THREE!
MAPS
TO:
STATE NATURAL
HISTORY MUSEUM

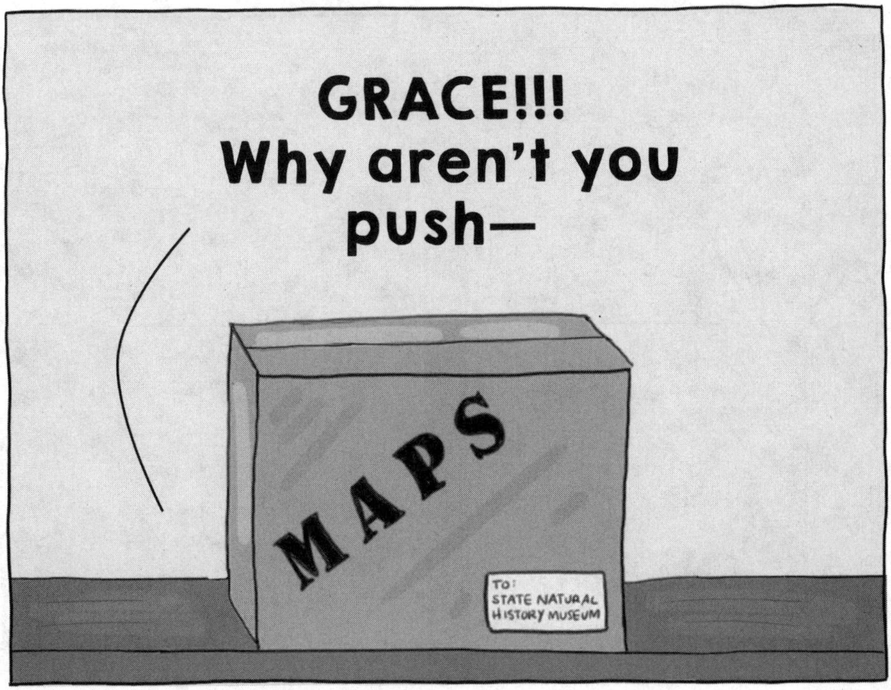
GRACE!!!
Why aren't you push—
MAPS
TO:
STATE NATURAL
HISTORY MUSEUM

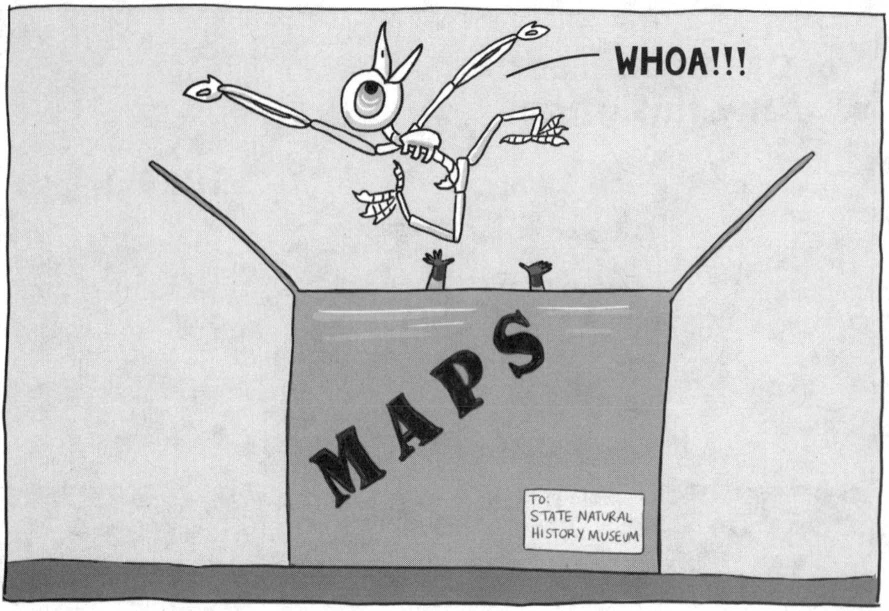
WHOA!!!
MAPS
TO:
STATE NATURAL
HISTORY MUSEUM

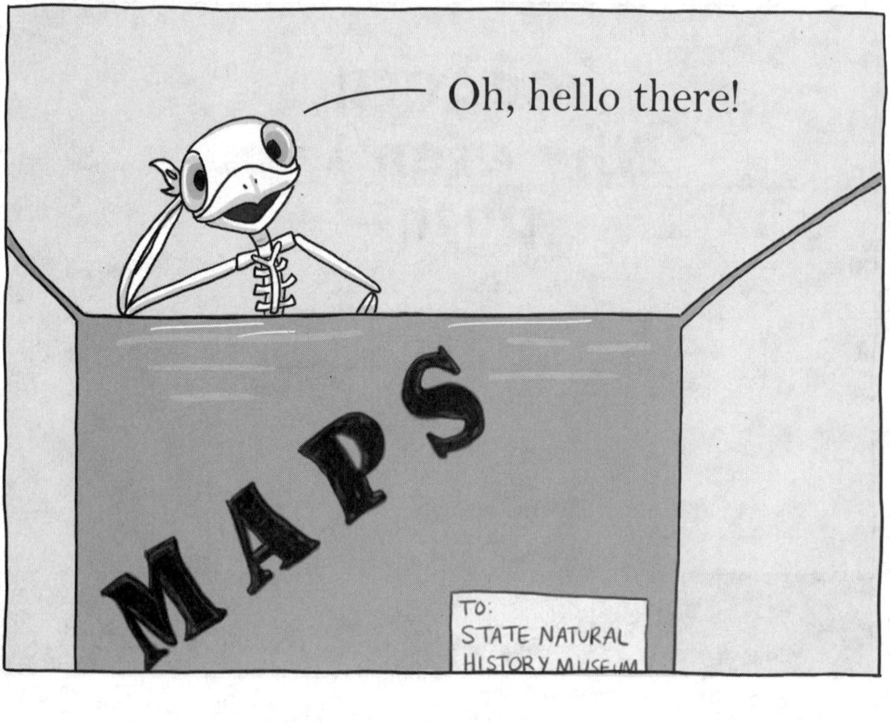
Oh, hello there!
MAPS
TO:
STATE NATURAL

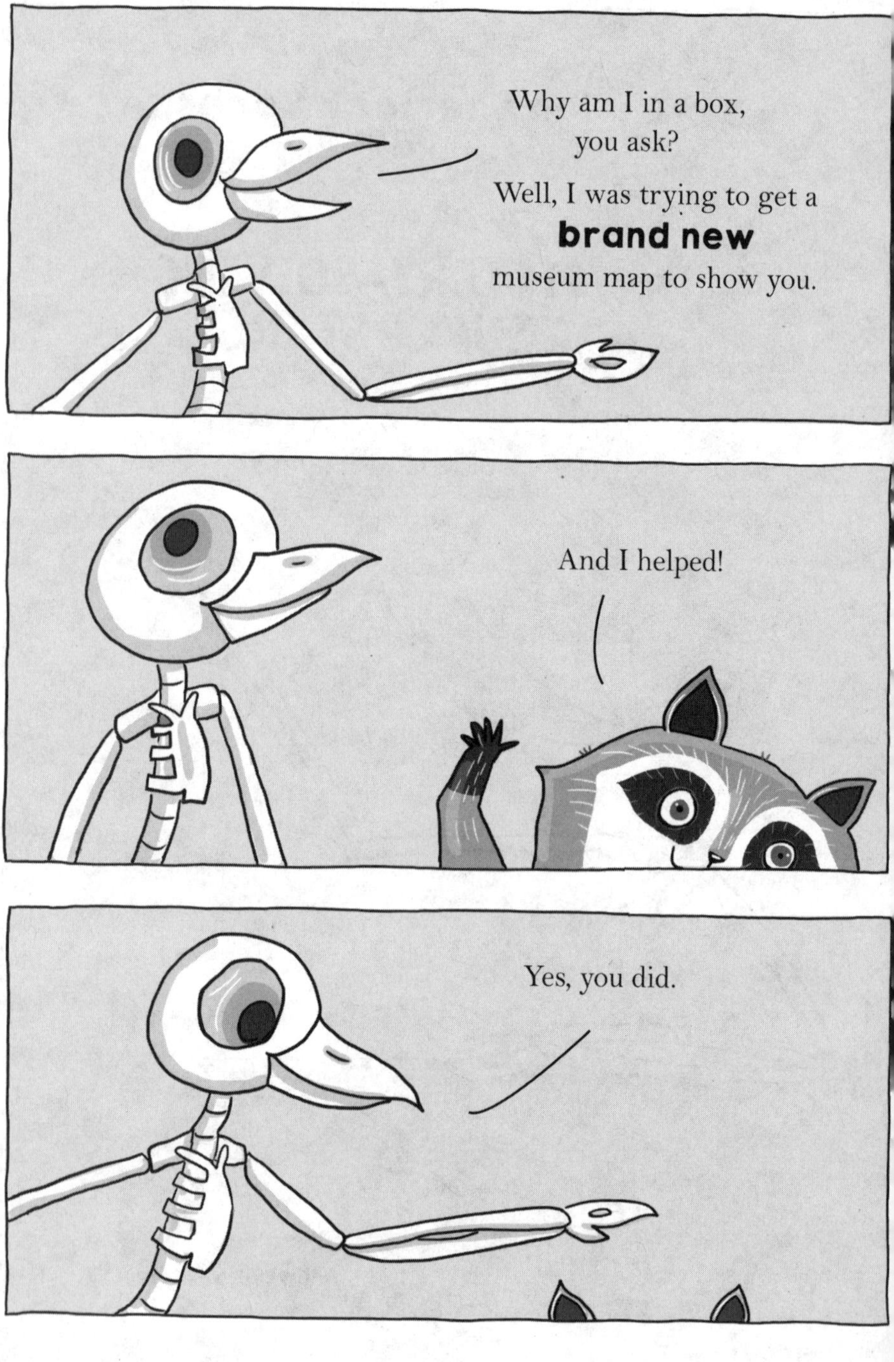
Why am I in a box, you ask?
Well, I was trying to get a **brand new** museum map to show you.
And I helped!
Yes, you did.

And by *helped* she means getting us stuck in this box.

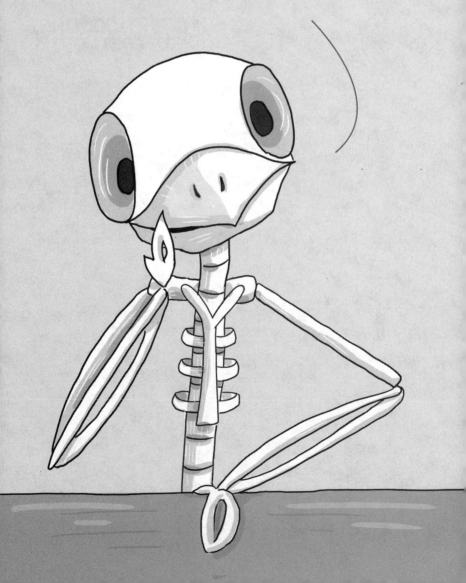

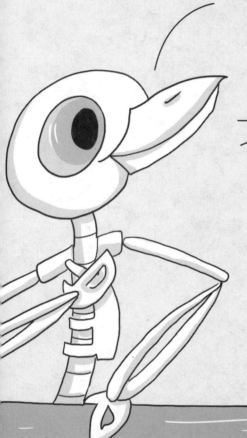

Allow me to start again...

I'm Sherlock Bones,
one of the

— **MYSTERY-SOLVING** —
SUPERSTARS

of this museum.

And these are my
trusty partners...

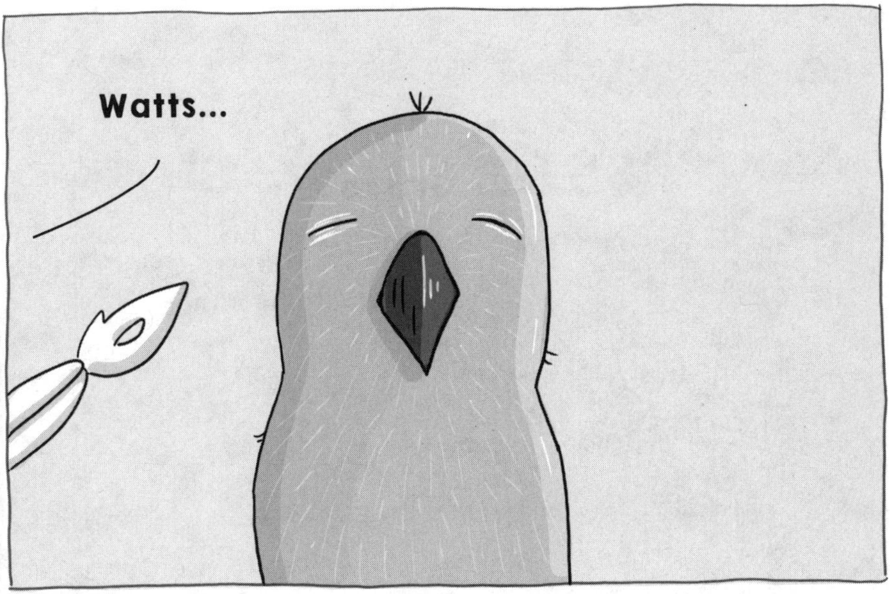
Watts...

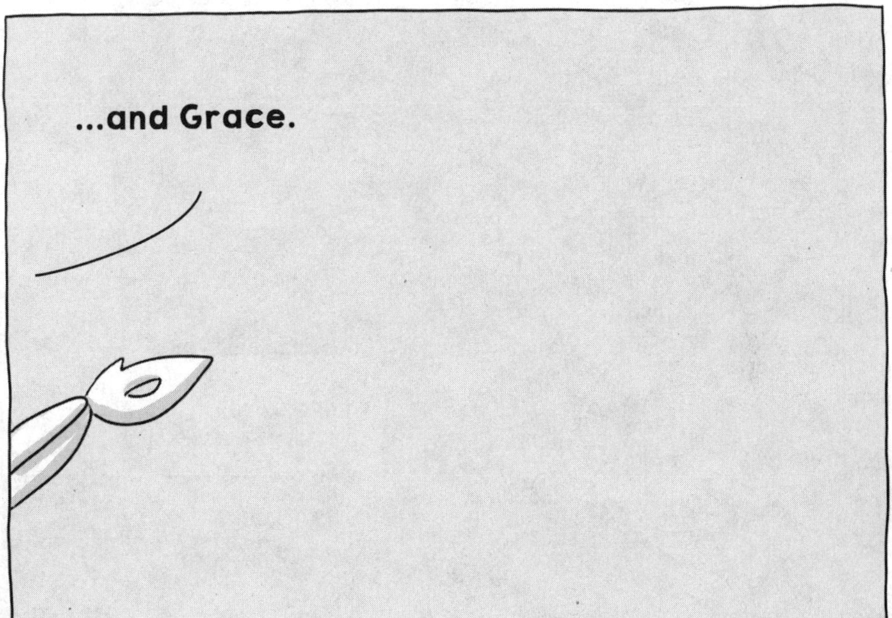
...and Grace.

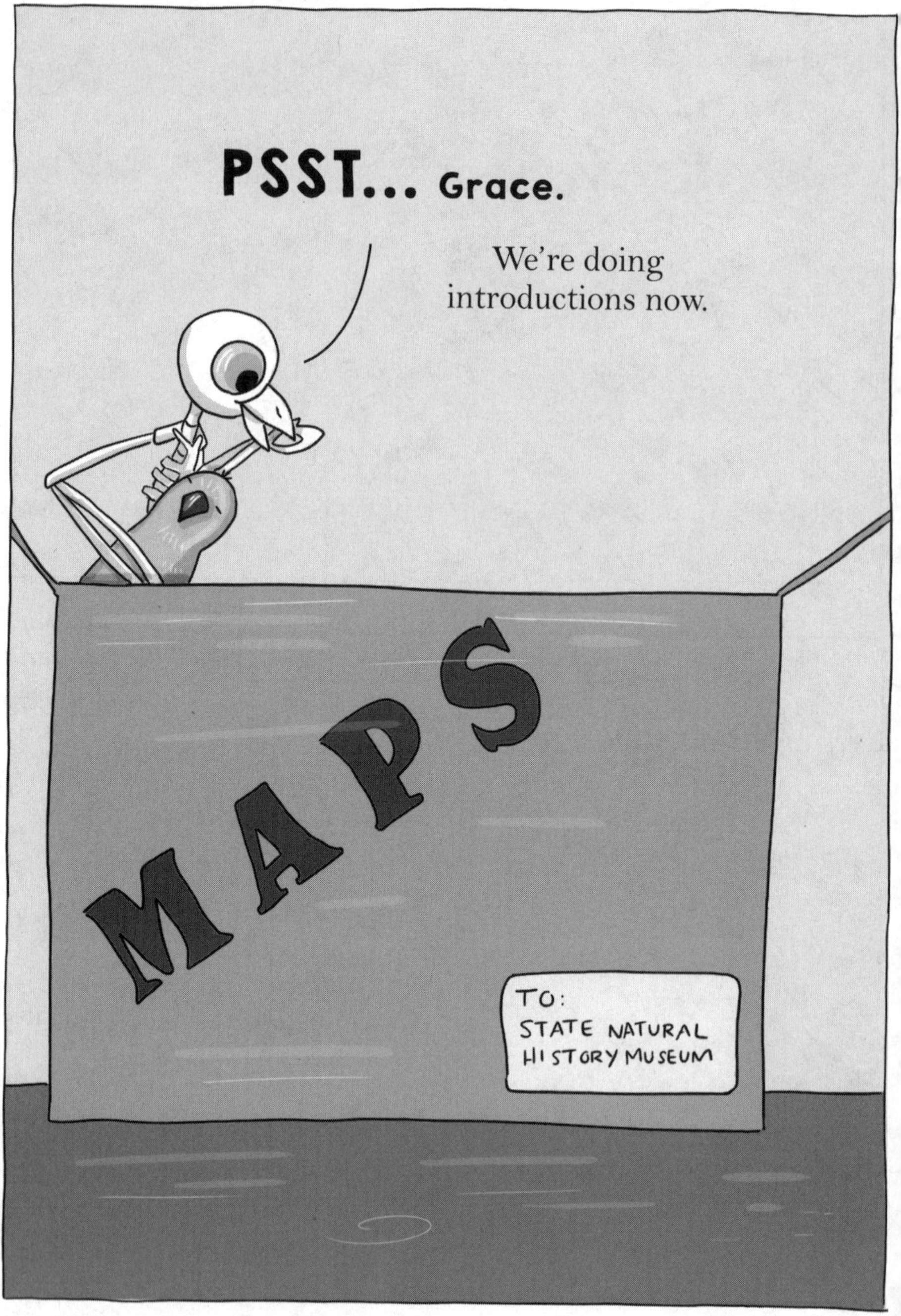
PSST... Grace.
We're doing introductions now.
MAPS
TO:
STATE NATURAL
HISTORY MUSEUM

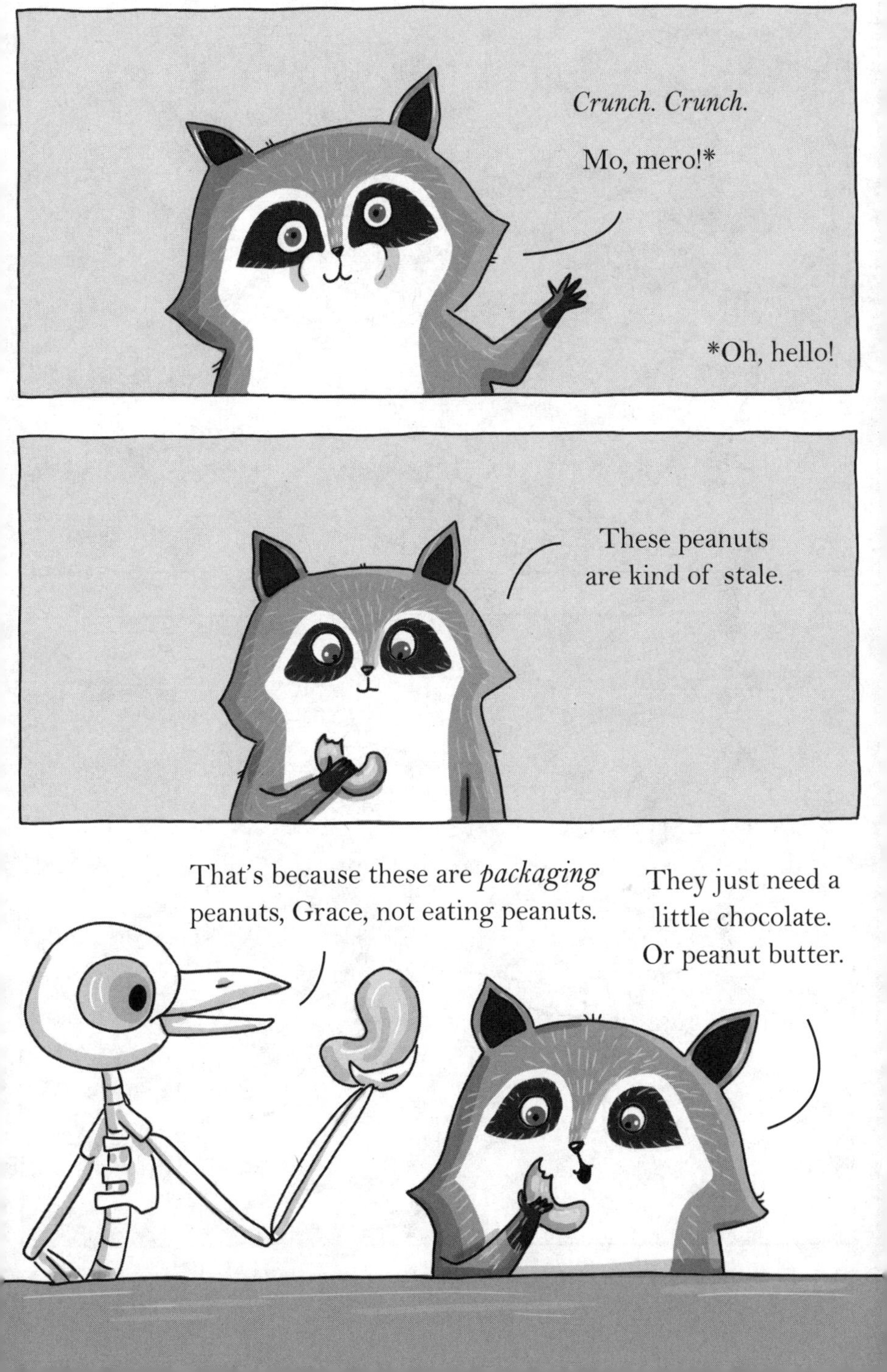
Crunch. Crunch.
Mo, mero!*
*Oh, hello!
These peanuts are kind of stale.
That's because these are *packaging* peanuts, Grace, not eating peanuts.
They just need a little chocolate. Or peanut butter.

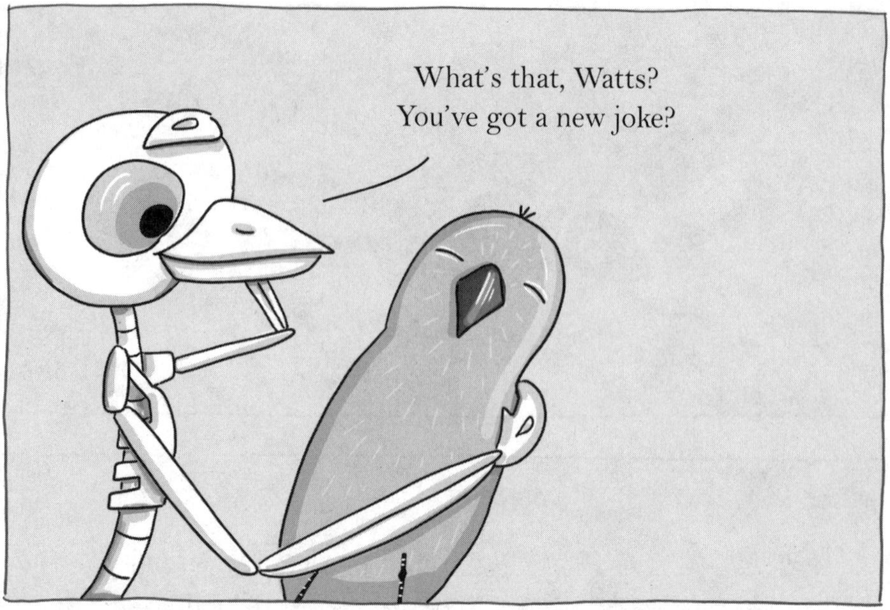
What's that, Watts?
You've got a new joke?

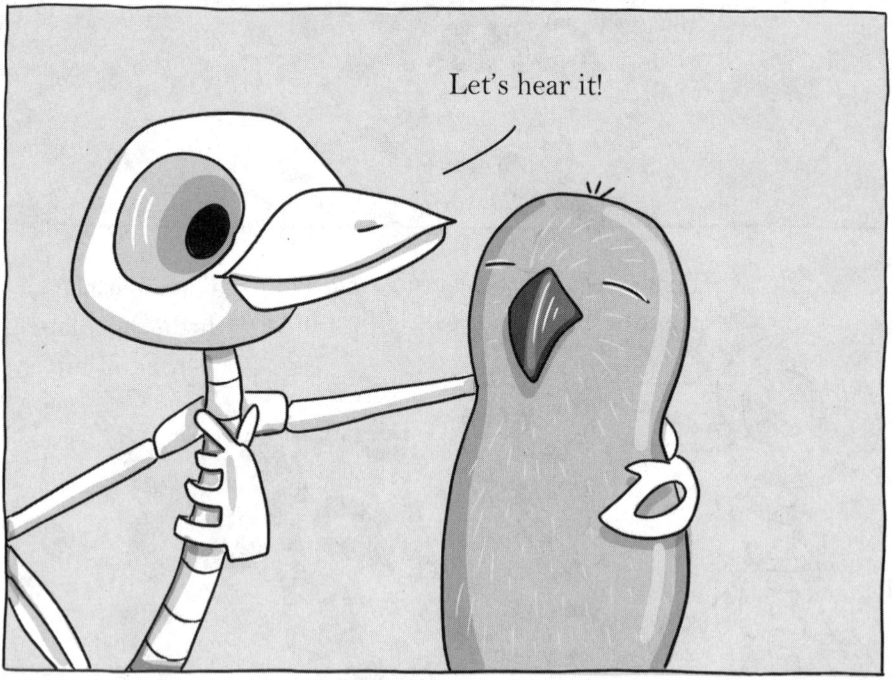
Let's hear it!

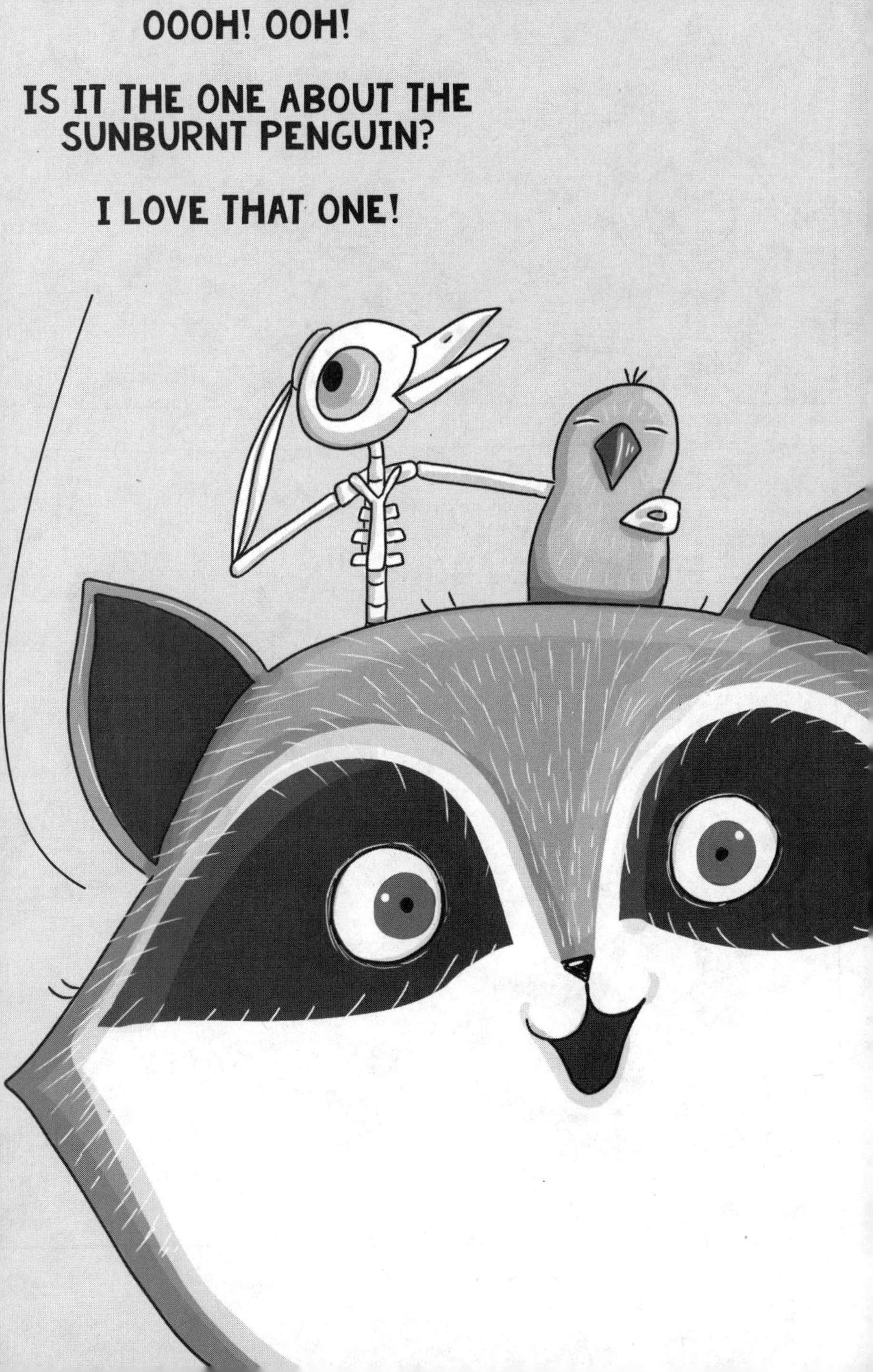
OOOH! OOH!
IS IT THE ONE ABOUT THE SUNBURNT PENGUIN?
I LOVE THAT ONE!

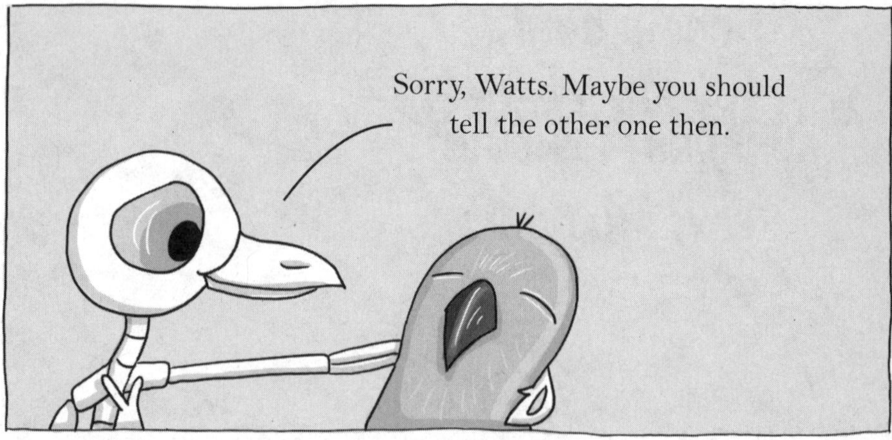
Sorry, Watts. Maybe you should tell the other one then.

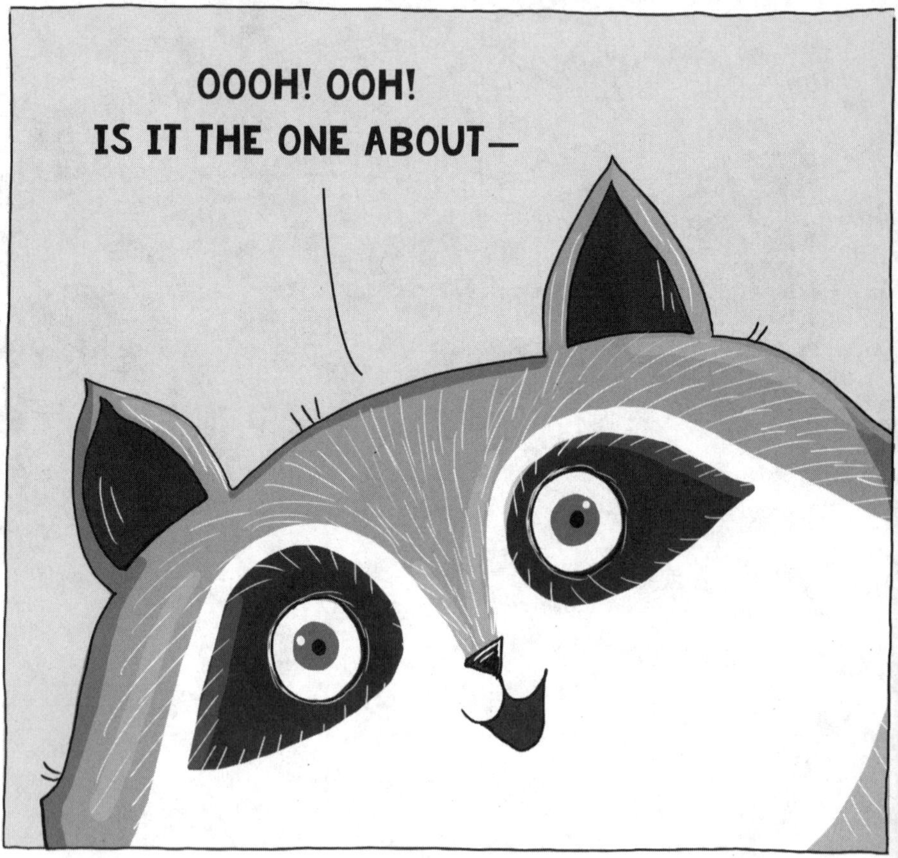
OOOH! OOH!
IS IT THE ONE ABOUT—

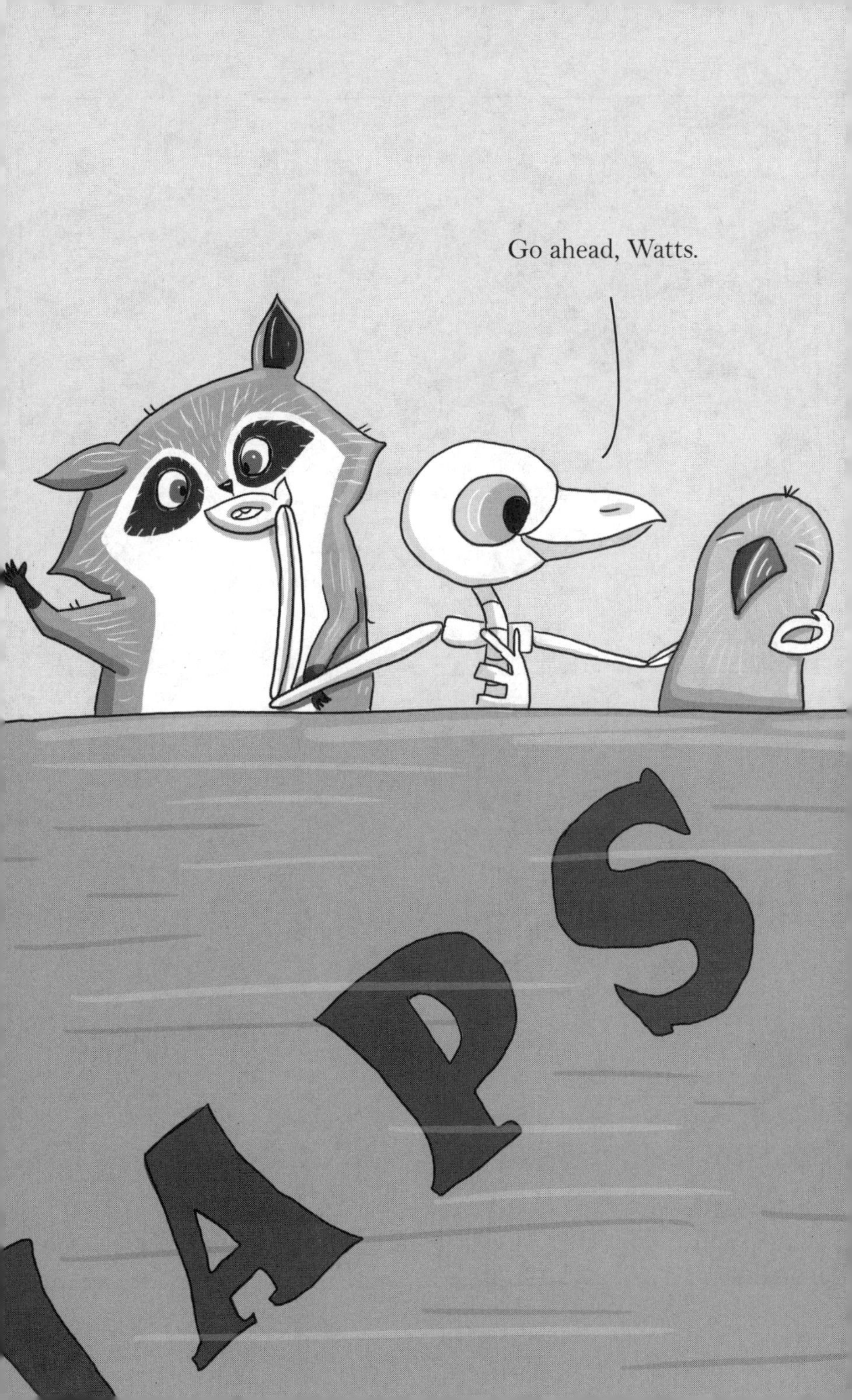
Go ahead, Watts.
APS

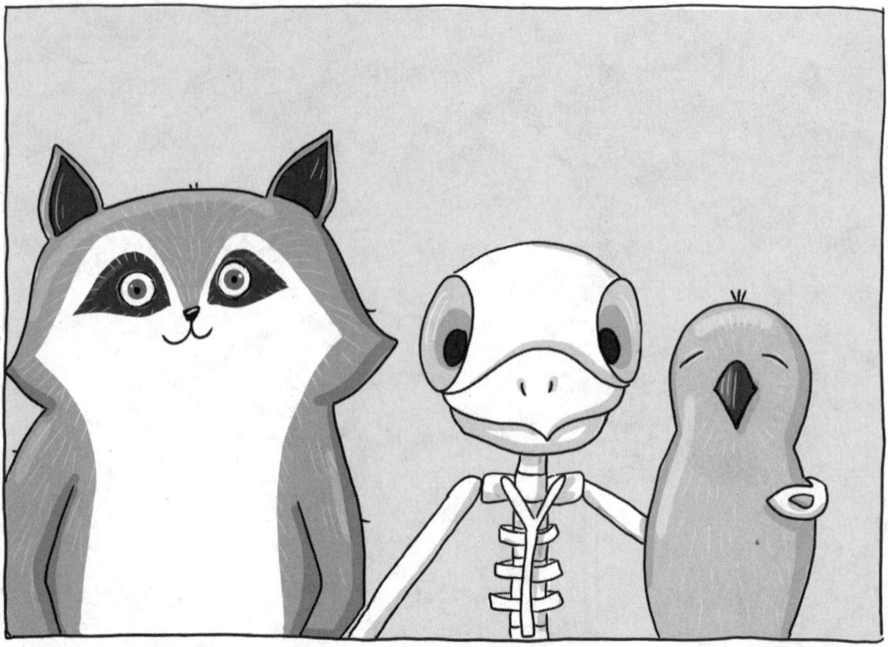

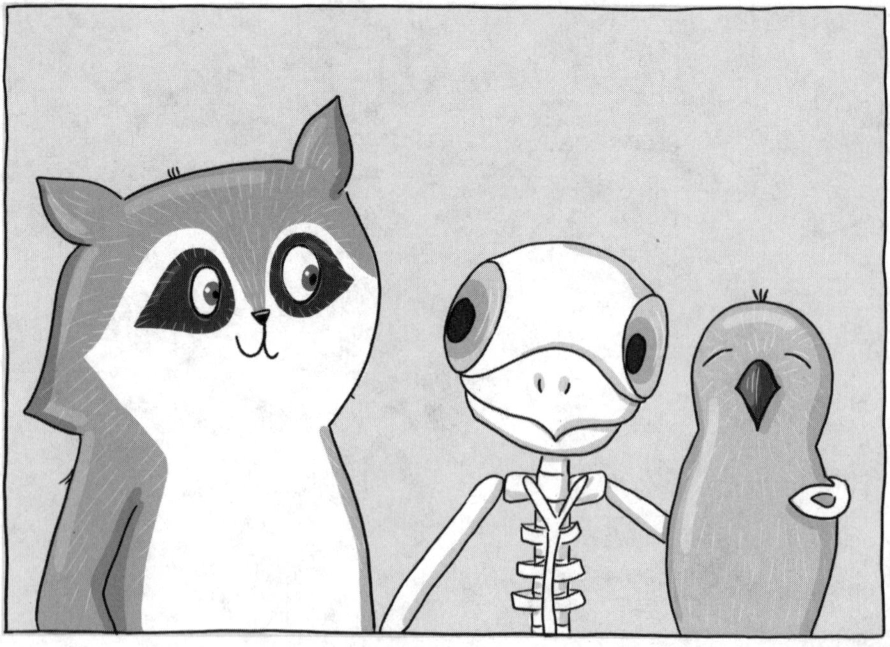

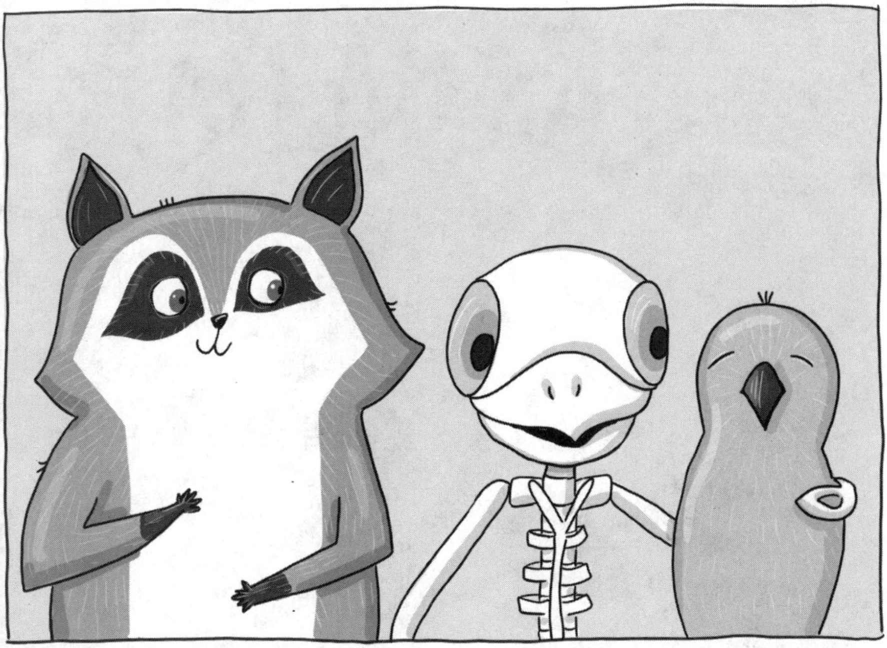

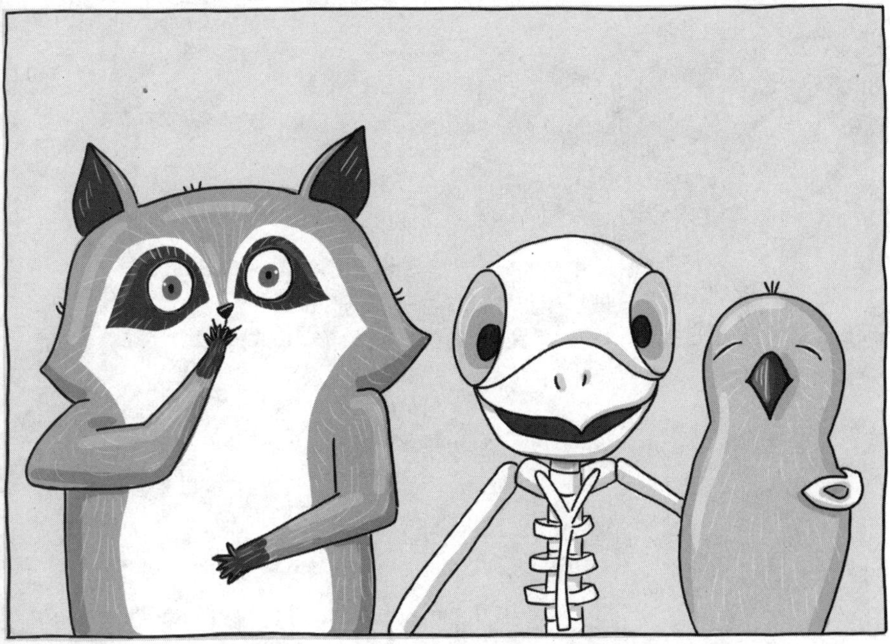

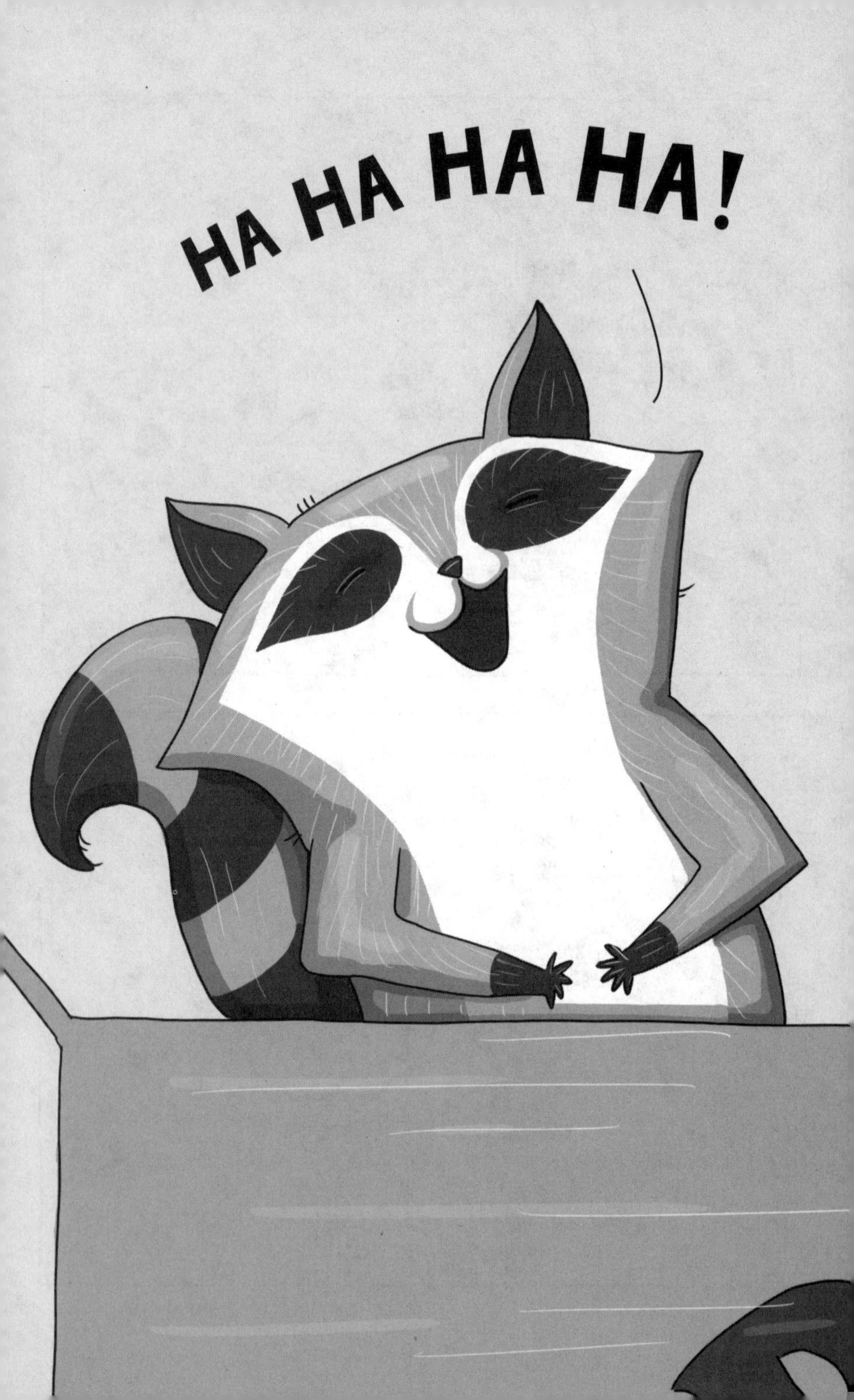
HA HA HA HA HA!

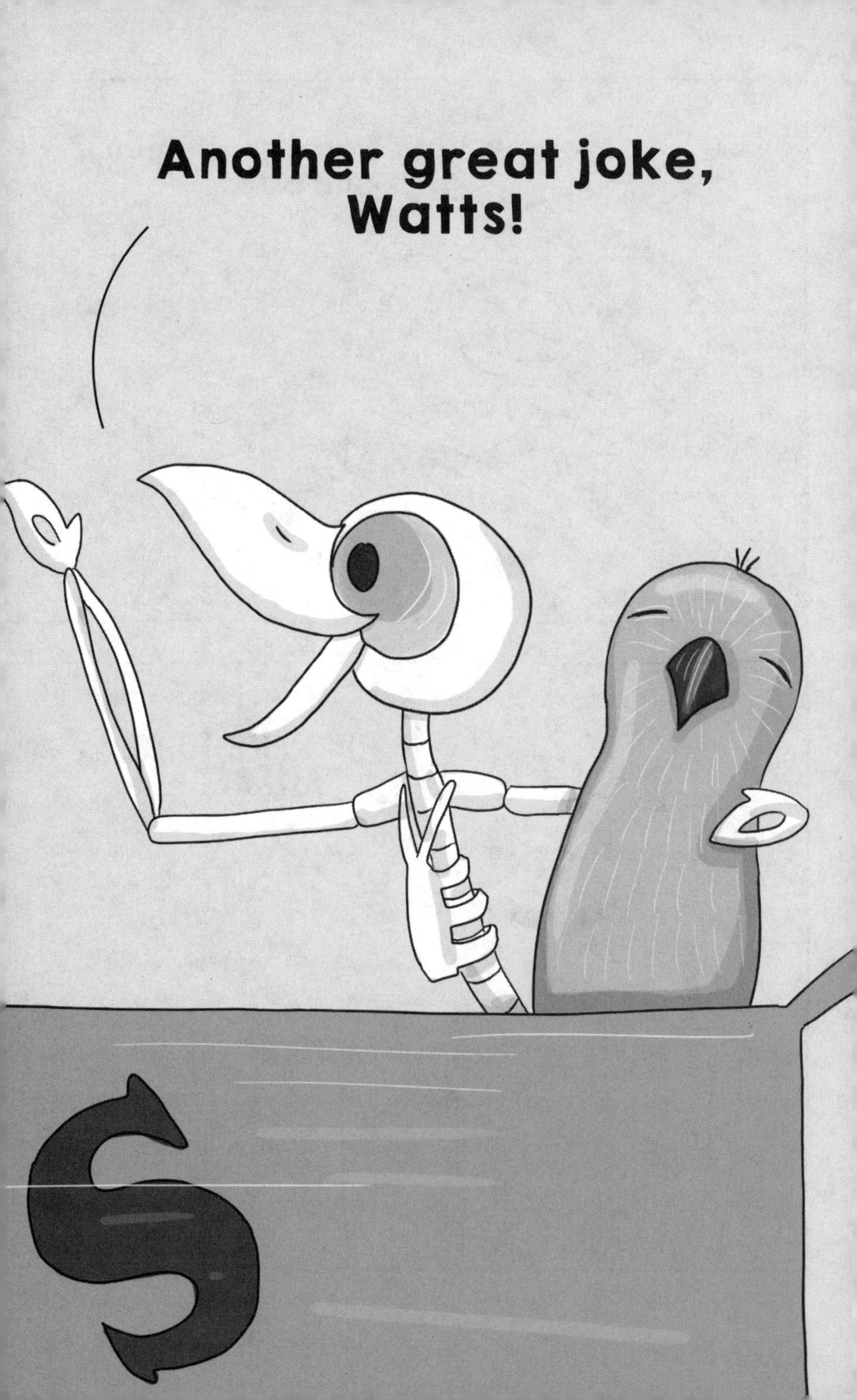
Another great joke, Watts!

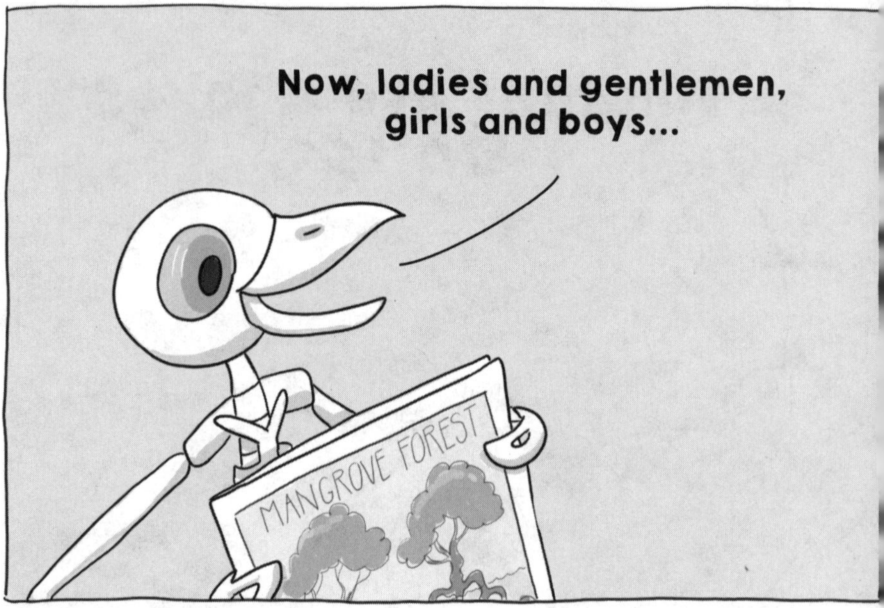
Now, ladies and gentlemen, girls and boys...
MANGROVE FOREST

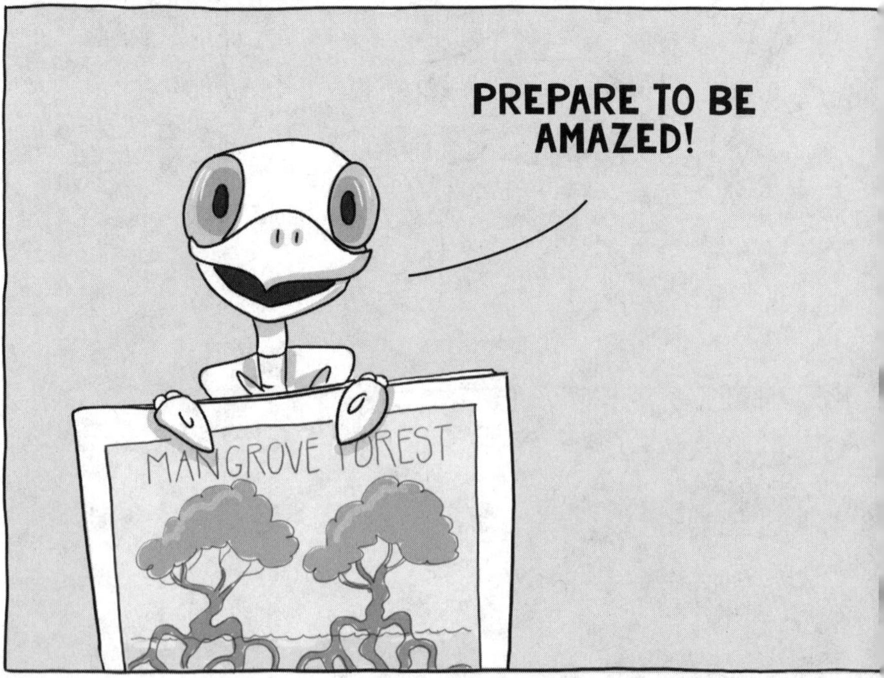
PREPARE TO BE AMAZED!
MANGROVE FOREST

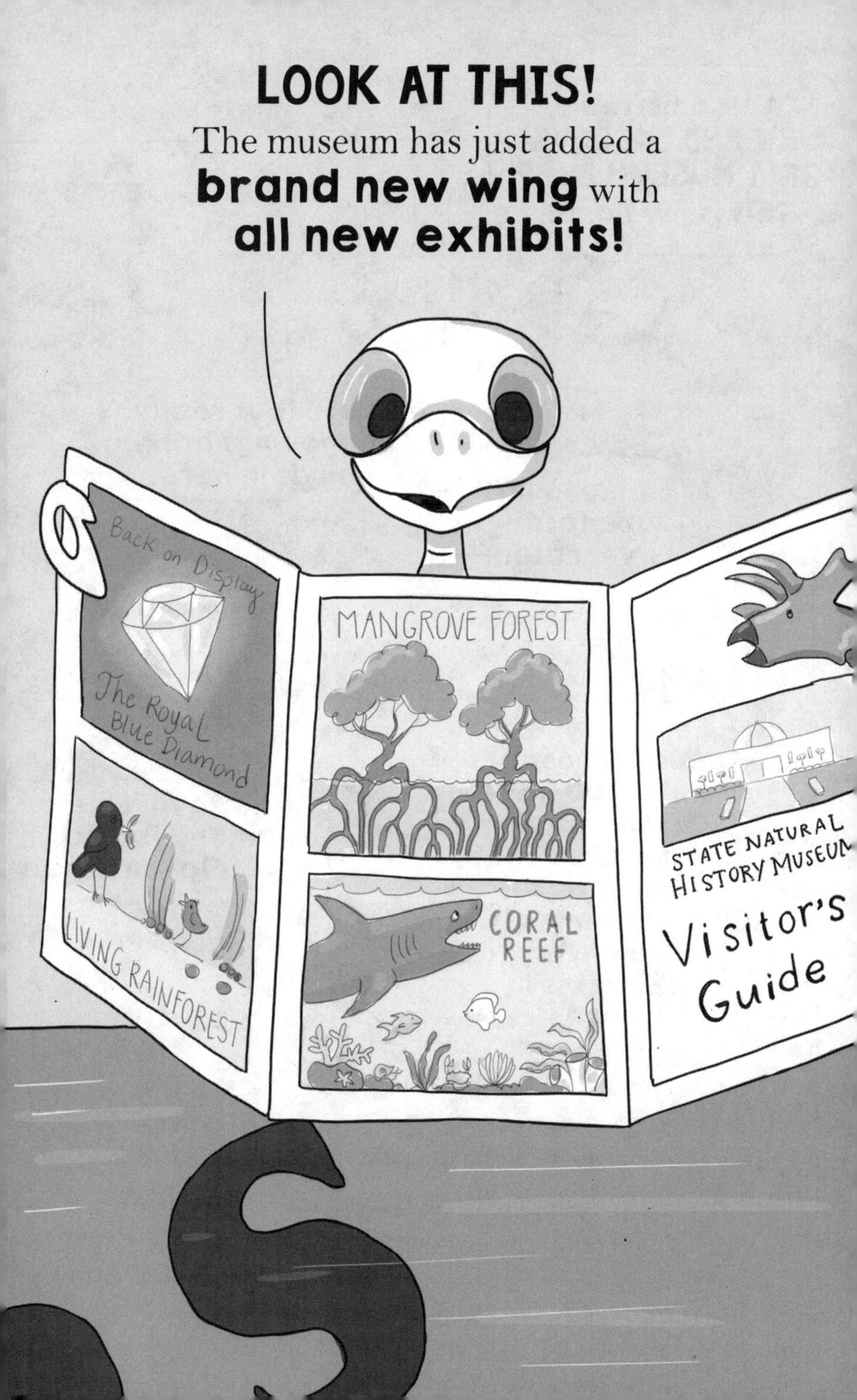
LOOK AT THIS!
The museum has just added a brand new wing with all new exhibits!
Back on Display
The Royal Blue Diamond
LIVING RAINFOREST
MANGROVE FOREST
CORAL REEF
STATE NATURAL HISTORY MUSEUM
Visitor's Guide

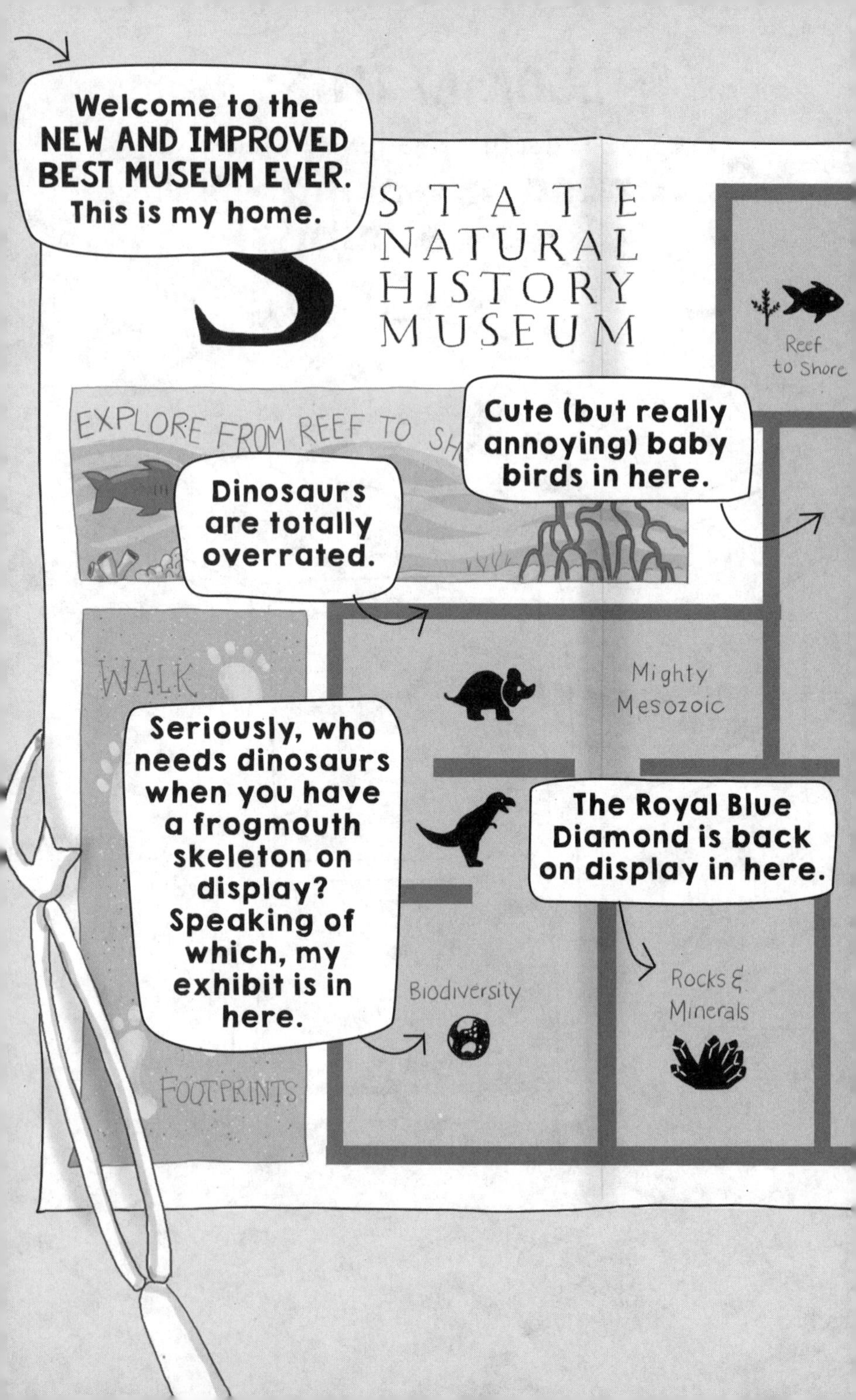
Welcome to the
NEW AND IMPROVED
BEST MUSEUM EVER.
This is my home.
STATE NATURAL HISTORY MUSEUM
Reef to Shore
EXPLORE FROM REEF TO SH
Cute (but really annoying) baby birds in here.
Dinosaurs are totally overrated.
WALK
FOOTPRINTS
Mighty Mesozoic
Seriously, who needs dinosaurs when you have a frogmouth skeleton on display? Speaking of which, my exhibit is in here.
The Royal Blue Diamond is back on display in here.
Biodiversity
Rocks & Minerals

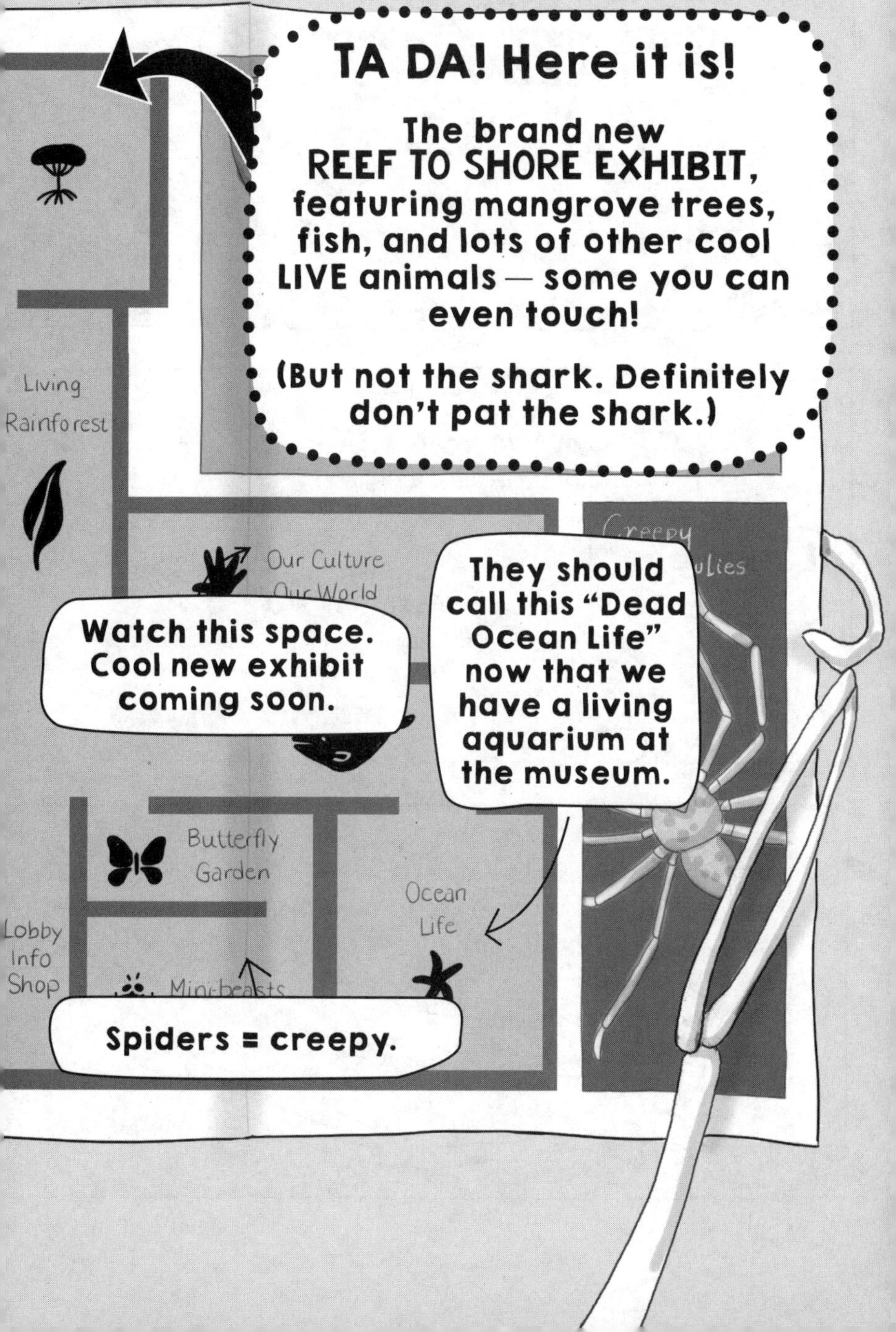
TA DA! Here it is!
The brand new REEF TO SHORE EXHIBIT, featuring mangrove trees, fish, and lots of other cool LIVE animals — some you can even touch!
(But not the shark. Definitely don't pat the shark.)
Living Rainforest
Our Culture Our World
Creepy
Watch this space. Cool new exhibit coming soon.
They should call this "Dead Ocean Life" now that we have a living aquarium at the museum.
Butterfly Garden
Ocean Life
Lobby Info Shop
Mini-beasts
Spiders = creepy.

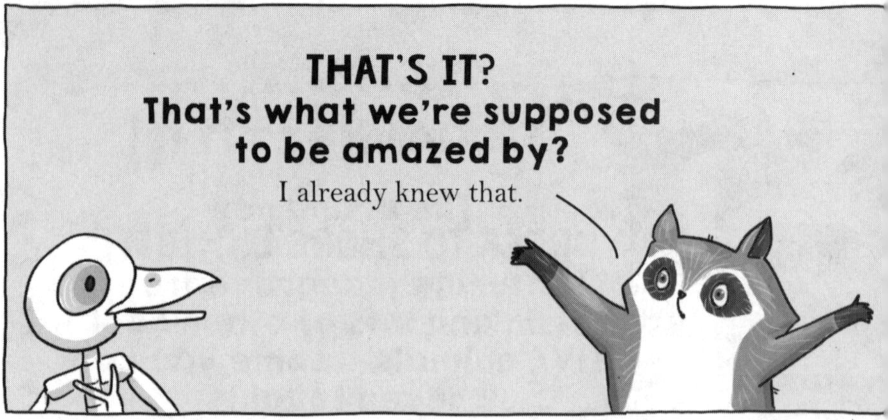
THAT'S IT?
That's what we're supposed to be amazed by?
I already knew that.

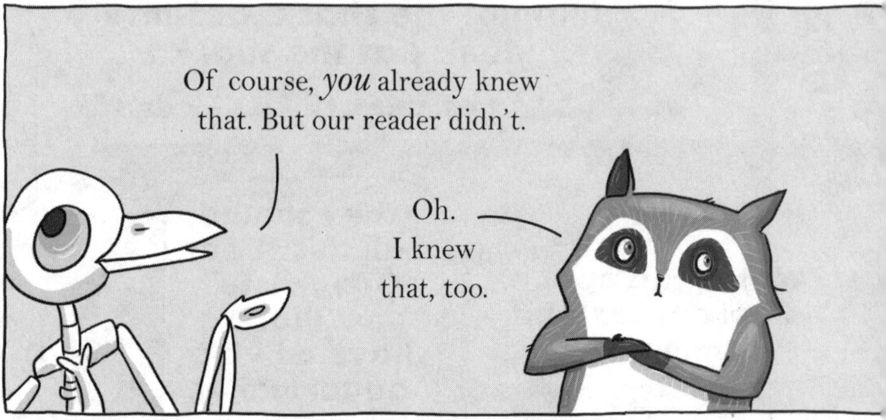
Of course, *you* already knew that. But our reader didn't.
Oh. I knew that, too.

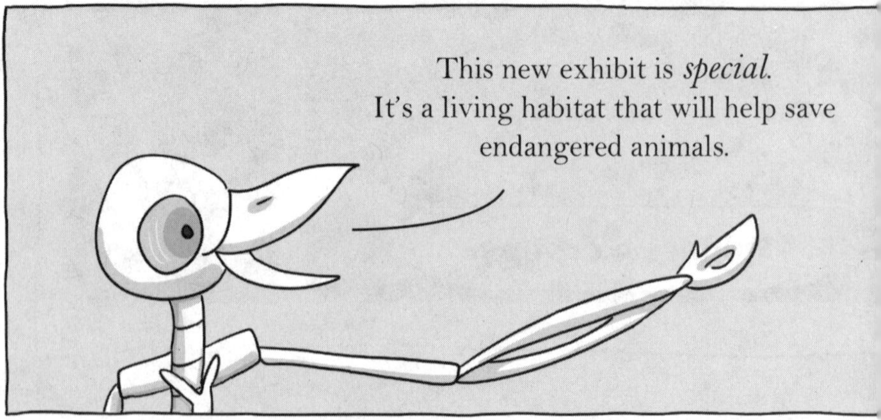
This new exhibit is *special.* It's a living habitat that will help save endangered animals.

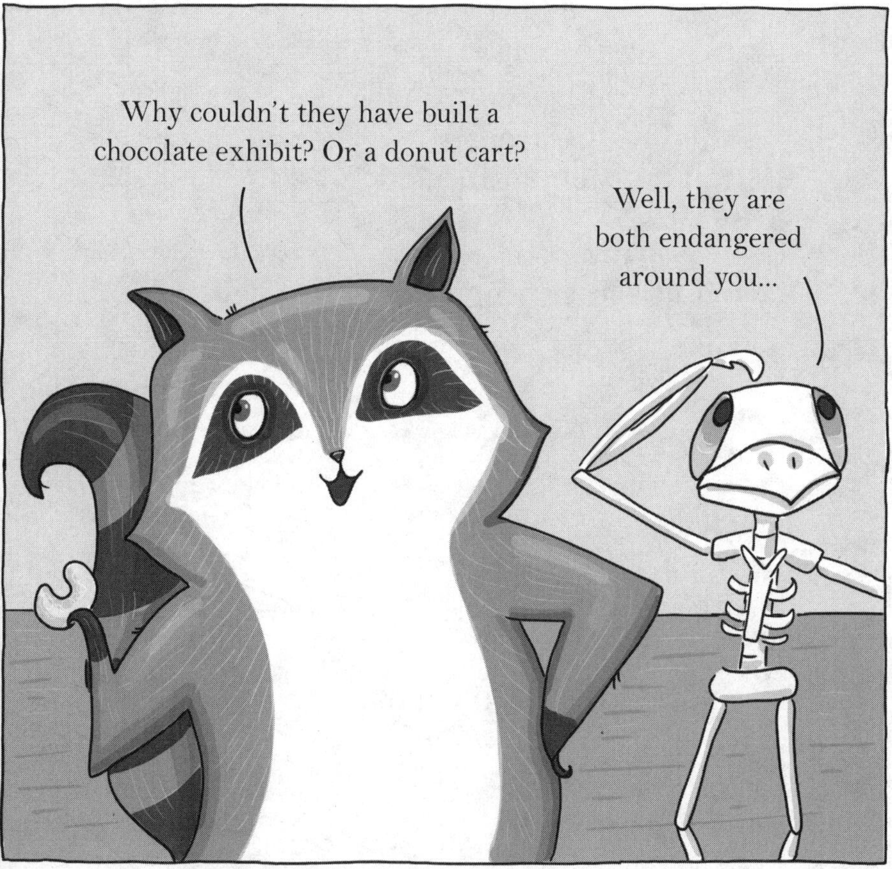
Why couldn't they have built a chocolate exhibit? Or a donut cart?
Well, they are both endangered around you...

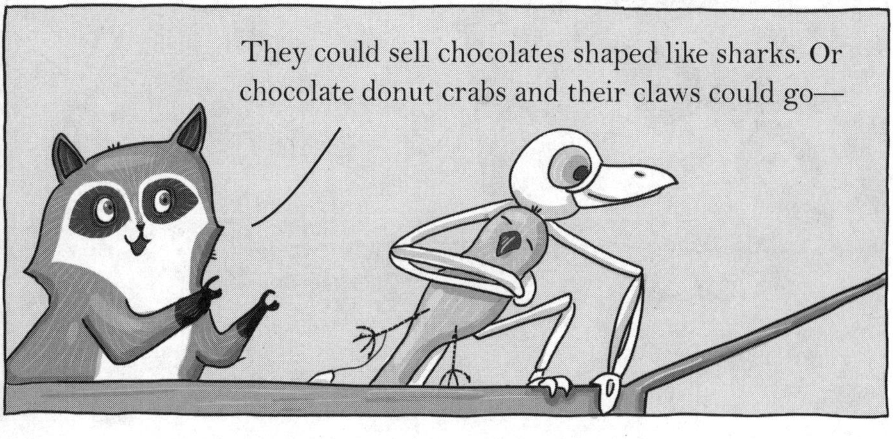
They could sell chocolates shaped like sharks. Or chocolate donut crabs and their claws could go—

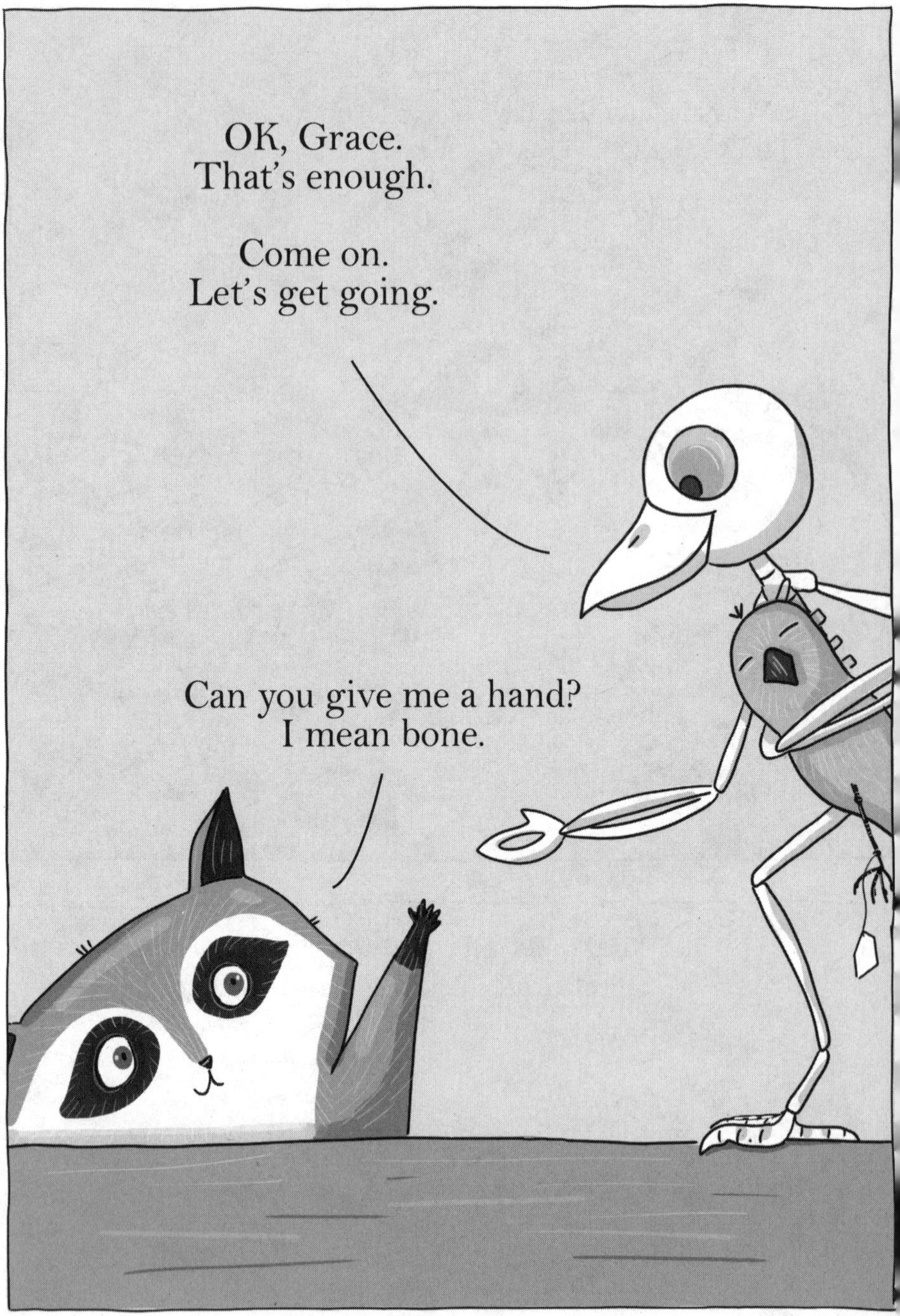
OK, Grace.
That's enough.
Come on.
Let's get going.
Can you give me a hand?
I mean bone.

Ugh. This could take a while.
Just skip ahead to page 36. That's where
Chapter 1 begins...
**and whatever you do,
don't look in this box.**

FOR:
State Natural
History Museu

ATTENTION:
Reef to Shore
Exhibit

CONTENTS:
Octopus
Enrichment
Program (Toys)

FOR:
State Natural
History Muse

ATTENTION:
Reef to Shore
Exhibit

CONTENTS:
Assorted
Aquarium Dis
Items

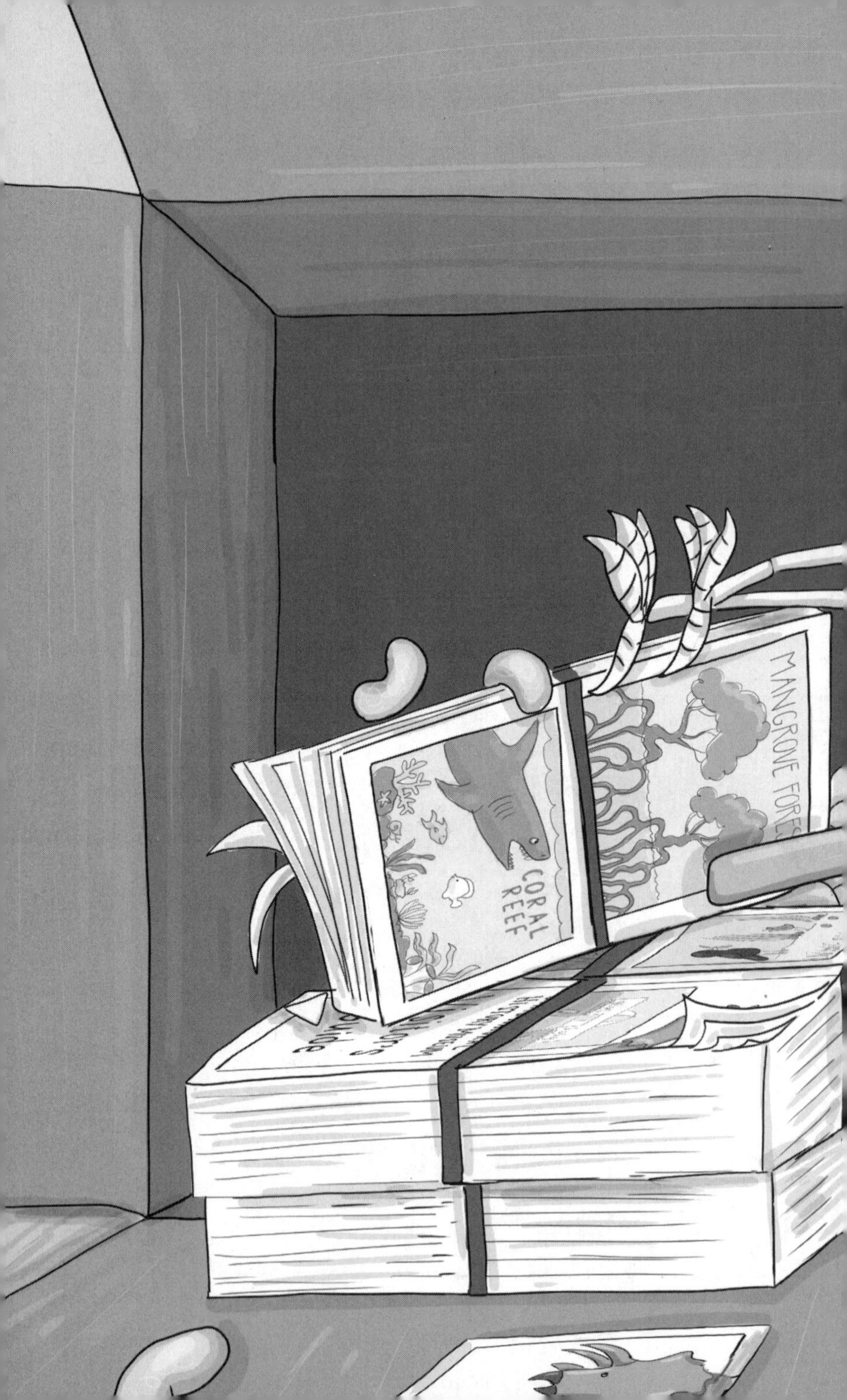
MANGROVE FORES
CORAL
REEF

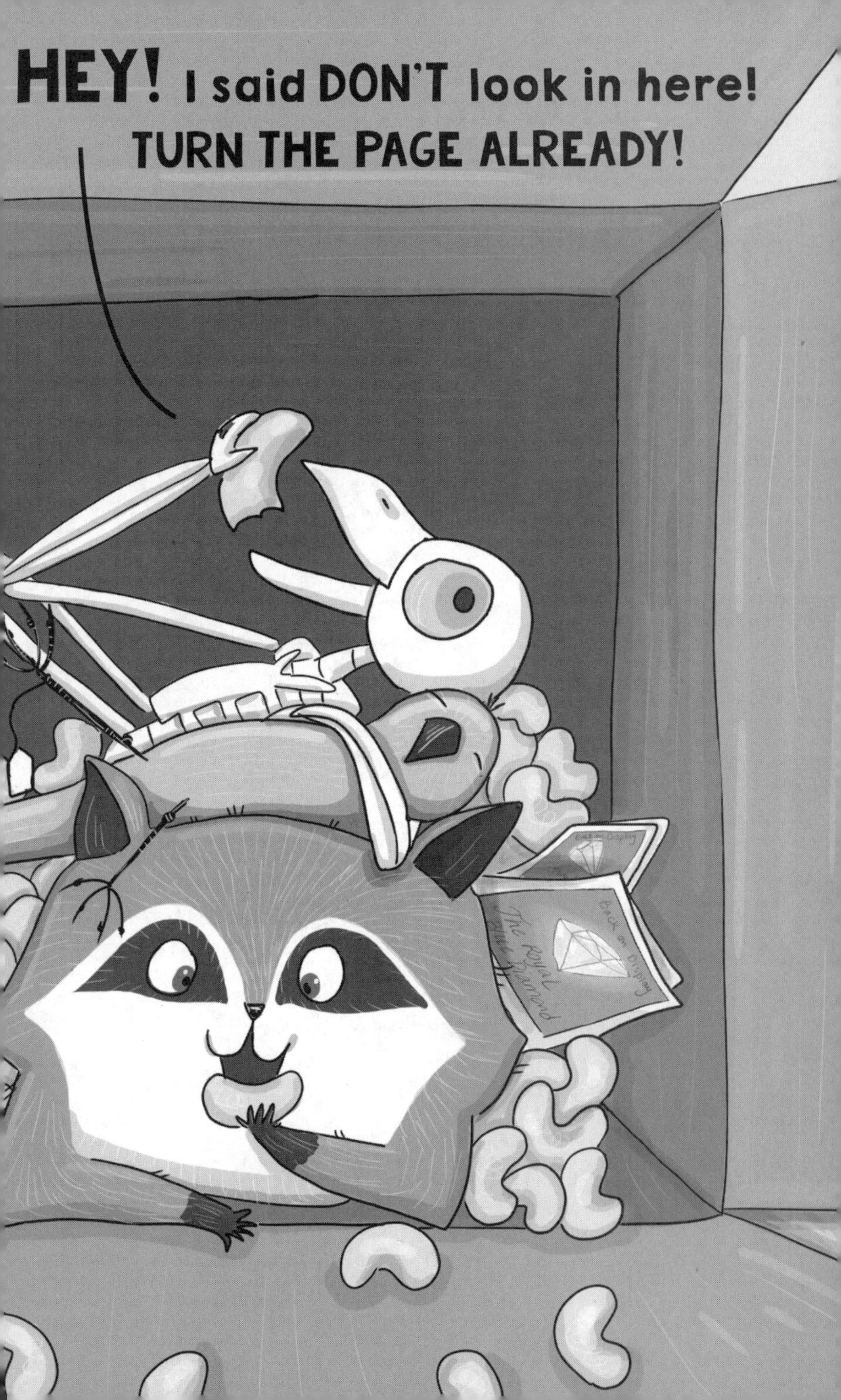
HEY! I said DON'T look in here!
TURN THE PAGE ALREADY!
Back on Display
The Royal Diamond

HISTORY MUSEUM

REEF to SHORE

MEET OUR THIEF IN THE RAINFOREST

TAKE A WALK IN OUR CULTURE OUR WORLD

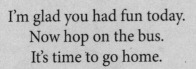

I'm glad you had fun today.
Now hop on the bus.
It's time to go home.

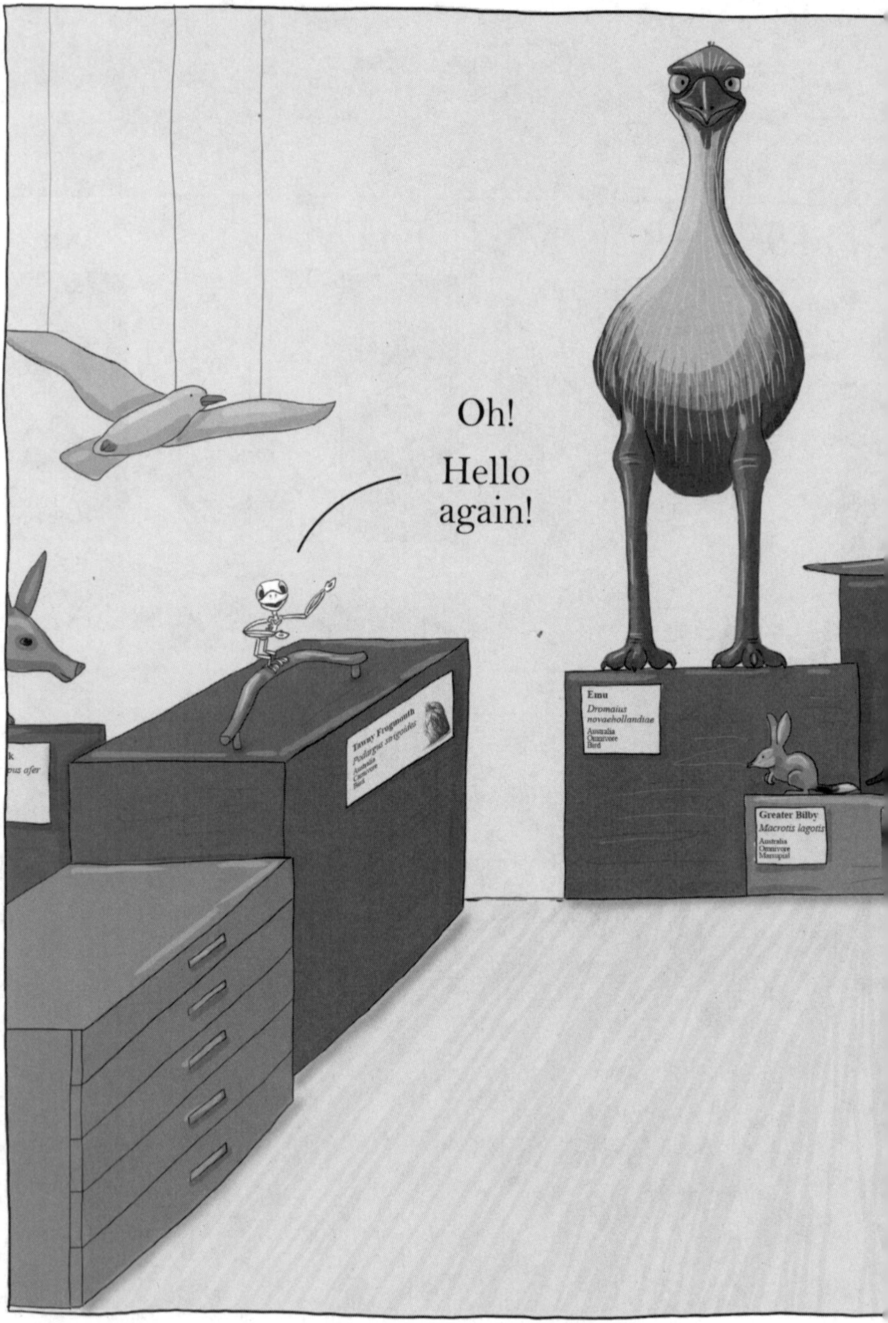

Oh!
Hello again!
Tawny Frogmouth
Podargus strigoides
Emu
Dromaius novaehollandiae
Australia
Omnivore
Bird
Greater Bilby
Macrotis lagotis
Australia
Omnivore
Marsupial

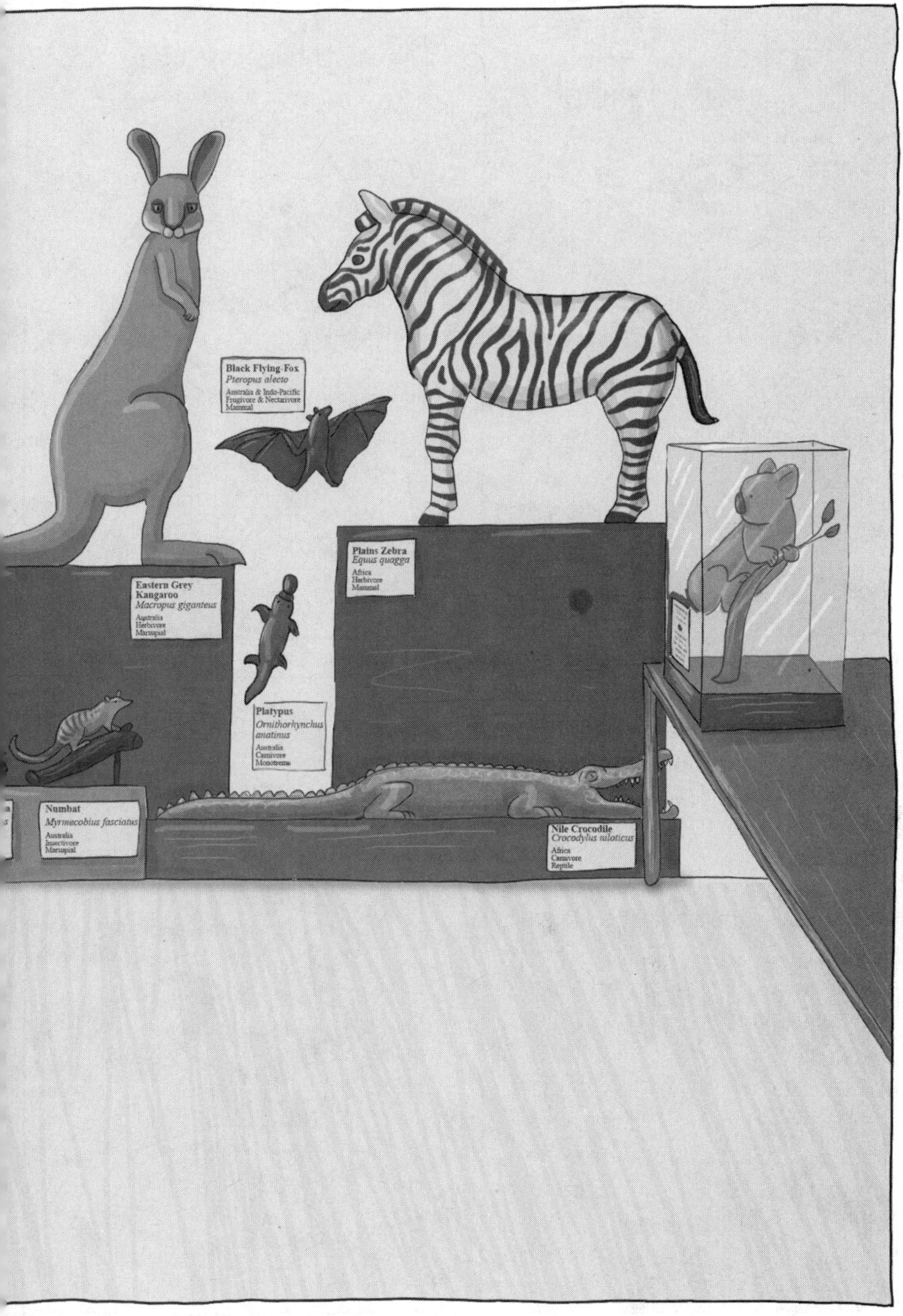
Black Flying-Fox
Pteropus alecto
Australia & Indo-Pacific
Frugivore & Nectarivore
Mammal
Eastern Grey Kangaroo
Macropus giganteus
Australia
Herbivore
Marsupial
Plains Zebra
Equus quagga
Africa
Herbivore
Mammal
Platypus
Ornithorhynchus anatinus
Australia
Carnivore
Monotreme
Numbat
Myrmecobius fasciatus
Australia
Insectivore
Marsupial
Nile Crocodile
Crocodylus niloticus
Africa
Carnivore
Reptile

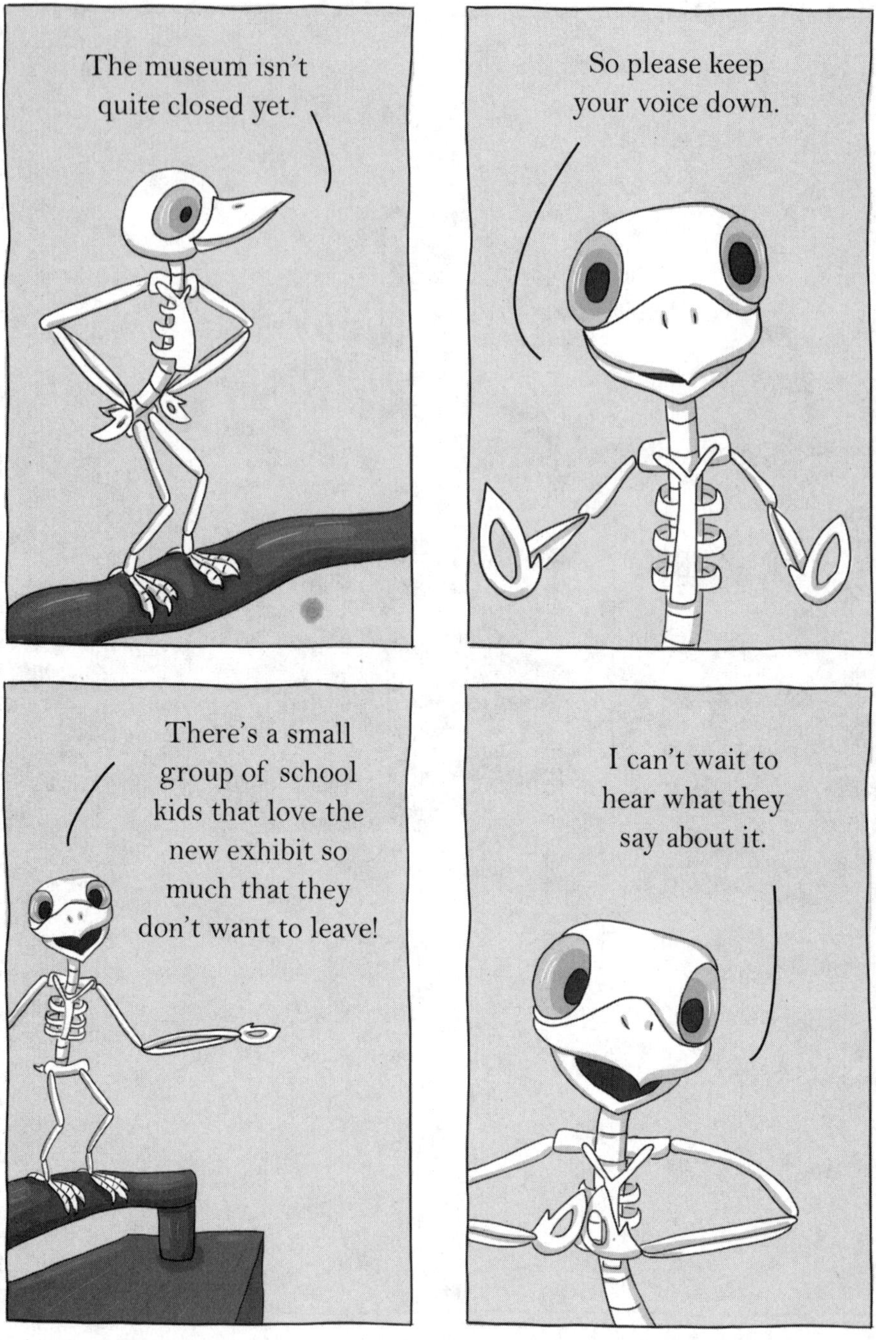
The museum isn't quite closed yet.
So please keep your voice down.
There's a small group of school kids that love the new exhibit so much that they don't want to leave!
I can't wait to hear what they say about it.

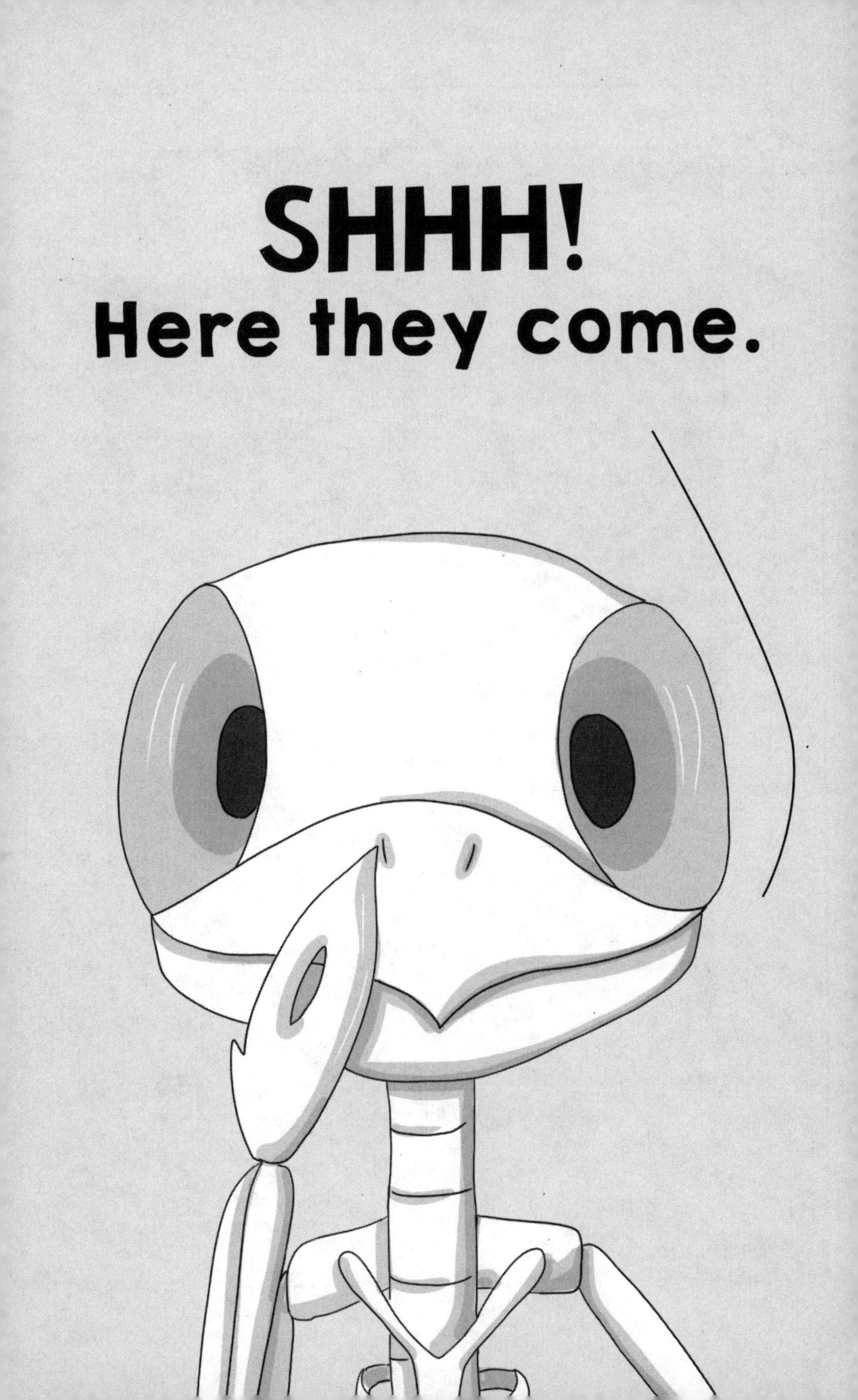
SHHH!
Here they come.

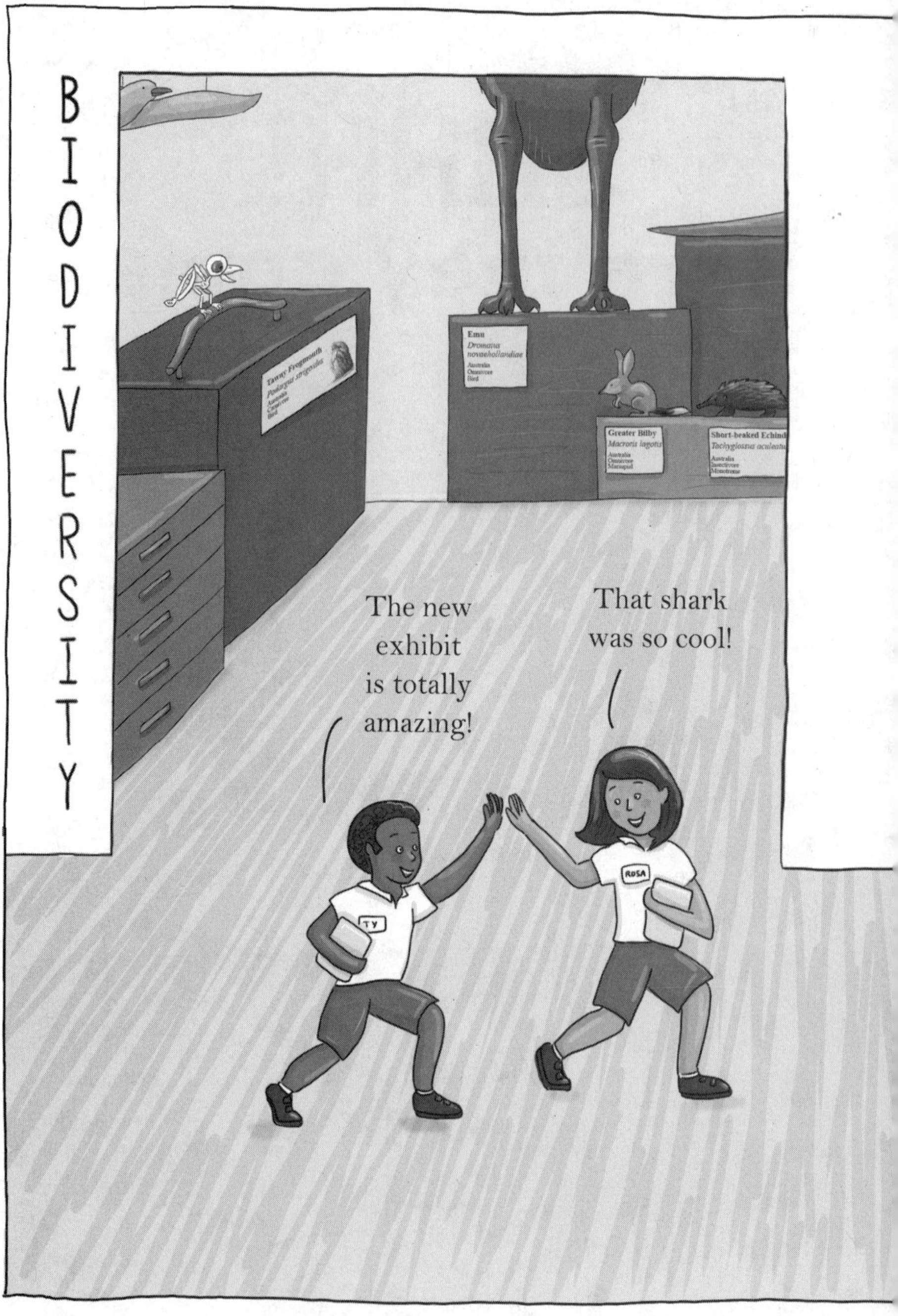
BIODIVERSITY
Tawny Frogmouth
Podargus strigoides
Emu
Dromaius novaehollandiae
Australia
Omnivore
Bird
Greater Bilby
Macrotis lagotis
Australia
Omnivore
Marsupial
Short-beaked Echind
Tachyglossus aculeatu
Australia
Insectivore
Monotreme
The new exhibit is totally amazing!
That shark was so cool!
TY
ROSA

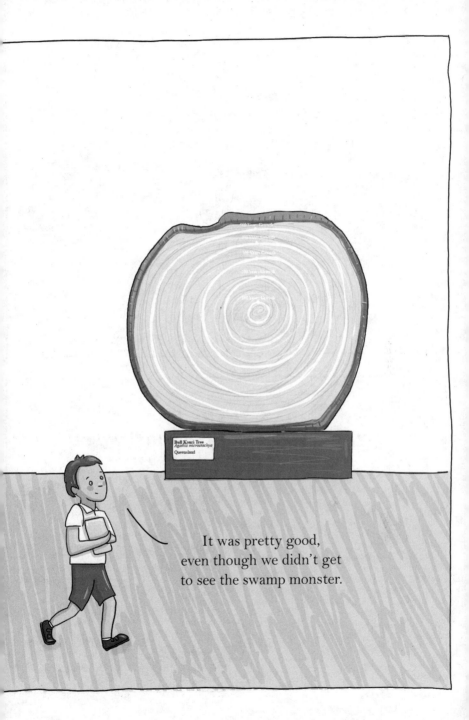

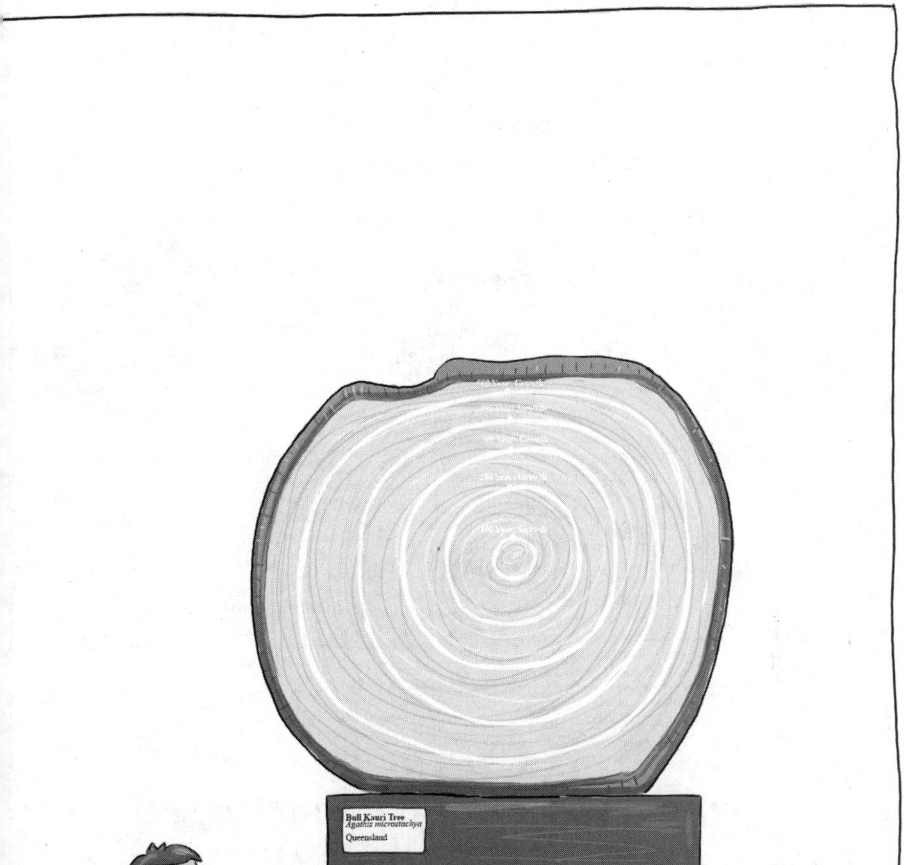
Bull Kauri Tree
Agathis microstachya
Queensland
It was pretty good, even though we didn't get to see the swamp monster.

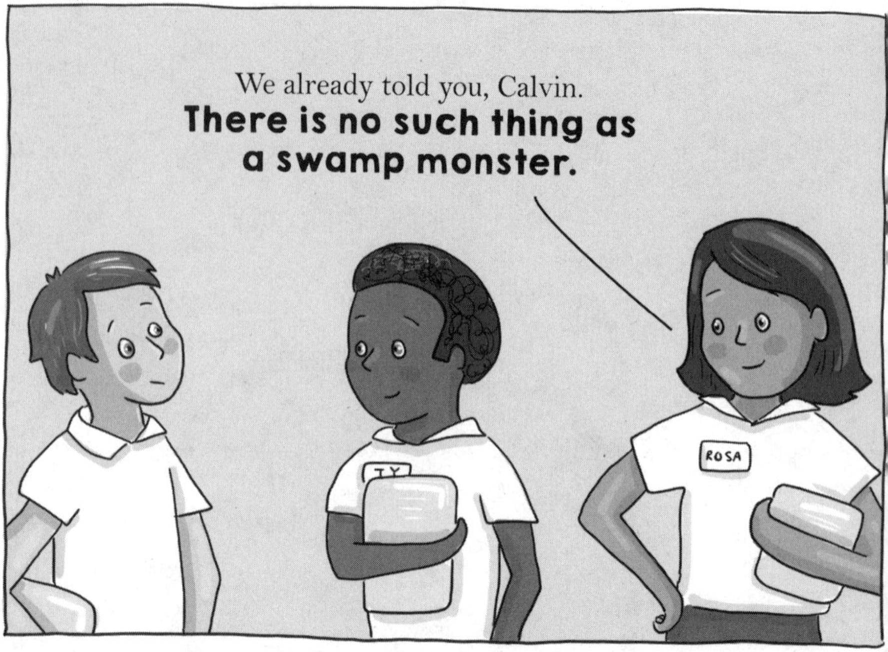
We already told you, Calvin.
There is no such thing as a swamp monster.
TY
ROSA

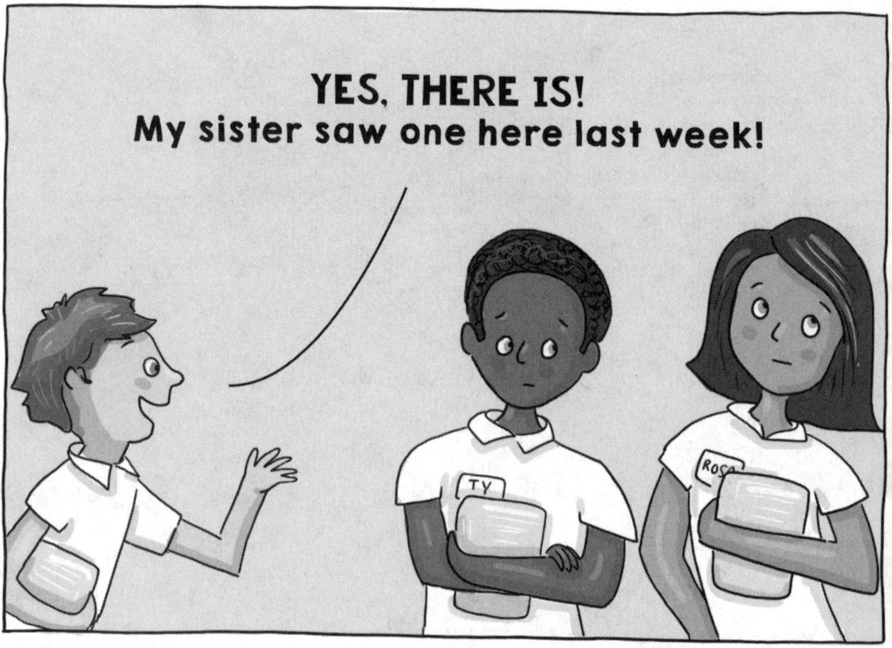
YES, THERE IS!
My sister saw one here last week!
TY

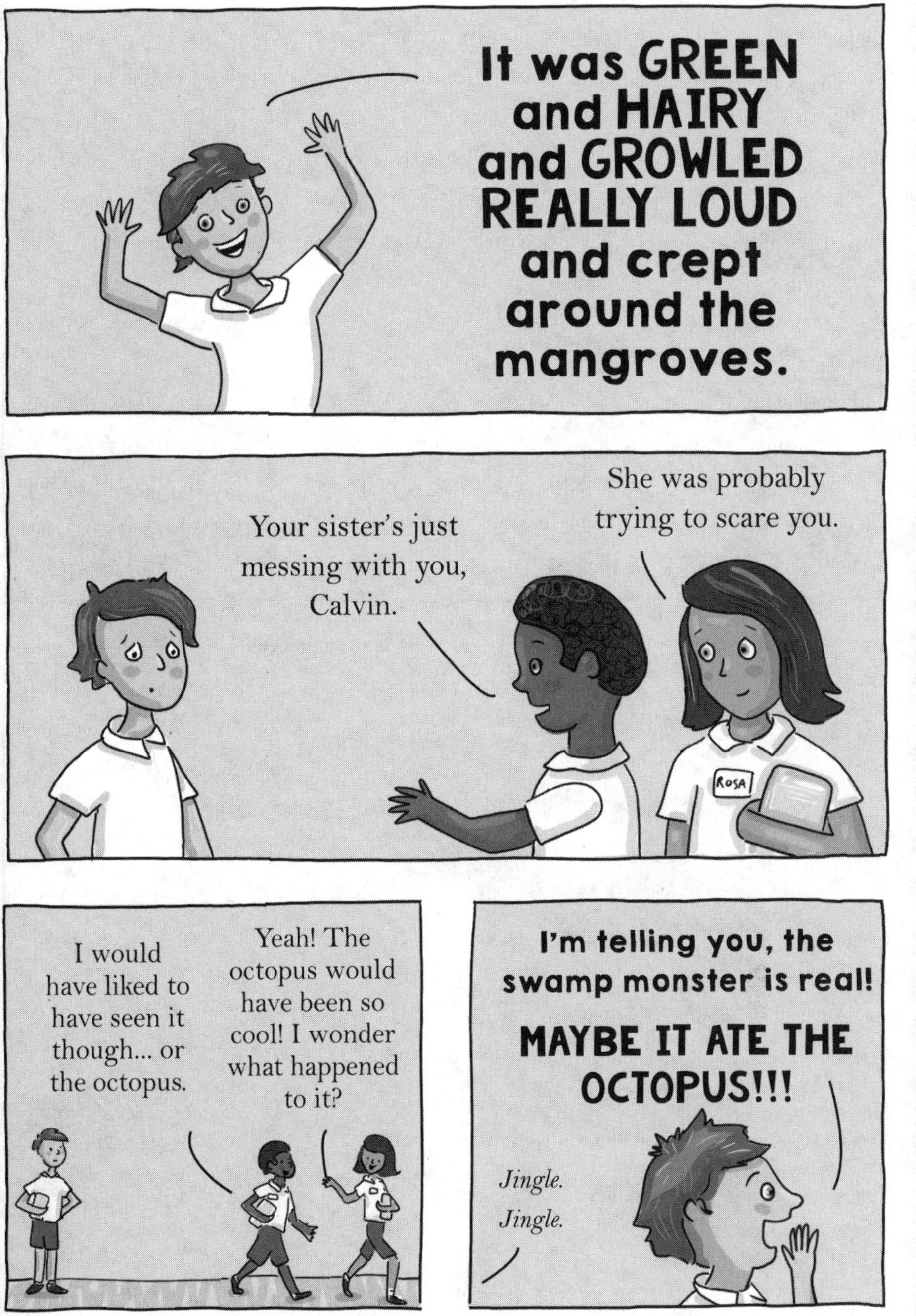
It was GREEN and HAIRY and GROWLED REALLY LOUD and crept around the mangroves.
She was probably trying to scare you.
Your sister's just messing with you, Calvin.
ROSA
I would have liked to have seen it though... or the octopus.
Yeah! The octopus would have been so cool! I wonder what happened to it?
I'm telling you, the swamp monster is real!
MAYBE IT ATE THE OCTOPUS!!!
Jingle.
Jingle.

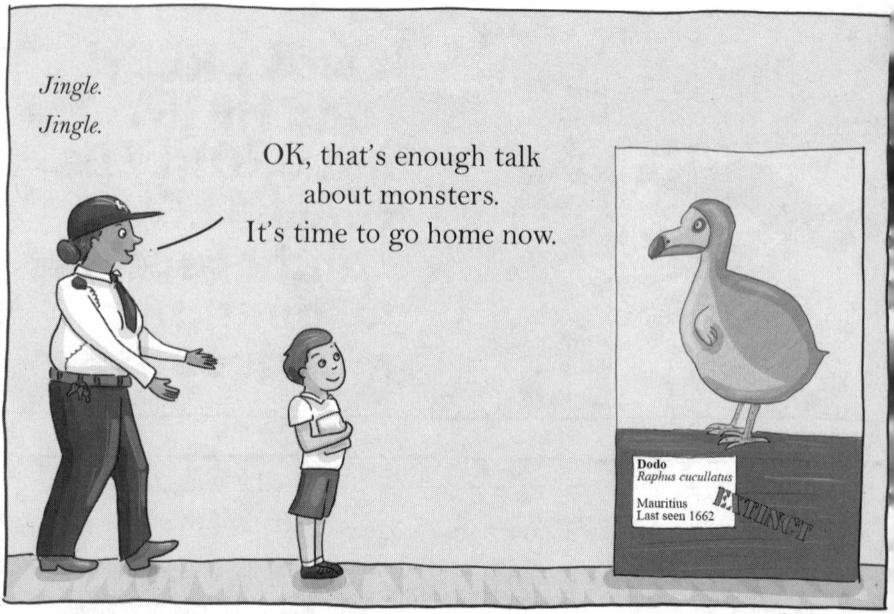
Jingle.
Jingle.
OK, that's enough talk about monsters. It's time to go home now.
Dodo
Raphus cucullatus
Mauritius
Last seen 1662
EXTINCT

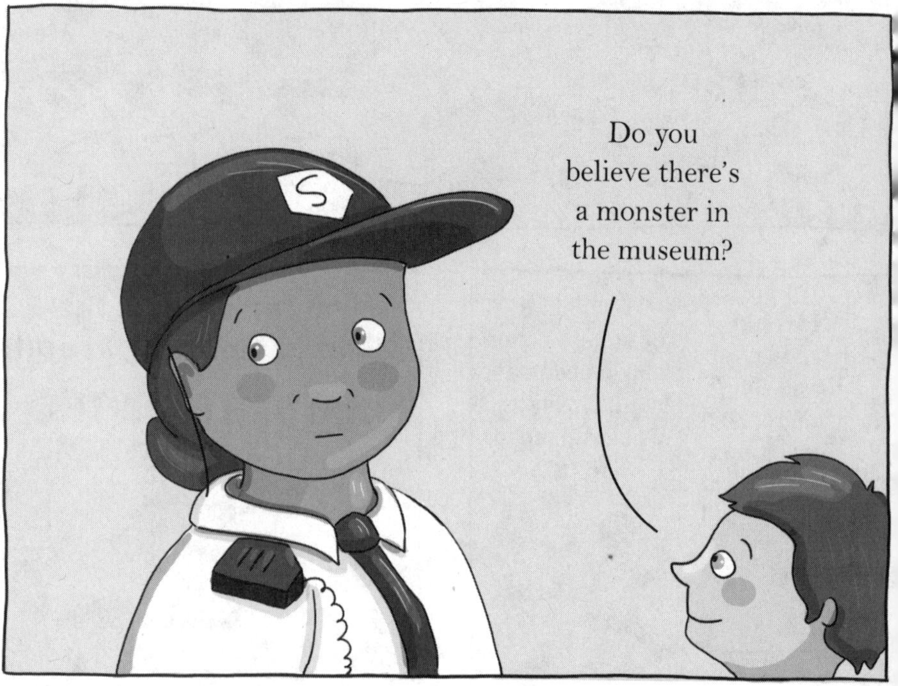
Do you believe there's a monster in the museum?

OH, LOOK!

The rest of your class is already on the bus.

Better hurry!

The museum is about to close.

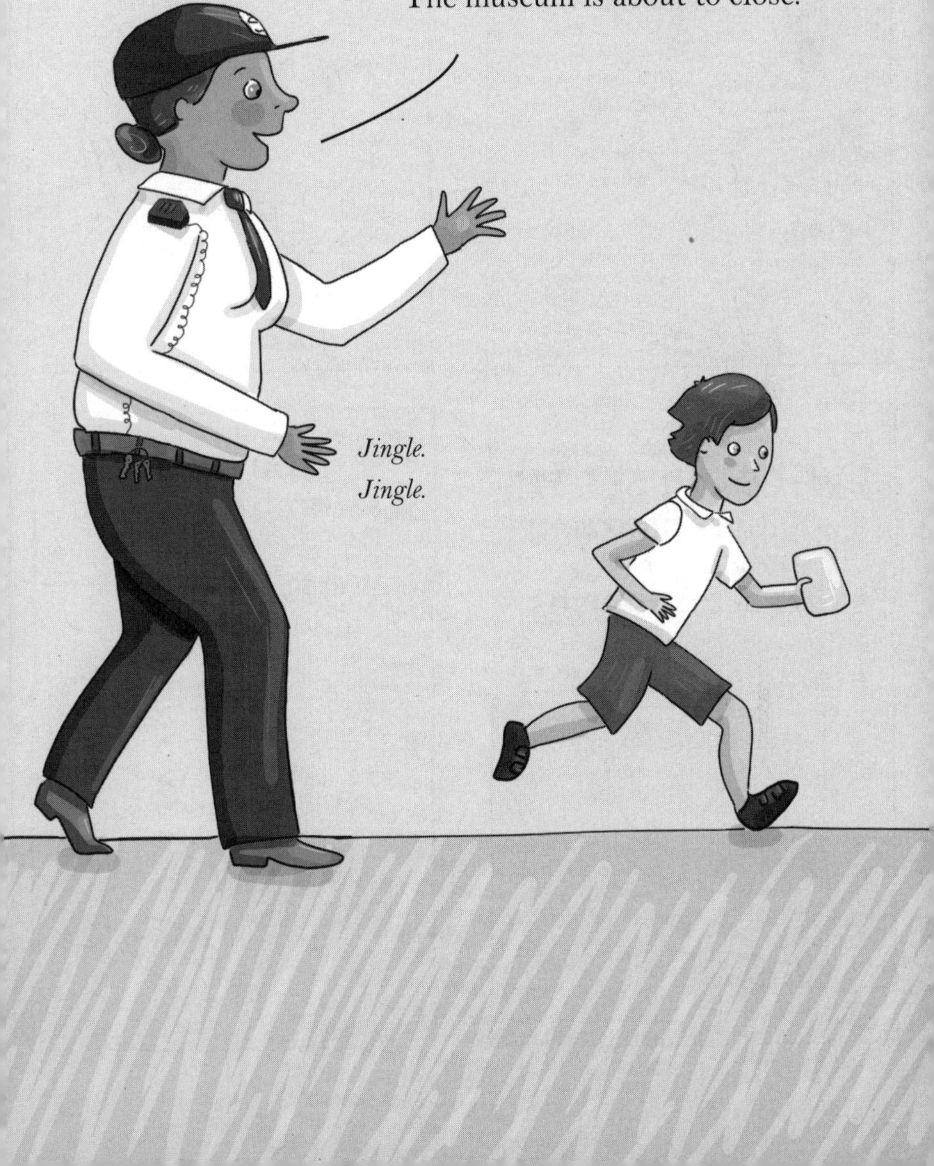

Jingle.
Jingle.

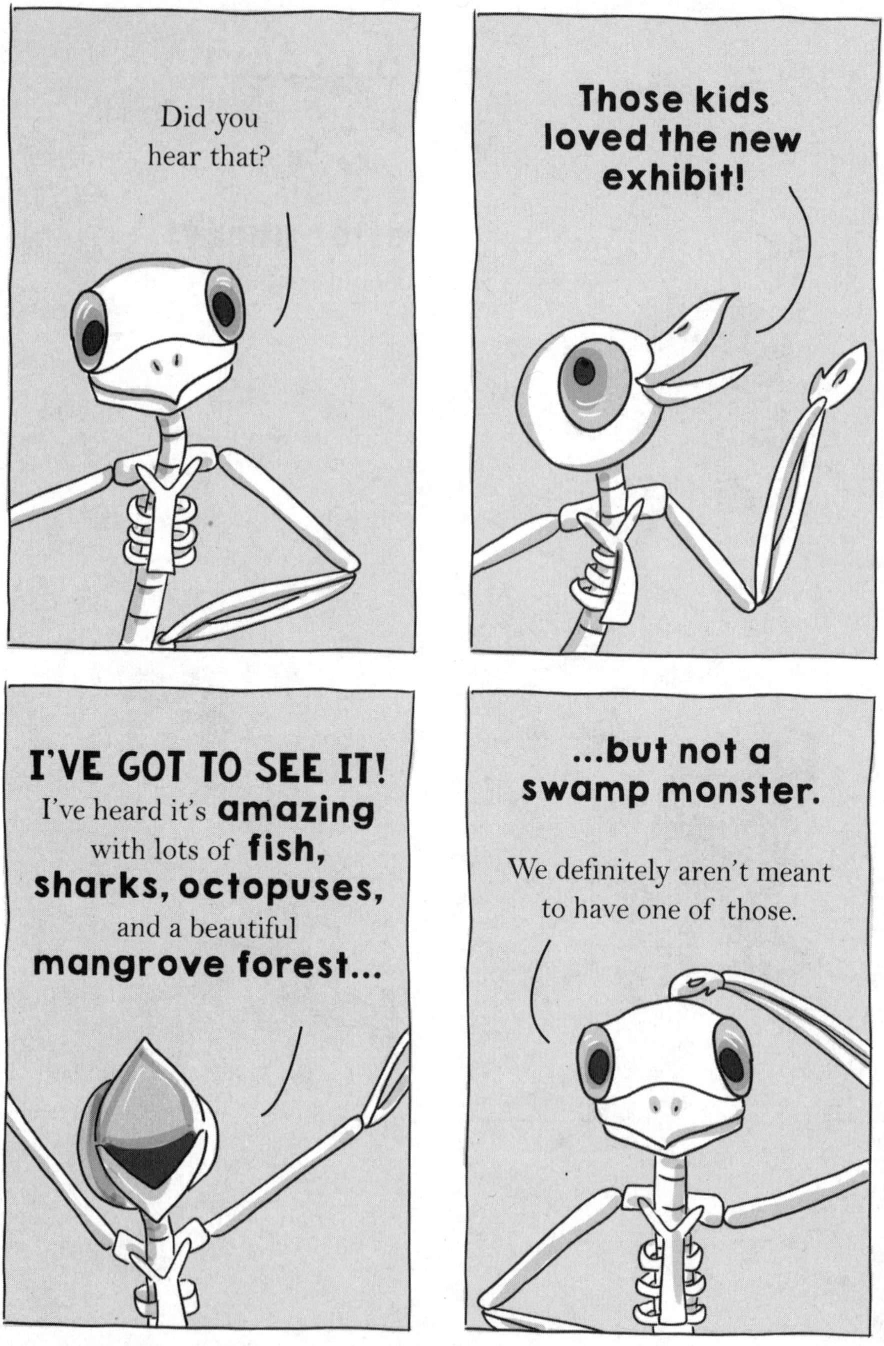
Did you hear that?
Those kids loved the new exhibit!
I'VE GOT TO SEE IT! I've heard it's amazing with lots of fish, sharks, octopuses, and a beautiful mangrove forest...
...but not a swamp monster.
We definitely aren't meant to have one of those.

Hey, Watts! Would it be worse if the kids **think** the museum has a swamp monster?

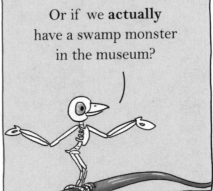

Or if we **actually** have a swamp monster in the museum?

Watts?

Heeellllllooo?

Where are you?

Well, of course you're in your drawer!

Tawny Frogmouth
Podargus strigoides
Australia
Carnivore
Bird

SPECIMENS

Caprimulgiformes:
Nightjars, frogmouths

Psittaciformes:
Parrots

Passeriformes:
Perching birds

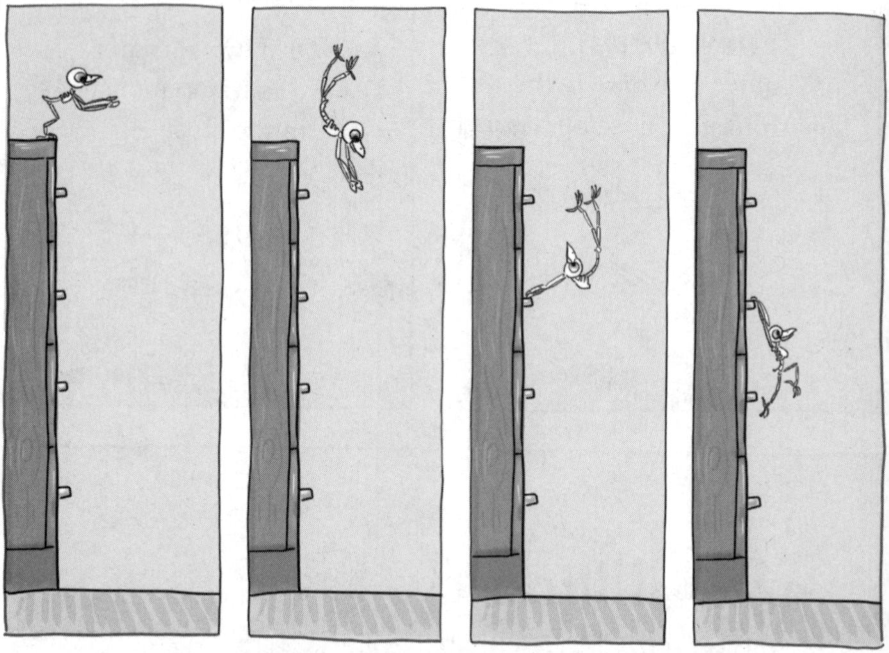

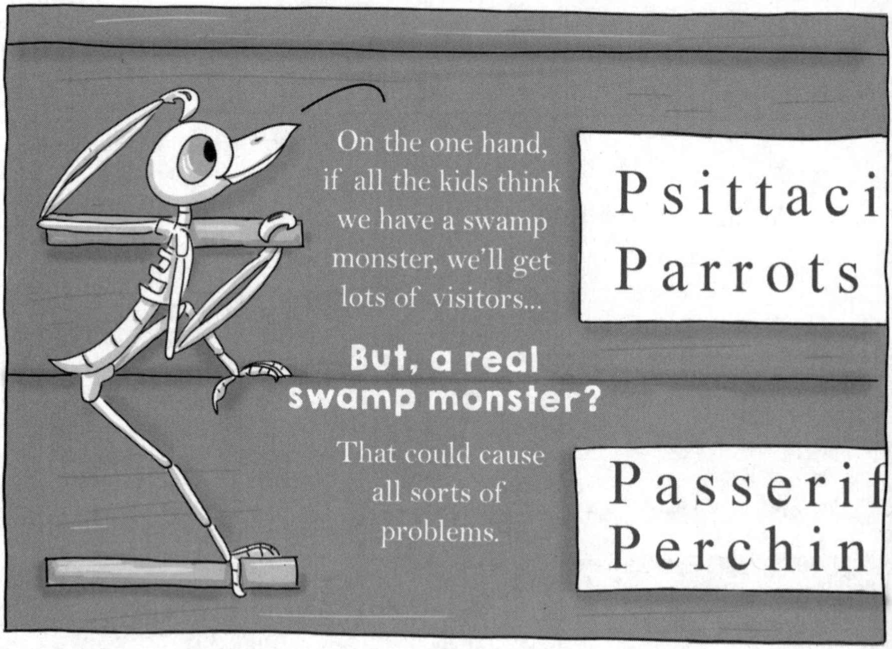
On the one hand, if all the kids think we have a swamp monster, we'll get lots of visitors...
But, a real swamp monster?
That could cause all sorts of problems.
Psittaci
Parrots
Passerif
Perchin

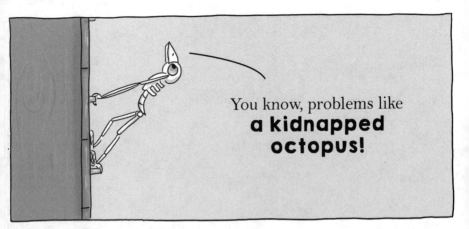

You know, problems like
**a kidnapped
octopus!**

Or would we call it
fish-napped?

Ugh. This stupid drawer
won't o—

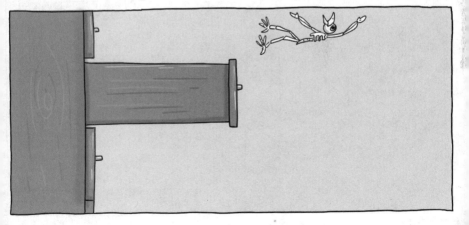

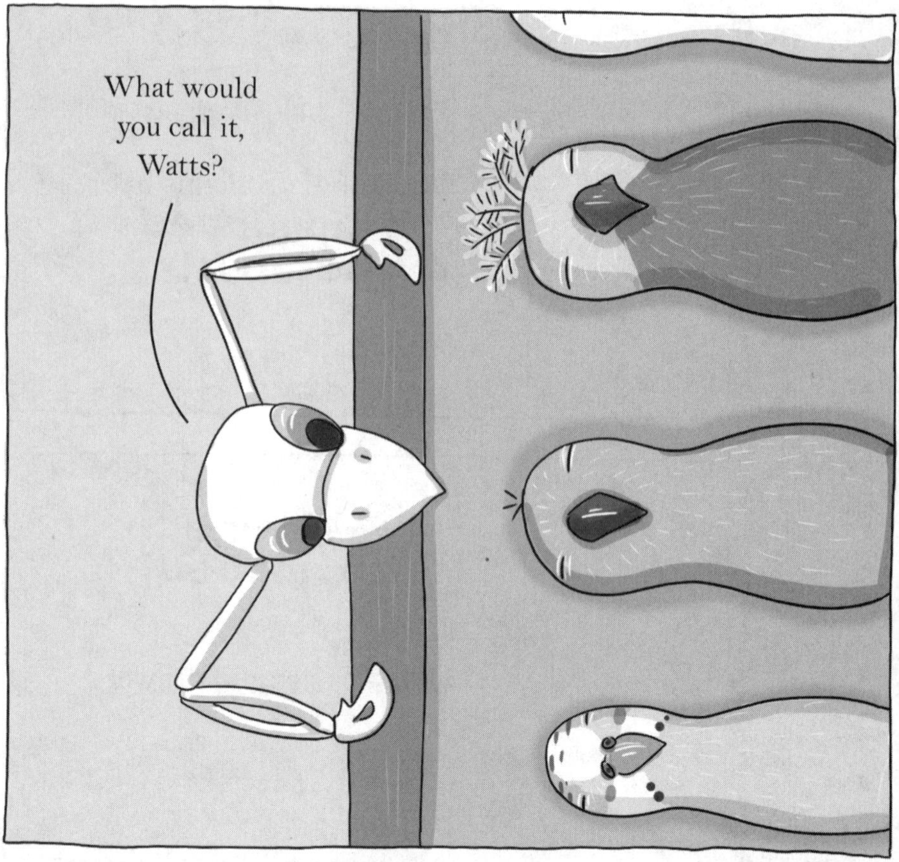
What would you call it, Watts?

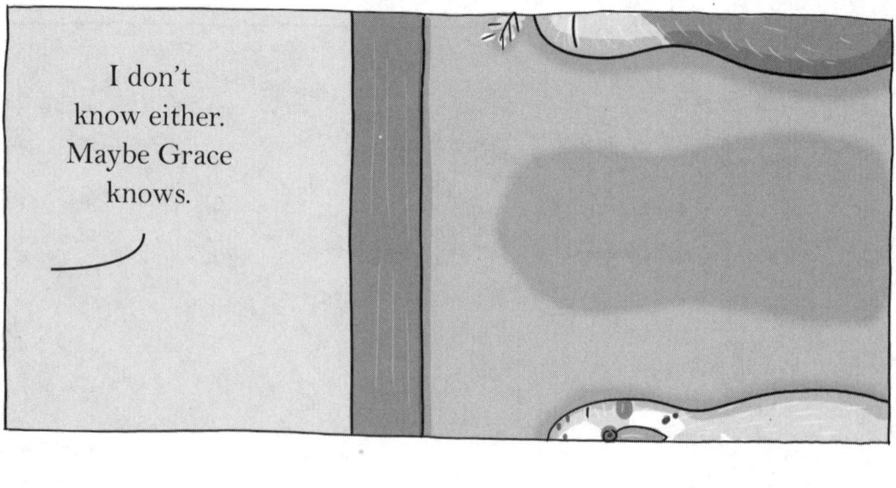
I don't know either. Maybe Grace knows.

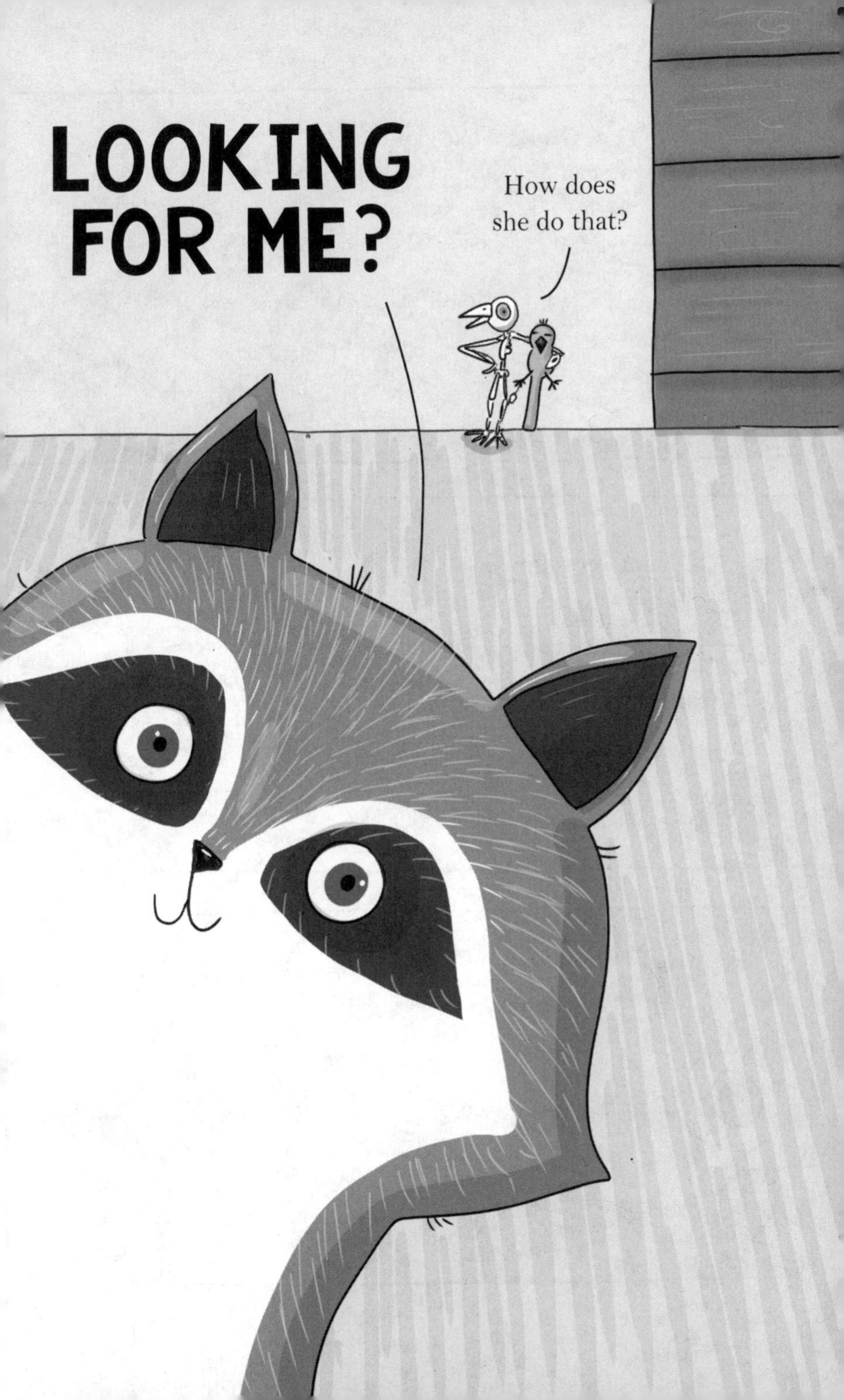
LOOKING FOR ME?
How does she do that?

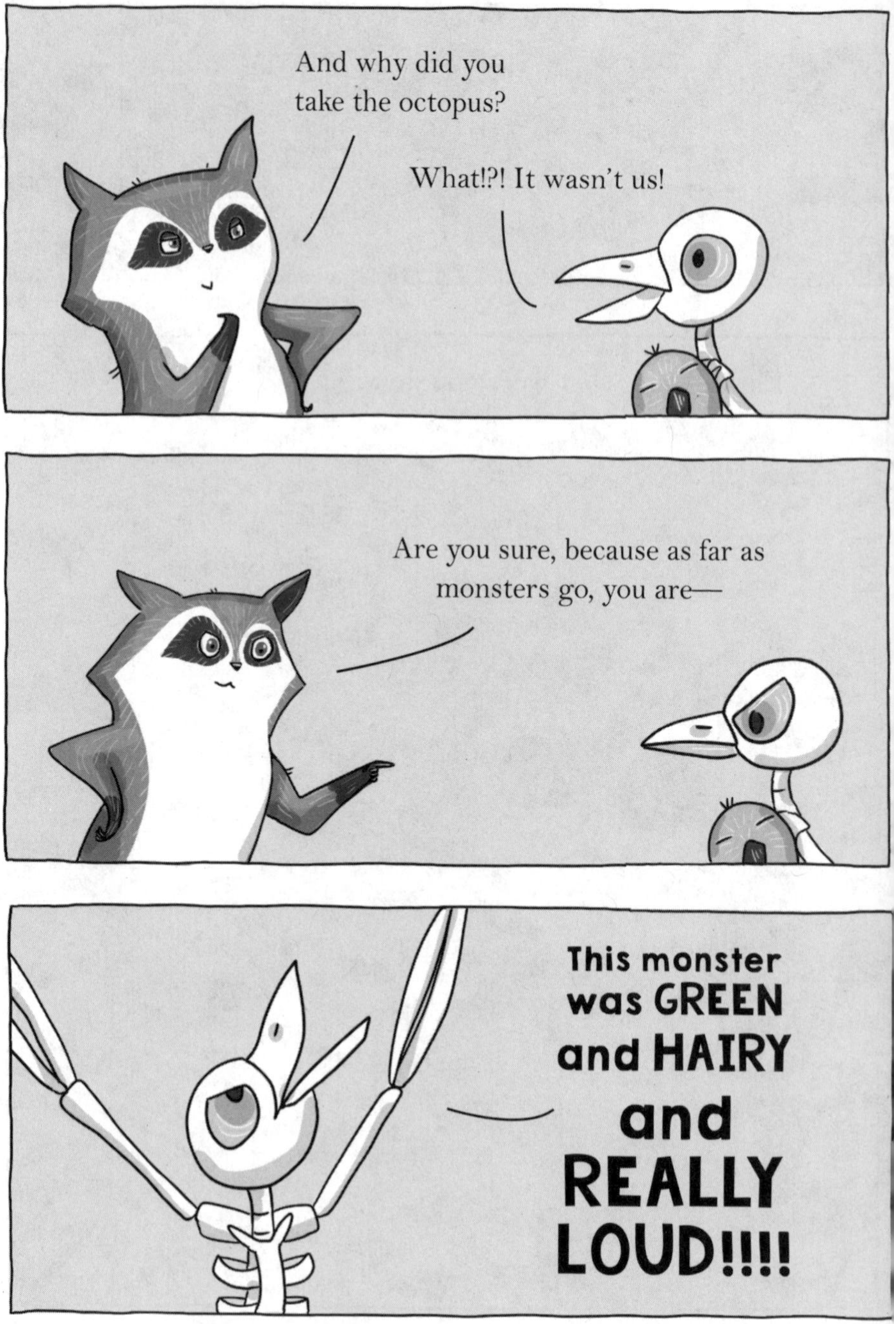
And why did you take the octopus?
What!?! It wasn't us!
Are you sure, because as far as monsters go, you are—
This monster was GREEN and HAIRY and REALLY LOUD!!!!

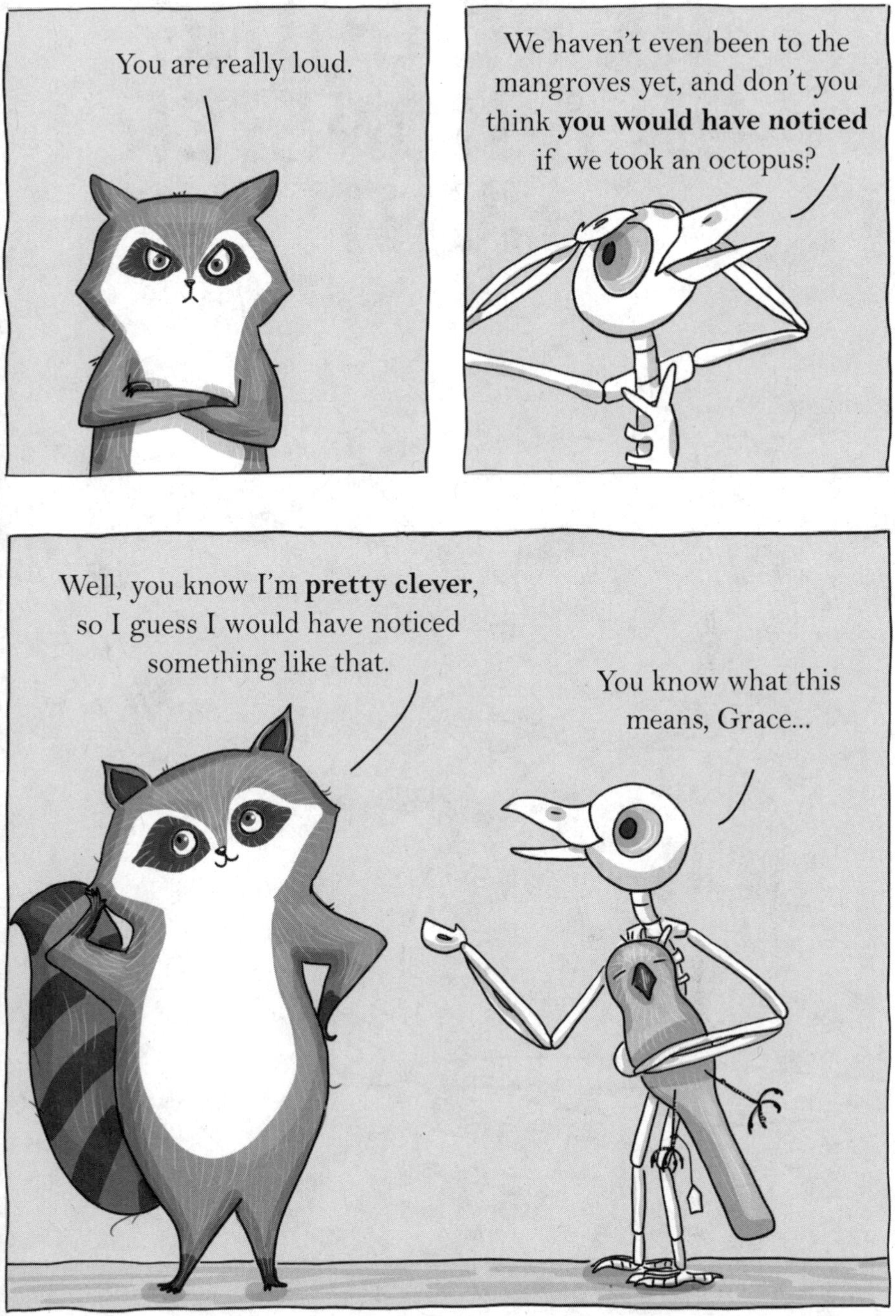
You are really loud.
We haven't even been to the mangroves yet, and don't you think **you would have noticed** if we took an octopus?
Well, you know I'm **pretty clever**, so I guess I would have noticed something like that.
You know what this means, Grace...

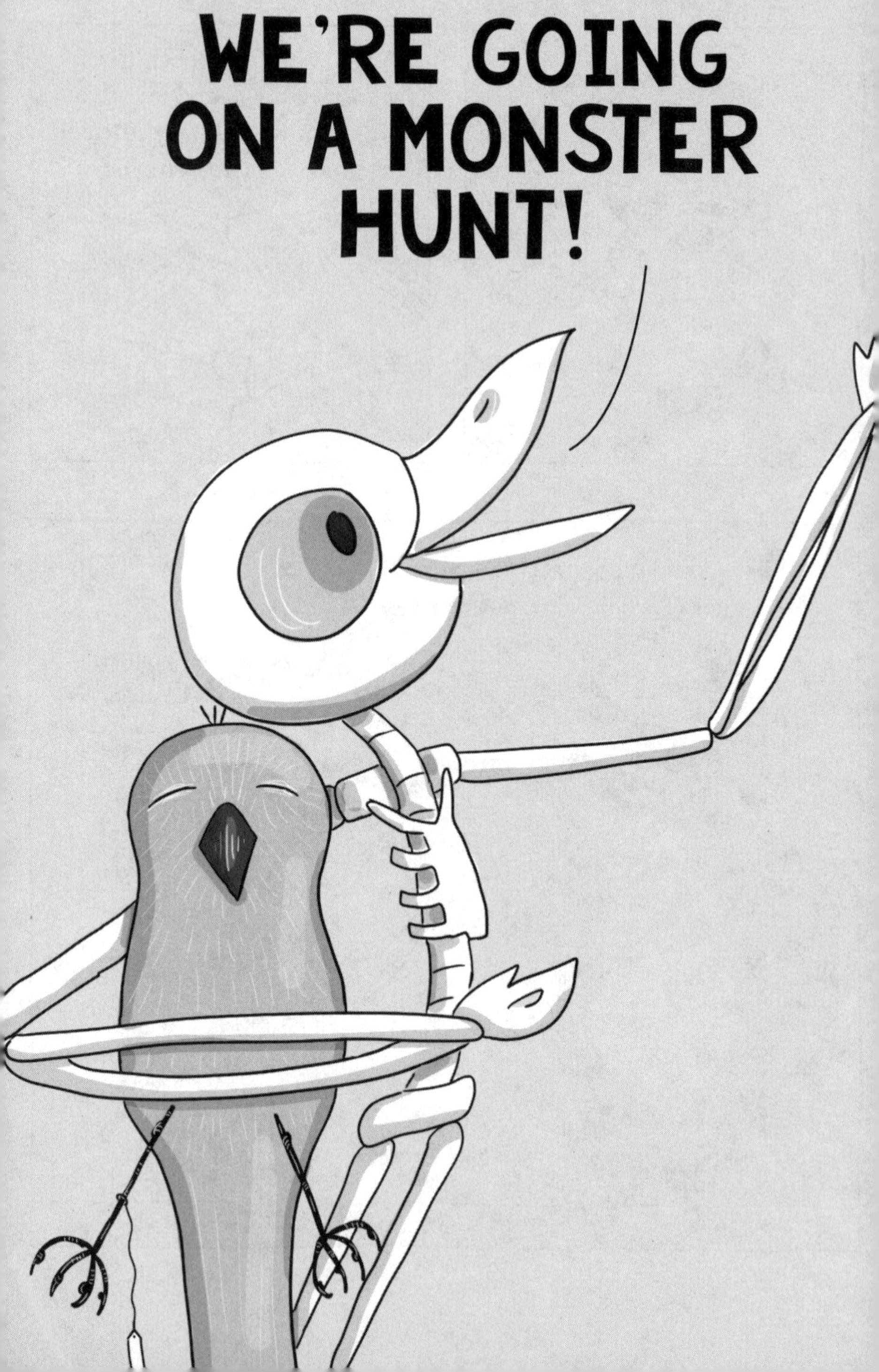
WE'RE GOING ON A MONSTER HUNT!

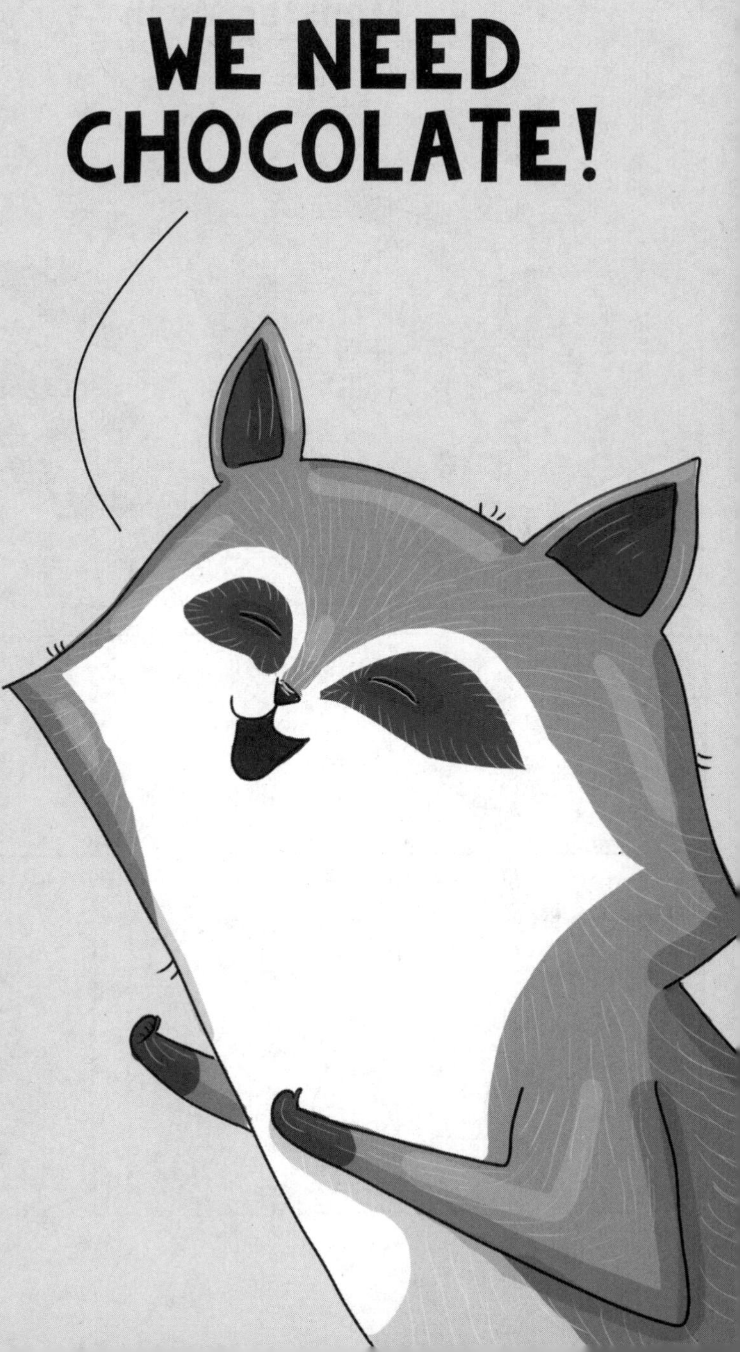
WE NEED CHOCOLATE!

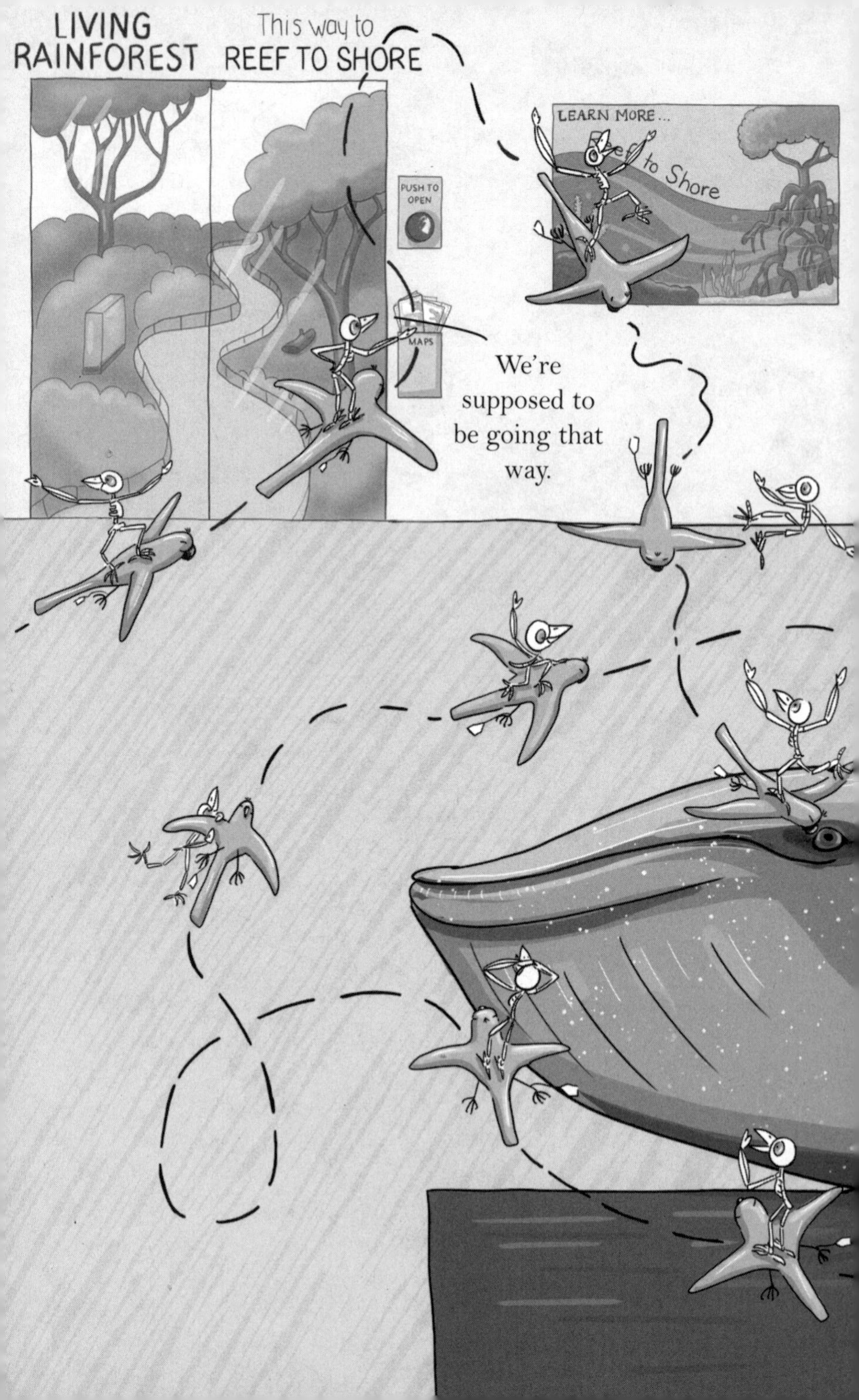
LIVING RAINFOREST
This way to REEF TO SHORE
PUSH TO OPEN
MAPS
LEARN MORE...
to Shore
We're supposed to be going that way.

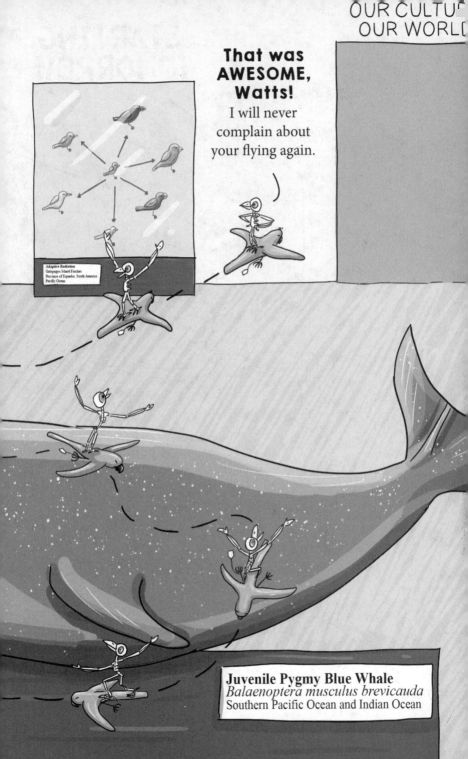

That was **AWESOME, Watts!**

I will never complain about your flying again.

Adaptive Radiation
Galapagos Island Finches
Province of Ecuador, South America
Pacific Ocean

Juvenile Pygmy Blue Whale
Balaenoptera musculus brevicauda
Southern Pacific Ocean and Indian Ocean

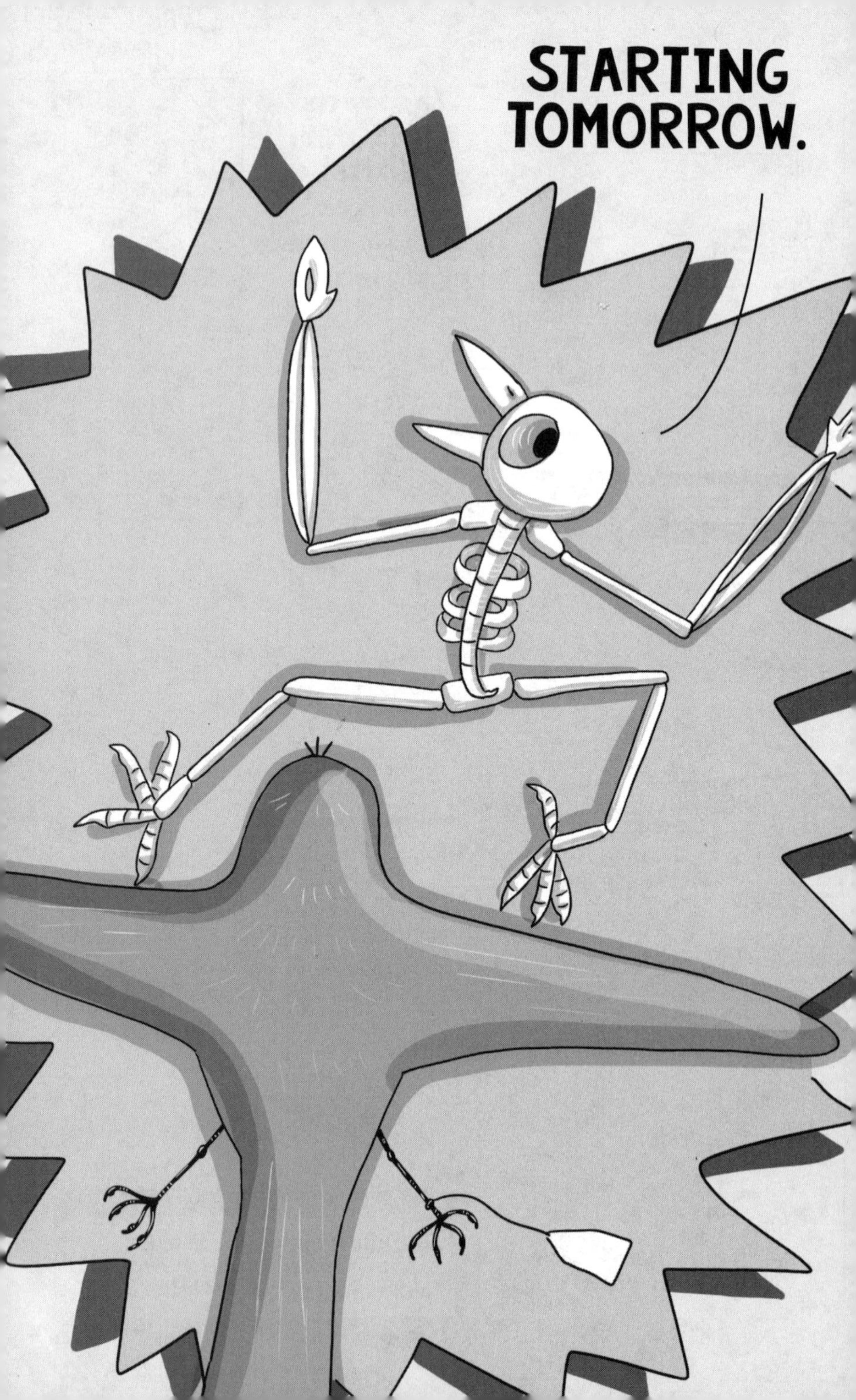
STARTING TOMORROW.

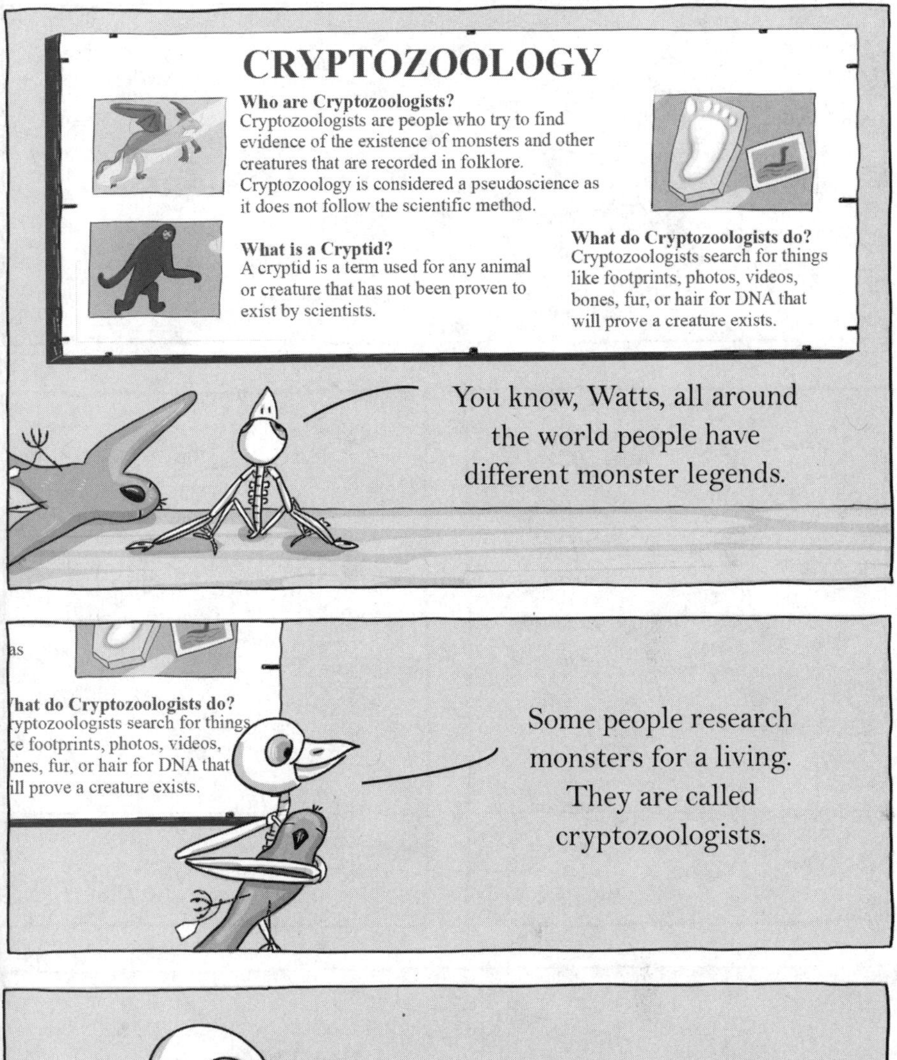
CRYPTOZOOLOGY
Who are Cryptozoologists?
Cryptozoologists are people who try to find evidence of the existence of monsters and other creatures that are recorded in folklore. Cryptozoology is considered a pseudoscience as it does not follow the scientific method.
What is a Cryptid?
A cryptid is a term used for any animal or creature that has not been proven to exist by scientists.
What do Cryptozoologists do?
Cryptozoologists search for things like footprints, photos, videos, bones, fur, or hair for DNA that will prove a creature exists.
You know, Watts, all around the world people have different monster legends.
as
hat do Cryptozoologists do?
ryptozoologists search for things
e footprints, photos, videos,
nes, fur, or hair for DNA that
ill prove a creature exists.
Some people research monsters for a living. They are called cryptozoologists.
Yes, I think it's a cool word too.

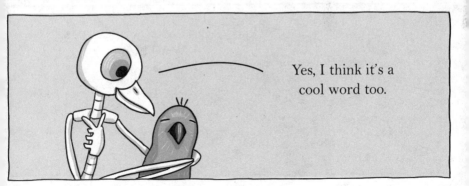

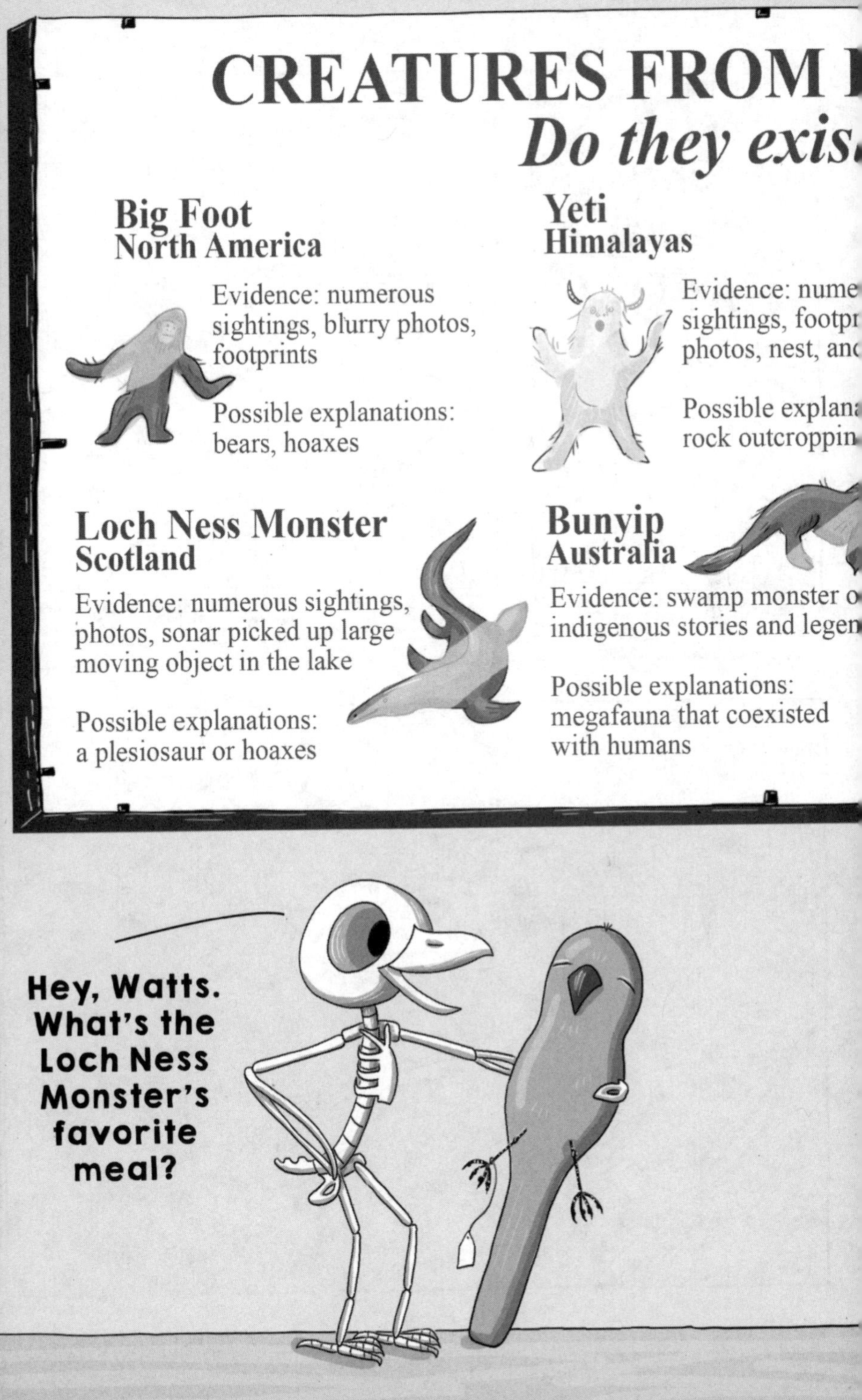

CREATURES FROM I
Do they exis

Big Foot
North America

Evidence: numerous sightings, blurry photos, footprints

Possible explanations: bears, hoaxes

Yeti
Himalayas

Evidence: nume sightings, footpr photos, nest, and

Possible explana rock outcroppin

Loch Ness Monster
Scotland

Evidence: numerous sightings, photos, sonar picked up large moving object in the lake

Possible explanations: a plesiosaur or hoaxes

Bunyip
Australia

Evidence: swamp monster o indigenous stories and legen

Possible explanations: megafauna that coexisted with humans

Hey, Watts. What's the Loch Ness Monster's favorite meal?

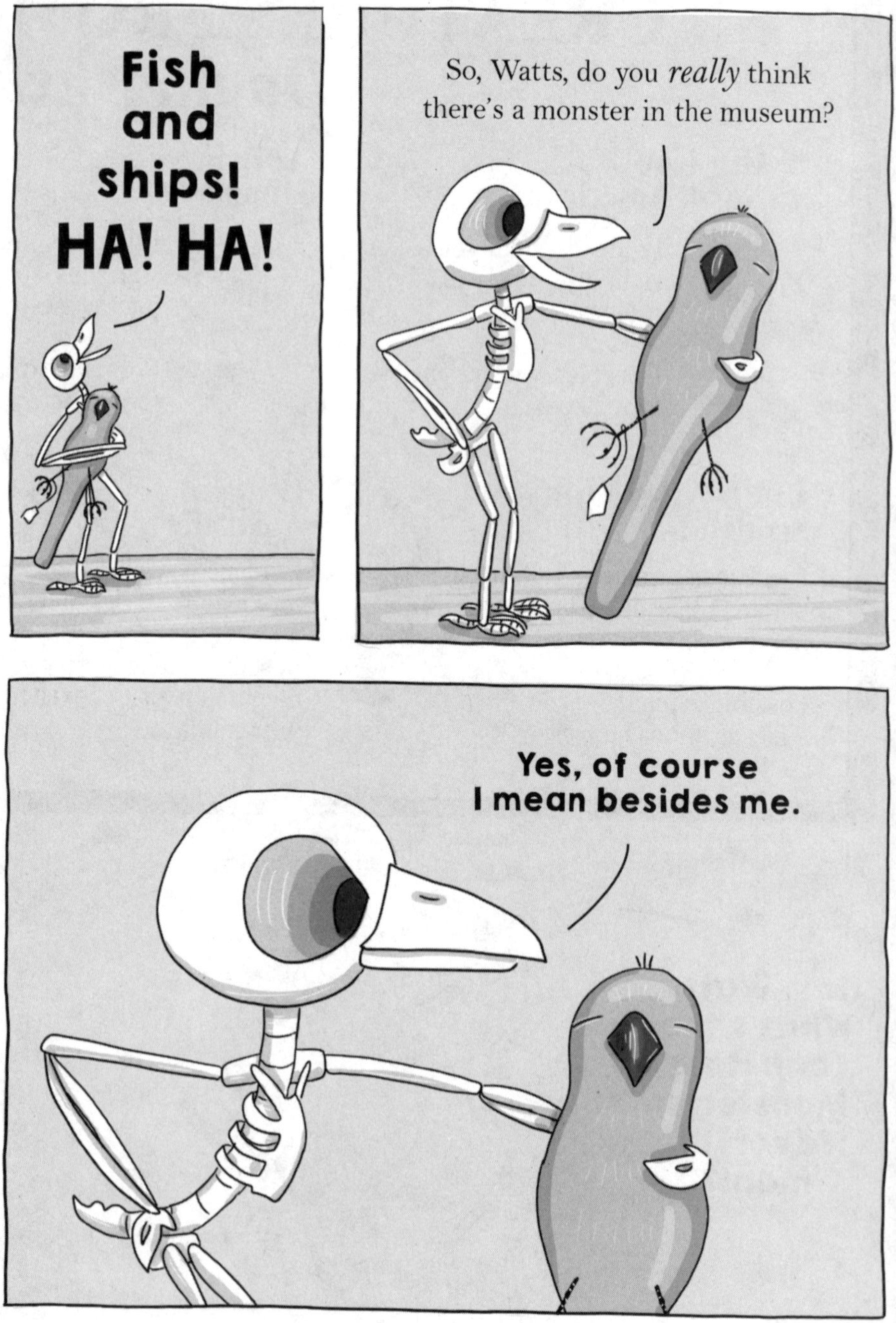
Fish and ships! HA! HA!
So, Watts, do you *really* think there's a monster in the museum?
Yes, of course I mean besides me.

CHAPTER 3
Feeling Blue

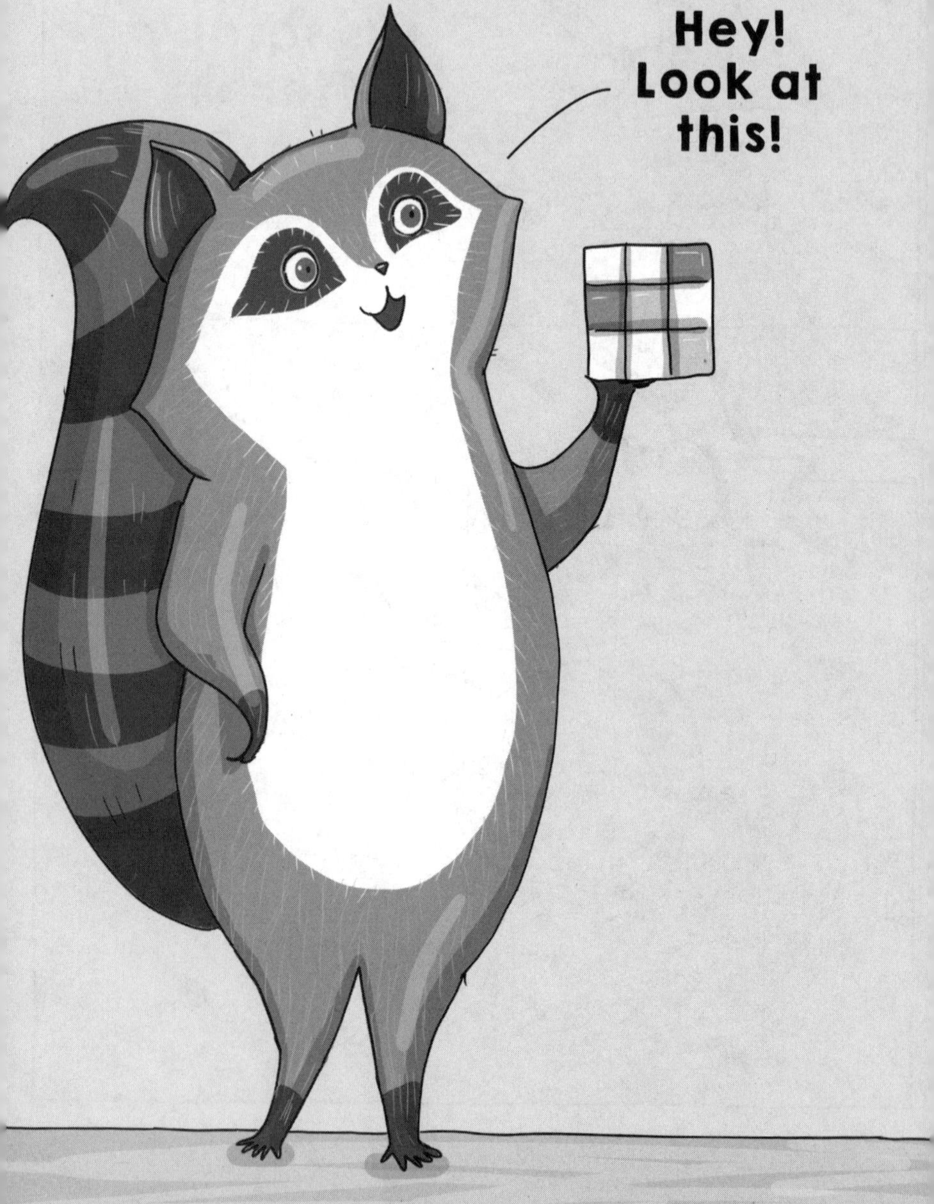
Hey!
Look at
this!

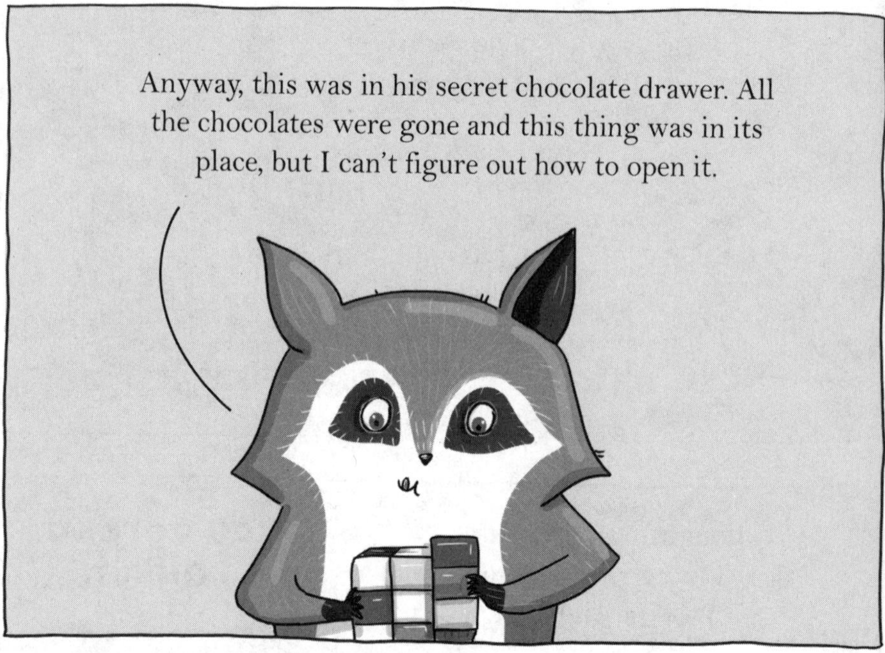
Anyway, this was in his secret chocolate drawer. All the chocolates were gone and this thing was in its place, but I can't figure out how to open it.

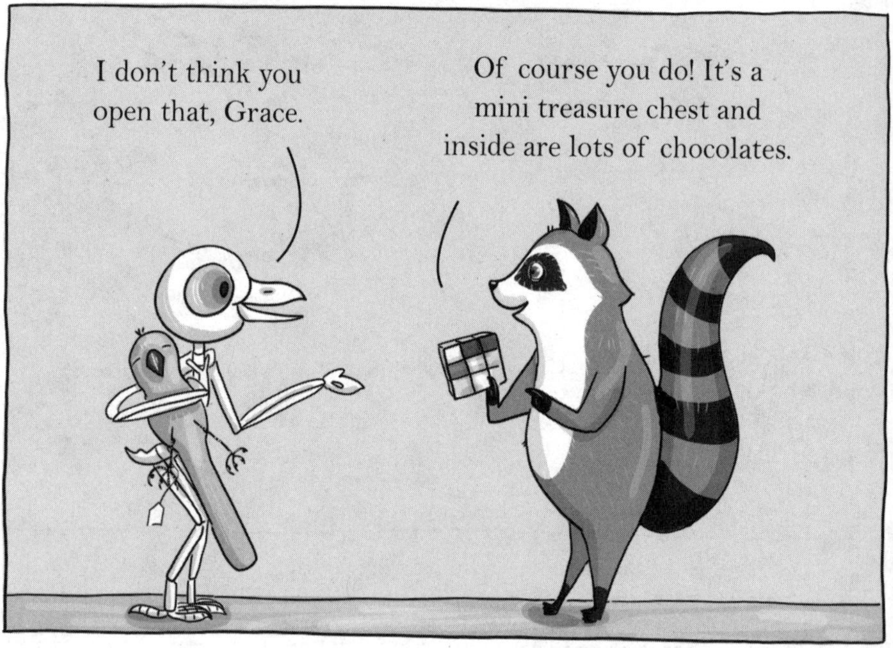
I don't think you open that, Grace.
Of course you do! It's a mini treasure chest and inside are lots of chocolates.

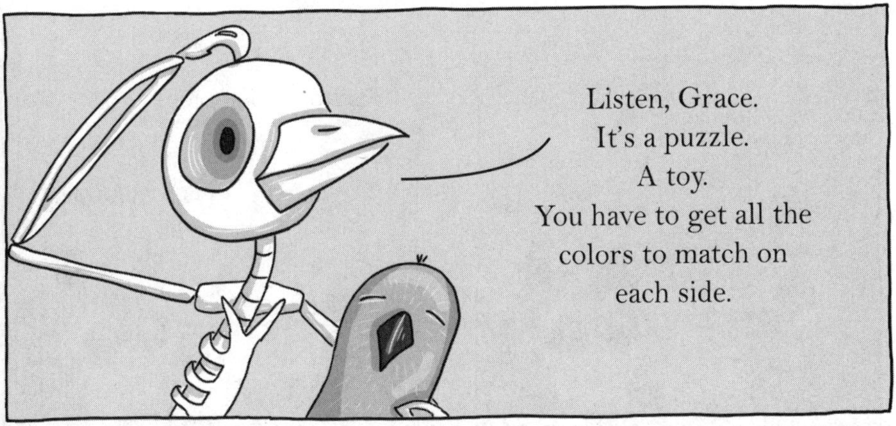
Listen, Grace.
It's a puzzle.
A toy.
You have to get all the
colors to match on
each side.

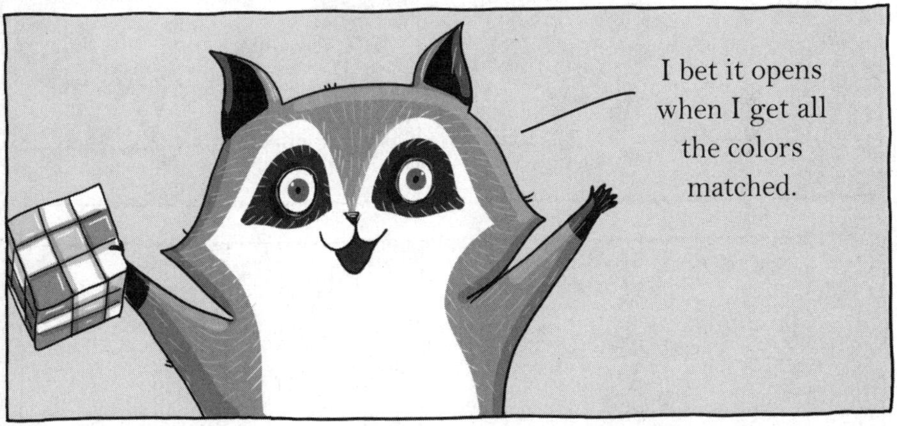
I bet it opens
when I get all
the colors
matched.

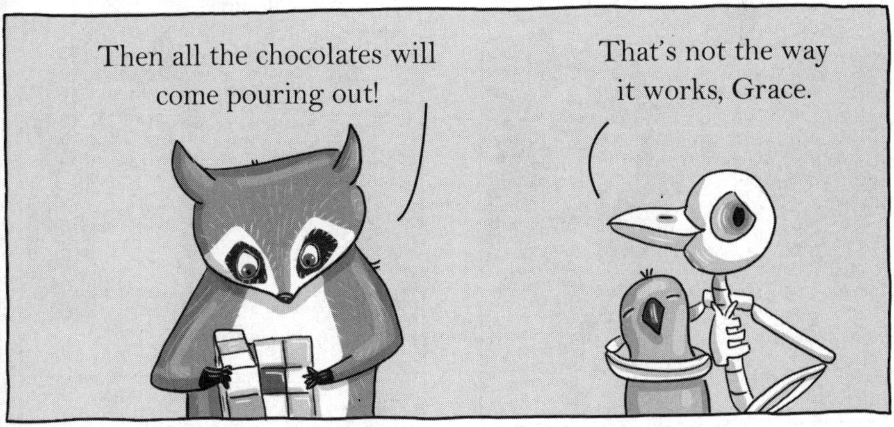
Then all the chocolates will
come pouring out!
That's not the way
it works, Grace.

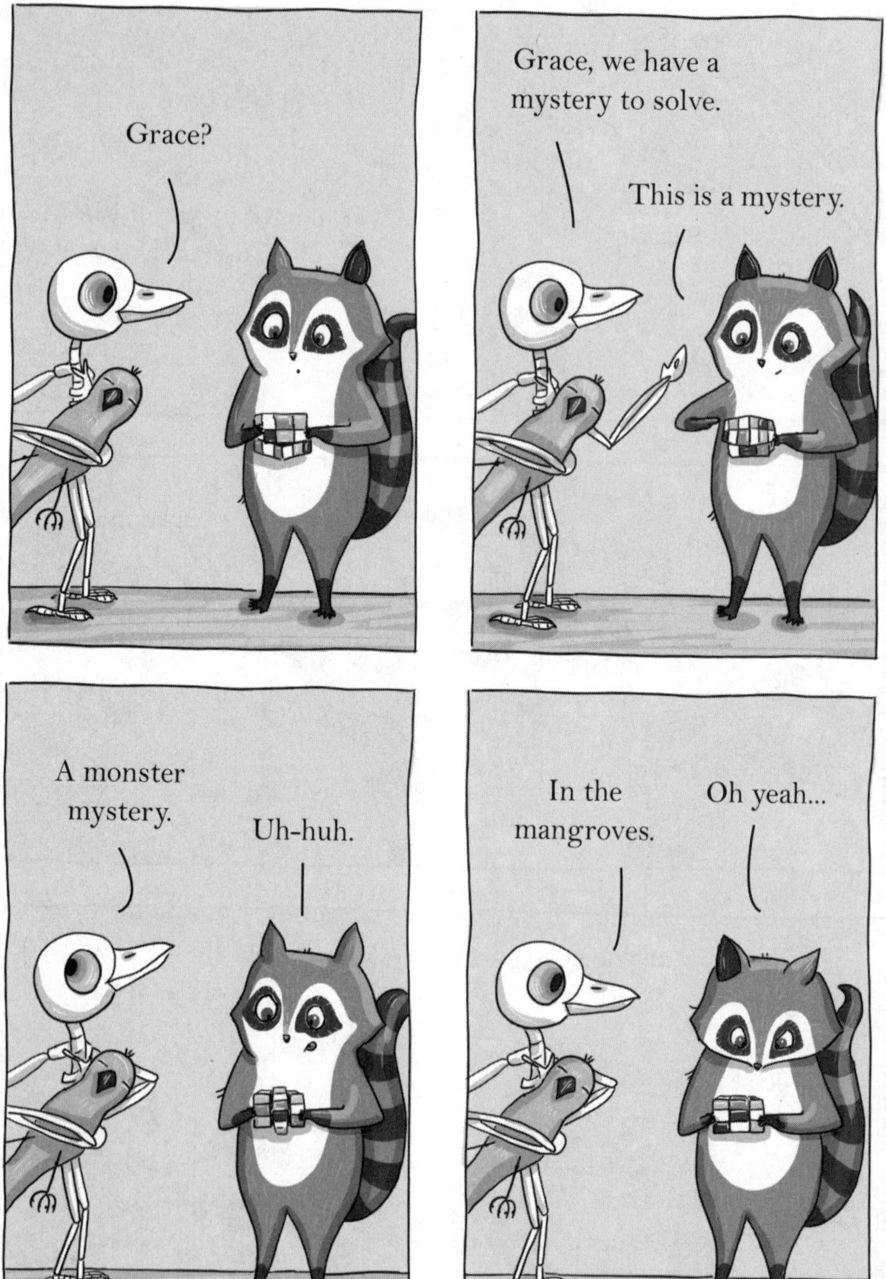
Grace?
Grace, we have a mystery to solve.
This is a mystery.
A monster mystery.
Uh-huh.
In the mangroves.
Oh yeah...

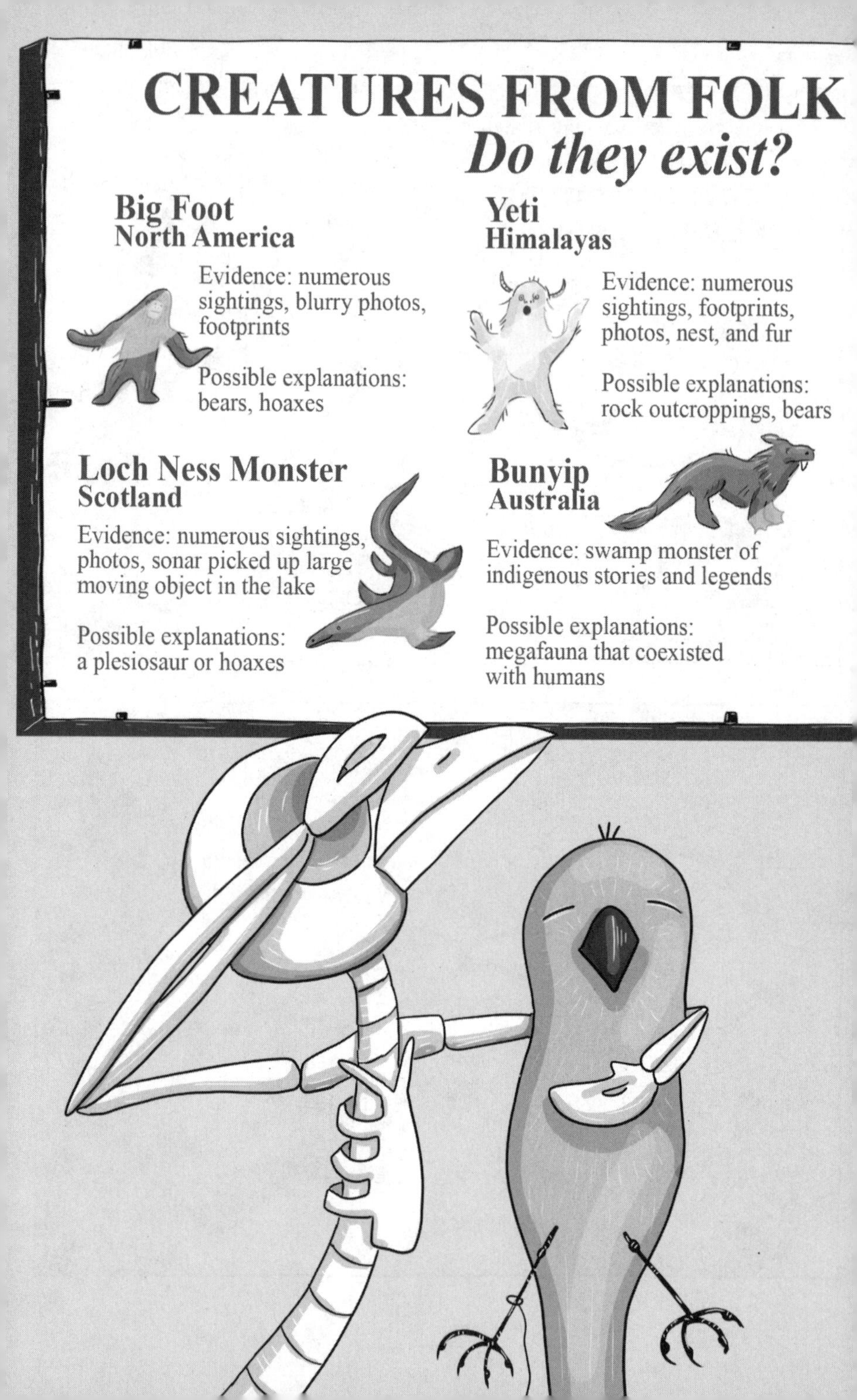

CREATURES FROM FOLK
Do they exist?

Big Foot
North America

Evidence: numerous sightings, blurry photos, footprints

Possible explanations: bears, hoaxes

Yeti
Himalayas

Evidence: numerous sightings, footprints, photos, nest, and fur

Possible explanations: rock outcroppings, bears

Loch Ness Monster
Scotland

Evidence: numerous sightings, photos, sonar picked up large moving object in the lake

Possible explanations: a plesiosaur or hoaxes

Bunyip
Australia

Evidence: swamp monster of indigenous stories and legends

Possible explanations: megafauna that coexisted with humans

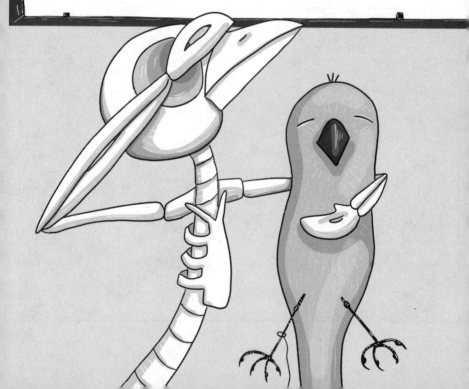

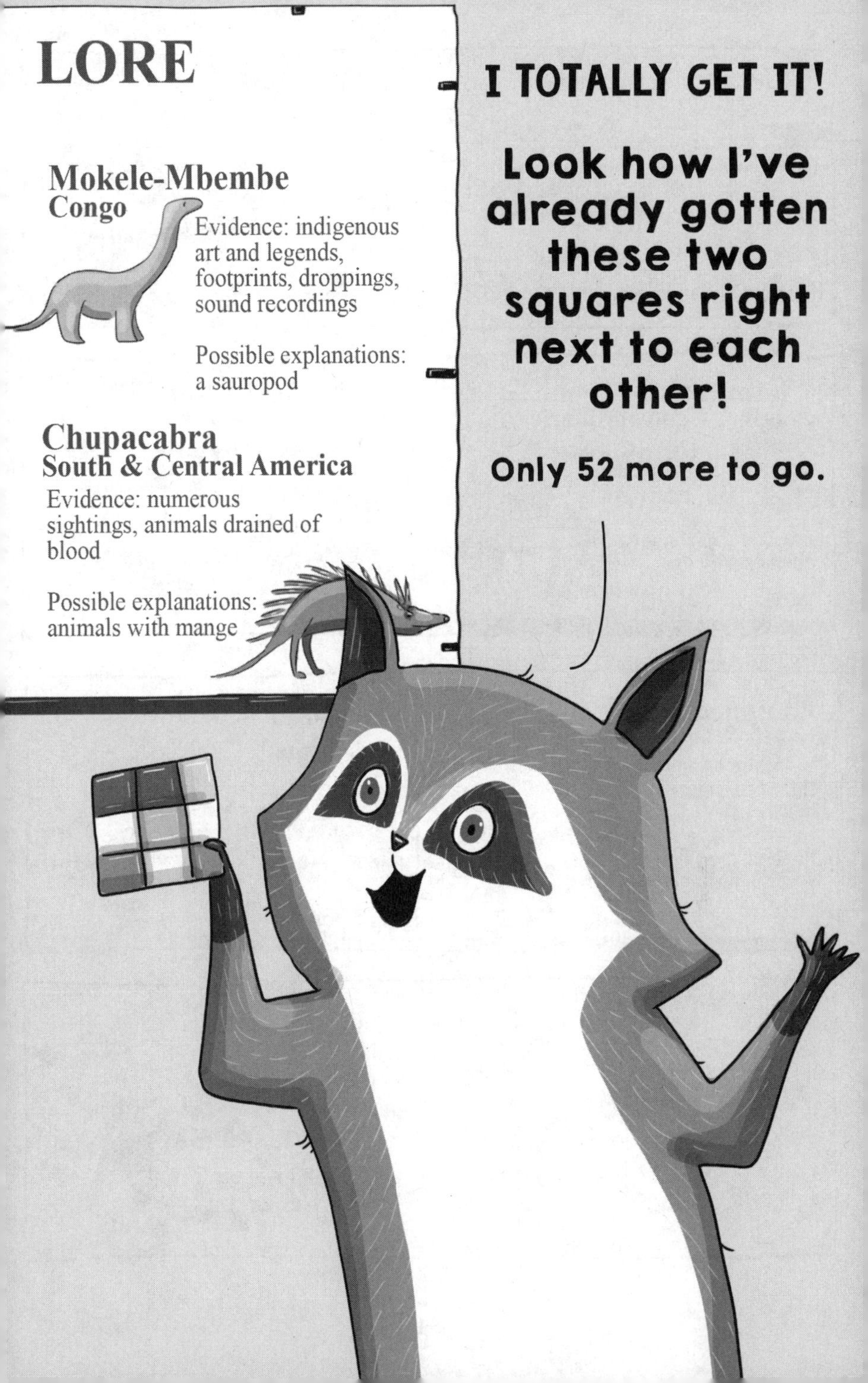
LORE
Mokele-Mbembe
Congo
Evidence: indigenous art and legends, footprints, droppings, sound recordings
Possible explanations: a sauropod
Chupacabra
South & Central America
Evidence: numerous sightings, animals drained of blood
Possible explanations: animals with mange
I TOTALLY GET IT!
Look how I've already gotten these two squares right next to each other!
Only 52 more to go.

Wooo... wooo...

creepy and scary...

blood-sucking monsters.

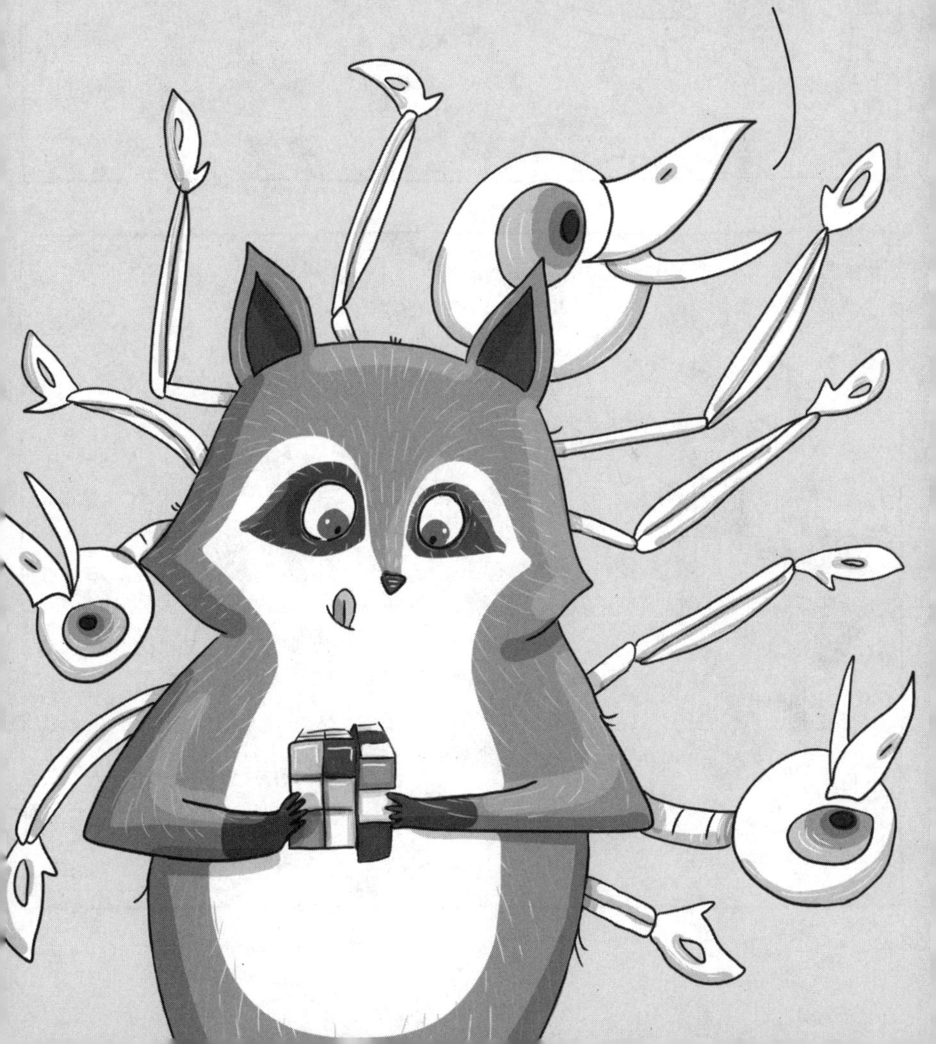

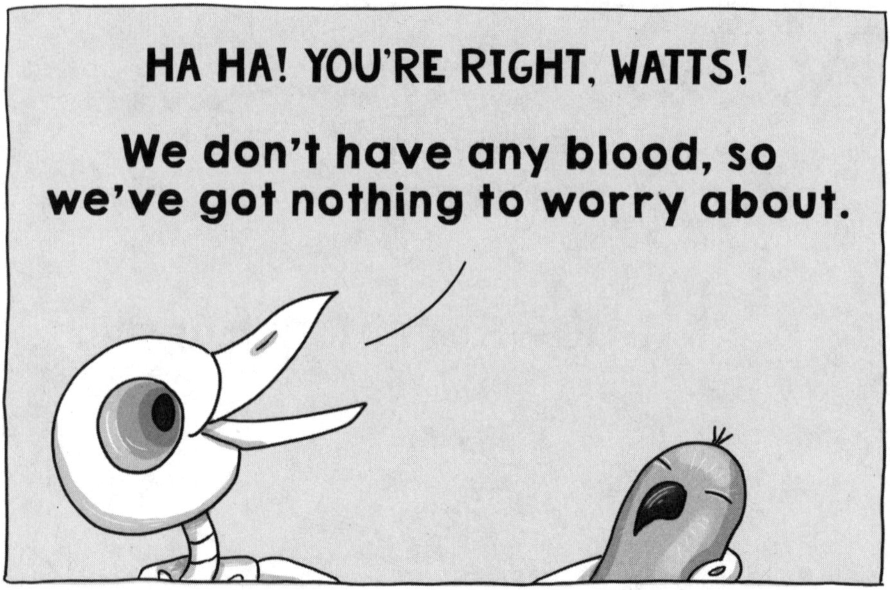

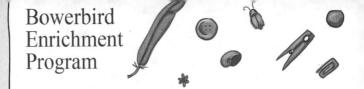

Bowerbird Enrichment Program

Every day we hide blue objects like these around the exhibit for the bo▨
Can you spot them all before the birds find them?

Touch Tank 1

Touch Tank 2

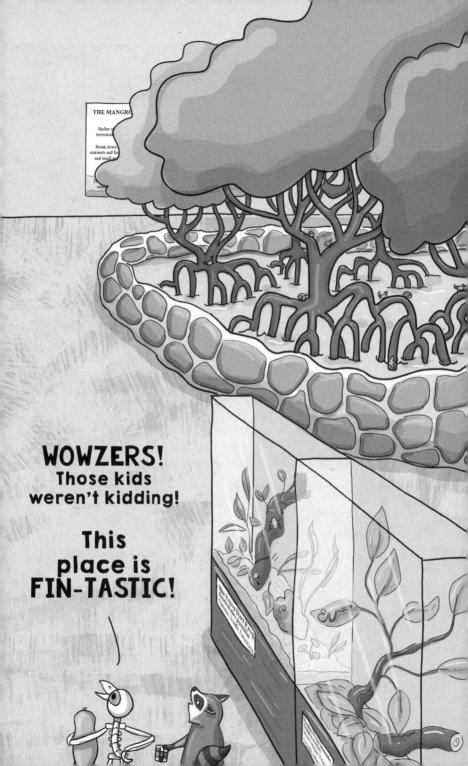

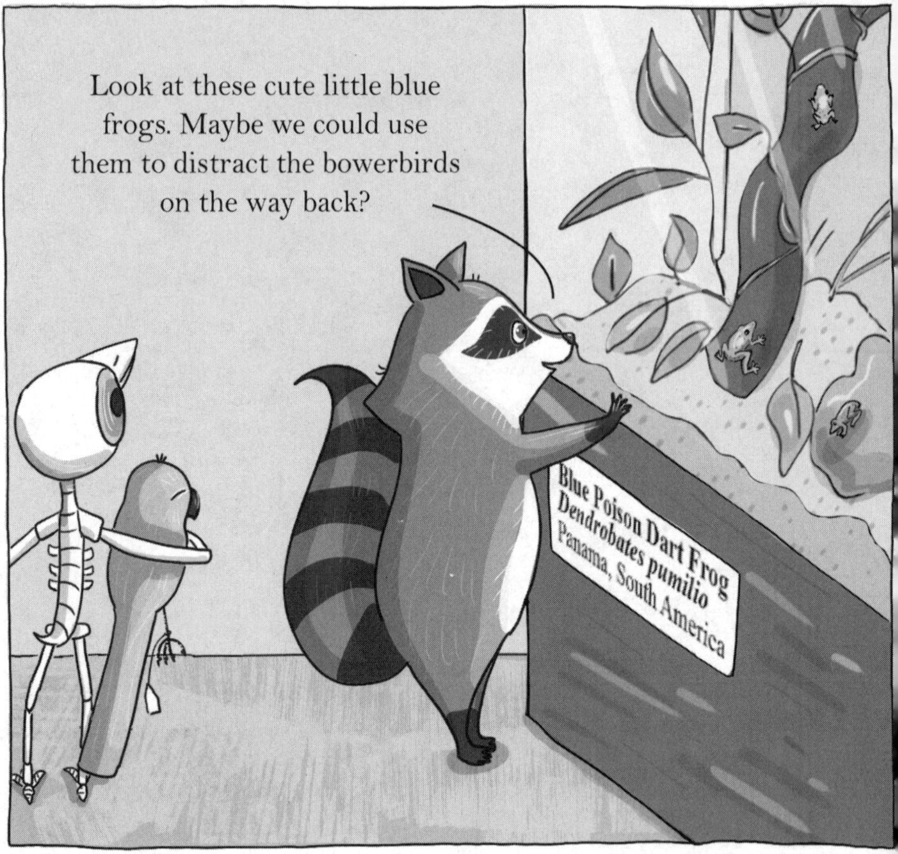
Look at these cute little blue frogs. Maybe we could use them to distract the bowerbirds on the way back?
Blue Poison Dart Frog
Dendrobates pumilio
Panama, South America

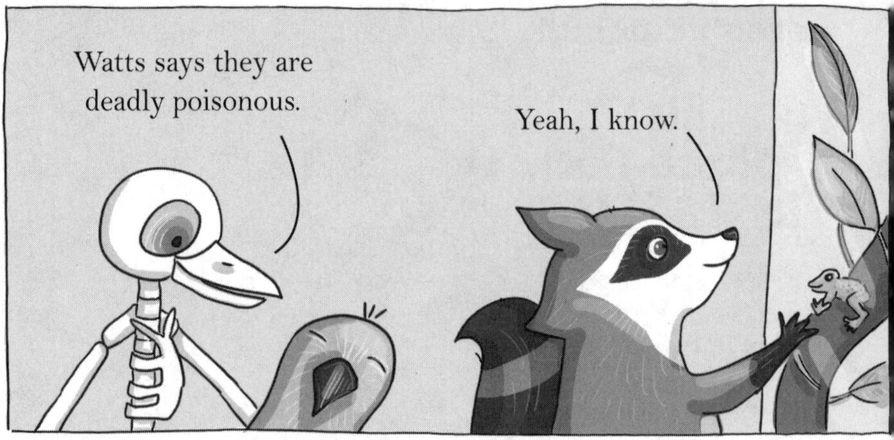
Watts says they are deadly poisonous.
Yeah, I know.

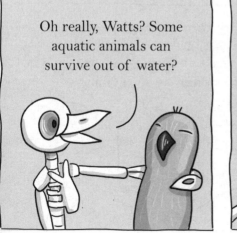

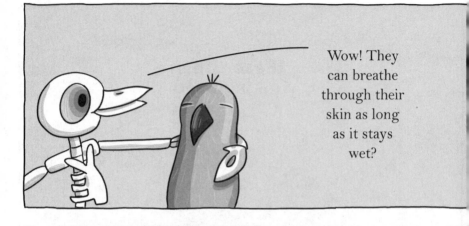

Wow! They can breathe through their skin as long as it stays wet?

That's just like some amphibians.

Oh, you know, frogs and salamanders...

Now stop distracting me, Watts. We need to investigate the mangroves before we do anything else.

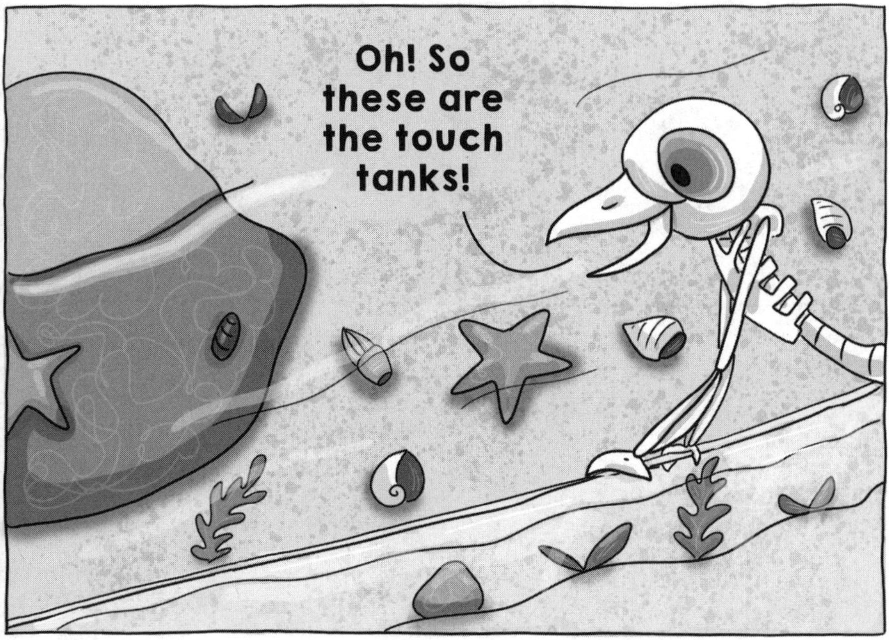
Oh! So these are the touch tanks!

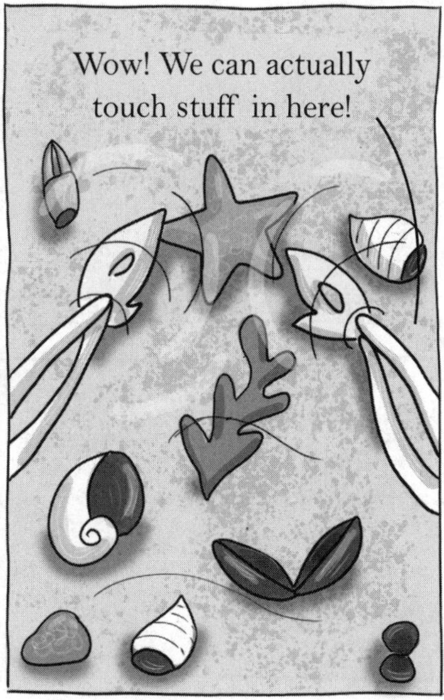
Wow! We can actually touch stuff in here!

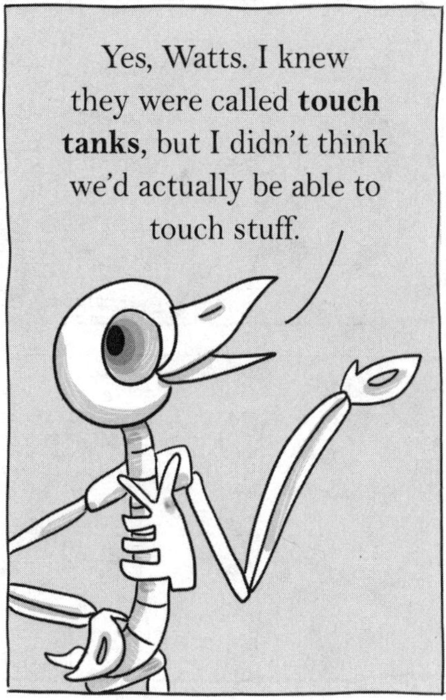
Yes, Watts. I knew they were called **touch tanks**, but I didn't think we'd actually be able to touch stuff.

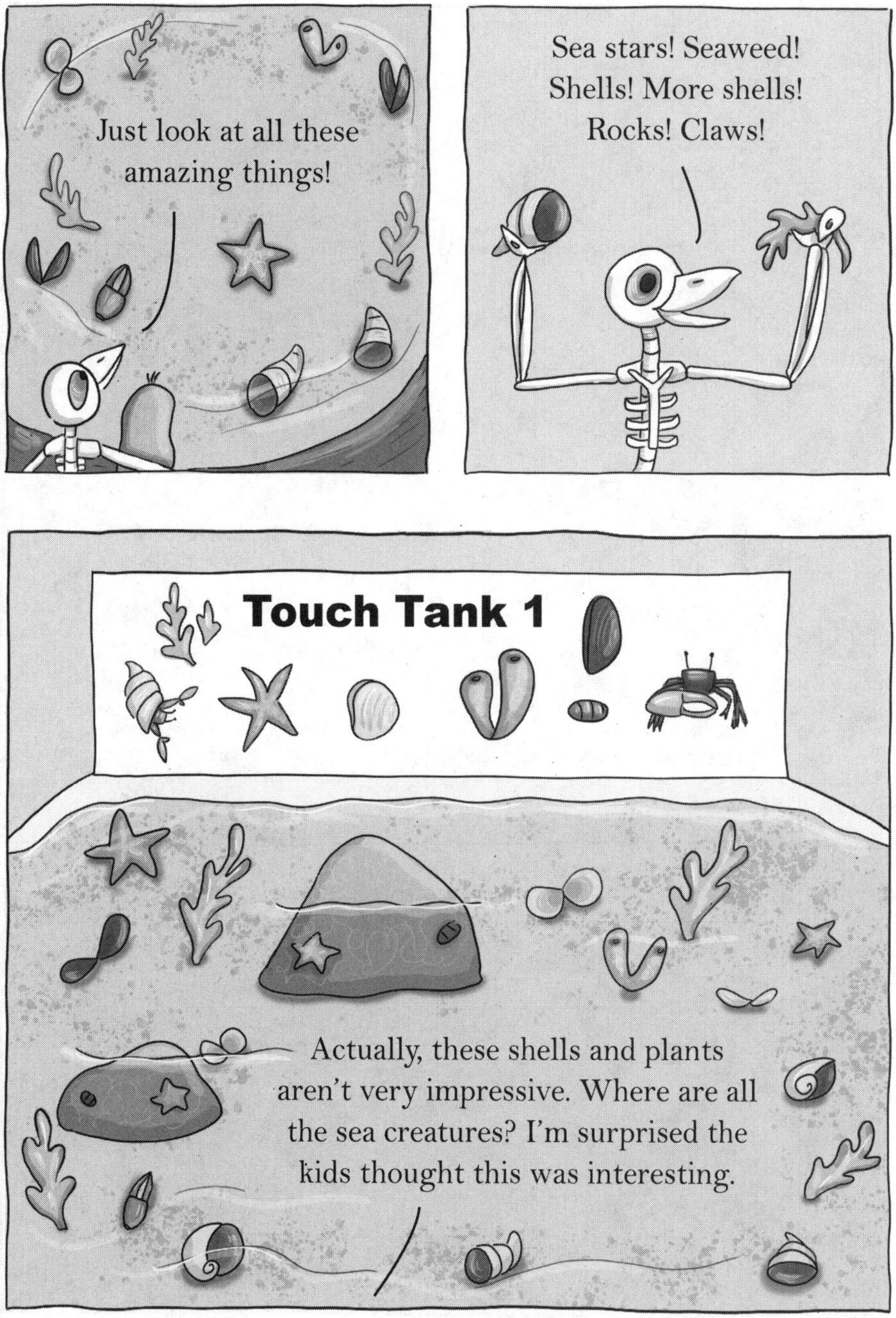
Just look at all these amazing things!
Sea stars! Seaweed! Shells! More shells! Rocks! Claws!
Touch Tank 1
Actually, these shells and plants aren't very impressive. Where are all the sea creatures? I'm surprised the kids thought this was interesting.

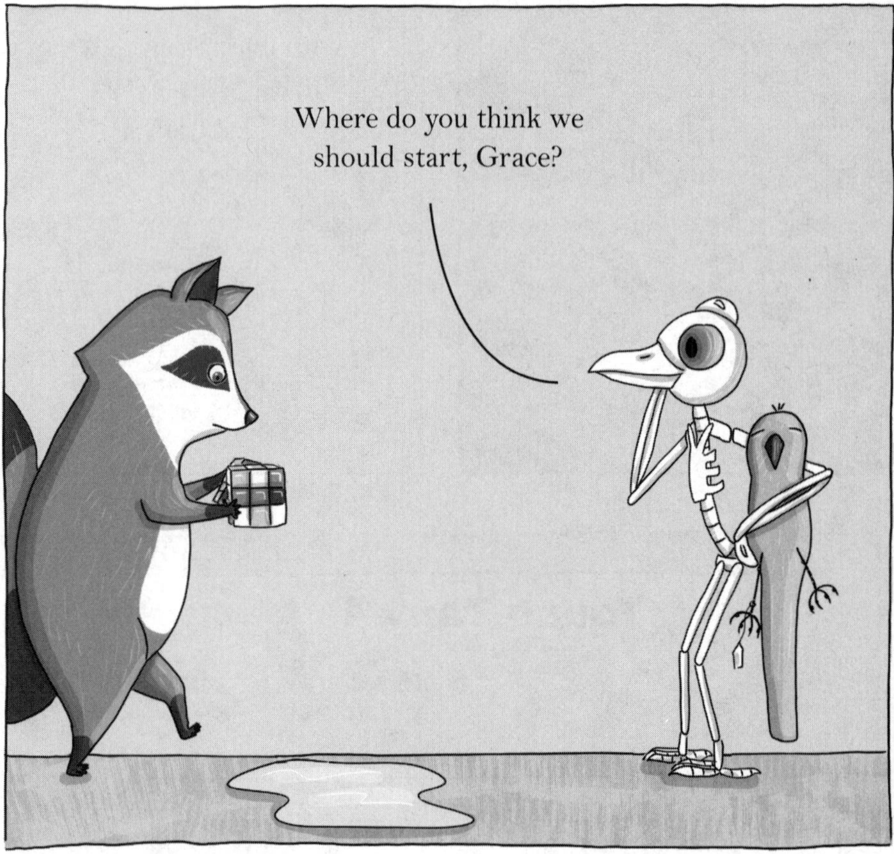
Where do you think we should start, Grace?

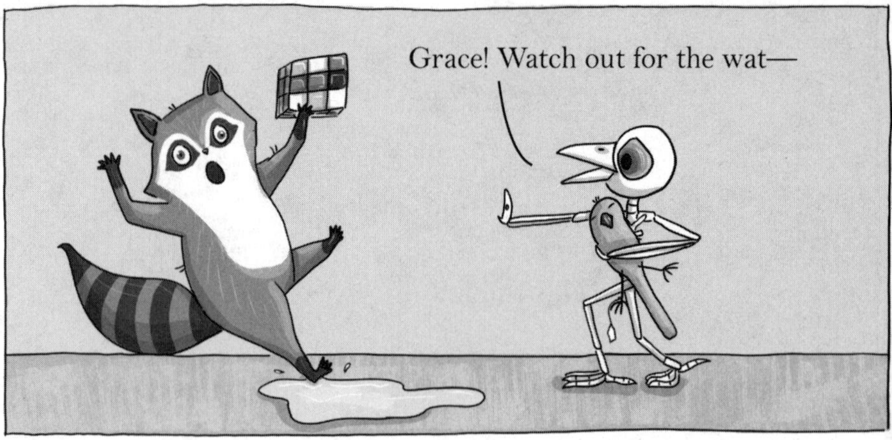
Grace! Watch out for the wat—

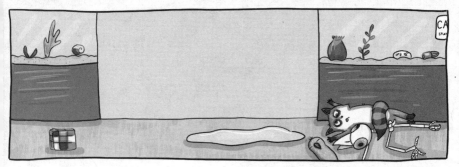

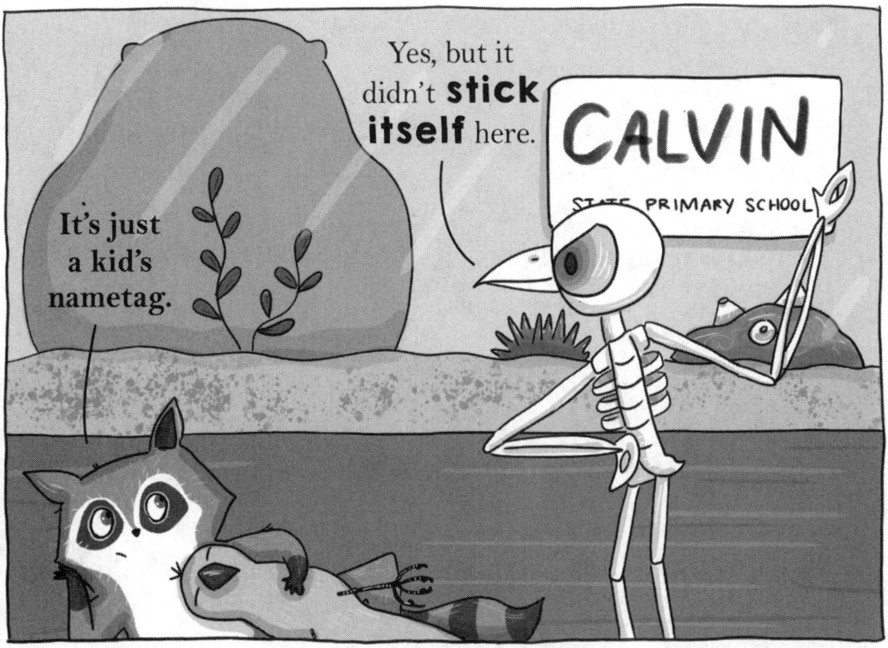
It's just a kid's nametag.
Yes, but it didn't **stick itself** here.
CALVIN
STATE PRIMARY SCHOOL

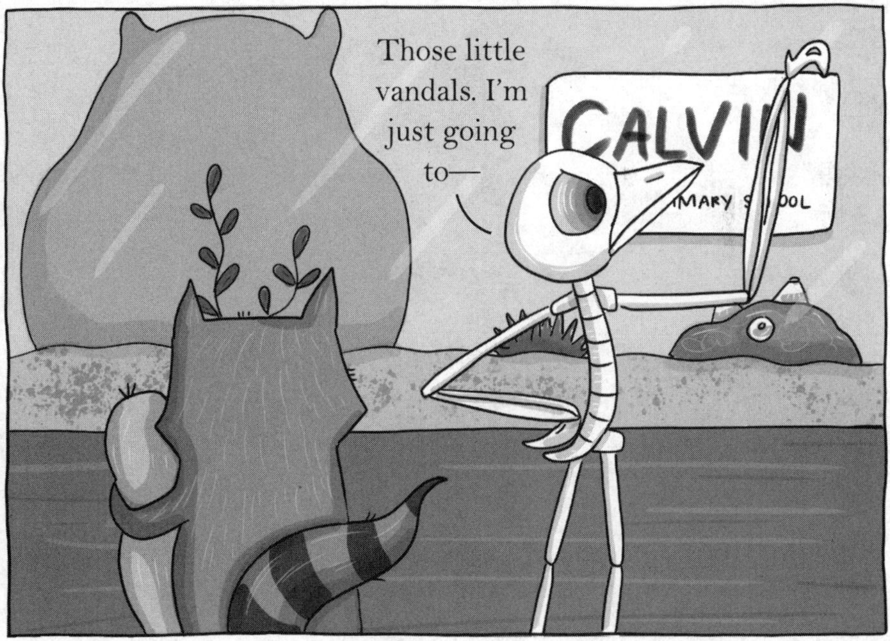
Those little vandals. I'm just going to—

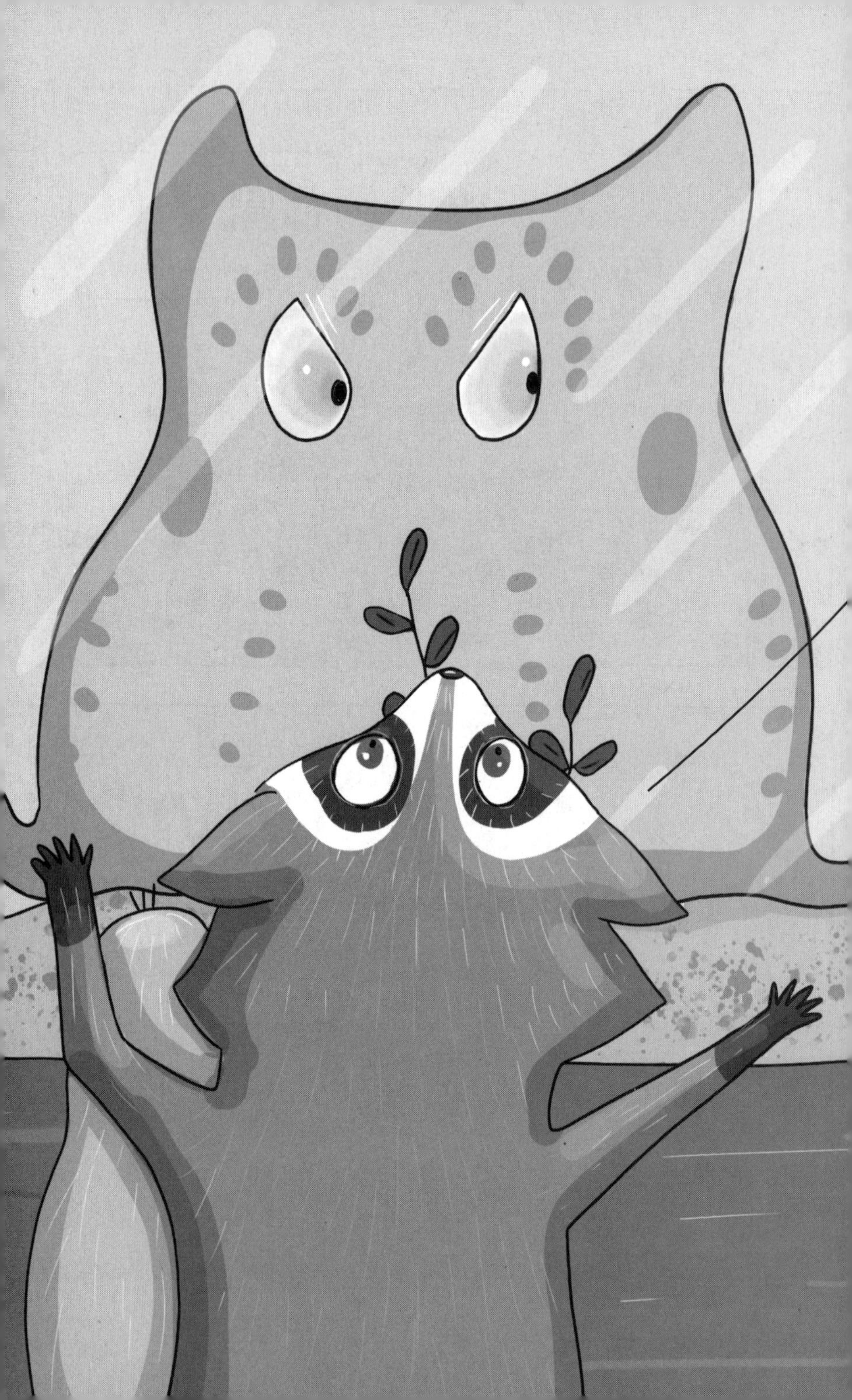

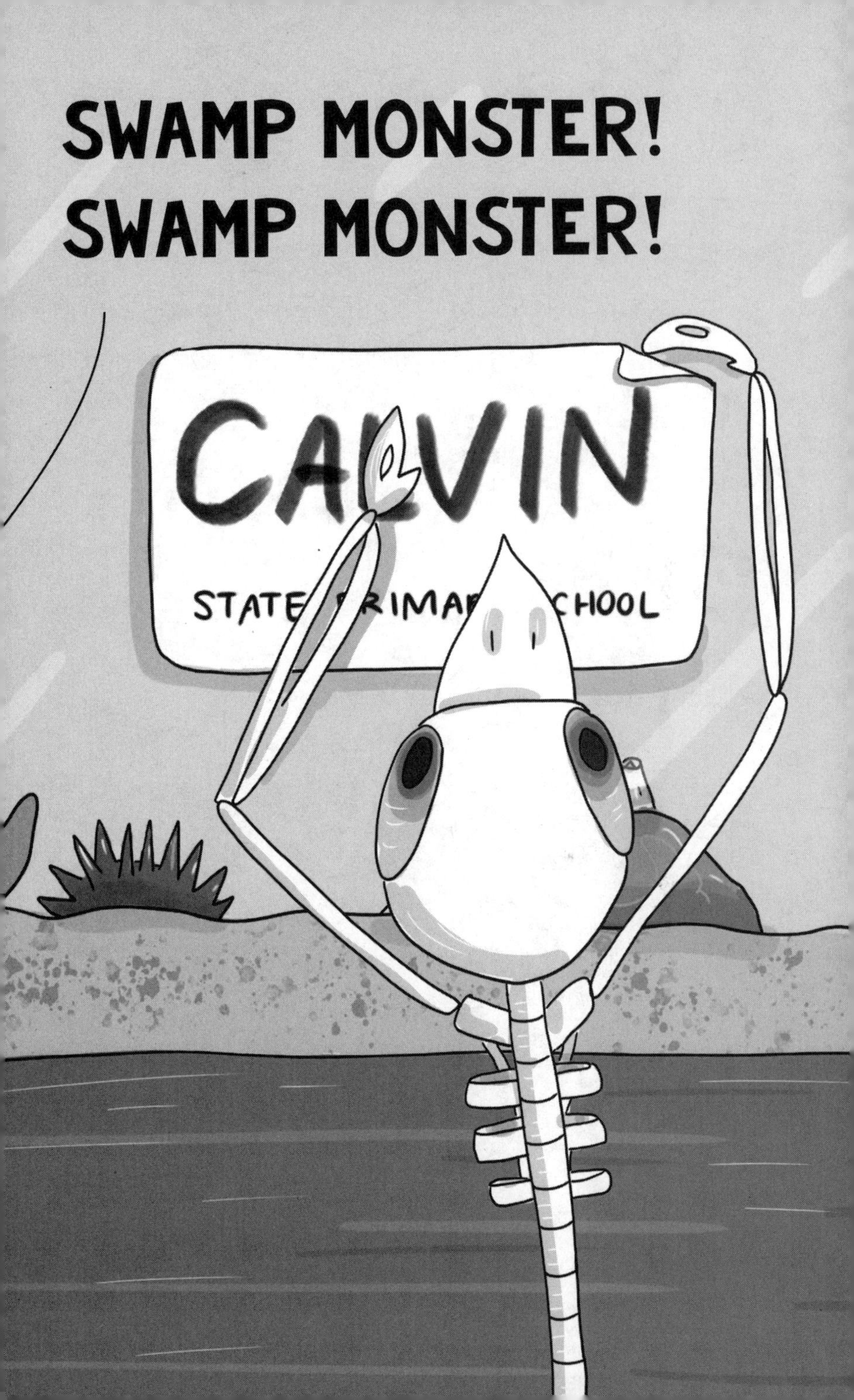
SWAMP MONSTER!
SWAMP MONSTER!
CALVIN

109

Touch Tank 2

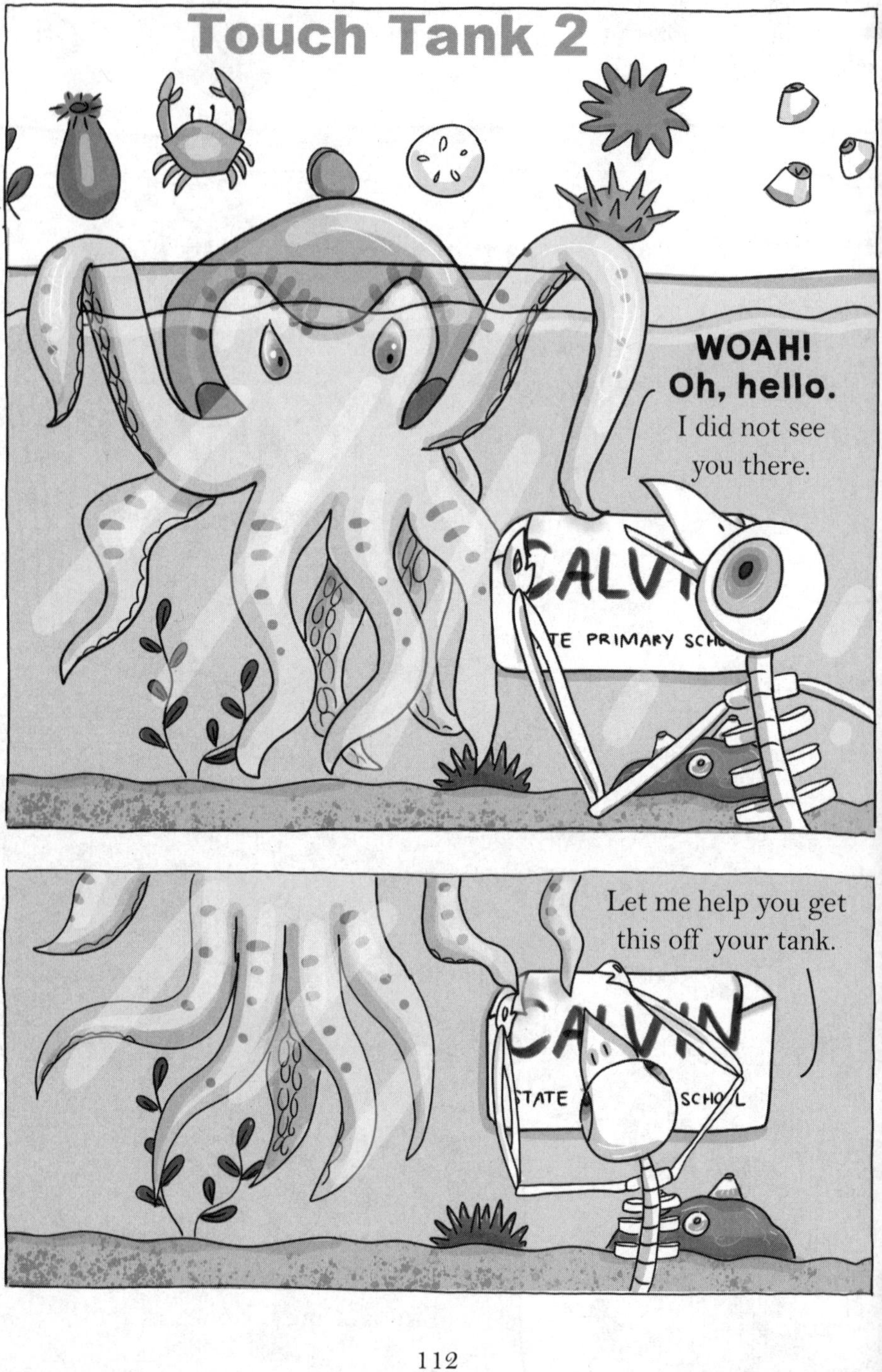
WOAH!
Oh, hello.
I did not see you there.
CALVIN
Let me help you get this off your tank.

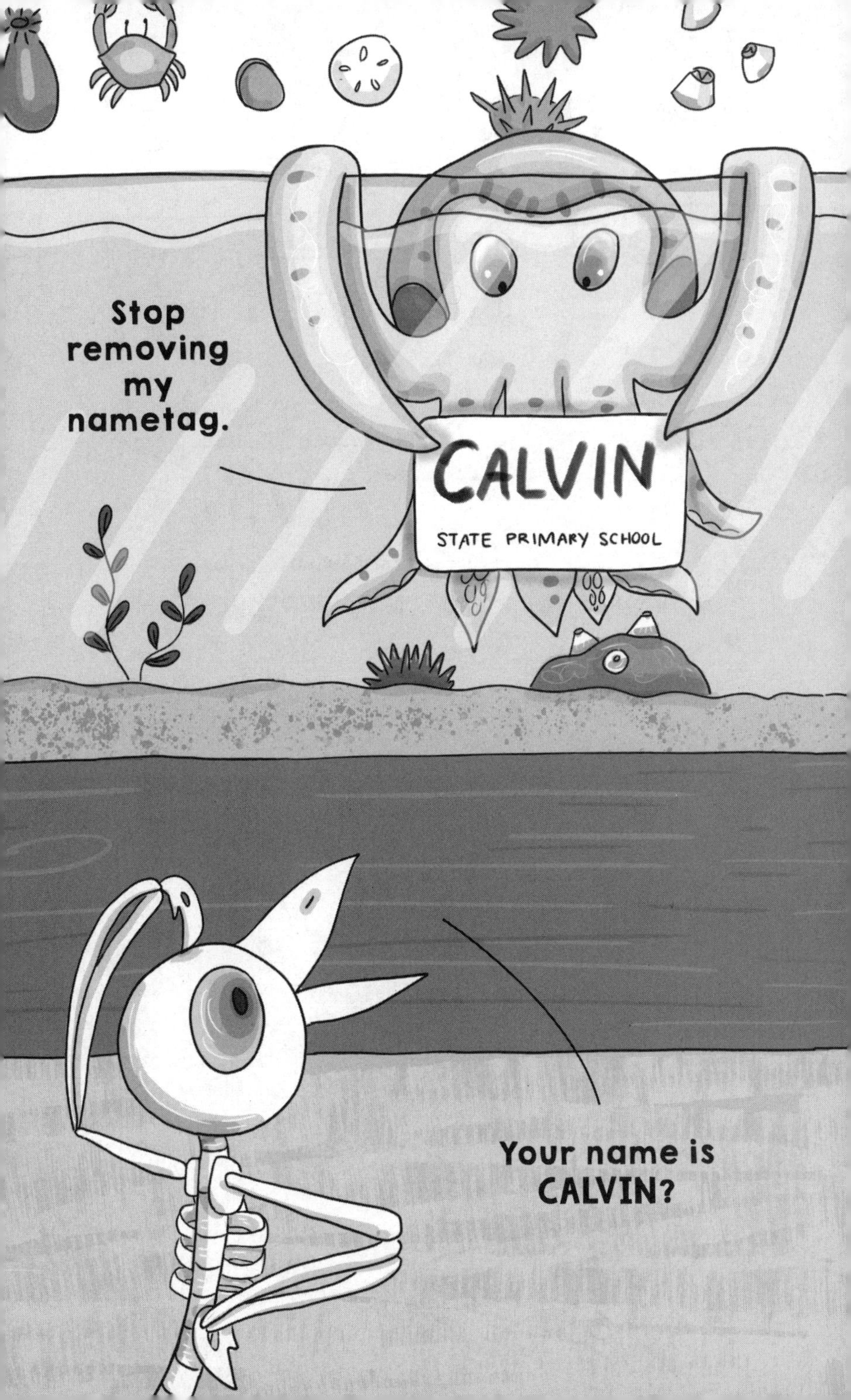
Stop removing my nametag.
CALVIN
STATE PRIMARY SCHOOL
Your name is CALVIN?

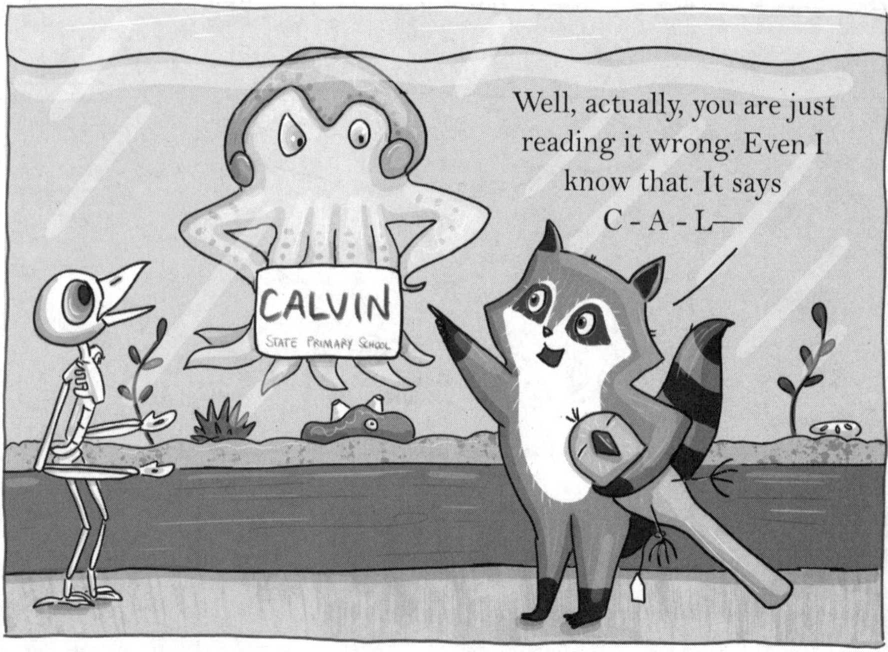

Well, actually, you are just reading it wrong. Even I know that. It says C - A - L—
CALVIN
STATE PRIMARY SCHOOL

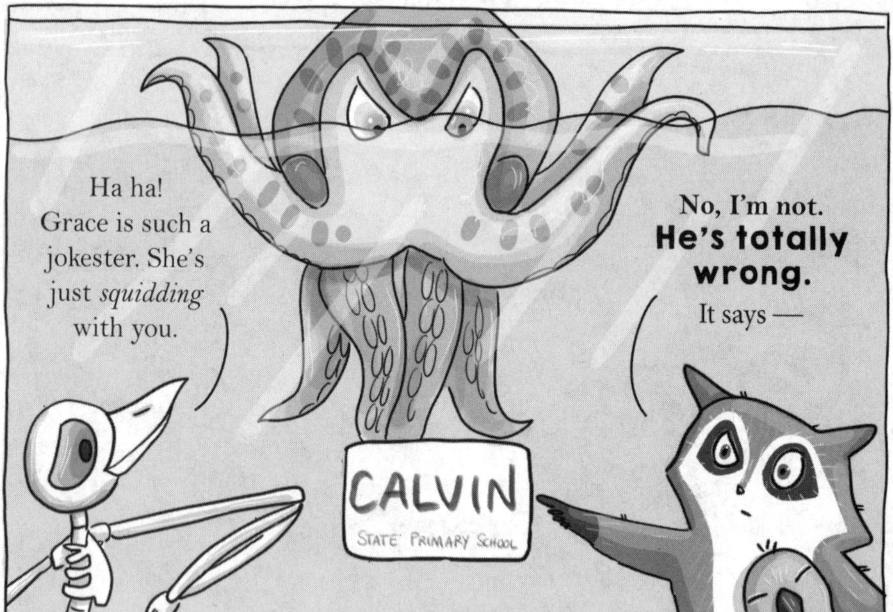

Ha ha! Grace is such a jokester. She's just *squidding* with you.
No, I'm not. **He's totally wrong.** It says —
CALVIN
STATE PRIMARY SCHOOL

Touch Tank 2

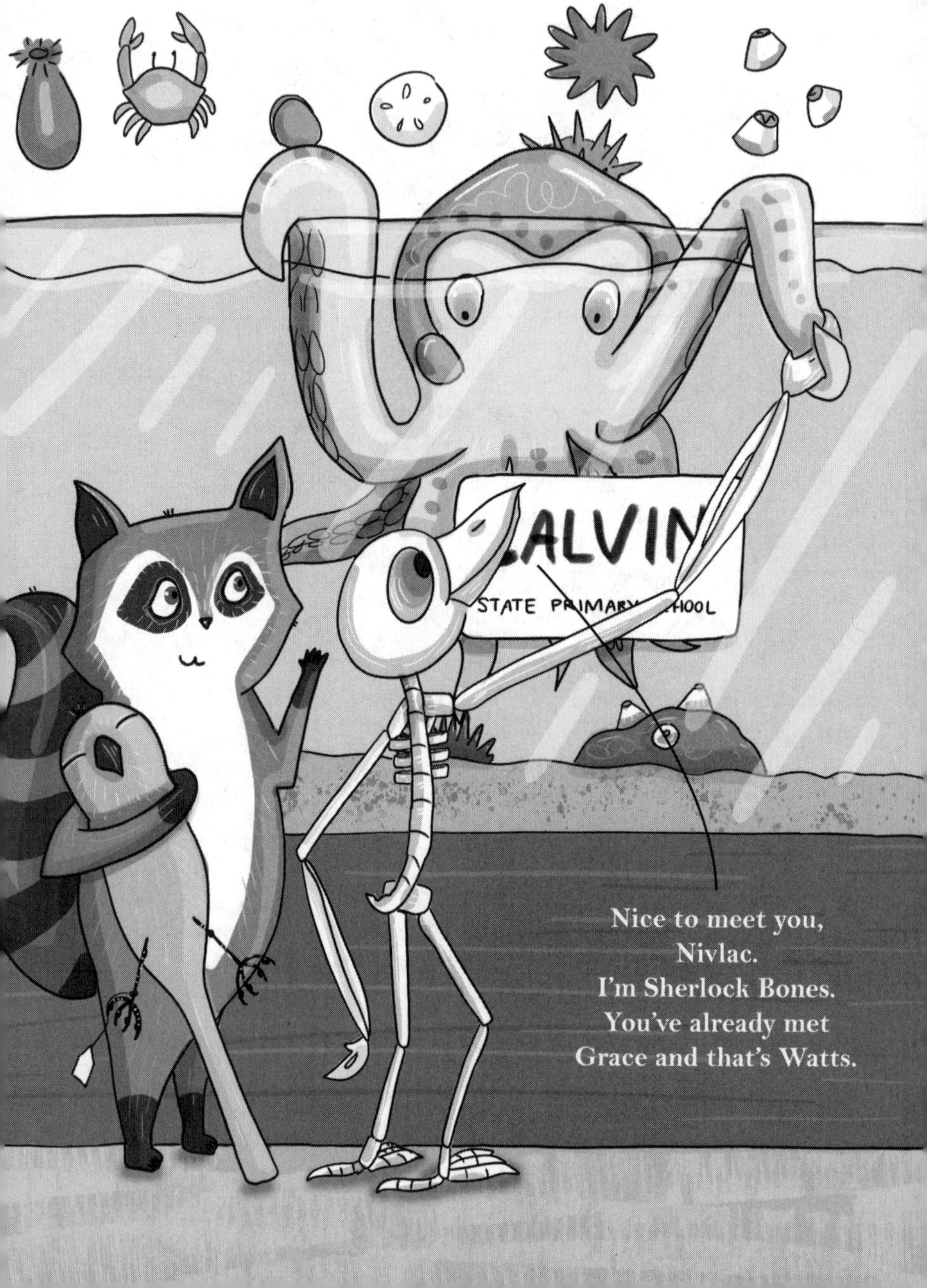
Nice to meet you,
Nivlac.
I'm Sherlock Bones.
You've already met
Grace and that's Watts.

119

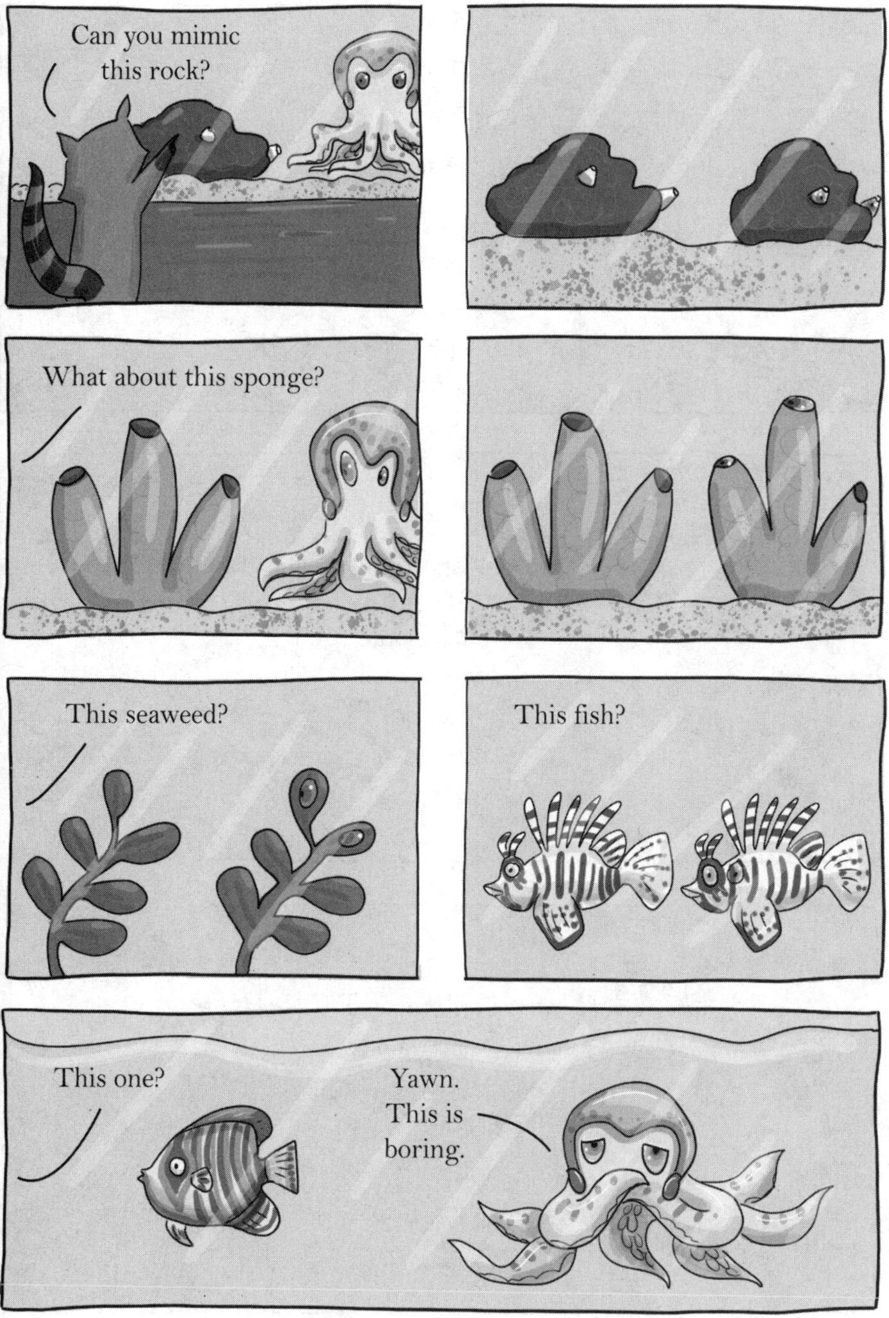
Can you mimic this rock?
What about this sponge?
This seaweed?
This fish?
This one?
Yawn. This is boring.

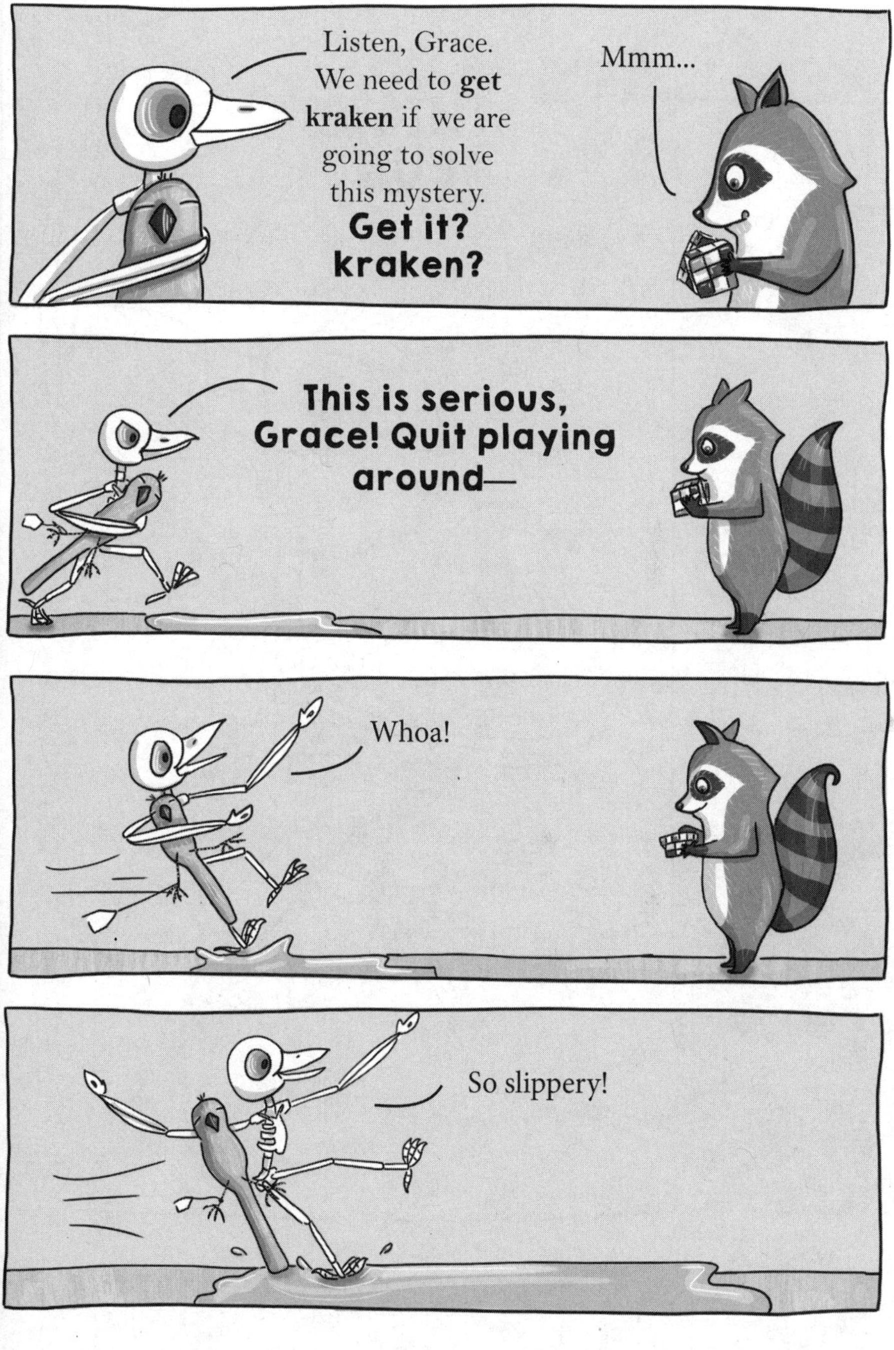
Listen, Grace. We need to **get kraken** if we are going to solve this mystery. **Get it? kraken?**
Mmm...
This is serious, Grace! Quit playing around—
Whoa!
So slippery!

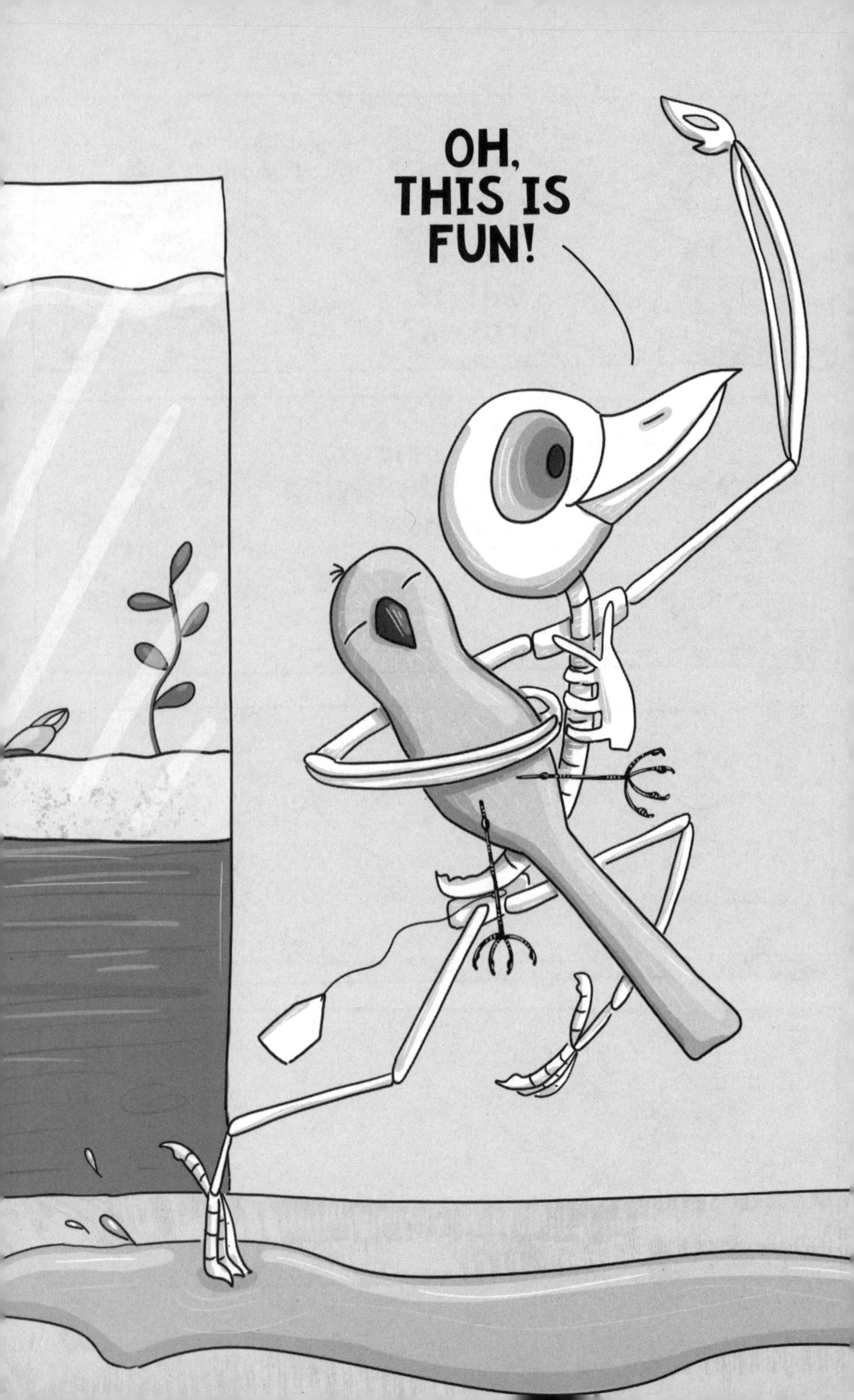
OH, THIS IS FUN!

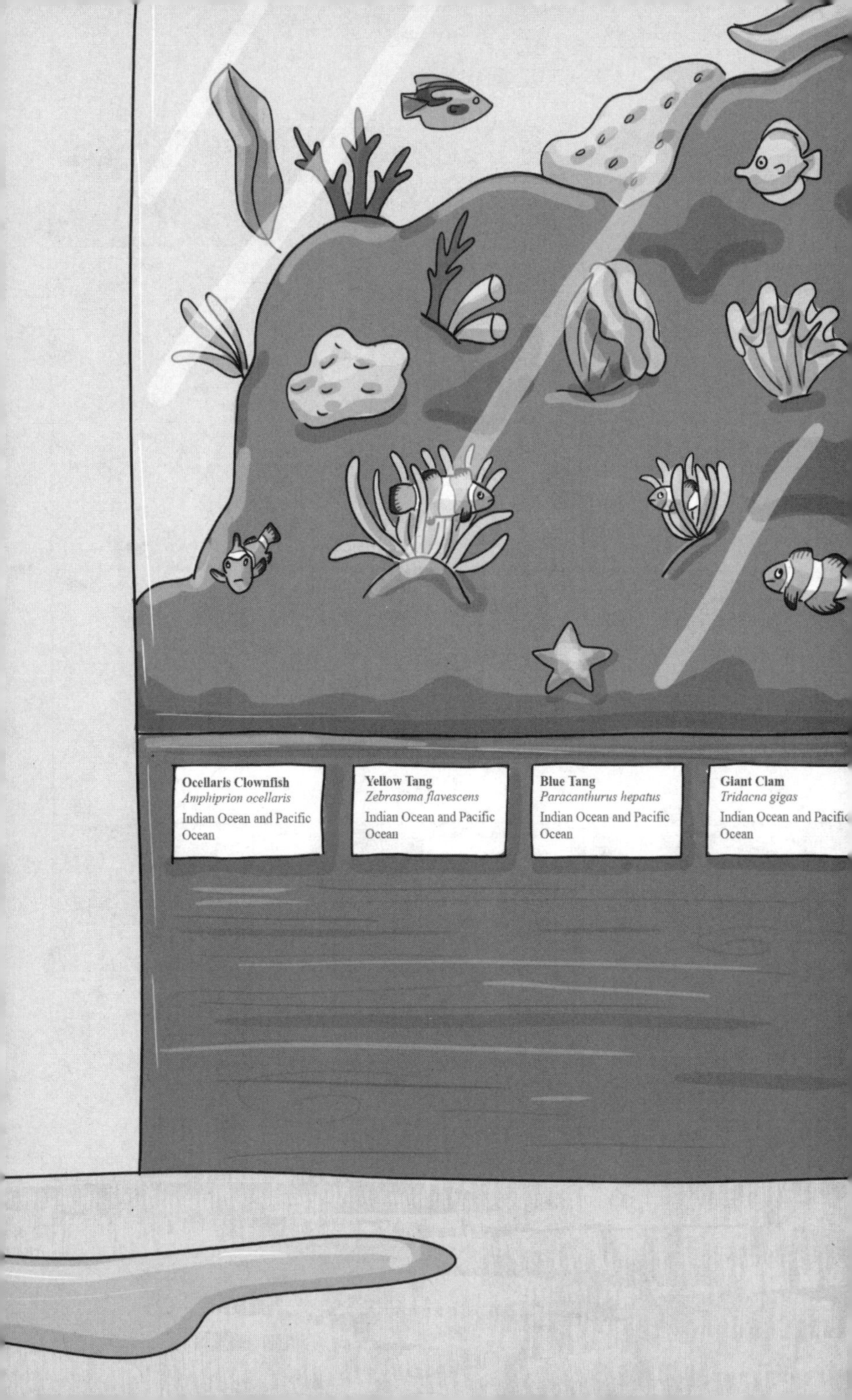
Ocellaris Clownfish
Amphiprion ocellaris
Indian Ocean and Pacific Ocean
Yellow Tang
Zebrasoma flavescens
Indian Ocean and Pacific Ocean
Blue Tang
Paracanthurus hepatus
Indian Ocean and Pacific Ocean
Giant Clam
Tridacna gigas
Indian Ocean and Pacific Ocean

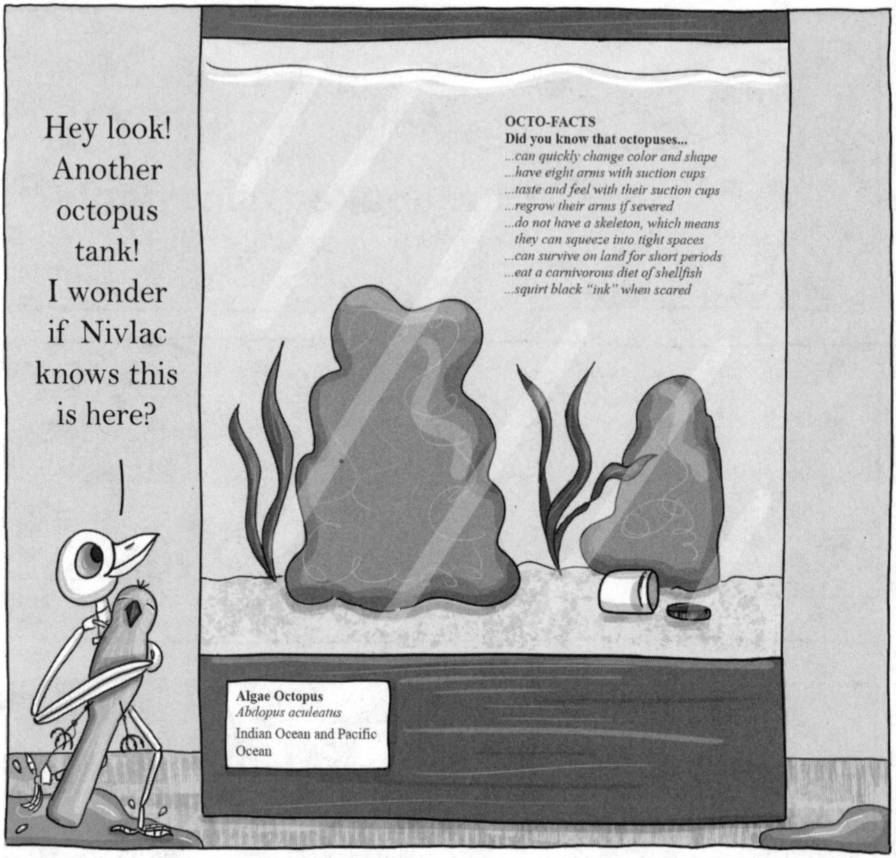
Hey look! Another octopus tank! I wonder if Nivlac knows this is here?
OCTO-FACTS
Did you know that octopuses...
...can quickly change color and shape
...have eight arms with suction cups
...taste and feel with their suction cups
...regrow their arms if severed
...do not have a skeleton, which means they can squeeze into tight spaces
...can survive on land for short periods
...eat a carnivorous diet of shellfish
...squirt black "ink" when scared
Algae Octopus
Abdopus aculeatus
Indian Ocean and Pacific Ocean

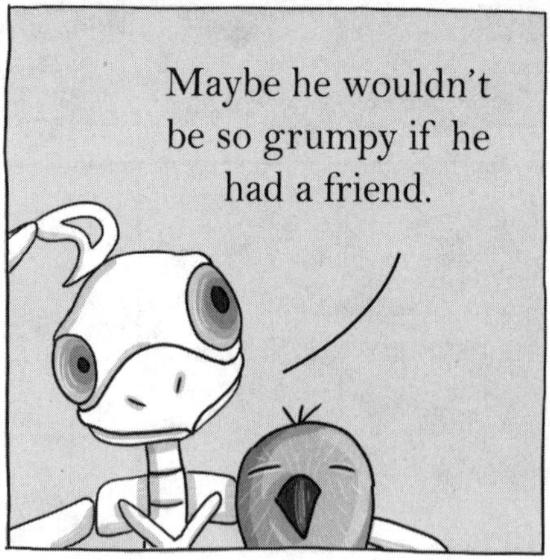
Maybe he wouldn't be so grumpy if he had a friend.

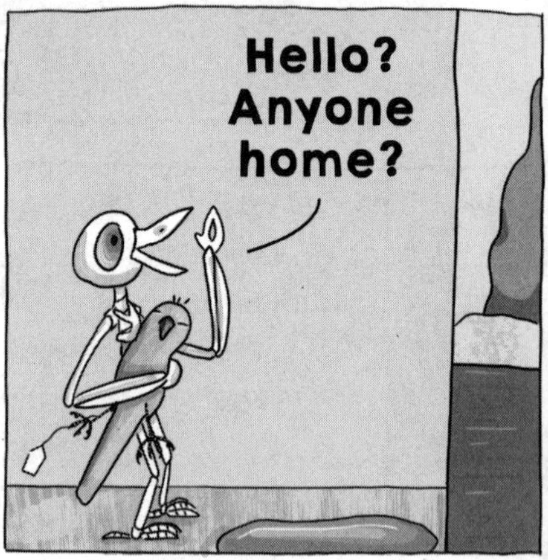
Hello? Anyone home?

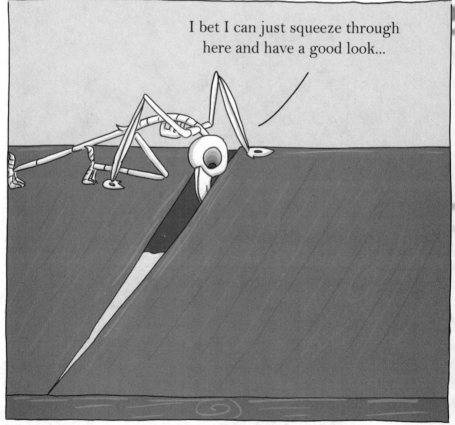

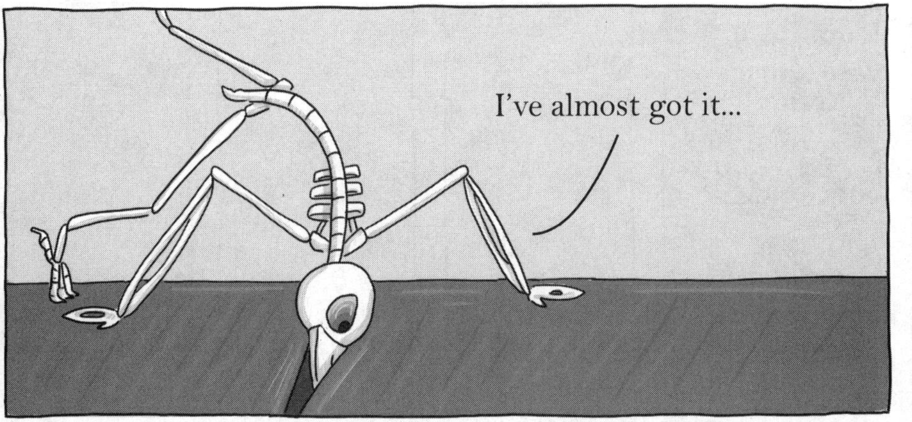
I've almost got it...

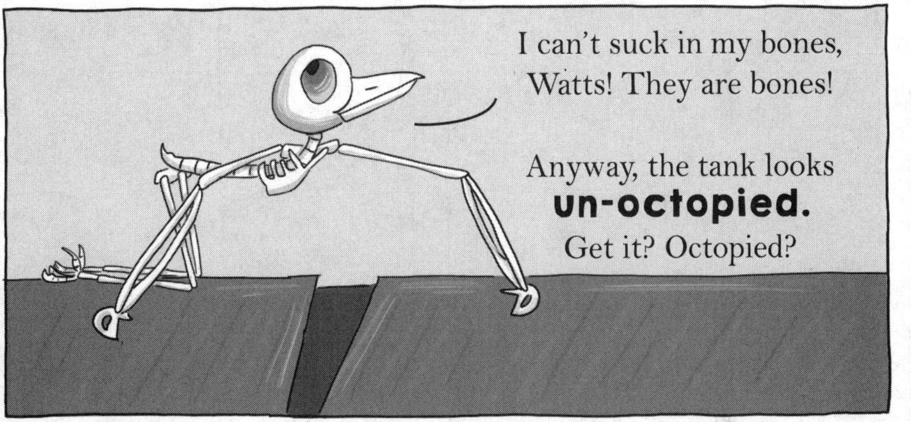
I can't suck in my bones, Watts! They are bones!
Anyway, the tank looks **un-octopied.** Get it? Octopied?

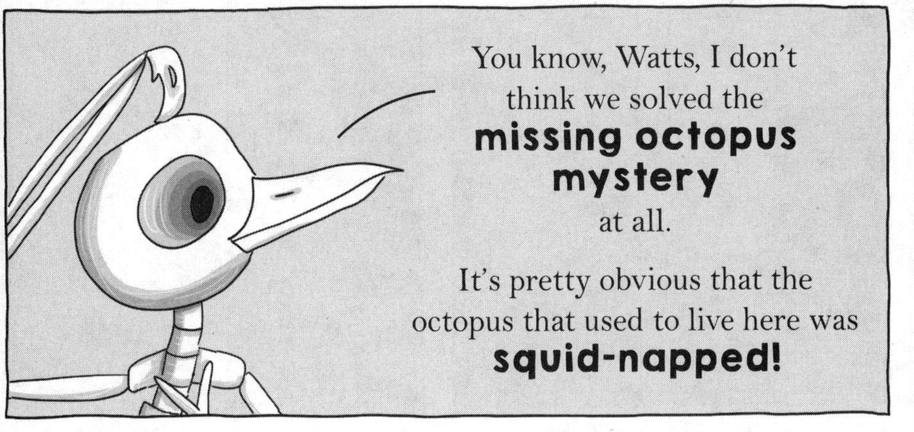
You know, Watts, I don't think we solved the **missing octopus mystery** at all.
It's pretty obvious that the octopus that used to live here was **squid-napped!**

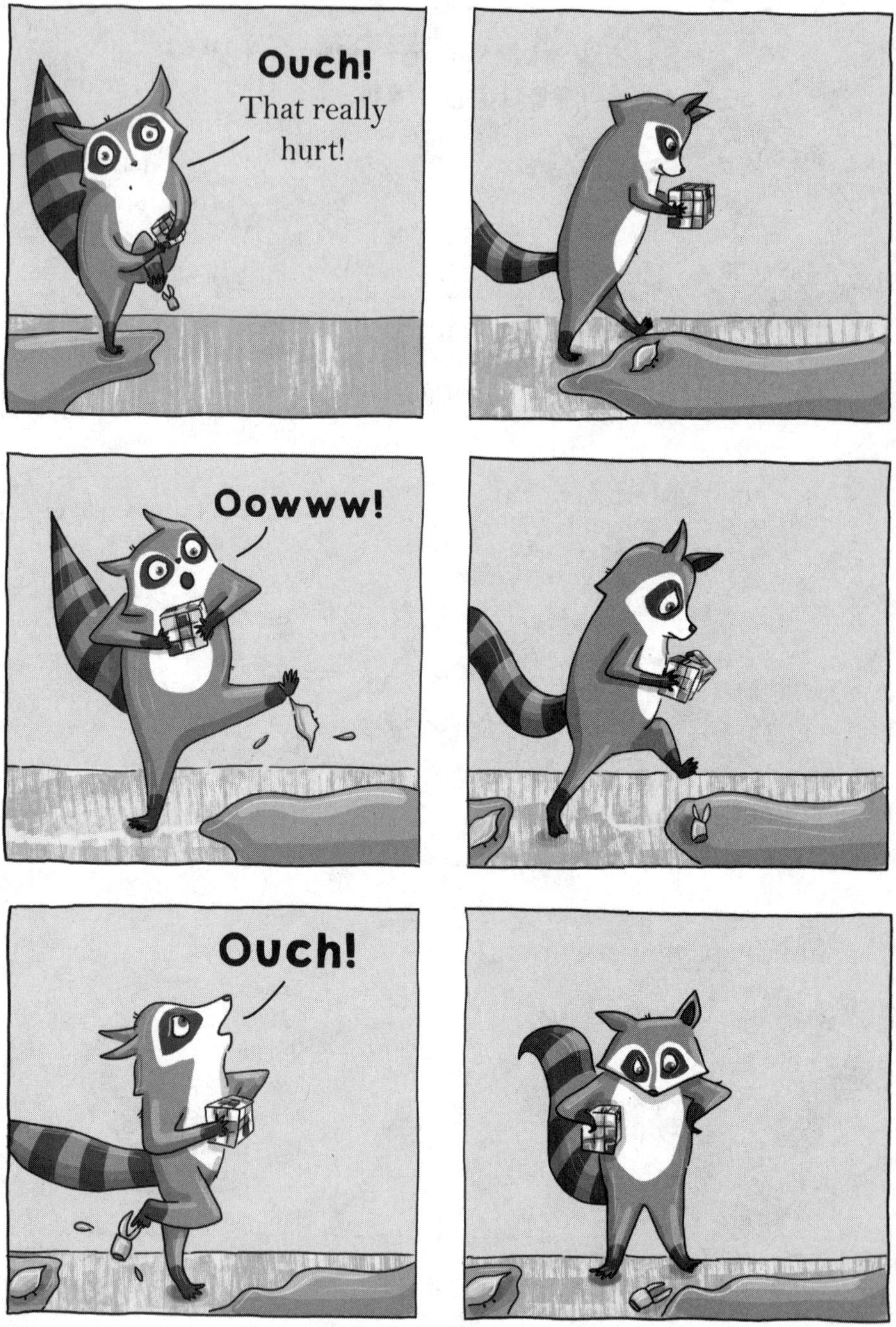
Ouch!
That really hurt!
Oowww!
Ouch!

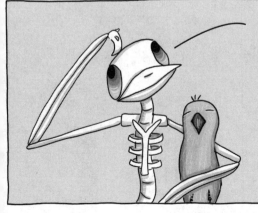

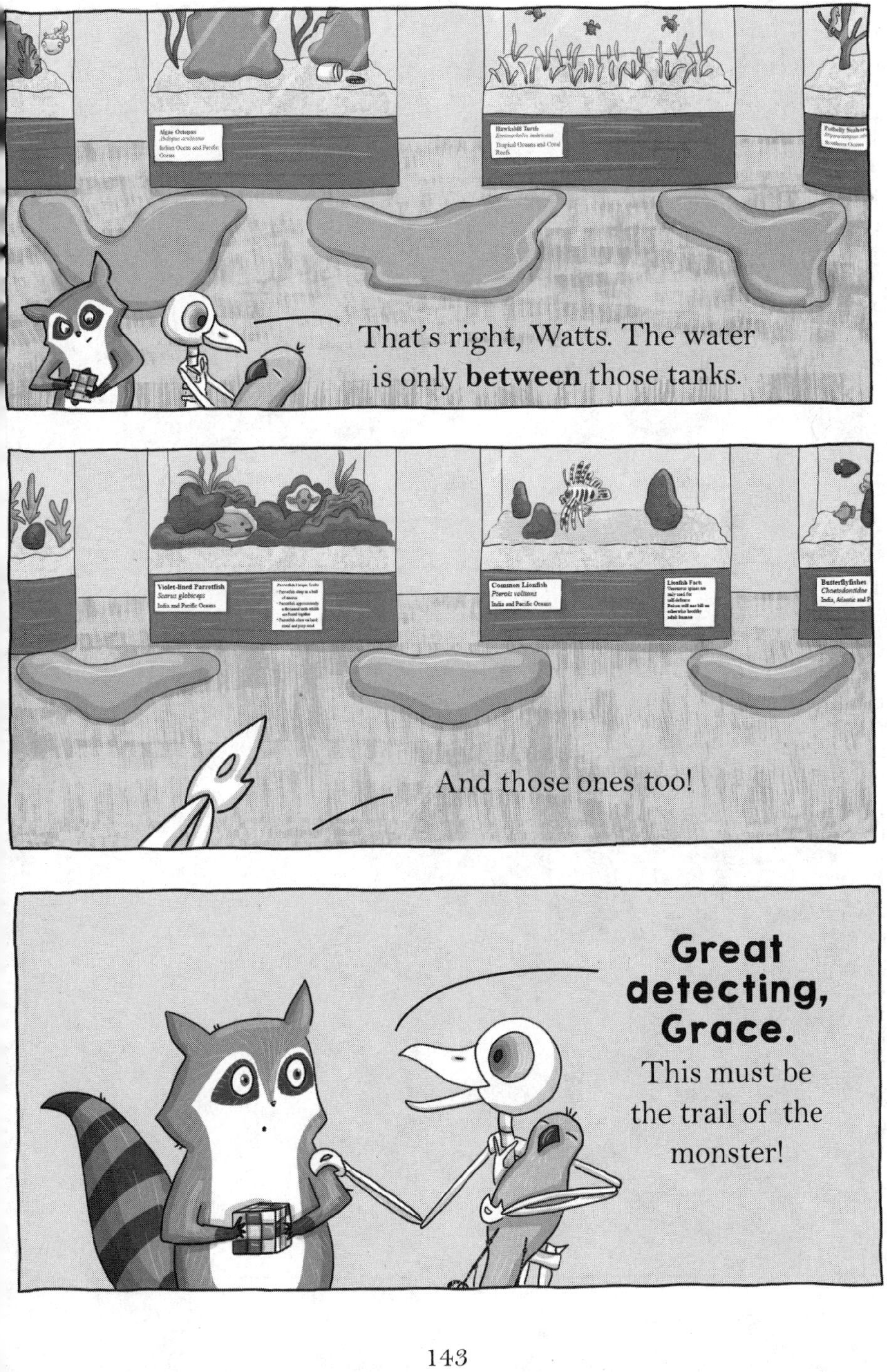
Algae Octopus
Hawksbill Turtle
That's right, Watts. The water is only **between** those tanks.
Violet-lined Parrotfish
Scarus globiceps
India and Pacific Oceans
Common Lionfish
Pterois volitans
India and Pacific Oceans
Butterflyfishes
Chaetodontidae
And those ones too!
Great detecting, Grace.
This must be the trail of the monster!

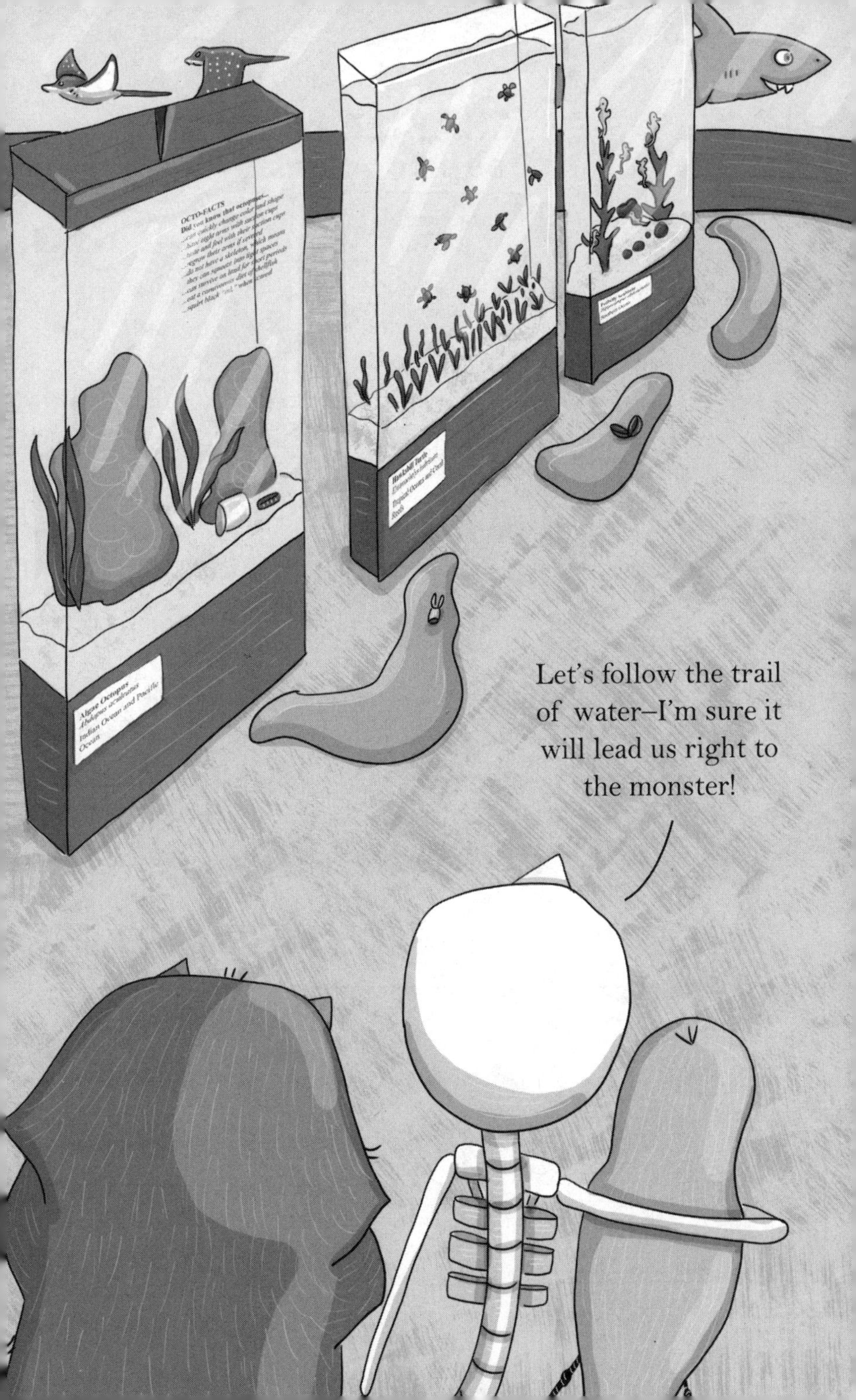
Let's follow the trail of water–I'm sure it will lead us right to the monster!

CHAPTER 6
Deep Boo Sea

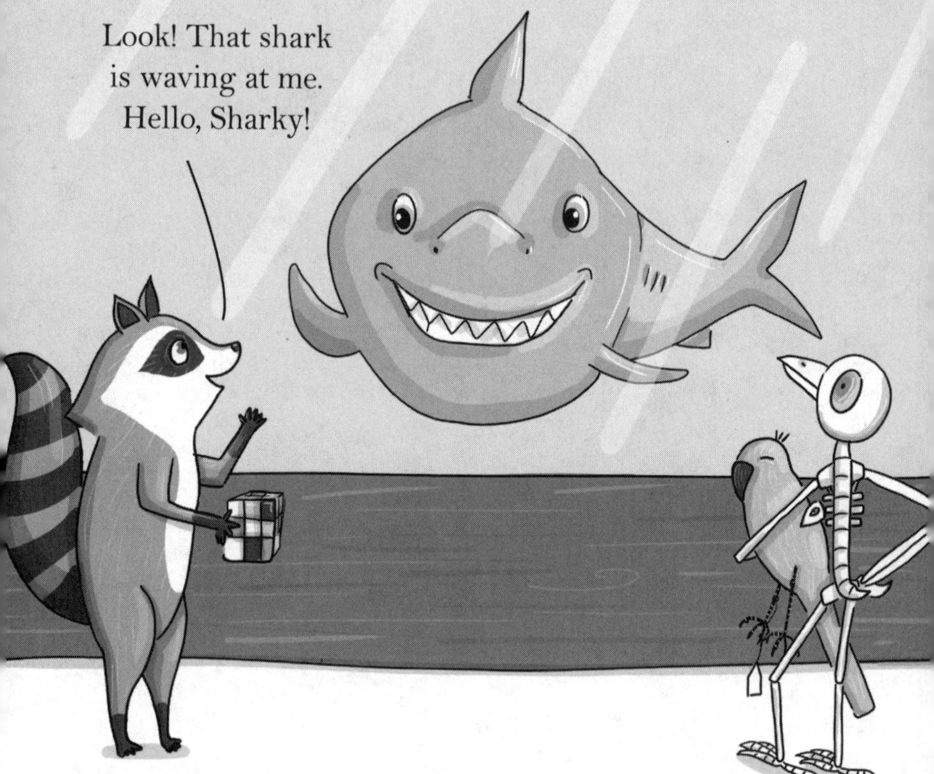
Look! That shark is waving at me. Hello, Sharky!

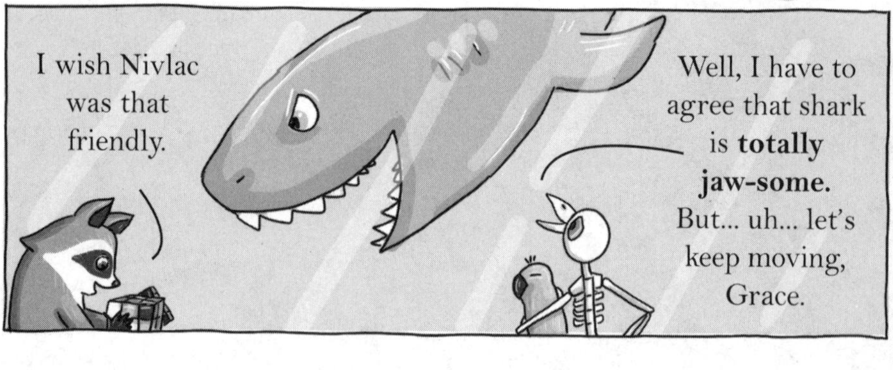
I wish Nivlac was that friendly.
Well, I have to agree that shark is **totally jaw-some.** But... uh... let's keep moving, Grace.

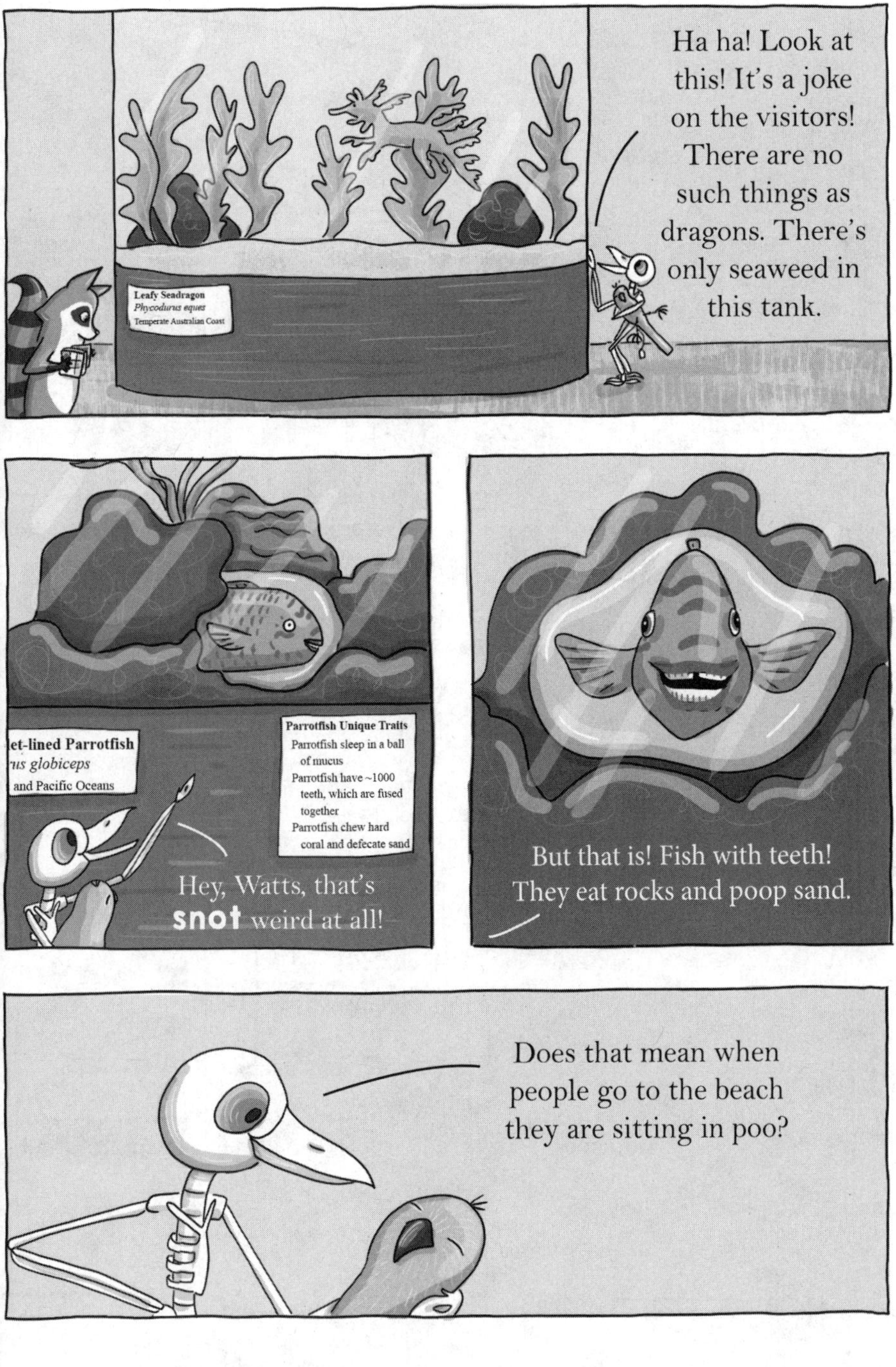
Ha ha! Look at this! It's a joke on the visitors! There are no such things as dragons. There's only seaweed in this tank.
Leafy Seadragon
Phycodurus eques
Temperate Australian Coast
et-lined Parrotfish
us globiceps
and Pacific Oceans
Parrotfish Unique Traits
Parrotfish sleep in a ball of mucus
Parrotfish have ~1000 teeth, which are fused together
Parrotfish chew hard coral and defecate sand
Hey, Watts, that's **snot** weird at all!
But that is! Fish with teeth! They eat rocks and poop sand.
Does that mean when people go to the beach they are sitting in poo?

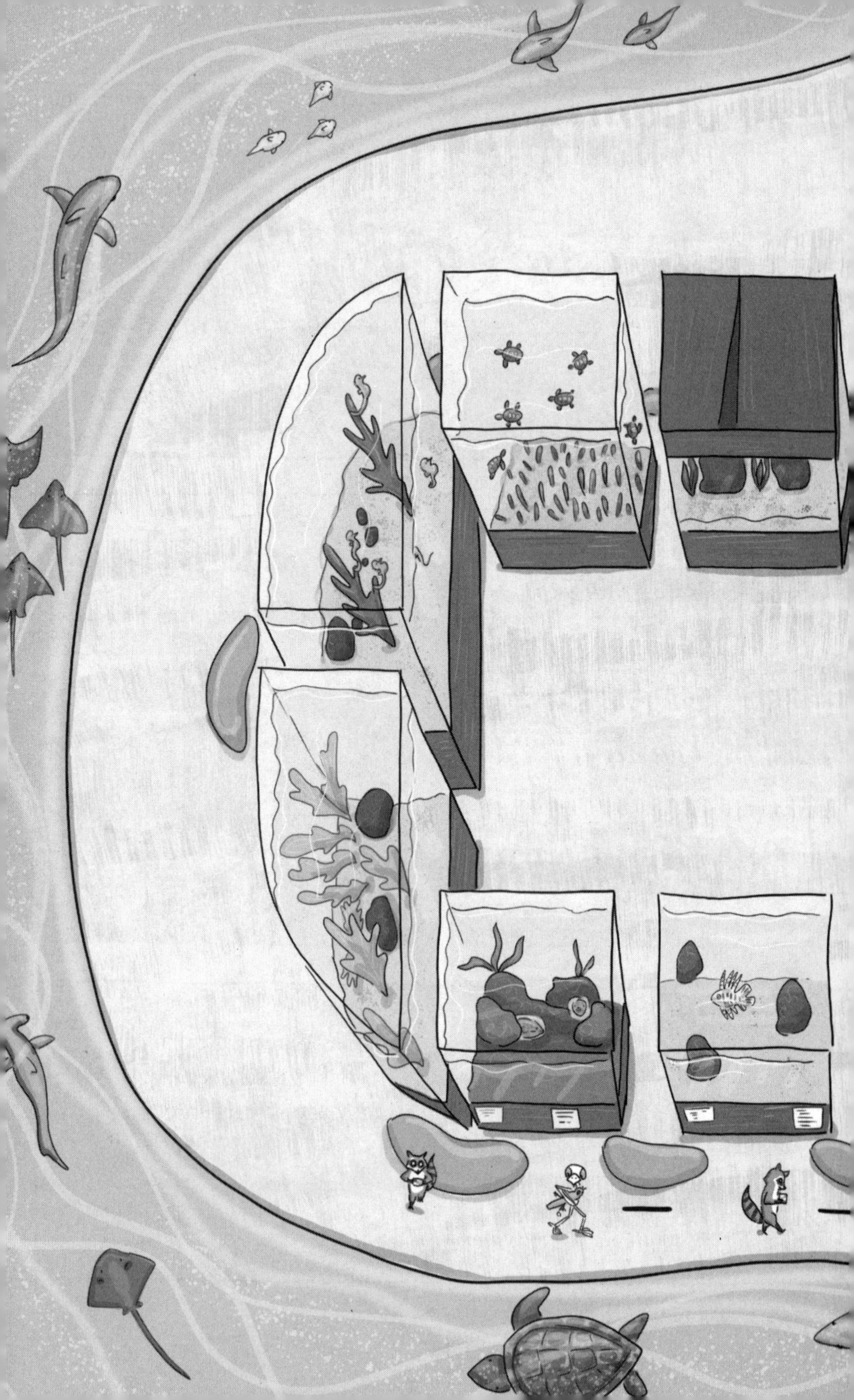

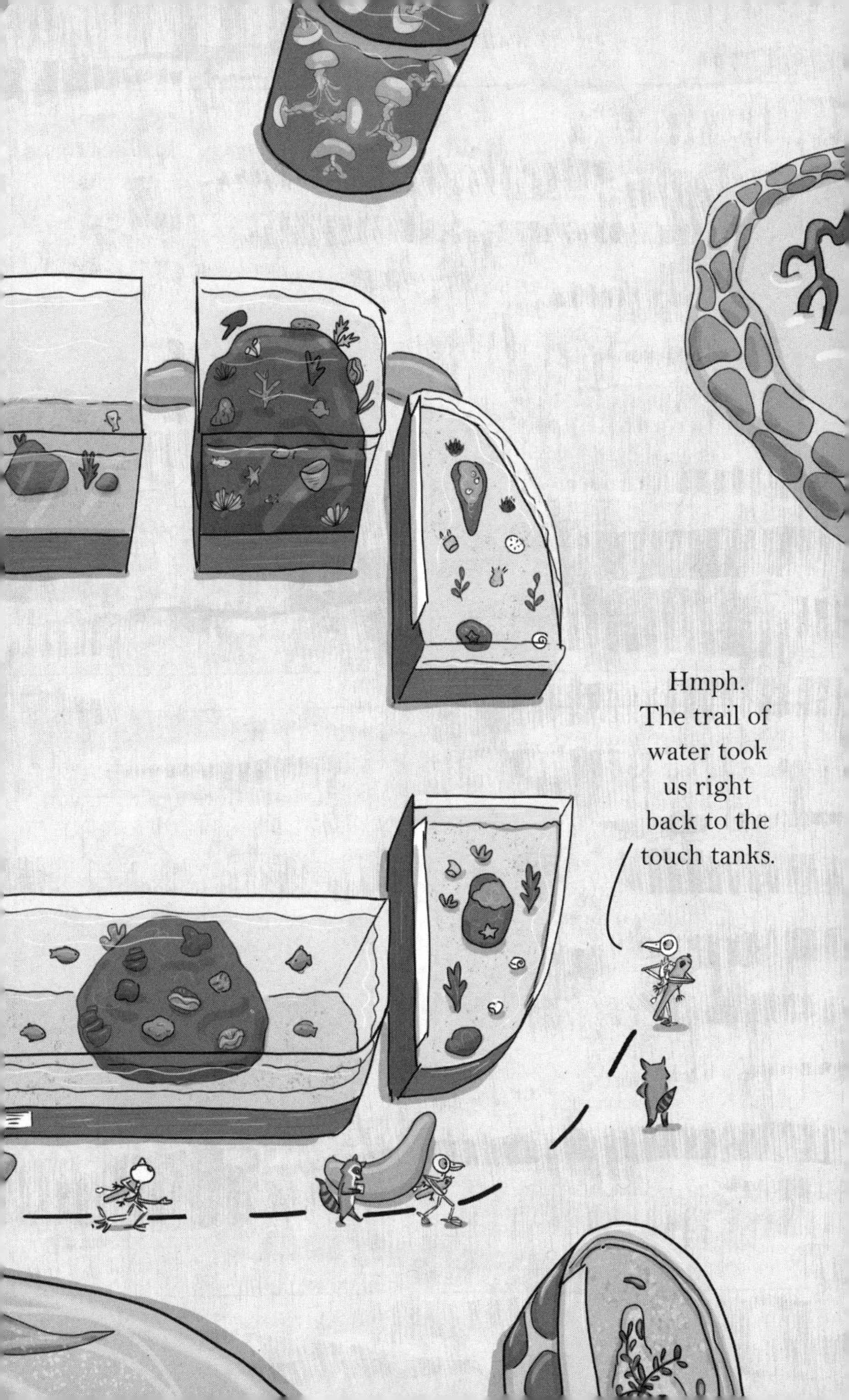
Hmph. The trail of water took us right back to the touch tanks.

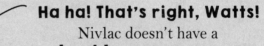

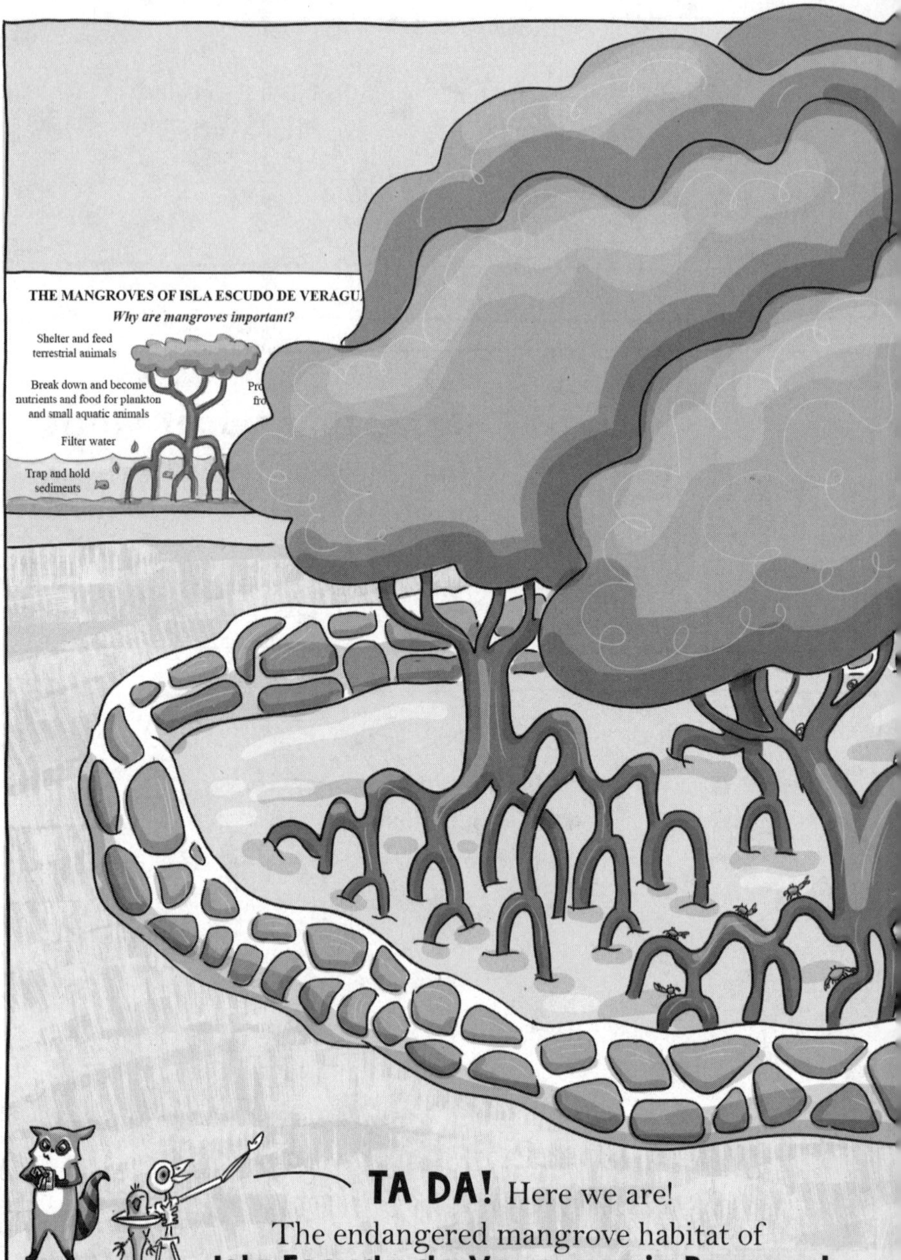
THE MANGROVES OF ISLA ESCUDO DE VERAGU
Why are mangroves important?
Shelter and feed terrestrial animals
Break down and become nutrients and food for plankton and small aquatic animals
Filter water
Trap and hold sediments
TA DA! Here we are!
The endangered mangrove habitat of
Isla Escuda de Veraguas in Panama!

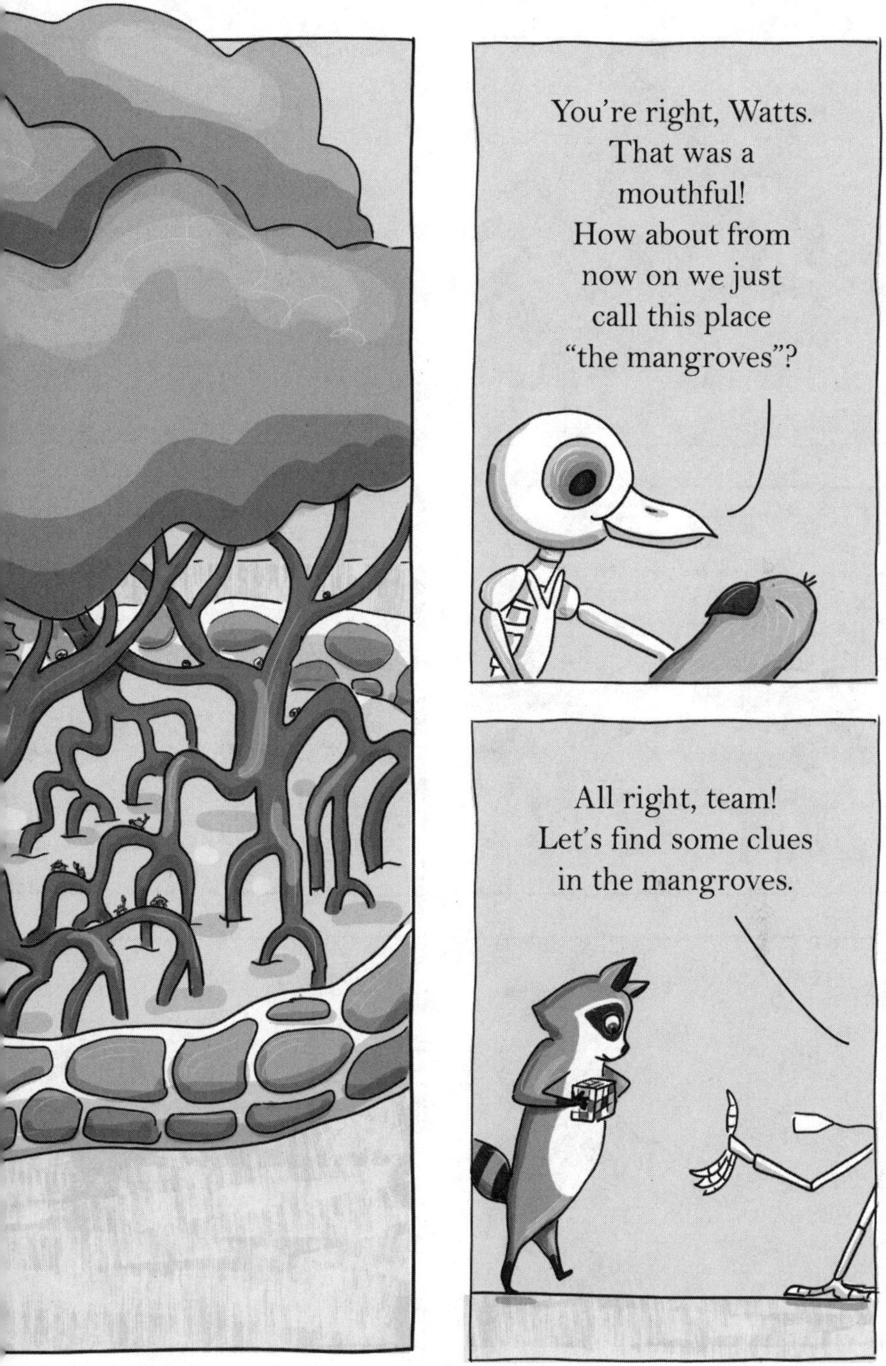
You're right, Watts.
That was a
mouthful!
How about from
now on we just
call this place
"the mangroves"?
All right, team!
Let's find some clues
in the mangroves.

157

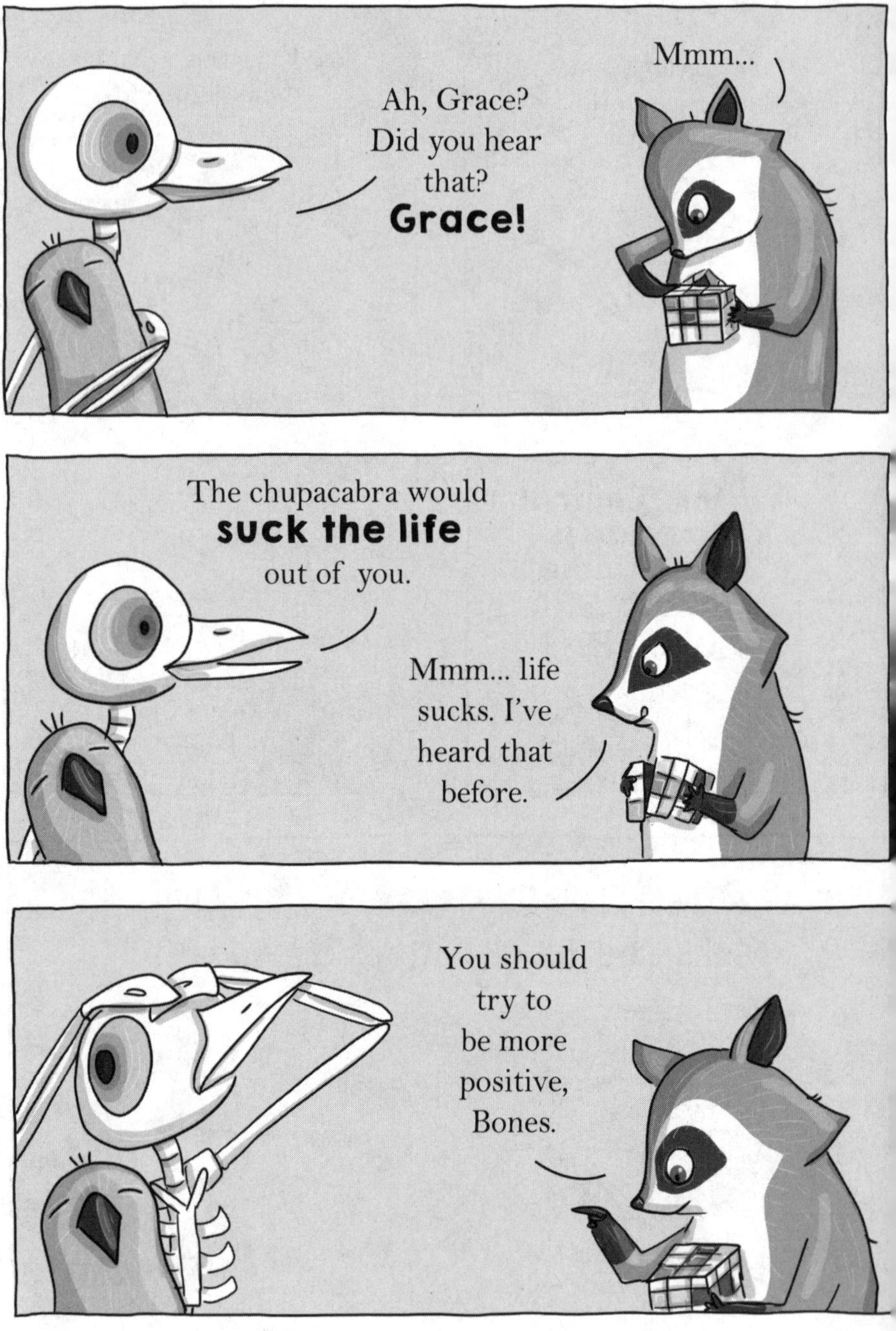
Mmm...
Ah, Grace? Did you hear that? **Grace!**
The chupacabra would **suck the life** out of you.
Mmm... life sucks. I've heard that before.
You should try to be more positive, Bones.

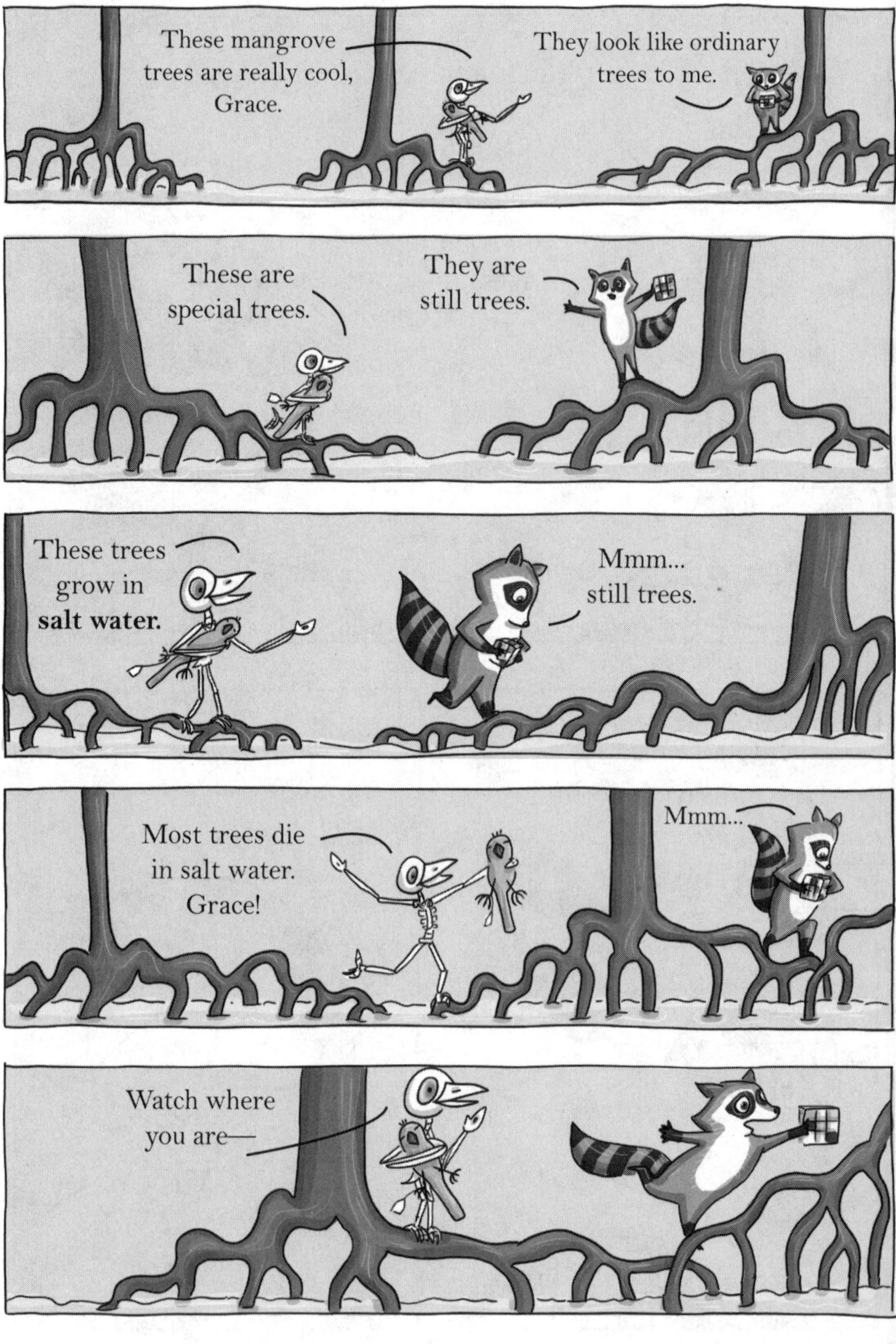
These mangrove trees are really cool, Grace.
They look like ordinary trees to me.
These are special trees.
They are still trees.
These trees grow in **salt water.**
Mmm... still trees.
Most trees die in salt water. Grace!
Mmm...
Watch where you are—

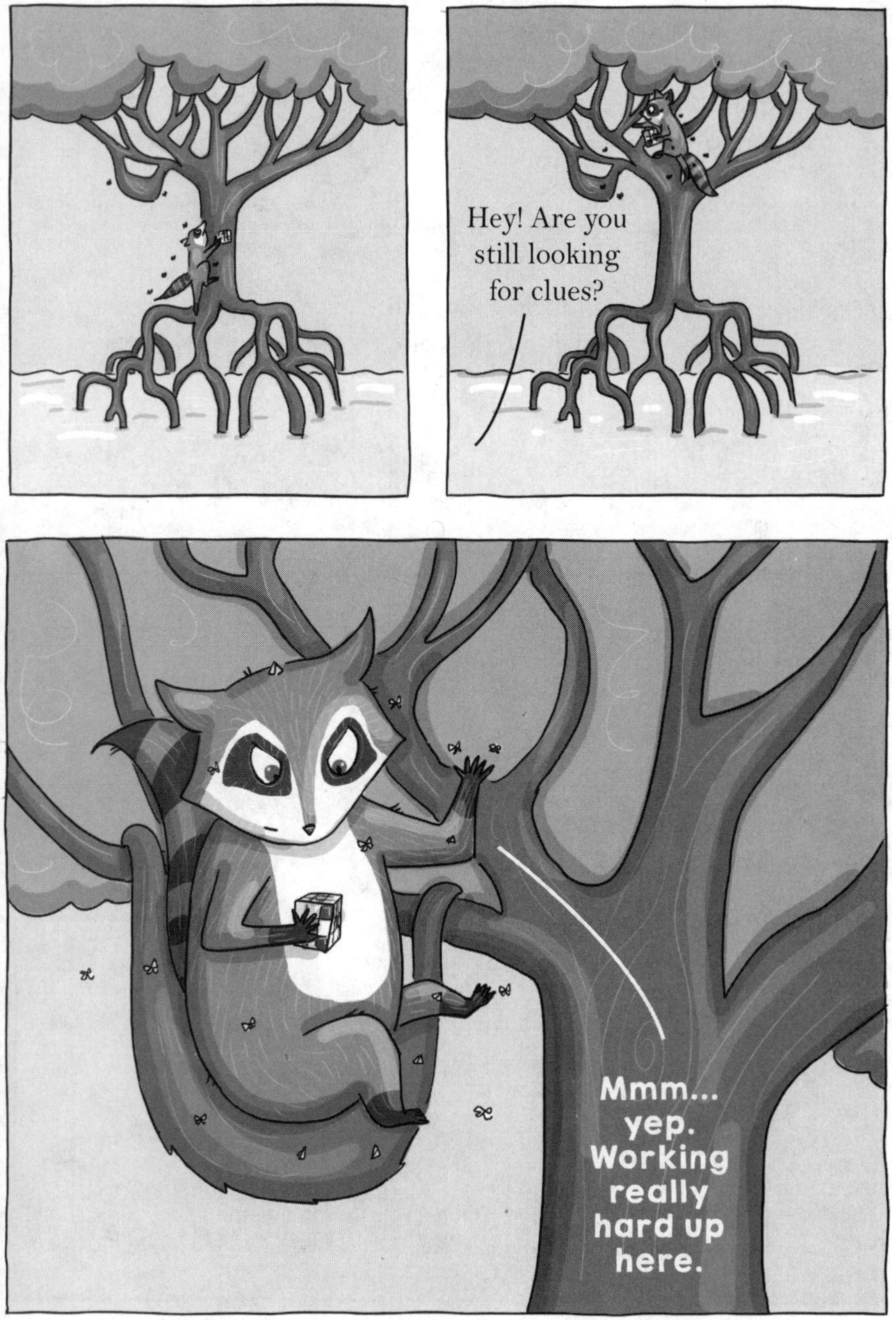
Hey! Are you still looking for clues?
Mmm... yep. Working really hard up here.

CHAPTER 7
Ink-redible

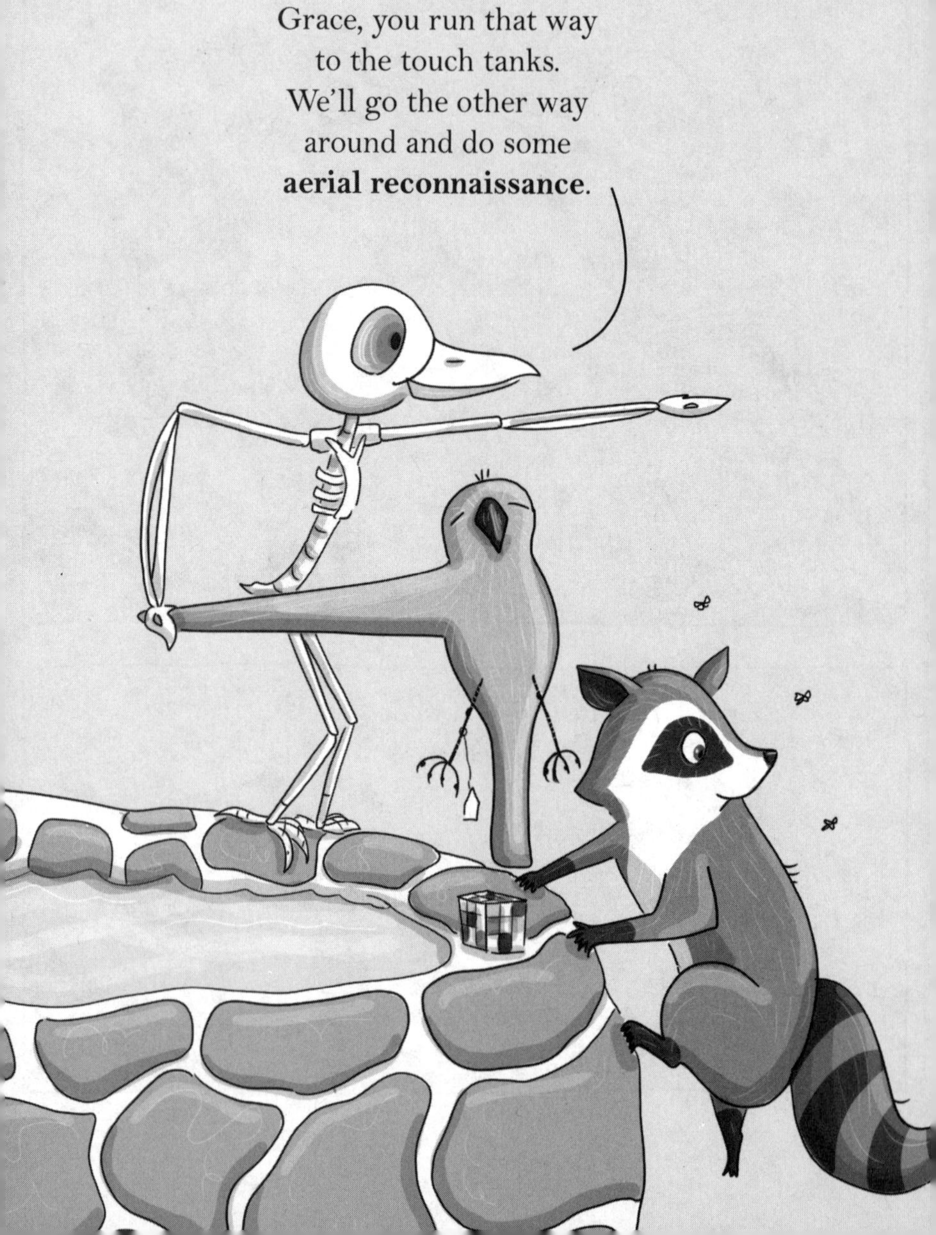

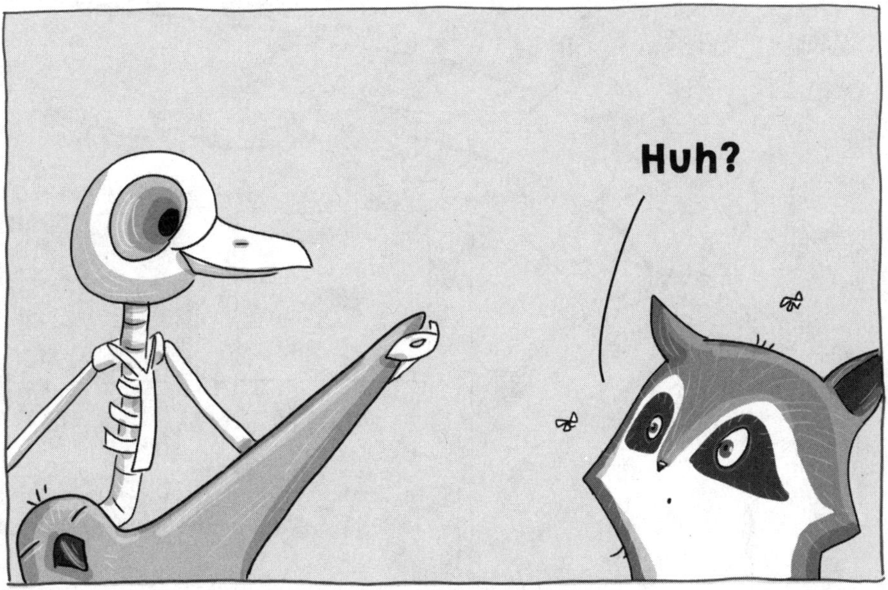
Huh?

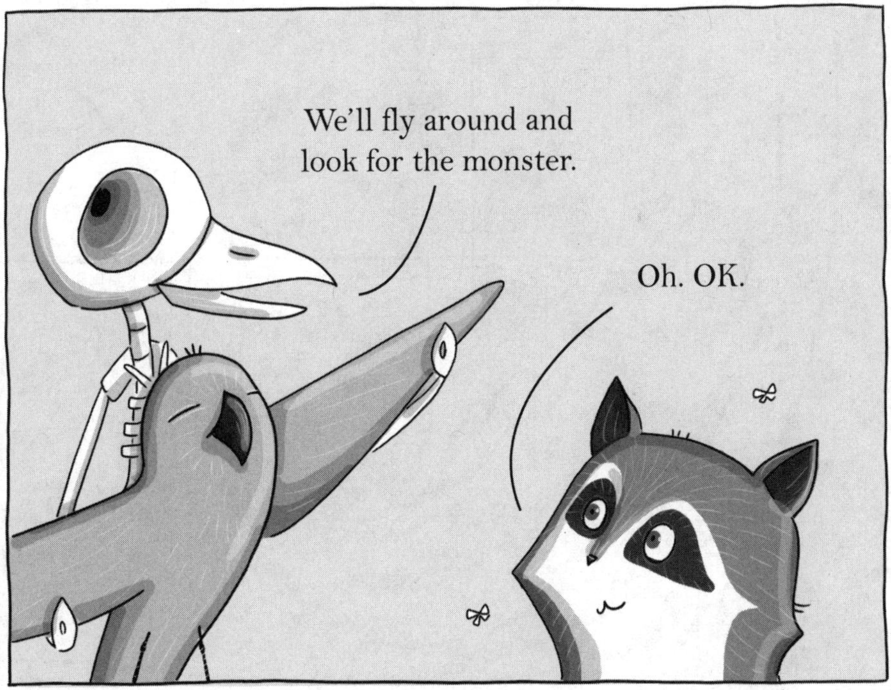
We'll fly around and look for the monster.
Oh. OK.

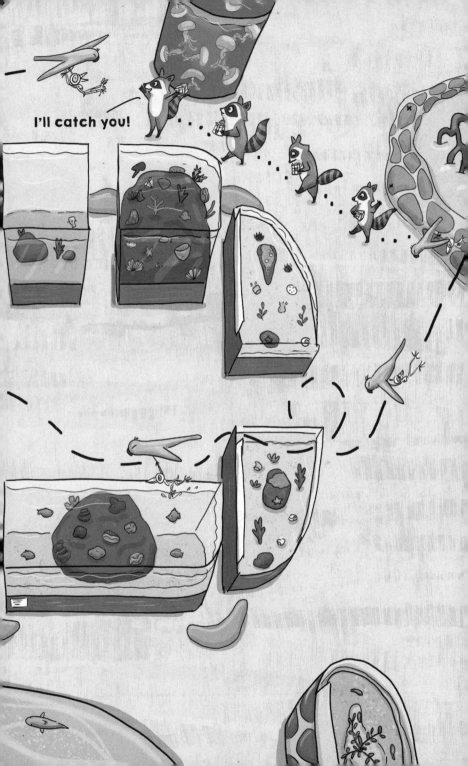

I'll catch you!

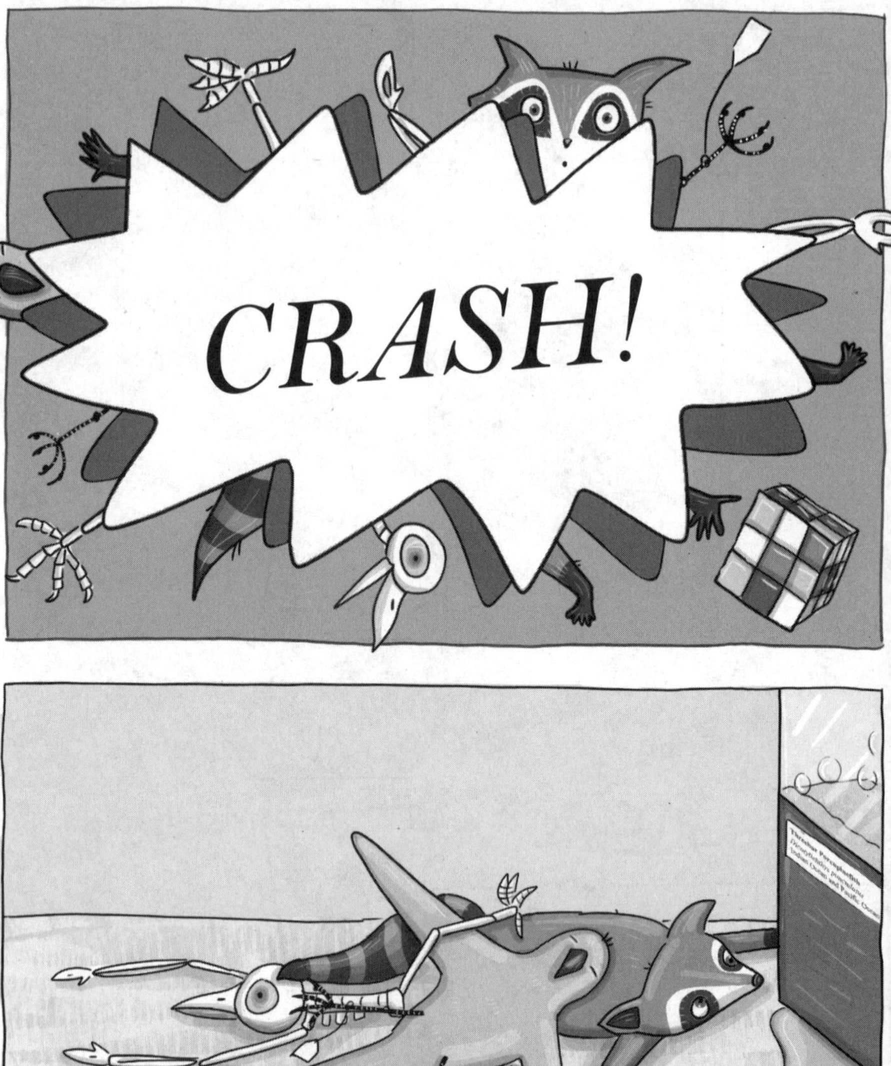
CRASH!

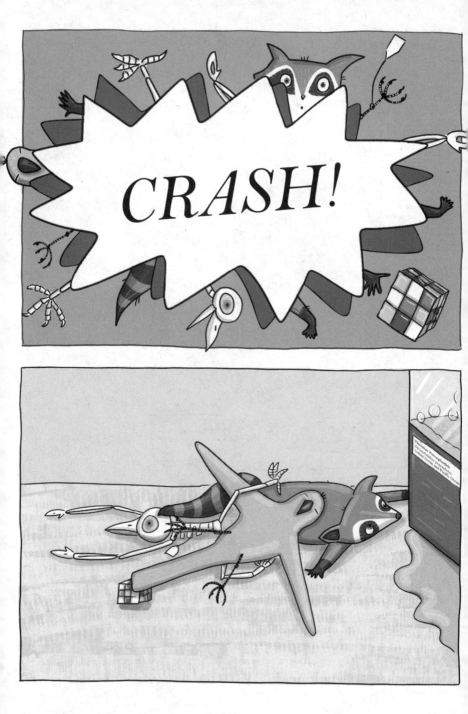

Oooh... it's connect-the-dots!

Hey, Bones! Come look at this fish!

179

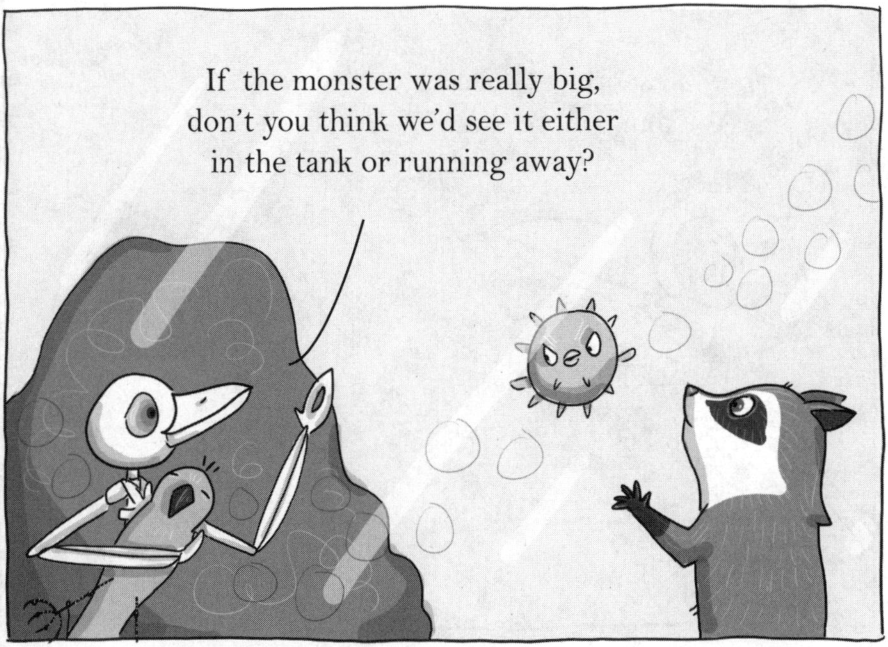
If the monster was really big, don't you think we'd see it either in the tank or running away?

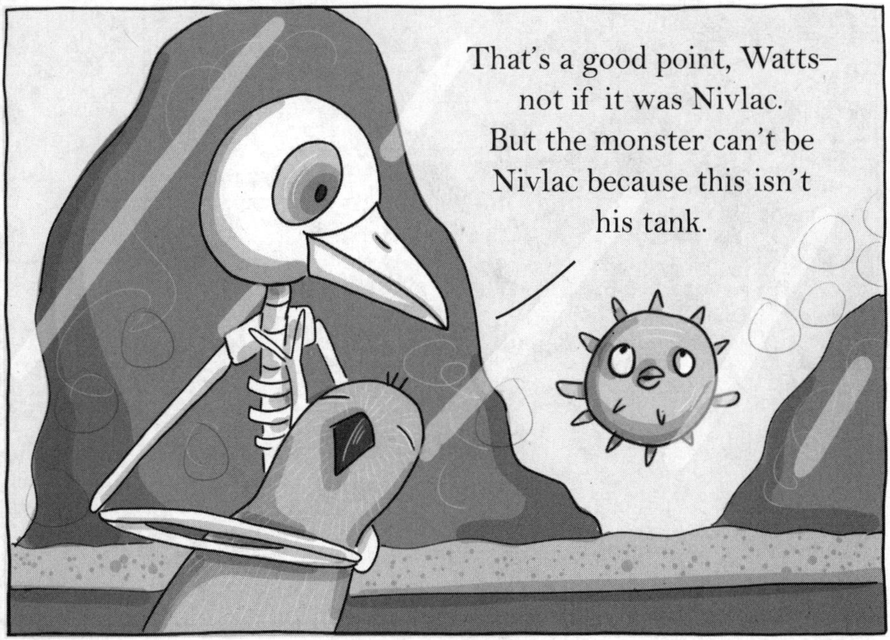
That's a good point, Watts– not if it was Nivlac. But the monster can't be Nivlac because this isn't his tank.

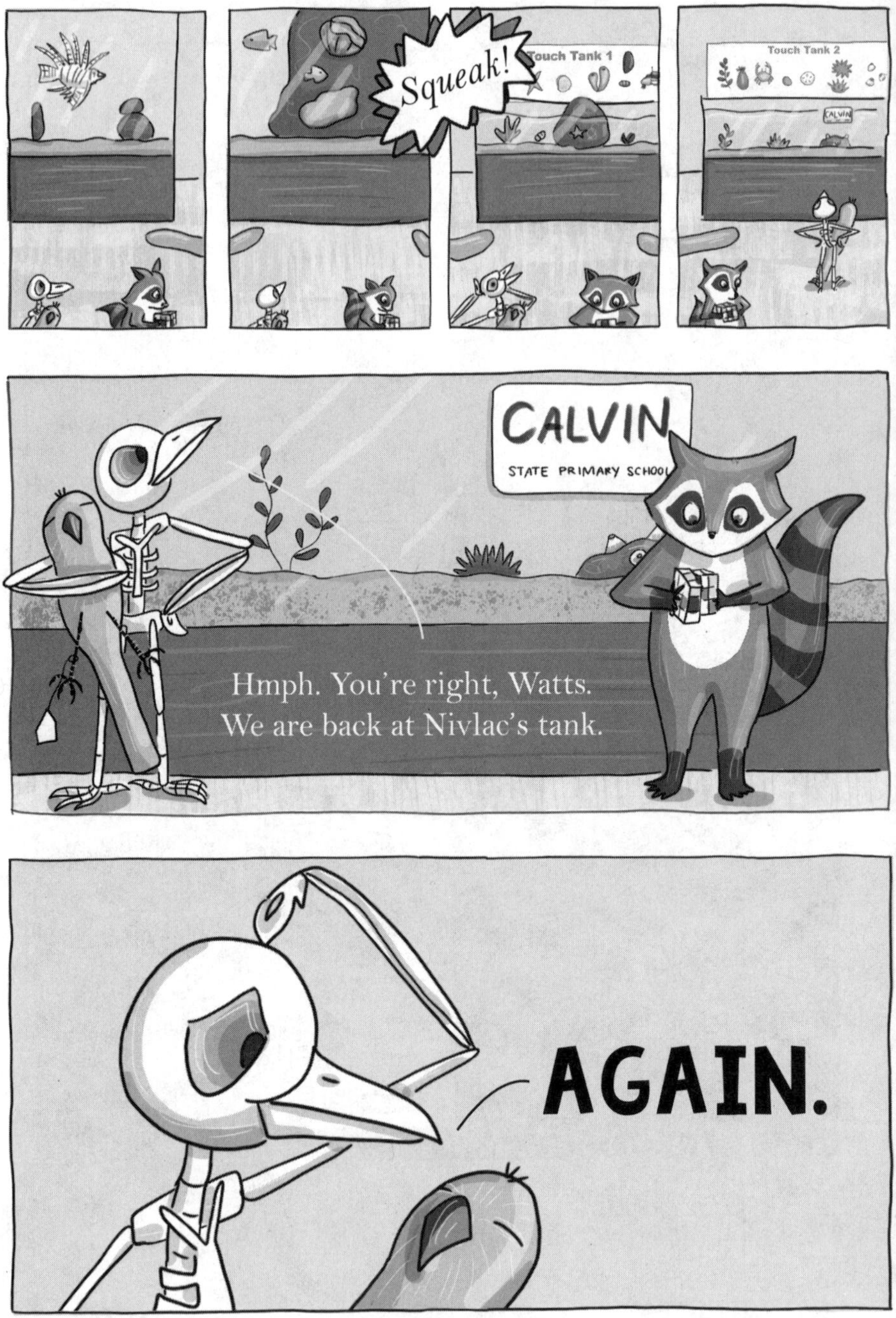
Squeak!
Touch Tank 1
Touch Tank 2
CALVIN
CALVIN
STATE PRIMARY SCHOO
Hmph. You’re right, Watts.
We are back at Nivlac’s tank.
AGAIN.

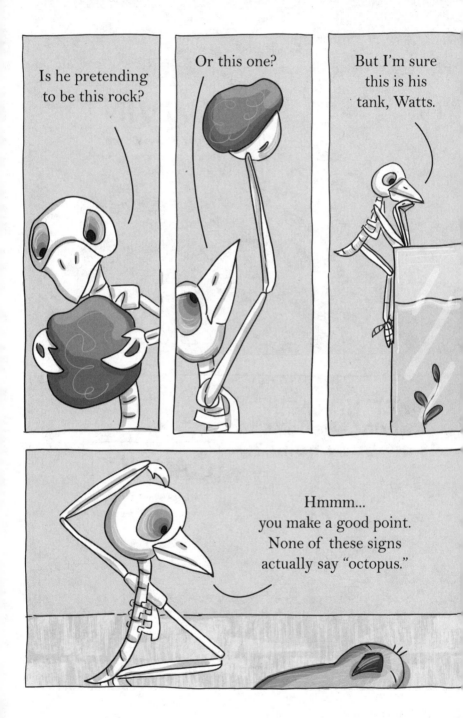

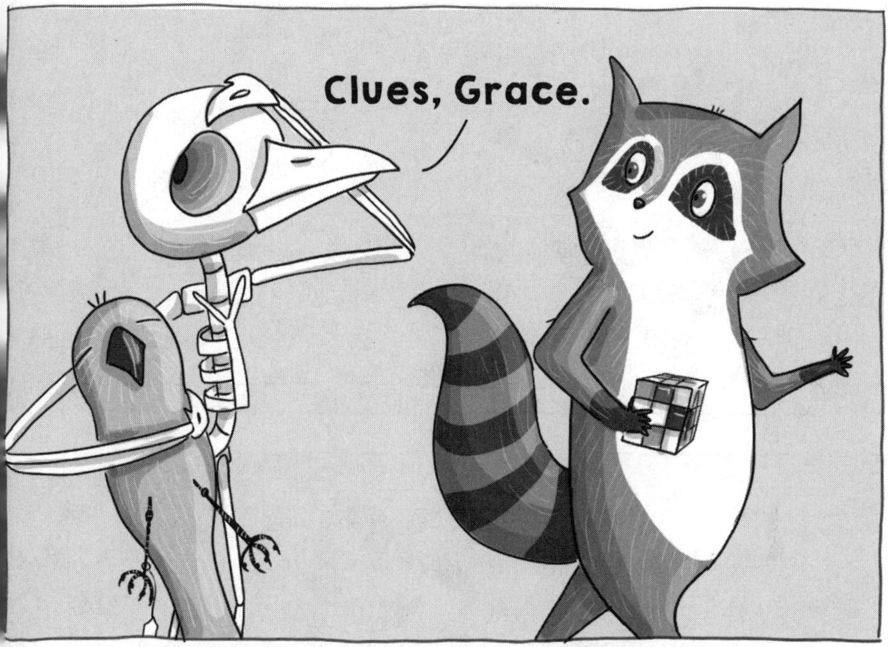
Clues, Grace.

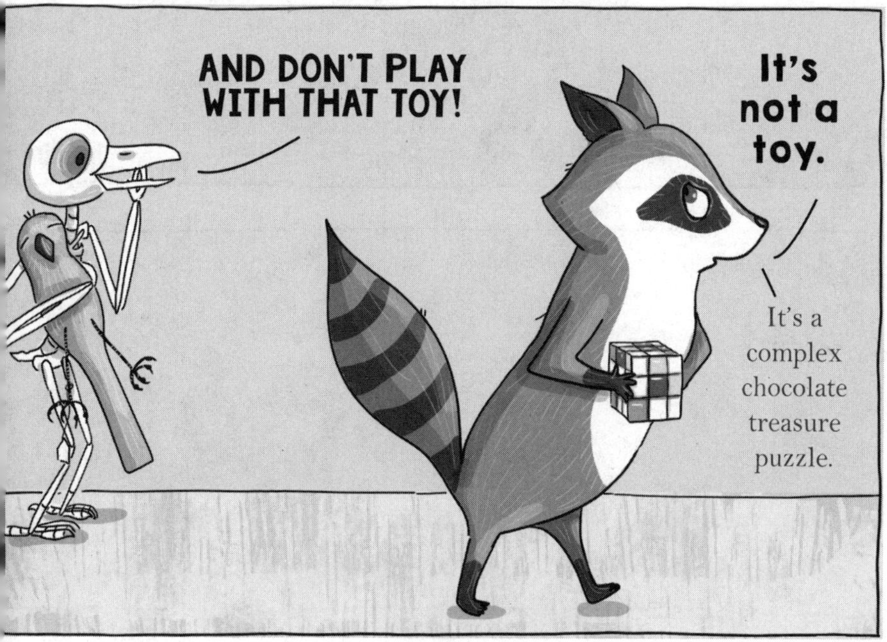
AND DON'T PLAY WITH THAT TOY!
It's not a toy.
It's a complex chocolate treasure puzzle.

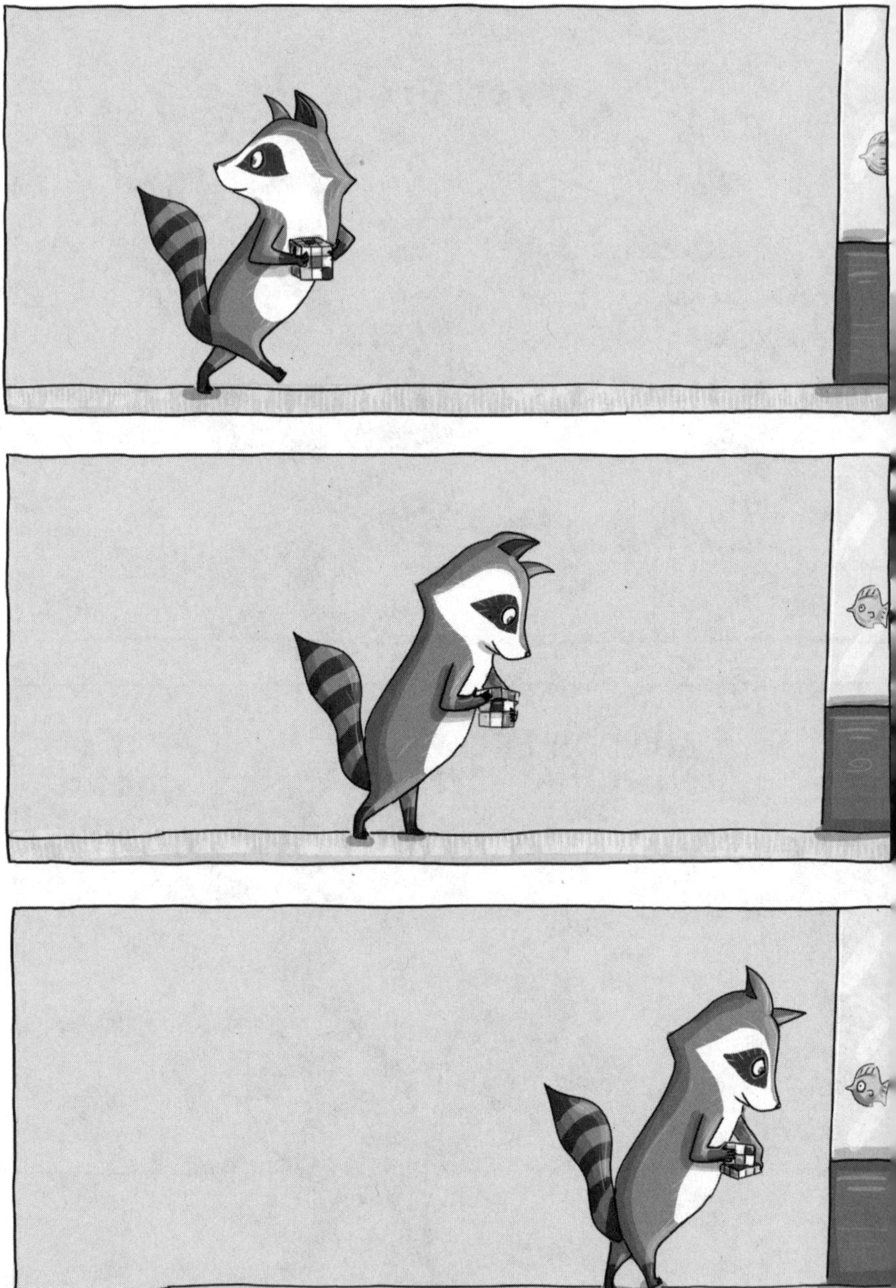

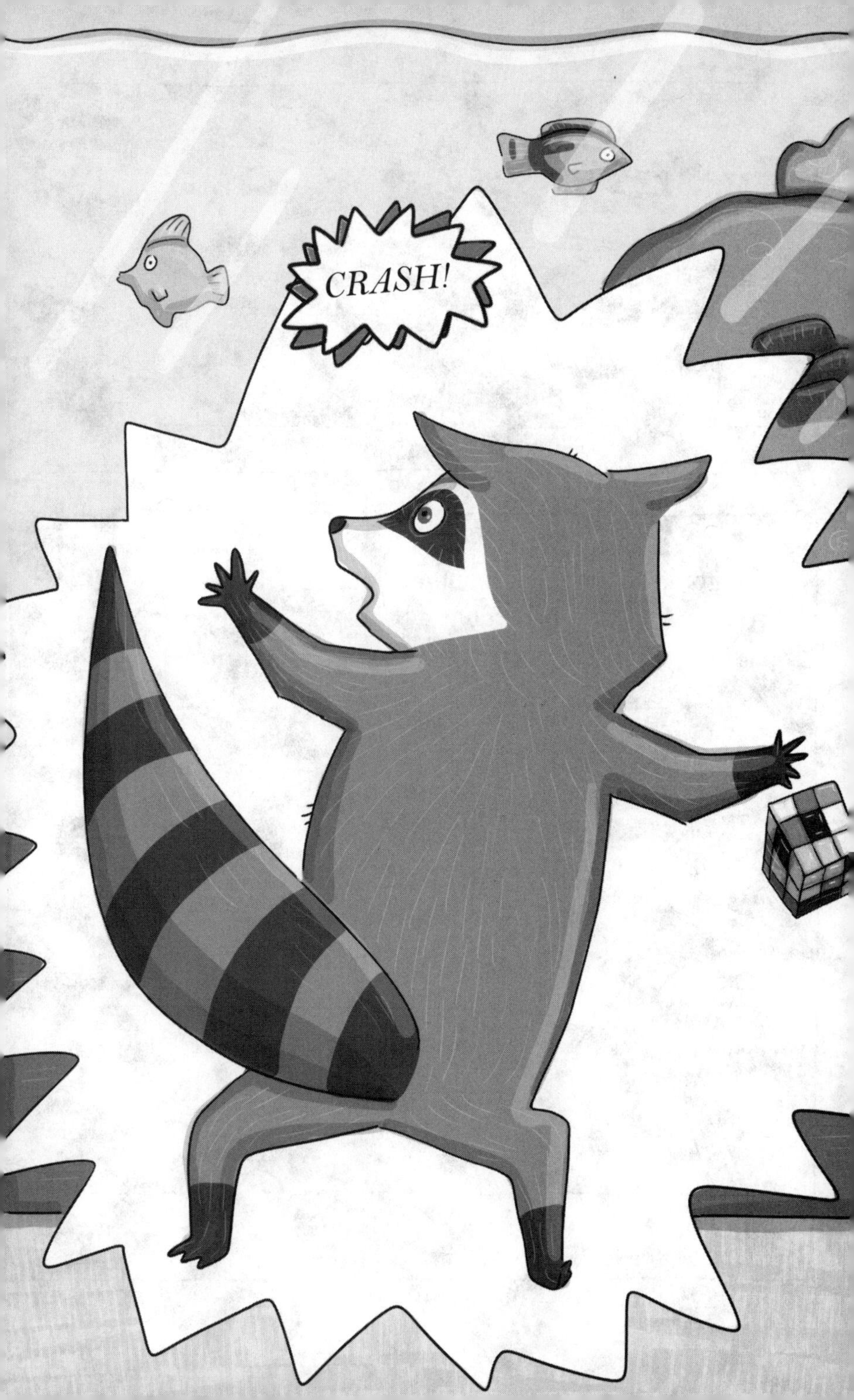
CRASH!

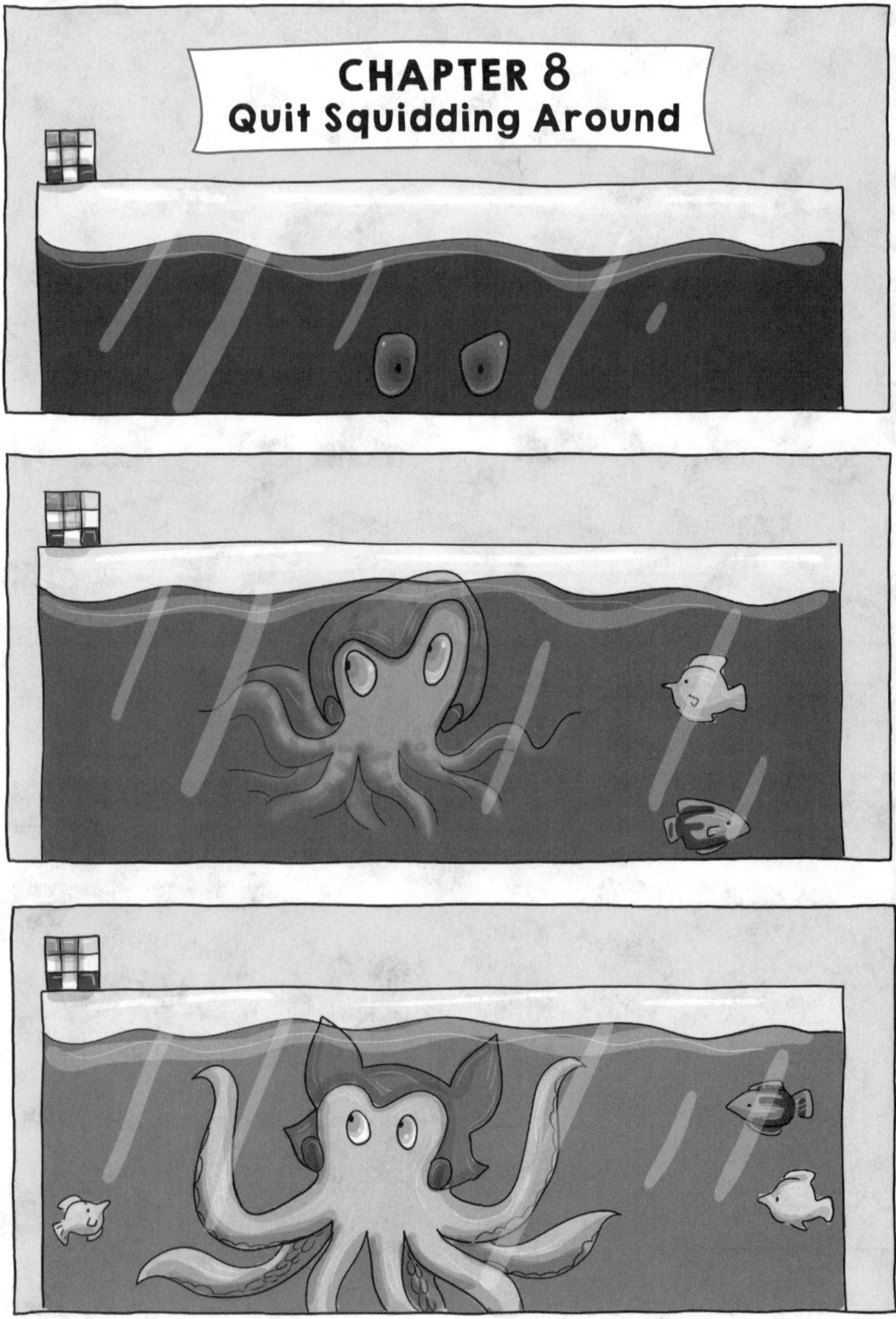
CHAPTER 8
Quit Squidding Around

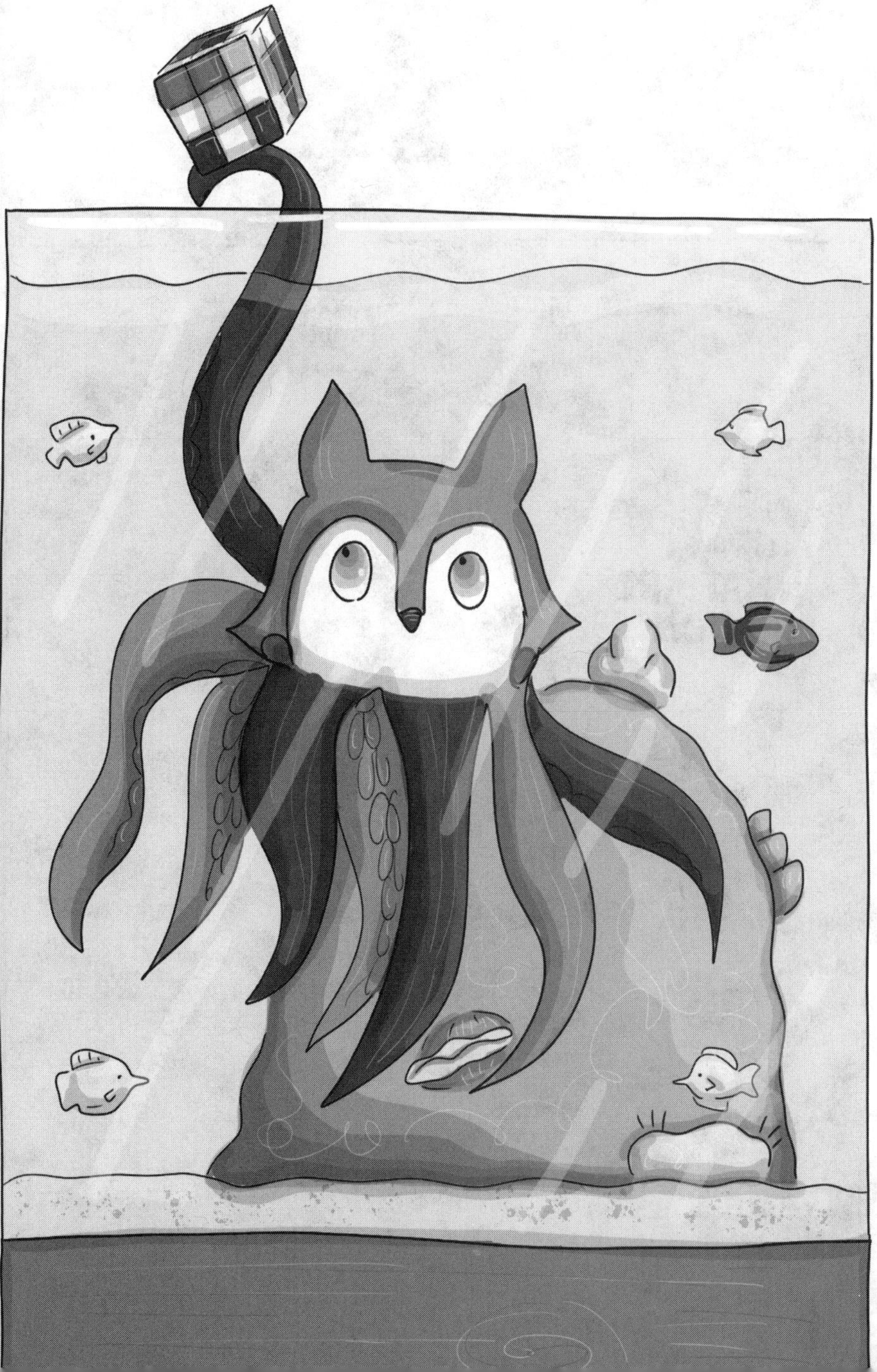

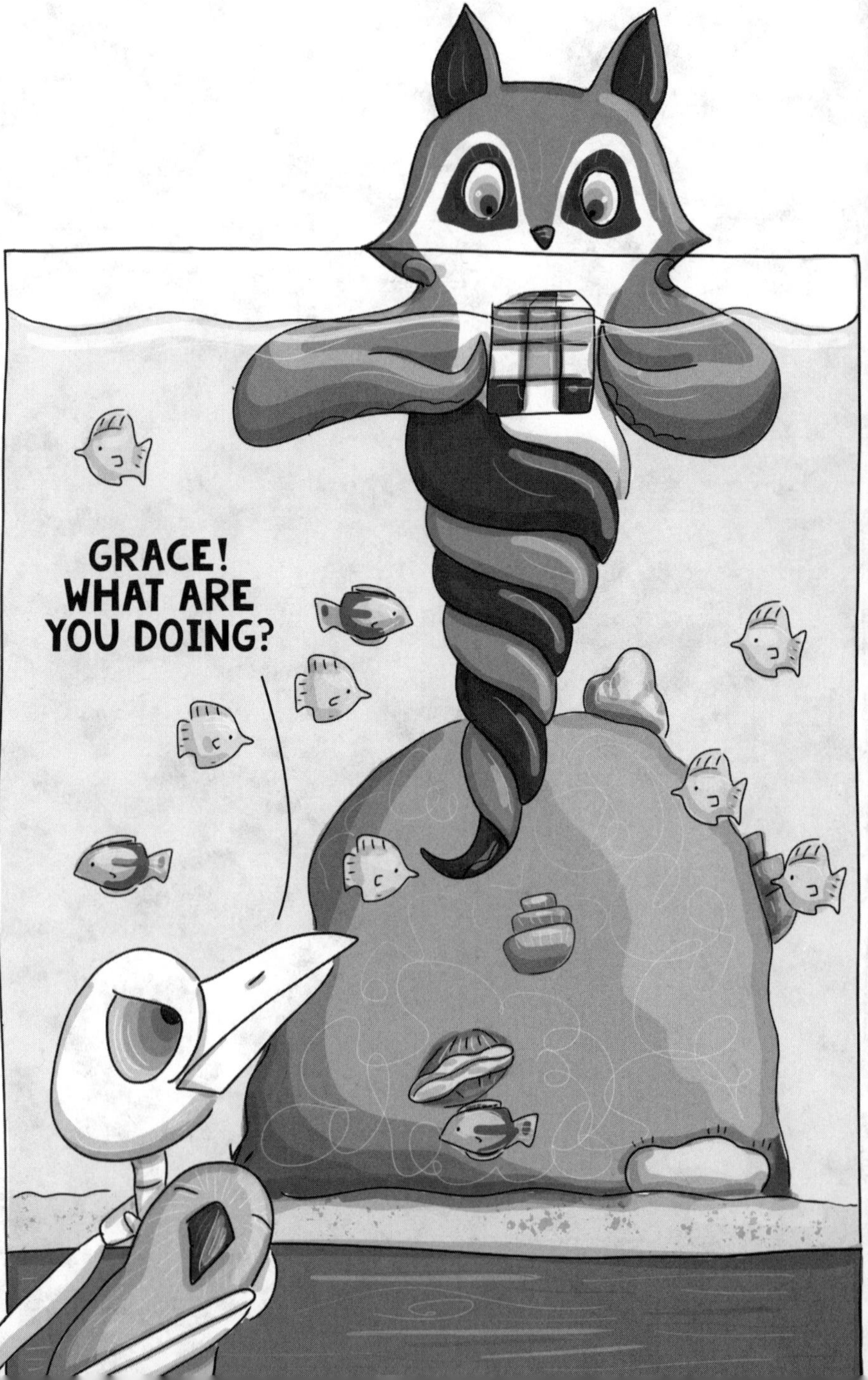
GRACE! WHAT ARE YOU DOING?

199

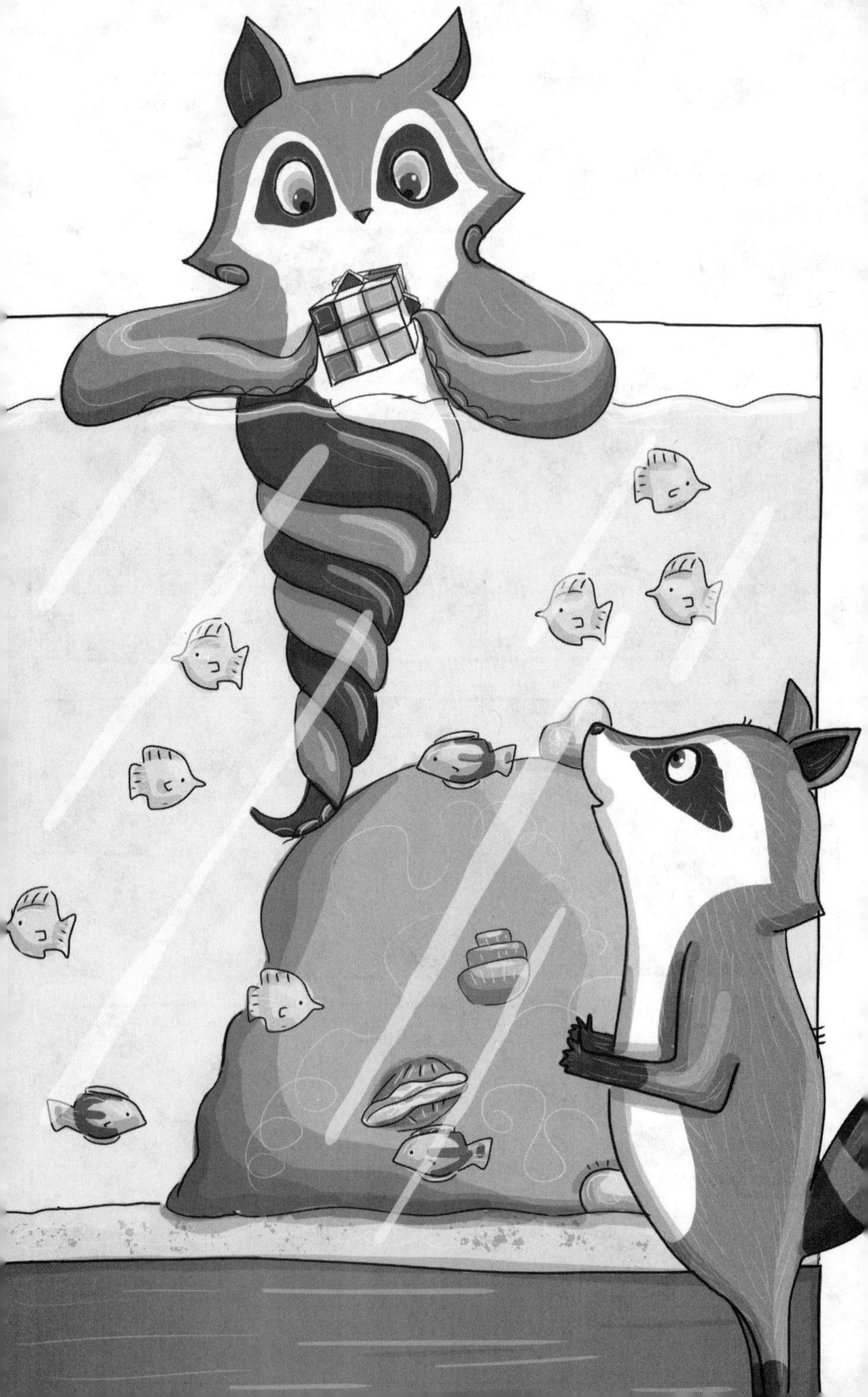

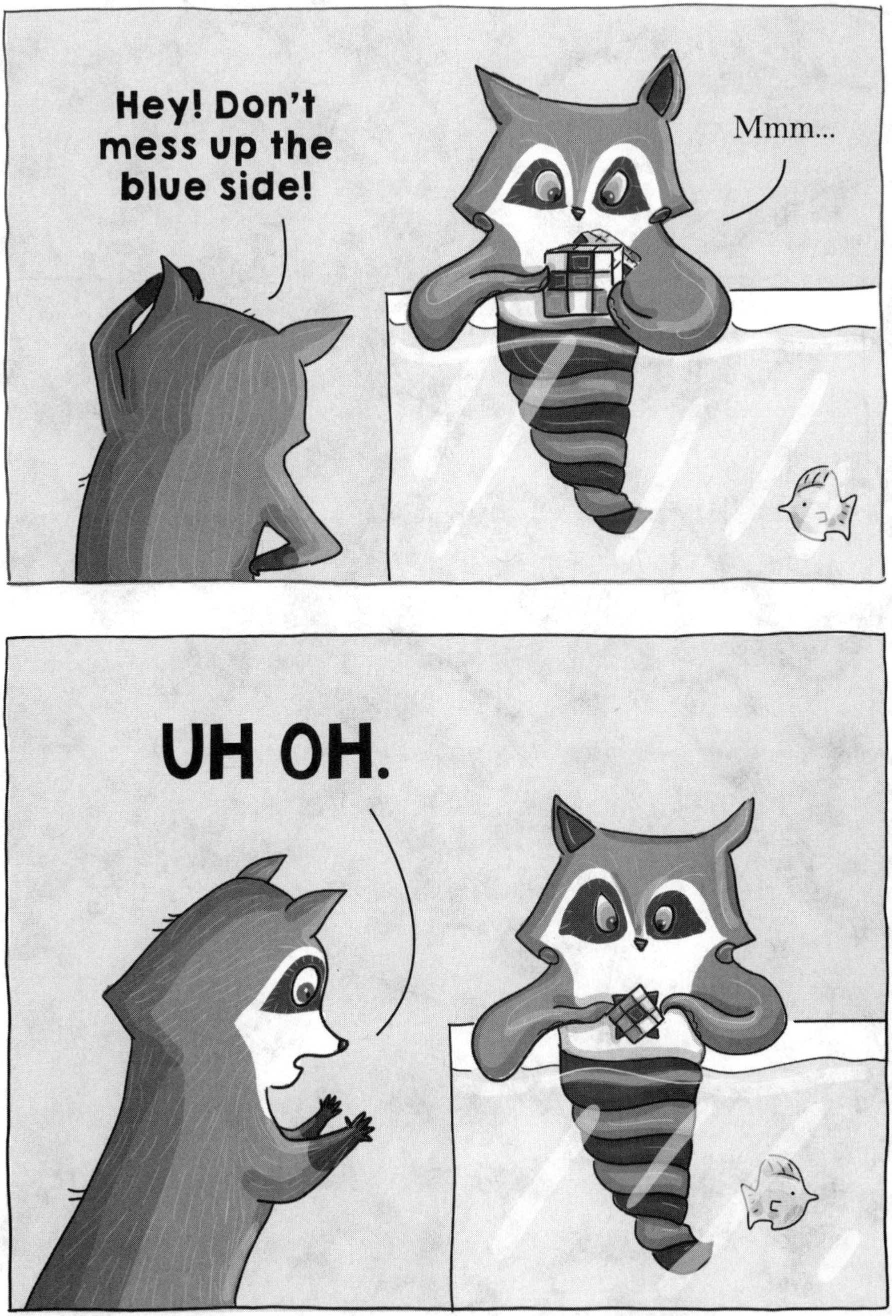
Hey! Don't mess up the blue side!
Mmm...
UH OH.

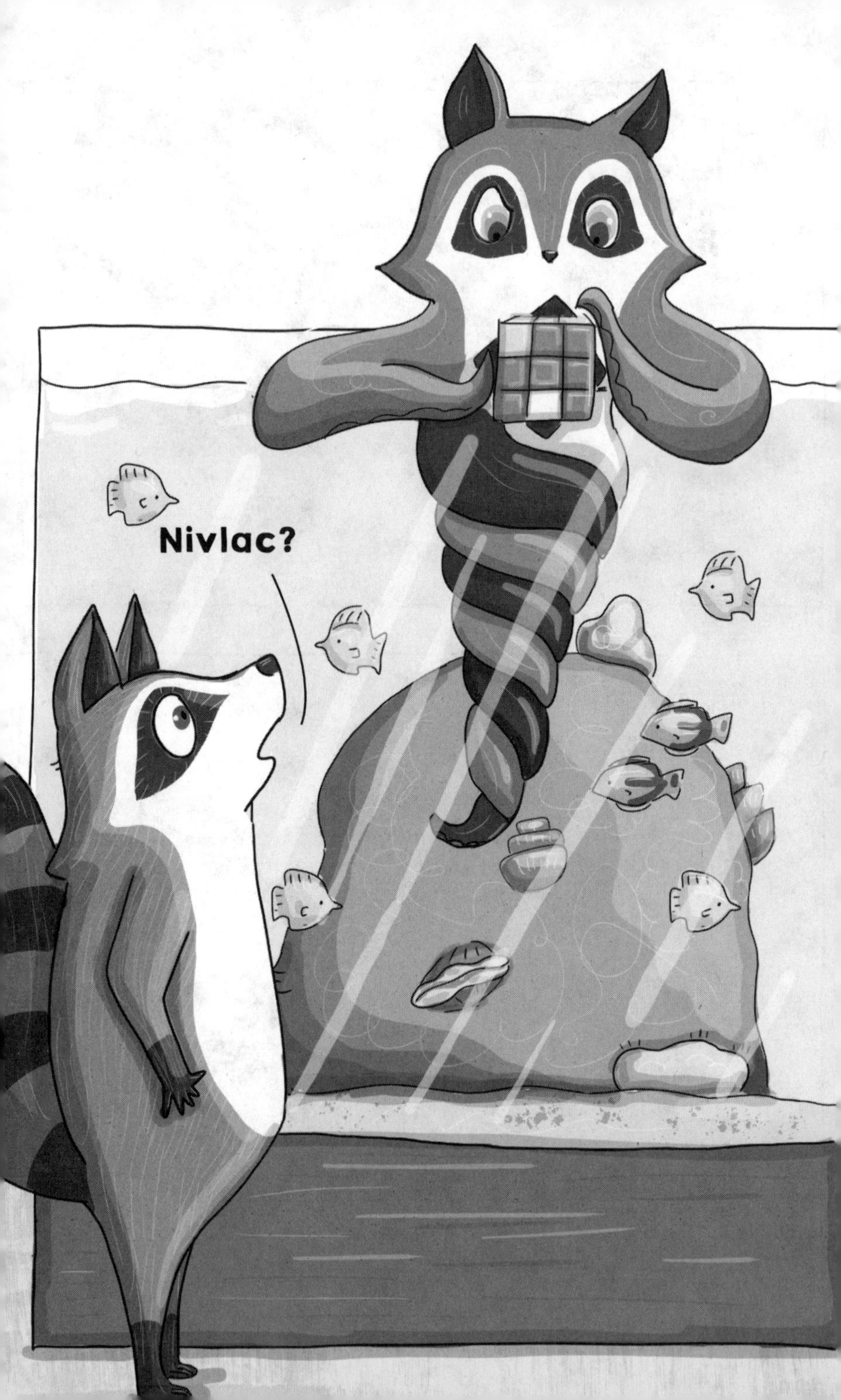
Nivlac?

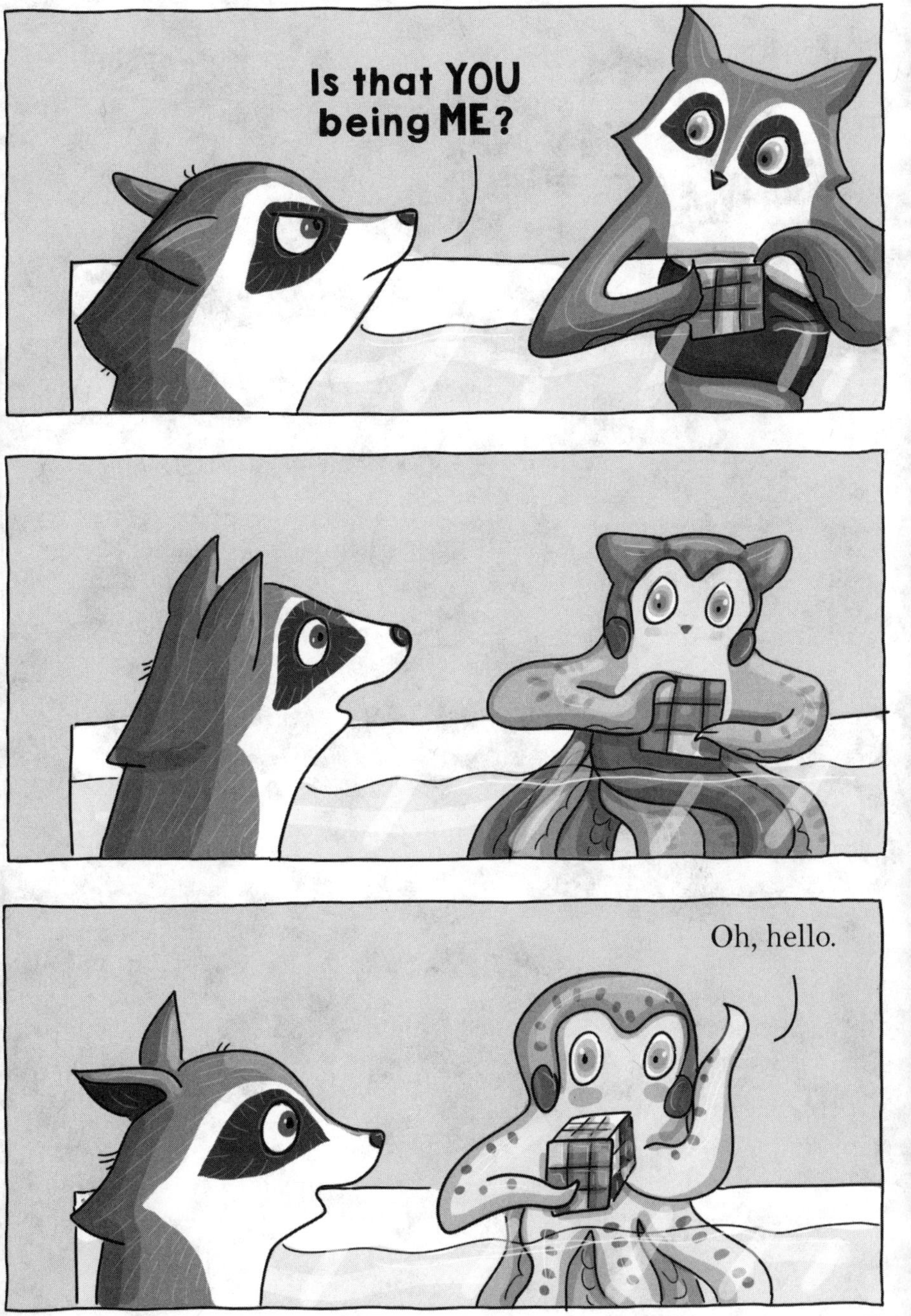
Is that YOU being ME?
Oh, hello.

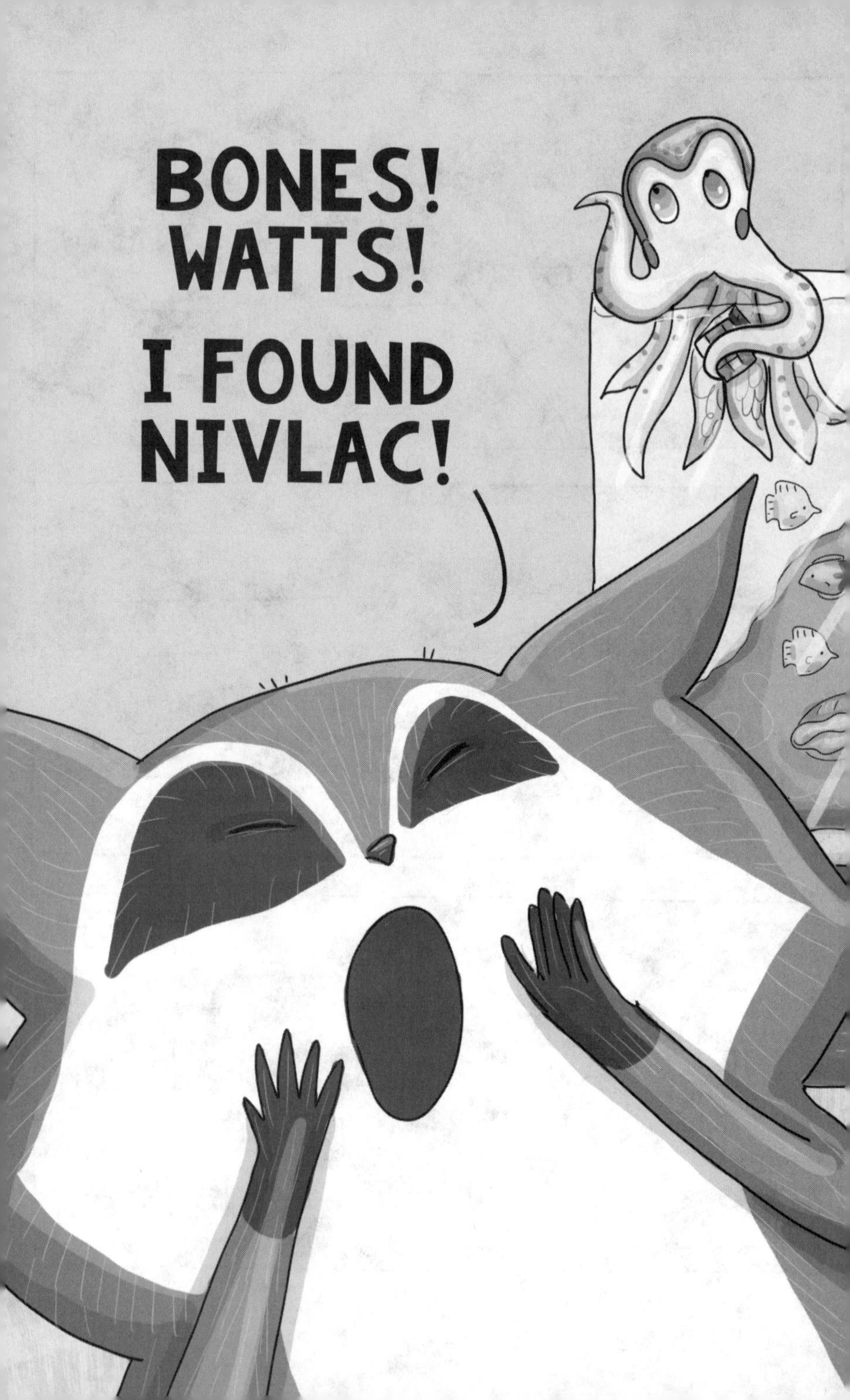
BONES! WATTS!
I FOUND NIVLAC!

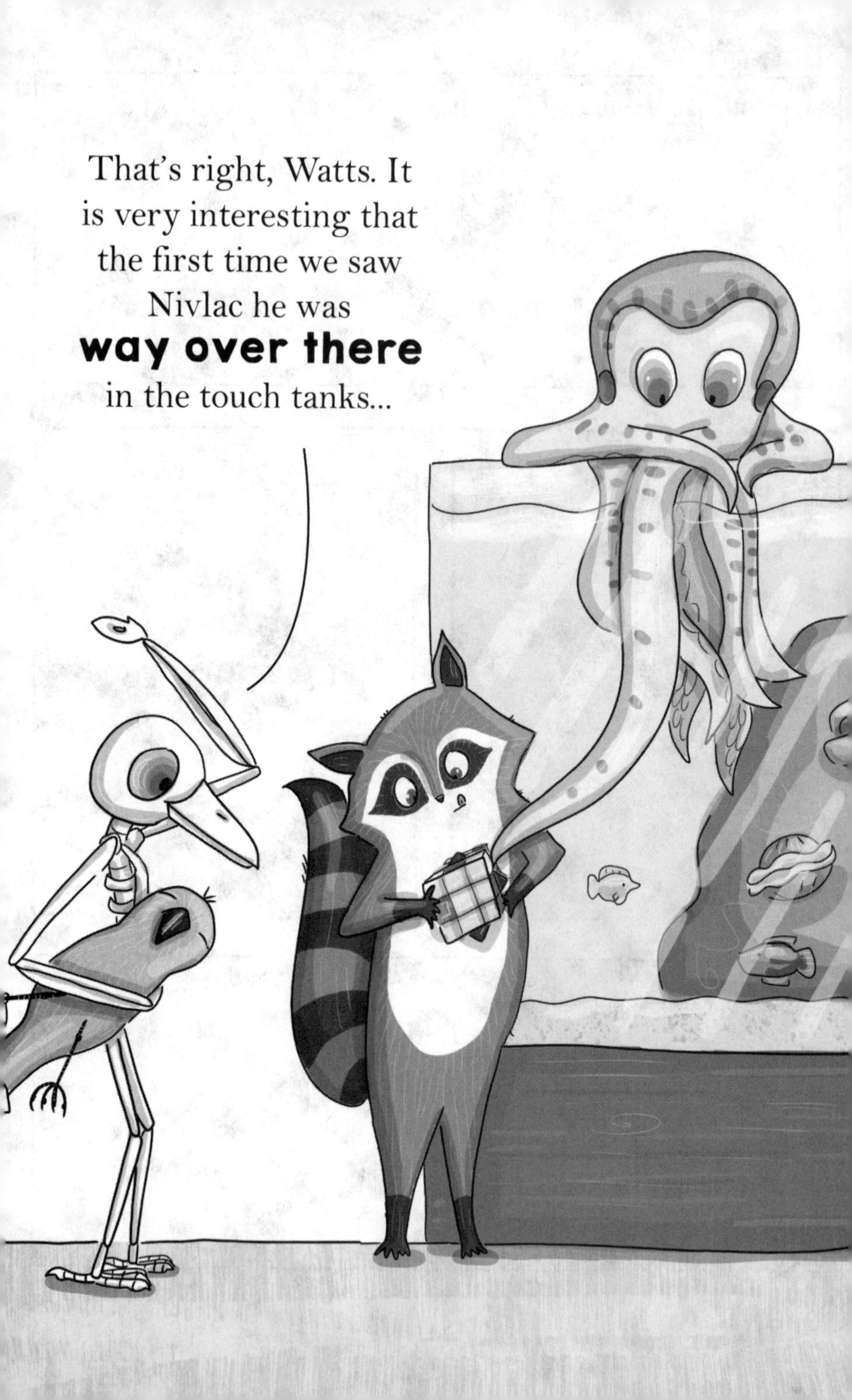
That's right, Watts. It is very interesting that the first time we saw Nivlac he was **way over there** in the touch tanks...

CHAPTER 9
You're Kraken Me Up

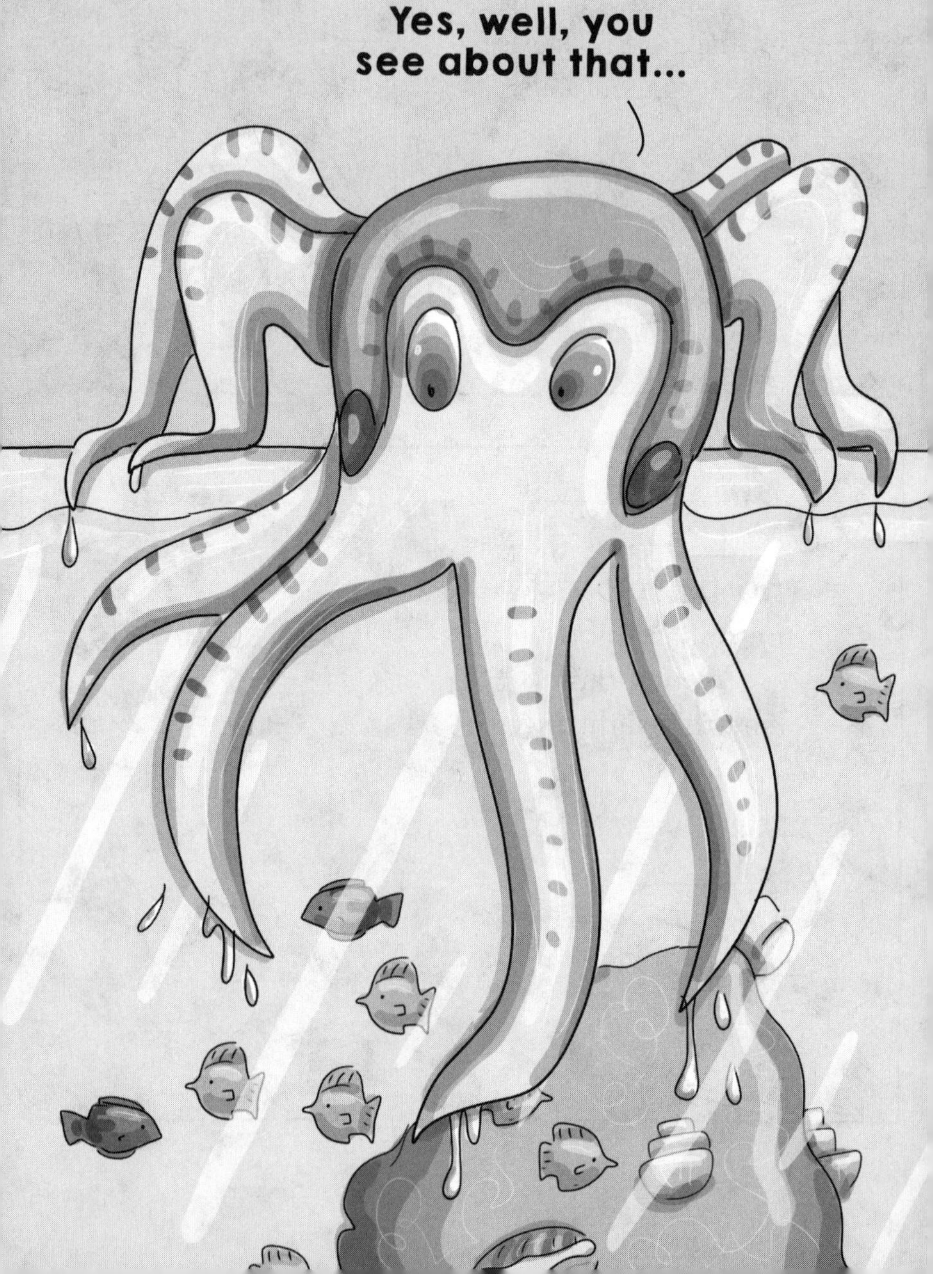

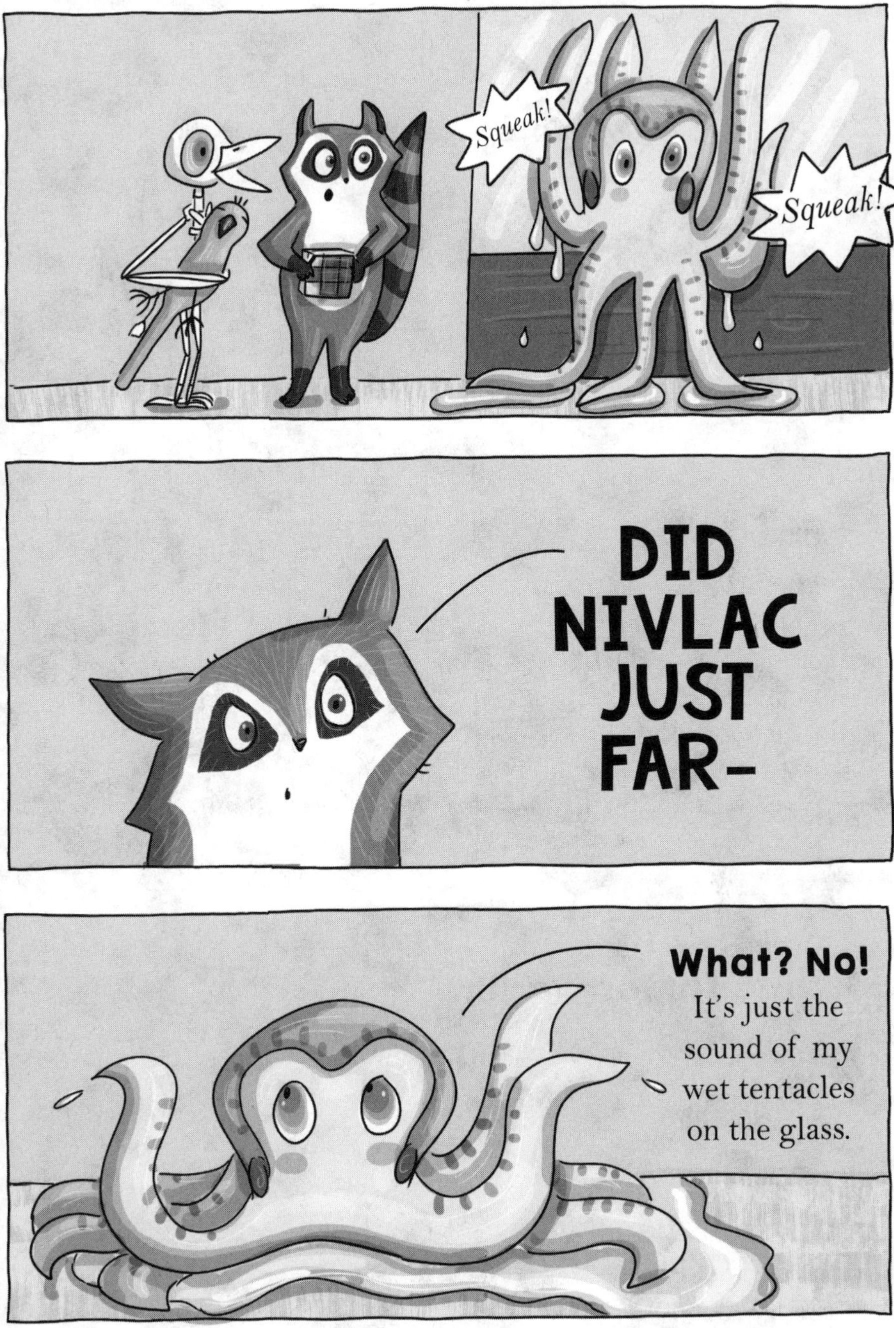
Squeak!
Squeak!
DID NIVLAC JUST FAR-
What? No!
It's just the sound of my wet tentacles on the glass.

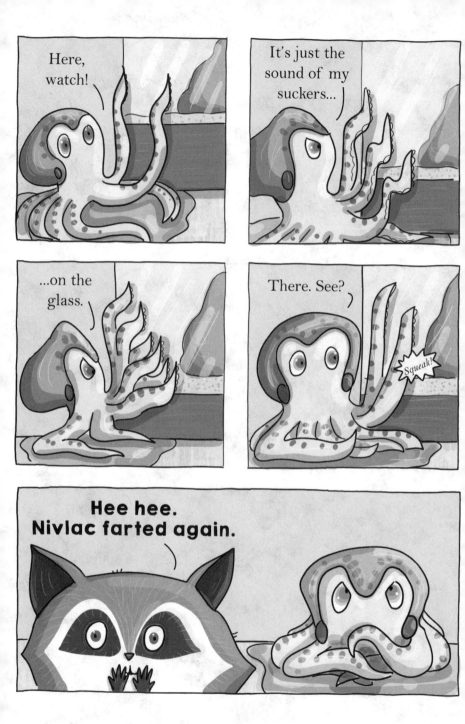

212

Look, it's really boring here!

I'm stuck in a tank all day and the only toy I've got is this jar.

Open the jar. Close the jar.

IT'S MAKING ME CRAZY!

I need to be out here, enjoying all the **wonderful** and **delicious** things this museum has to offer.

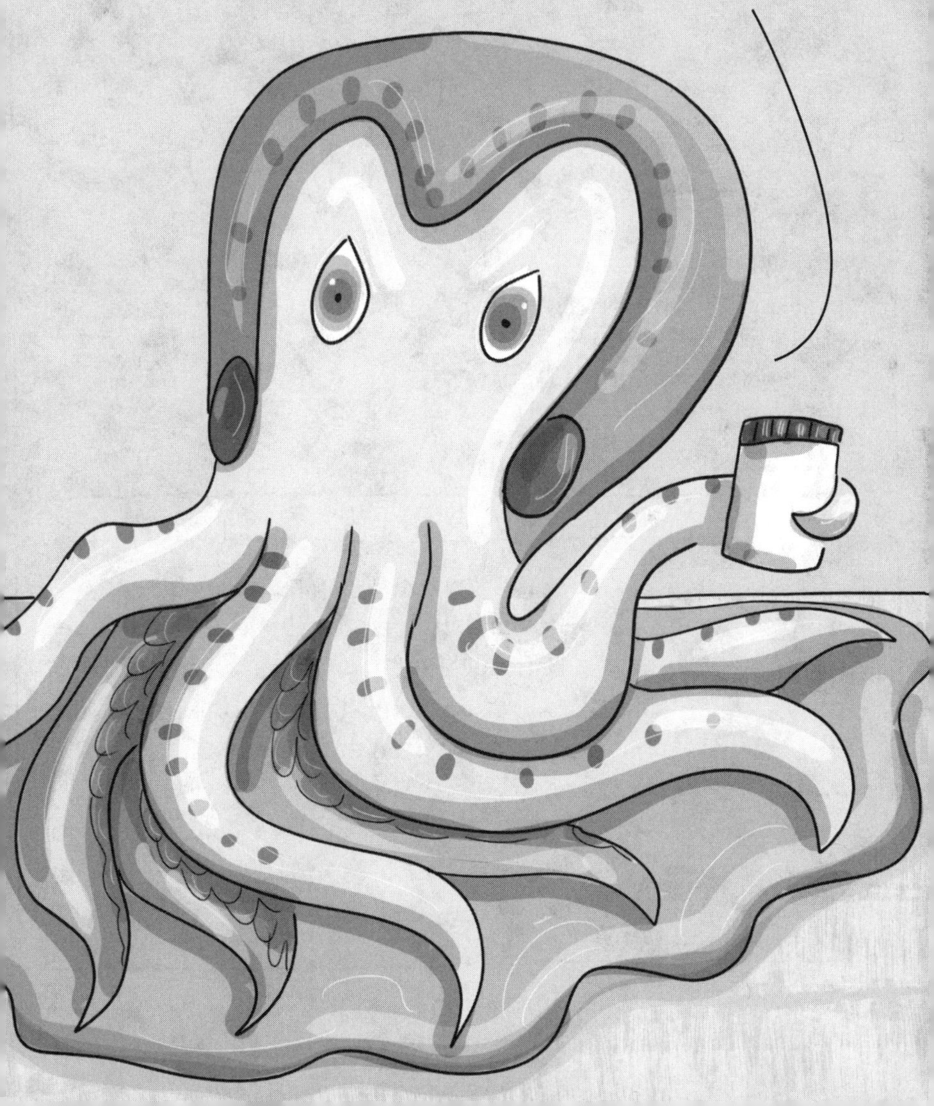

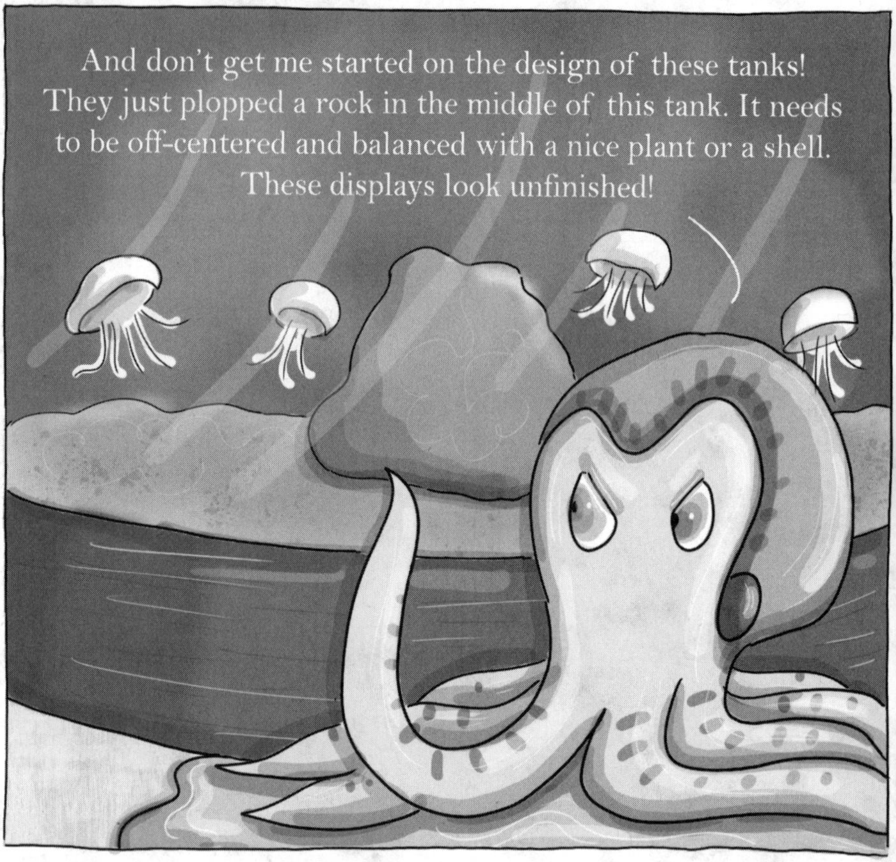
And don't get me started on the design of these tanks! They just plopped a rock in the middle of this tank. It needs to be off-centered and balanced with a nice plant or a shell. These displays look unfinished!

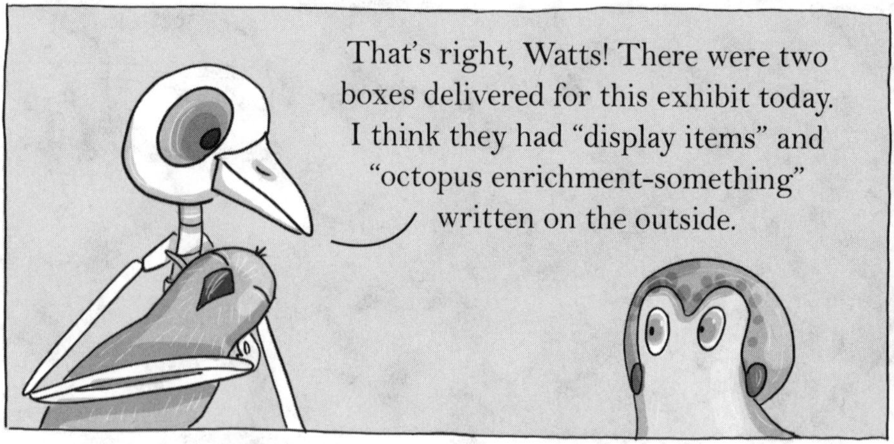
That's right, Watts! There were two boxes delivered for this exhibit today. I think they had "display items" and "octopus enrichment-something" written on the outside.

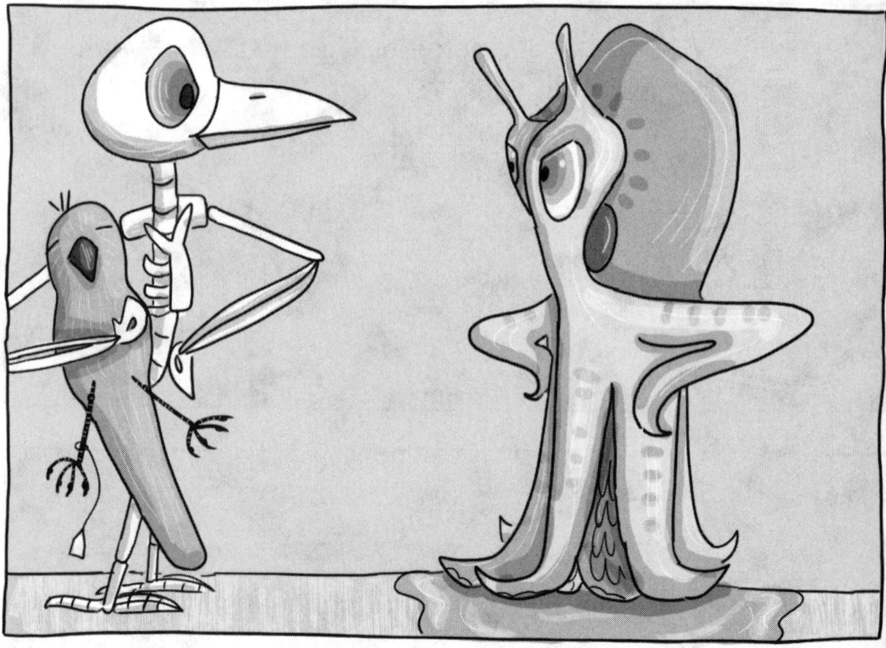

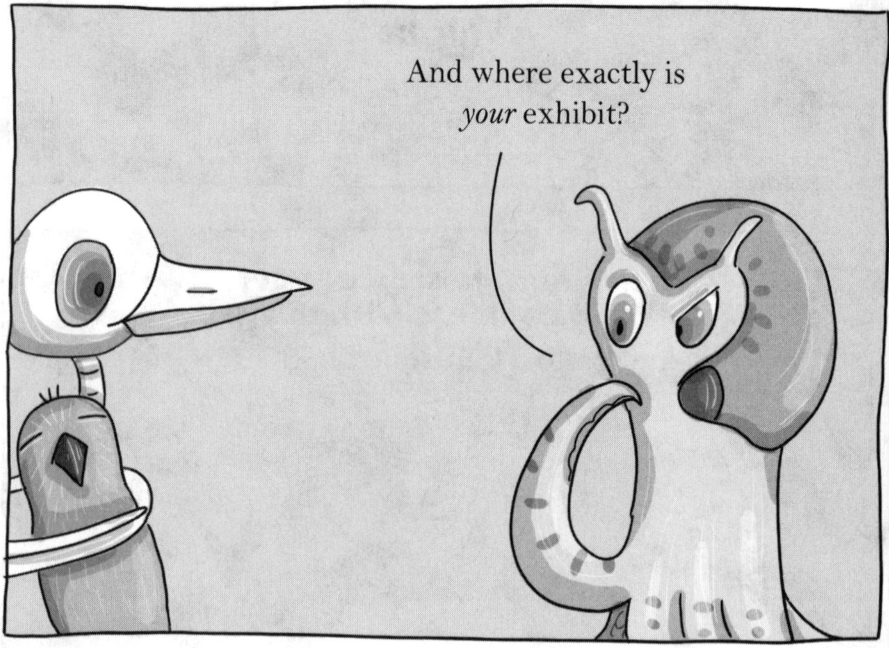
And where exactly is
your exhibit?

218

Let's get you back
to your proper tank.

So, what does this cube do?
I find it fascinating.

It's a magic cube. Here,
have a look. If you match
all the colors, chocolates
will come pouring out!

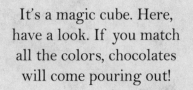

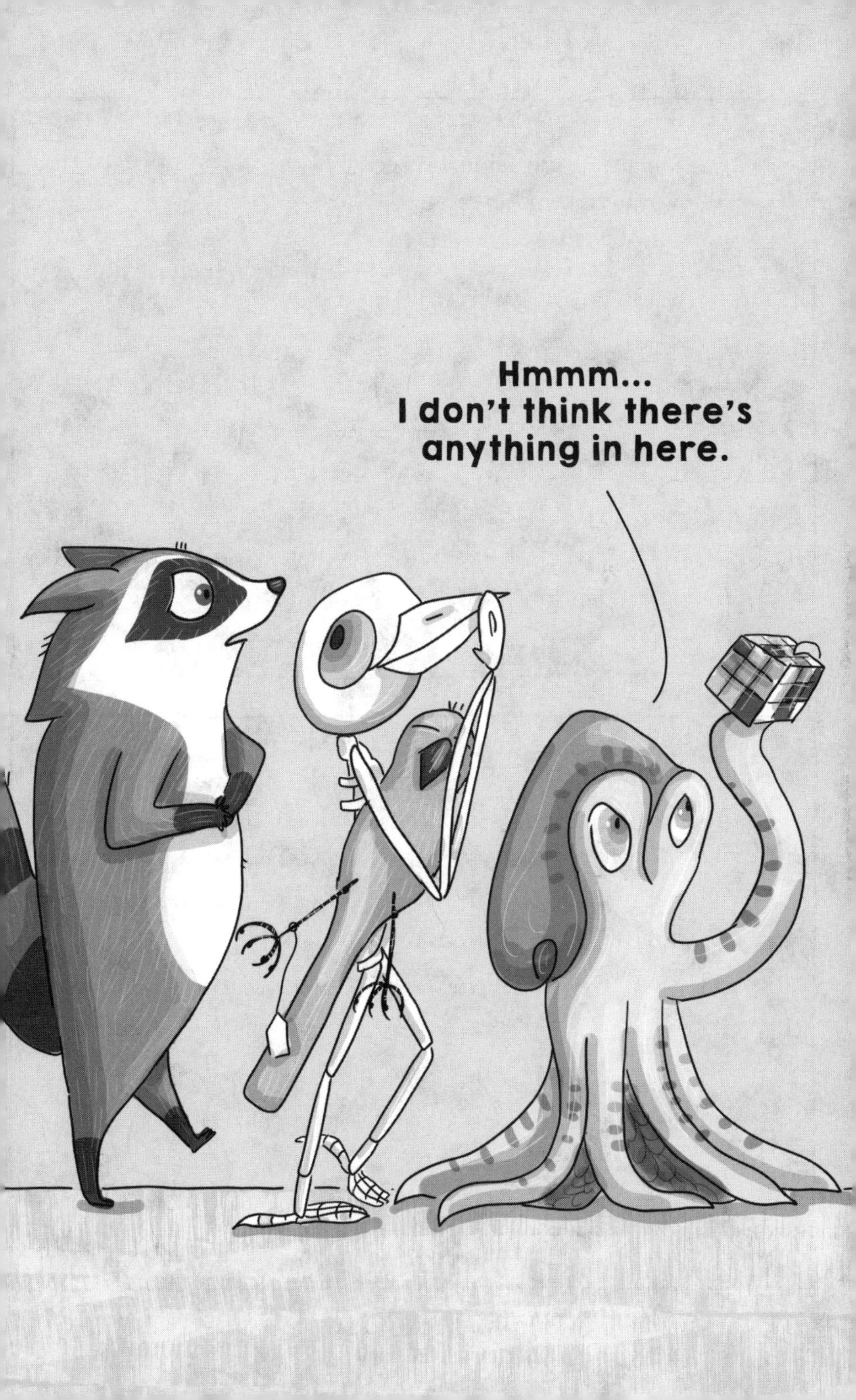
Hmmm...
I don't think there's
anything in here.

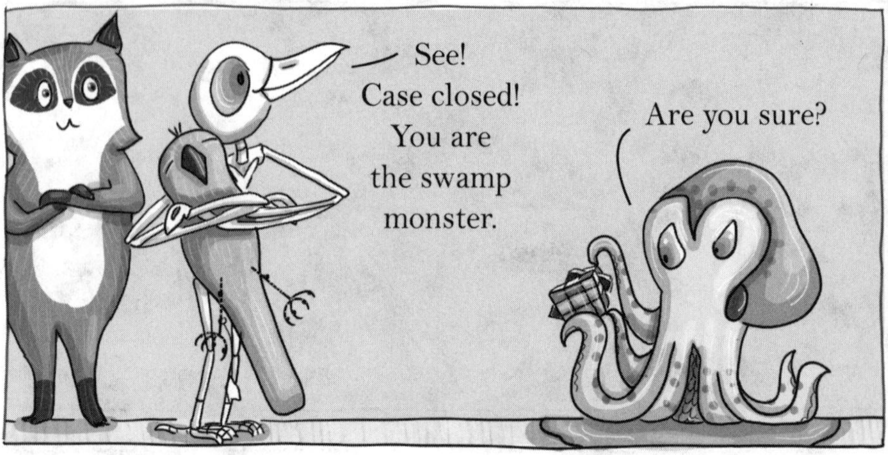
See!
Case closed!
You are
the swamp
monster.
Are you sure?

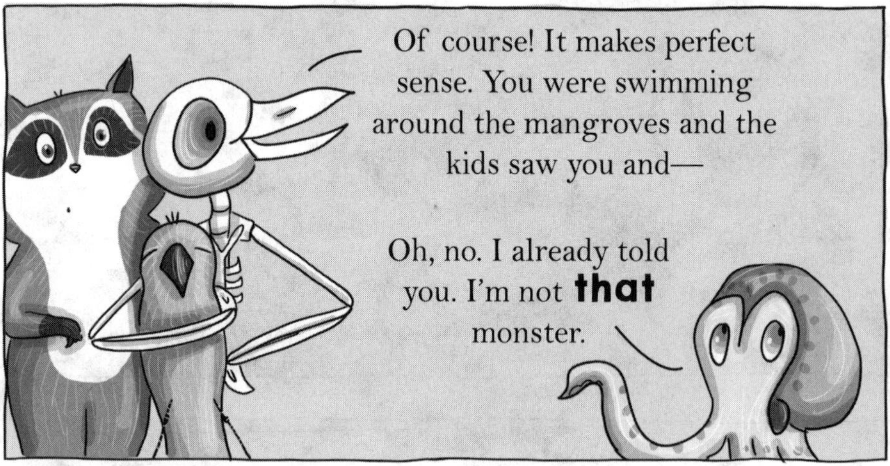
Of course! It makes perfect sense. You were swimming around the mangroves and the kids saw you and—
Oh, no. I already told you. I'm not **that** monster.

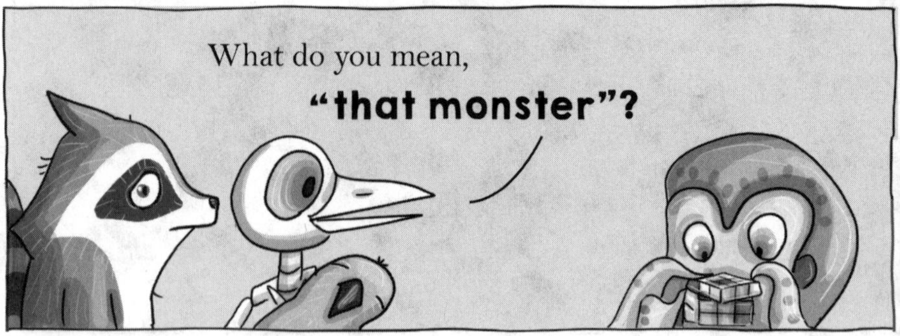
What do you mean,
"that monster"?

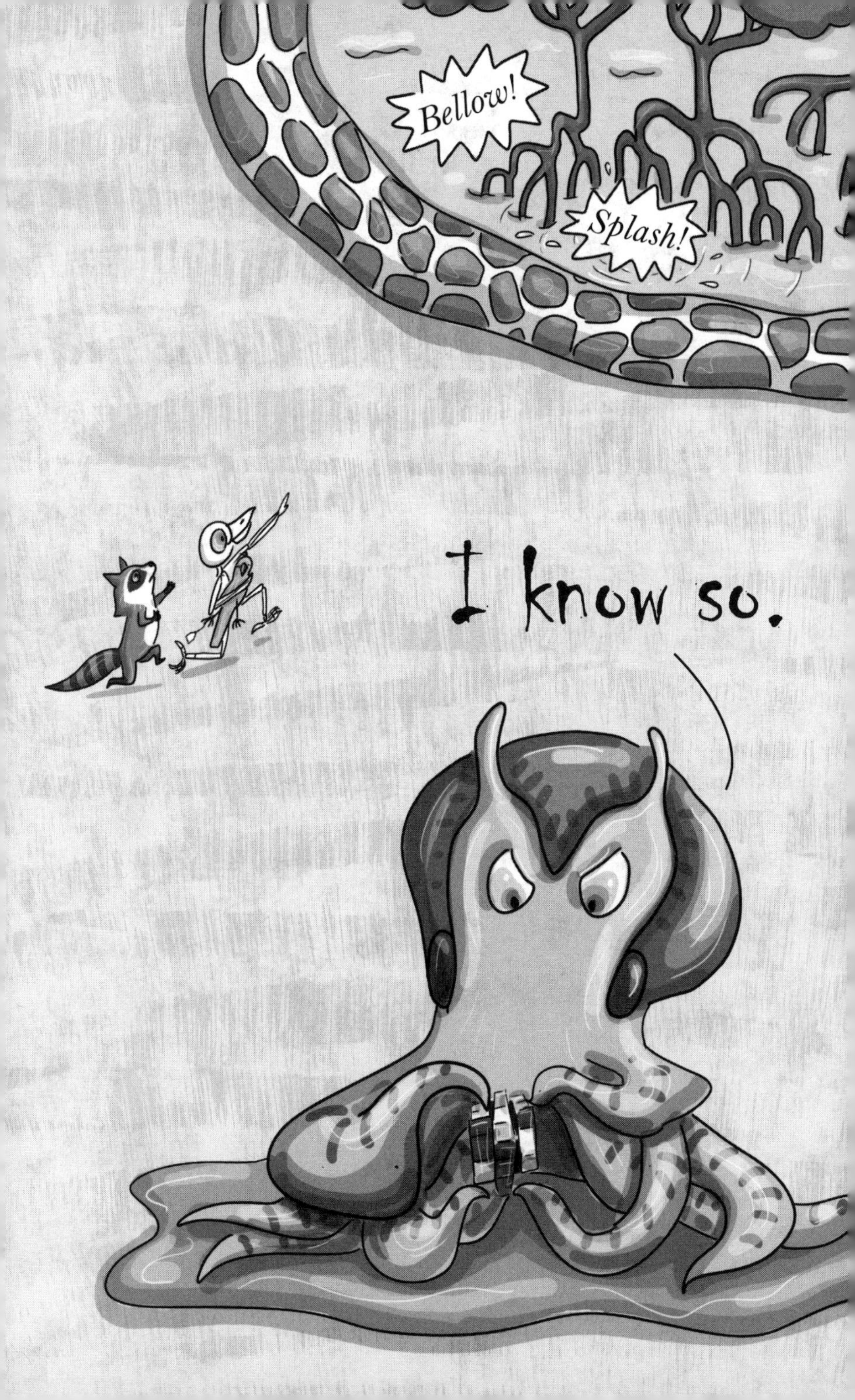
Bellow!
Splash!
I know so.

CHAPTER 10
You're Krilling Me

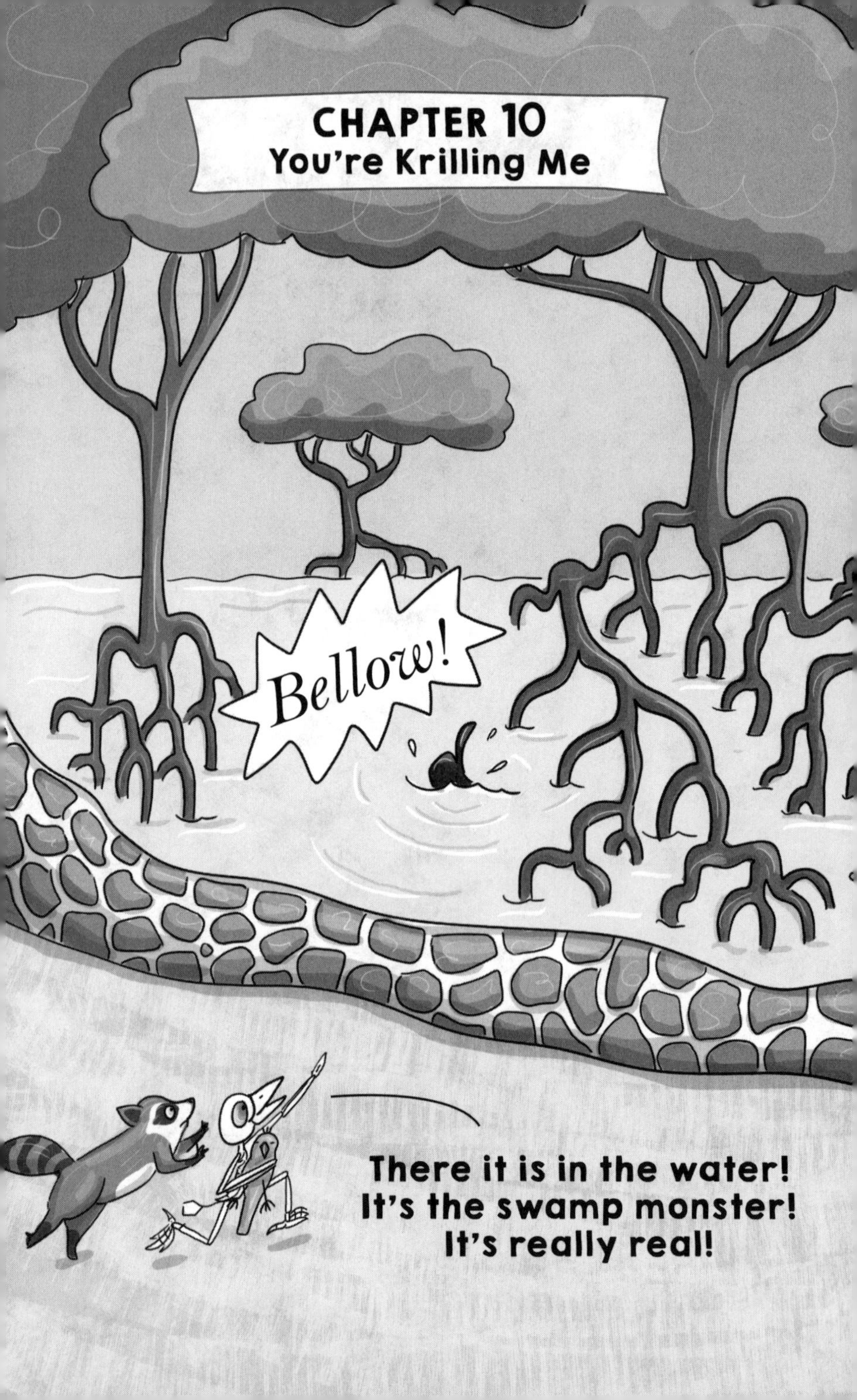

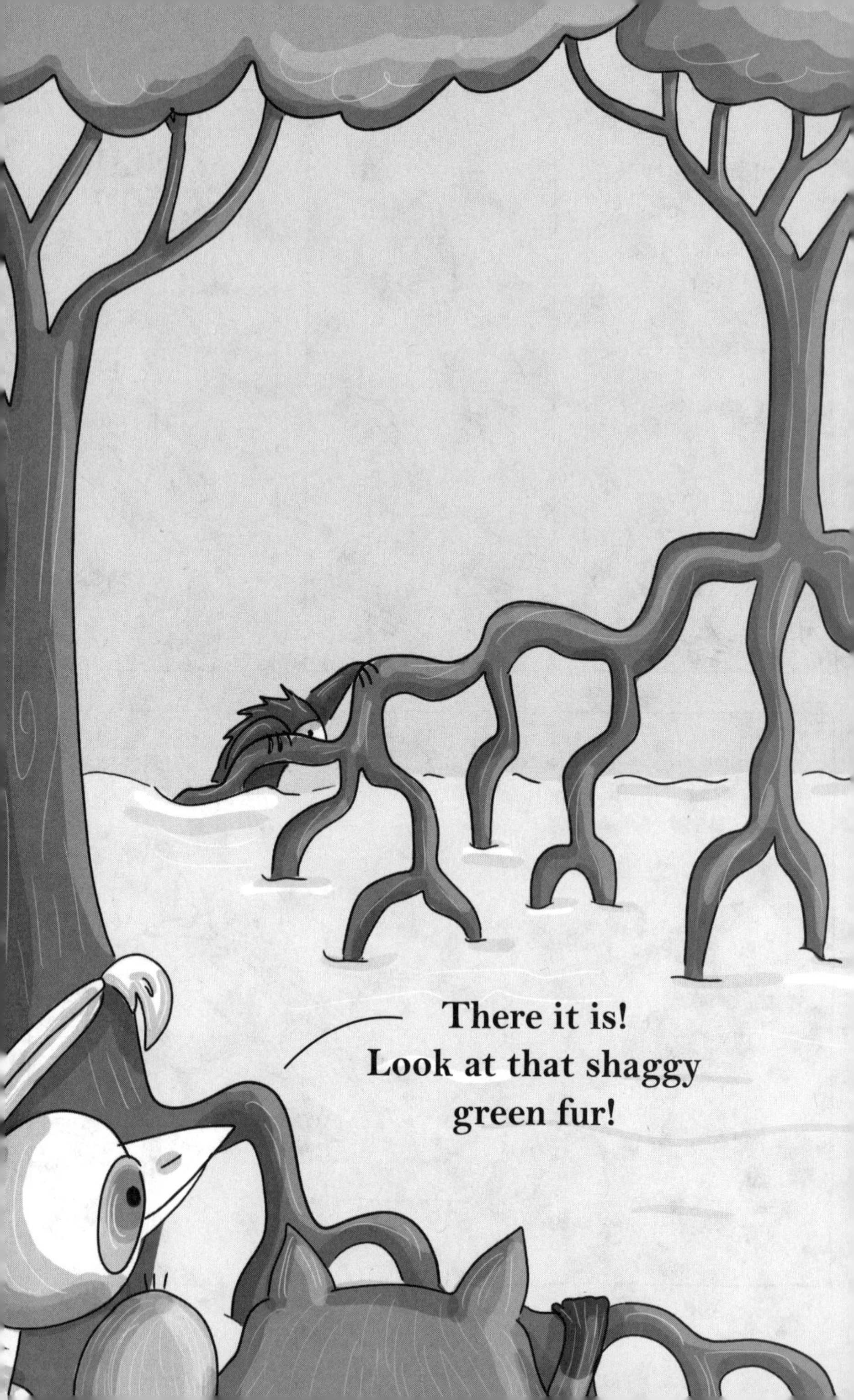
There it is!
Look at that shaggy
green fur!

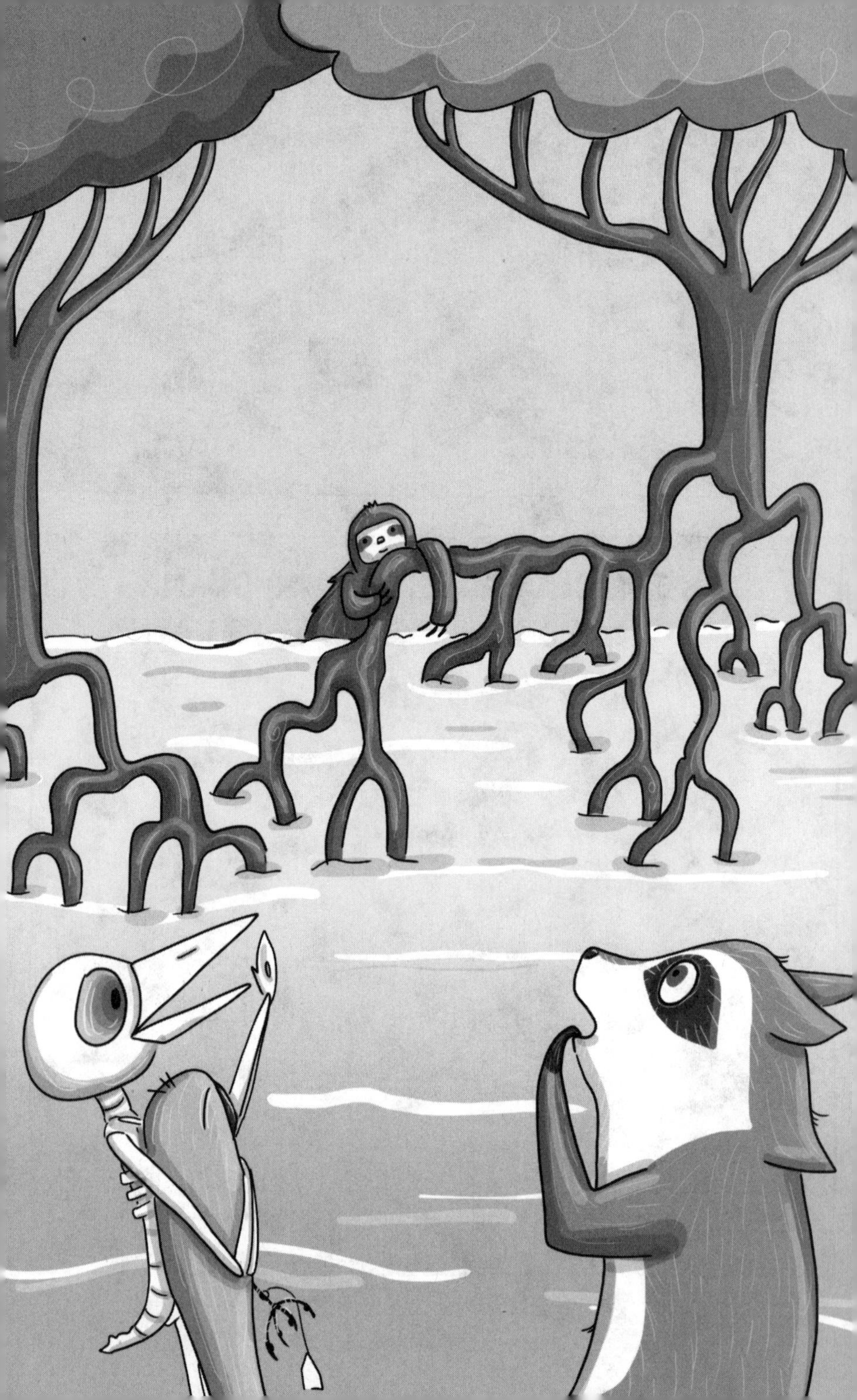

240

WELCOME TO THE MANGROVES OF ISLA ESCUDO DE VERAGUAS

We are growing trees to help reforest the island to protect endemic animals that are at risk because of habitat destruction

These endemic animals live only on this island and nowhere else in the world!

Escudo Fruit-Eating Bat
Artibeus incomitatus

Pygmy Three-Toed Sloth
Bradypus pygmaeus

Maritime Worm Salamander
Oedipina maritima

Sloths & Moths
It's a thing

Larvae feed on poo until they are are adults and fly back to the sloth

Moths live in sloth fur and eat the algae that turns sloth coats green

Once a week sloths climb down the tree to poo and moths lay their eggs in the poo

This isn't a swamp monster, Grace. It's an endangered pygmy sloth. They live only in the red mangrove forests on one teeny tiny island in Panama. This little critter must have hitchhiked its way into the museum on one of the trees.

Then why hasn't anyone noticed it before?

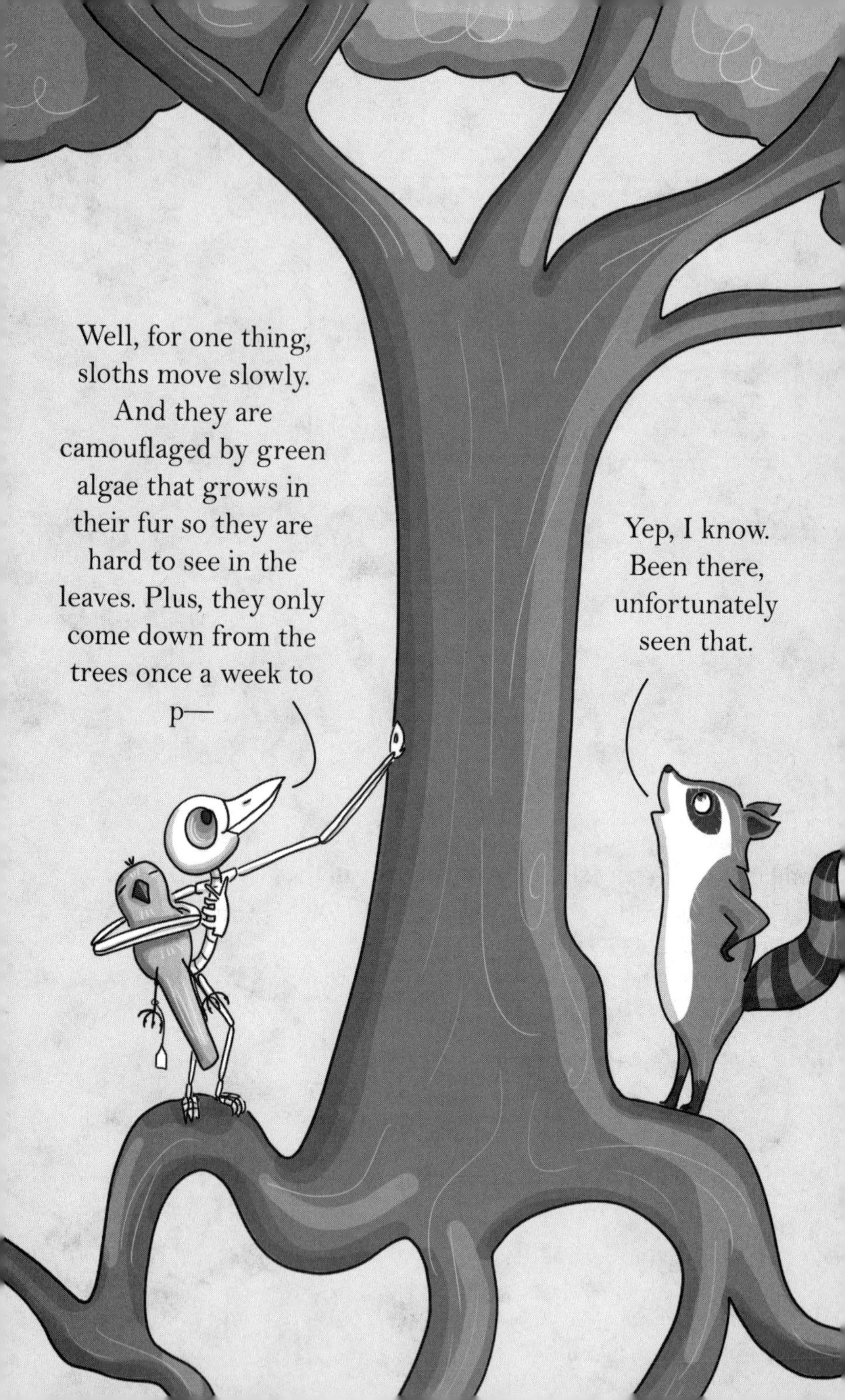
Well, for one thing, sloths move slowly. And they are camouflaged by green algae that grows in their fur so they are hard to see in the leaves. Plus, they only come down from the trees once a week to p—
Yep, I know. Been there, unfortunately seen that.

Sure, Watts, I agree with Grace too...but you have to admit the **how-are-we-going-to-get-the-museum-to-notice-the-really-well-camouflaged-sloth mystery** is fun to say.

Why do we need the museum to find the sloth anyway? It seems happy here.

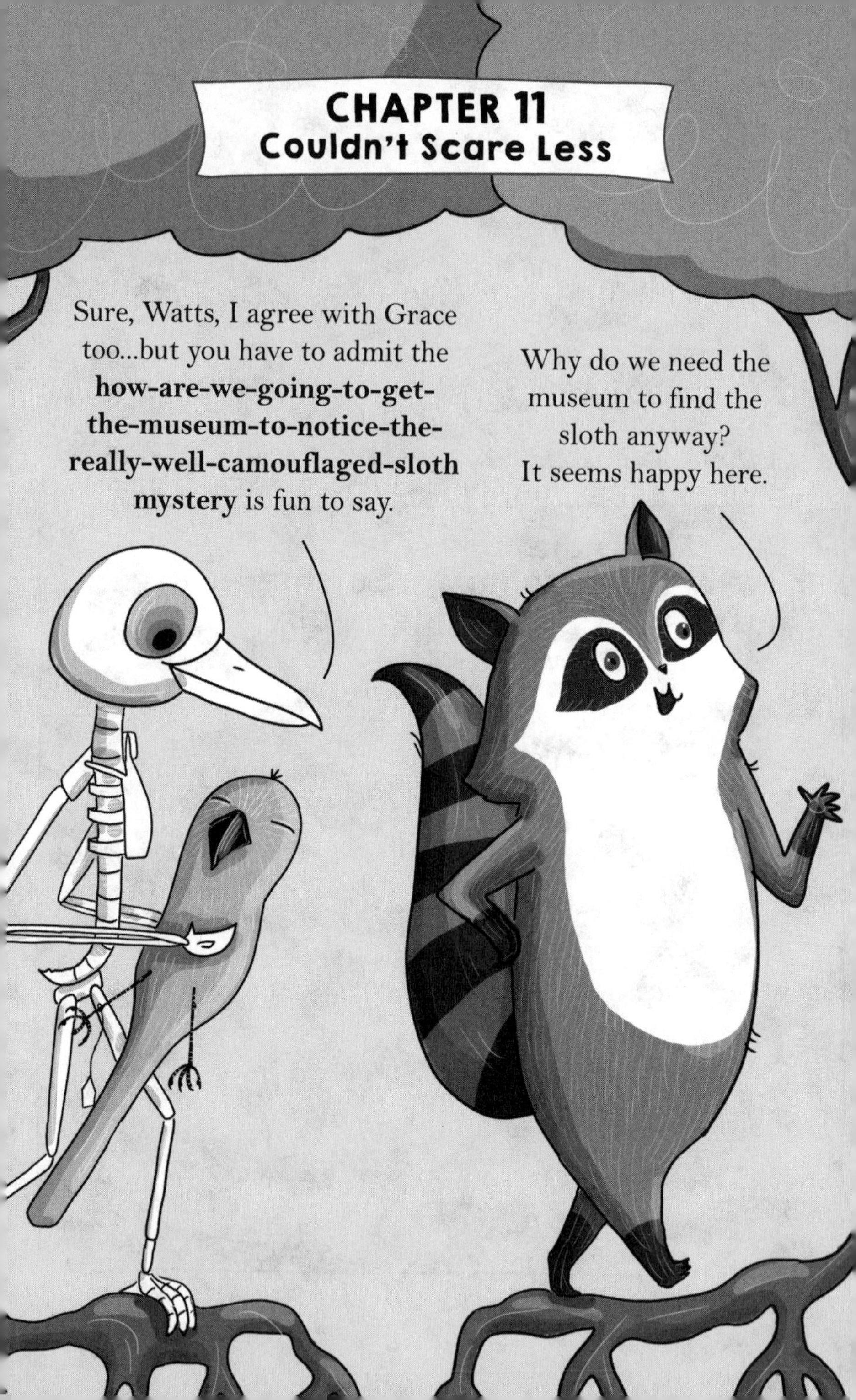

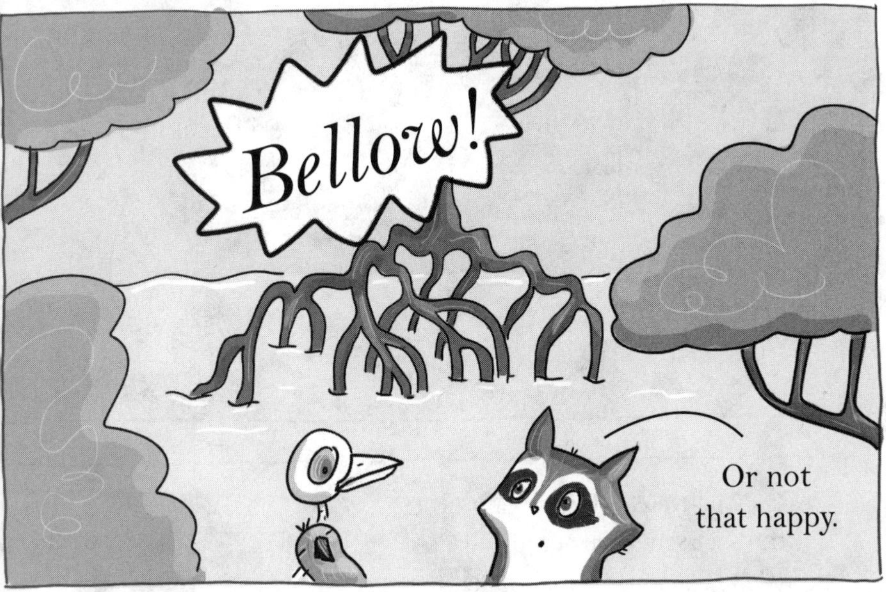
Bellow!
Or not that happy.

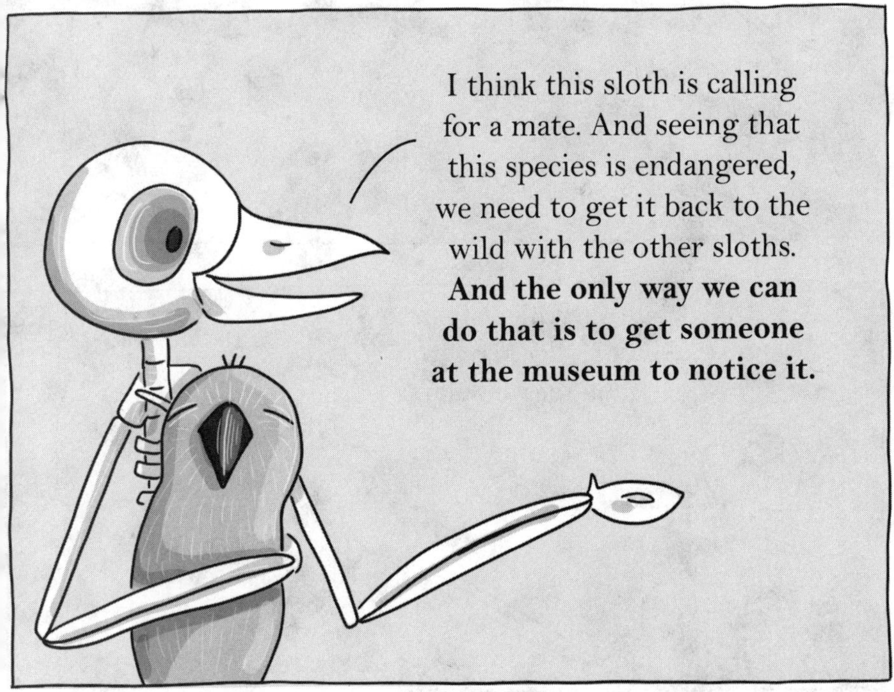
I think this sloth is calling for a mate. And seeing that this species is endangered, we need to get it back to the wild with the other sloths. **And the only way we can do that is to get someone at the museum to notice it.**

LIVING RAINFOREST & MAIN HALL

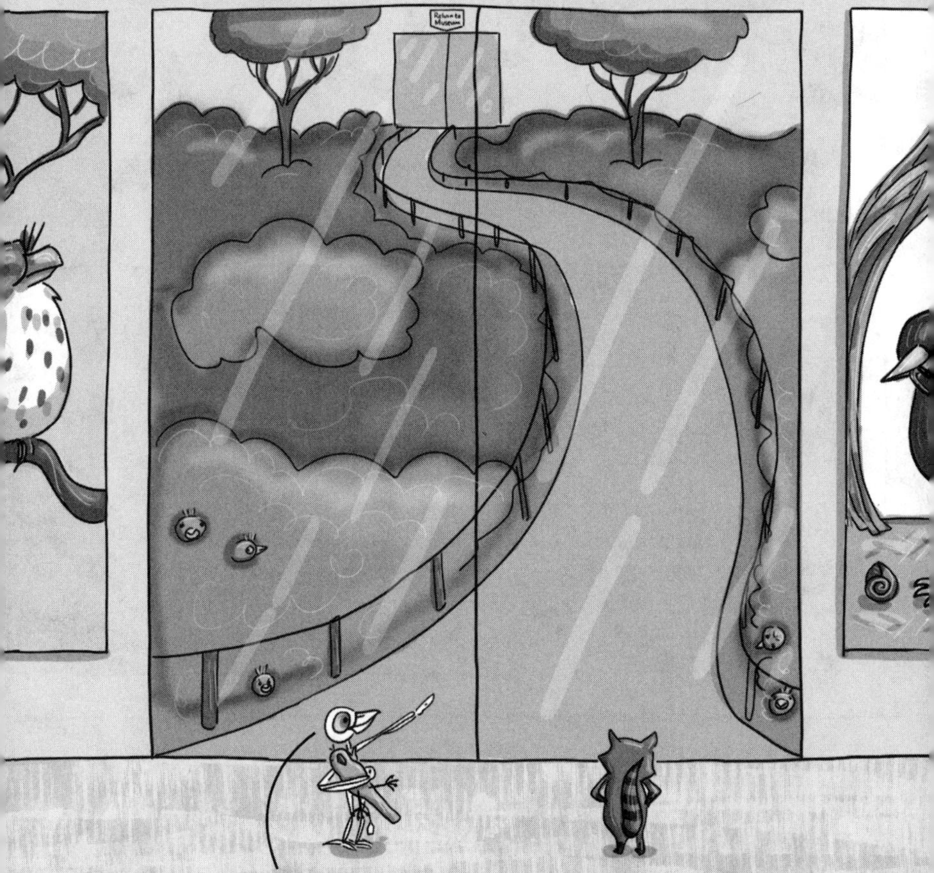

Here's the plan:
I'll distract the bowerbirds by waving Watts around on this side of the doors.

You run through the forest gallery, open the doors to the main hallway, find a good hiding spot, then bark loudly.

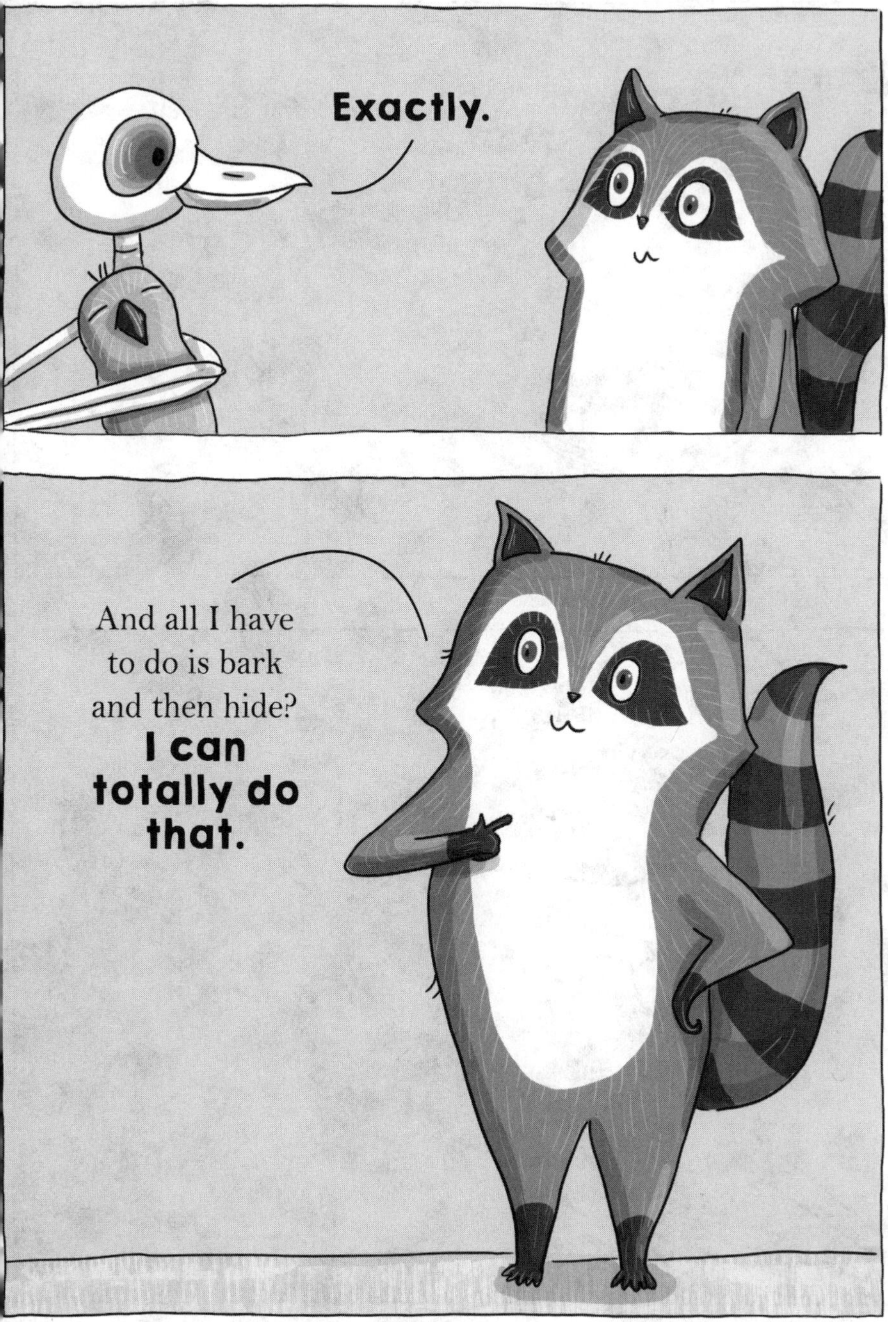
Exactly.
And all I have to do is bark and then hide?
I can totally do that.

**The museum can't get rid of a ghost...
but they can get rid of a raccoon.**

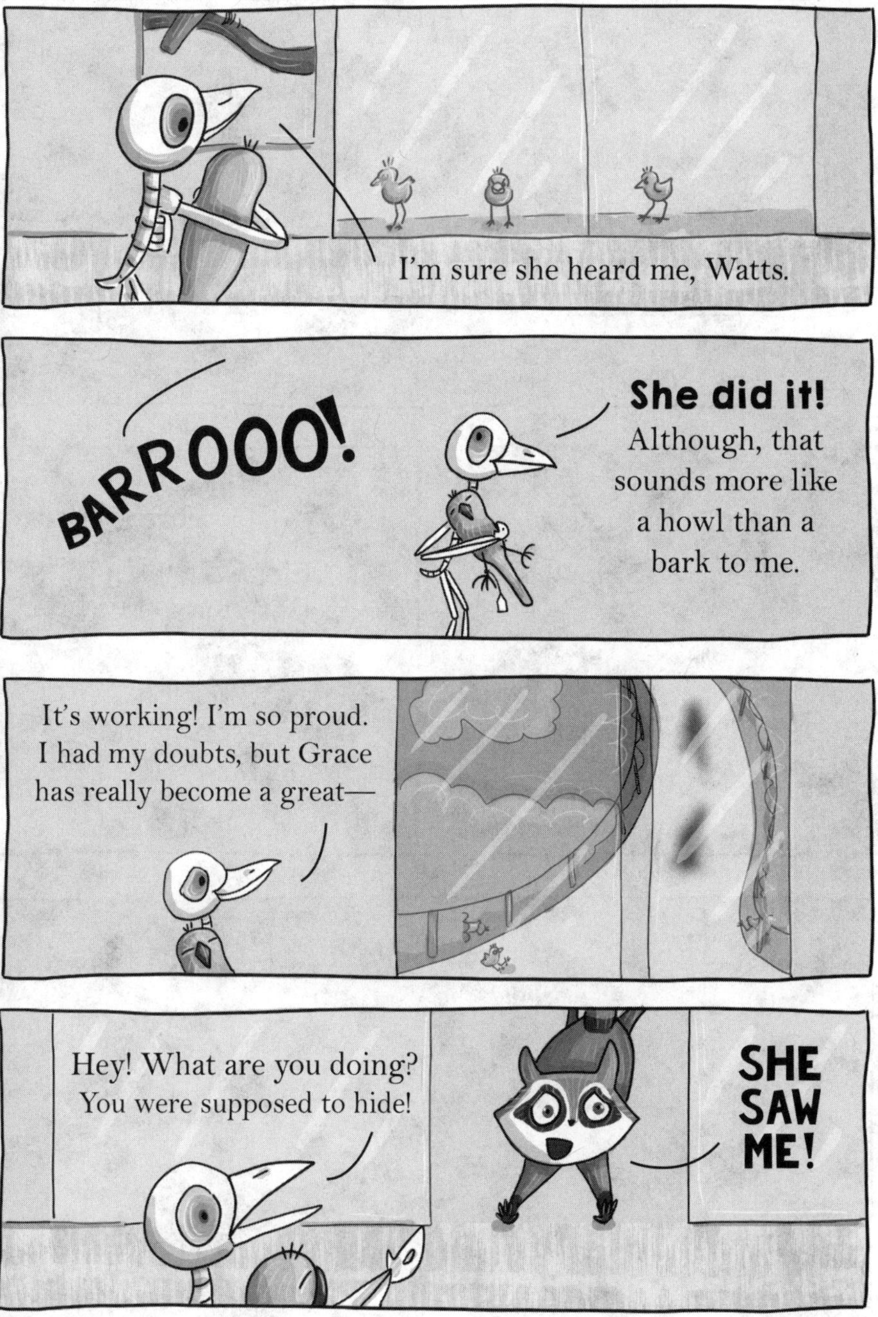
I'm sure she heard me, Watts.
BARROOO!
She did it!
Although, that sounds more like a howl than a bark to me.
It's working! I'm so proud. I had my doubts, but Grace has really become a great—
Hey! What are you doing? You were supposed to hide!
SHE SAW ME!

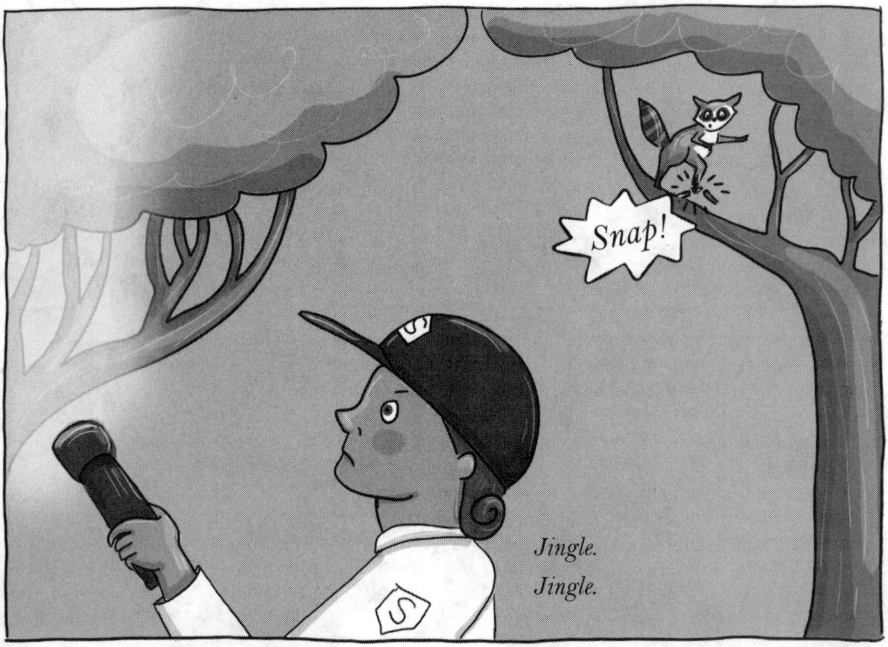
Snap!
Jingle.
Jingle.

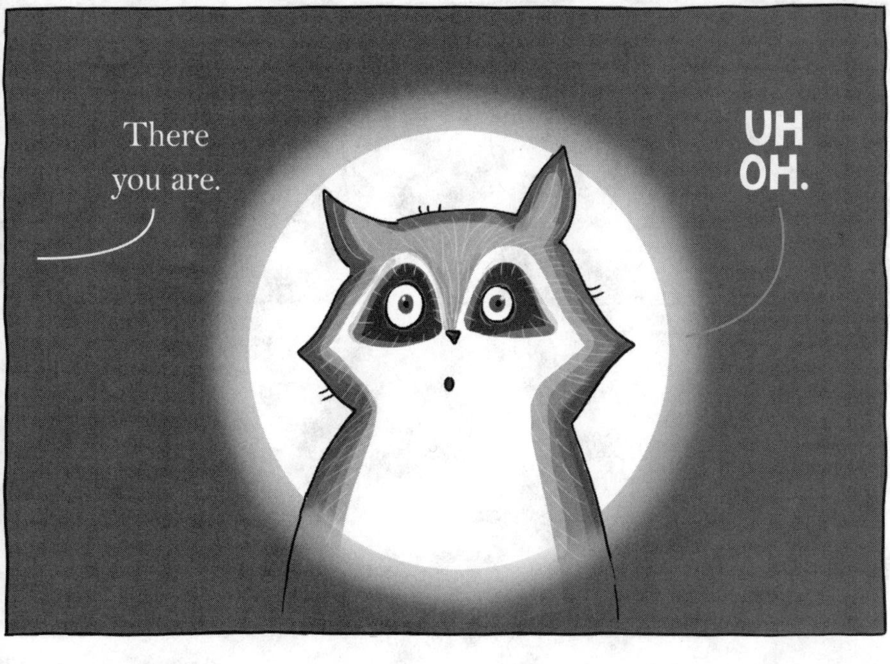
There you are.
UH OH.

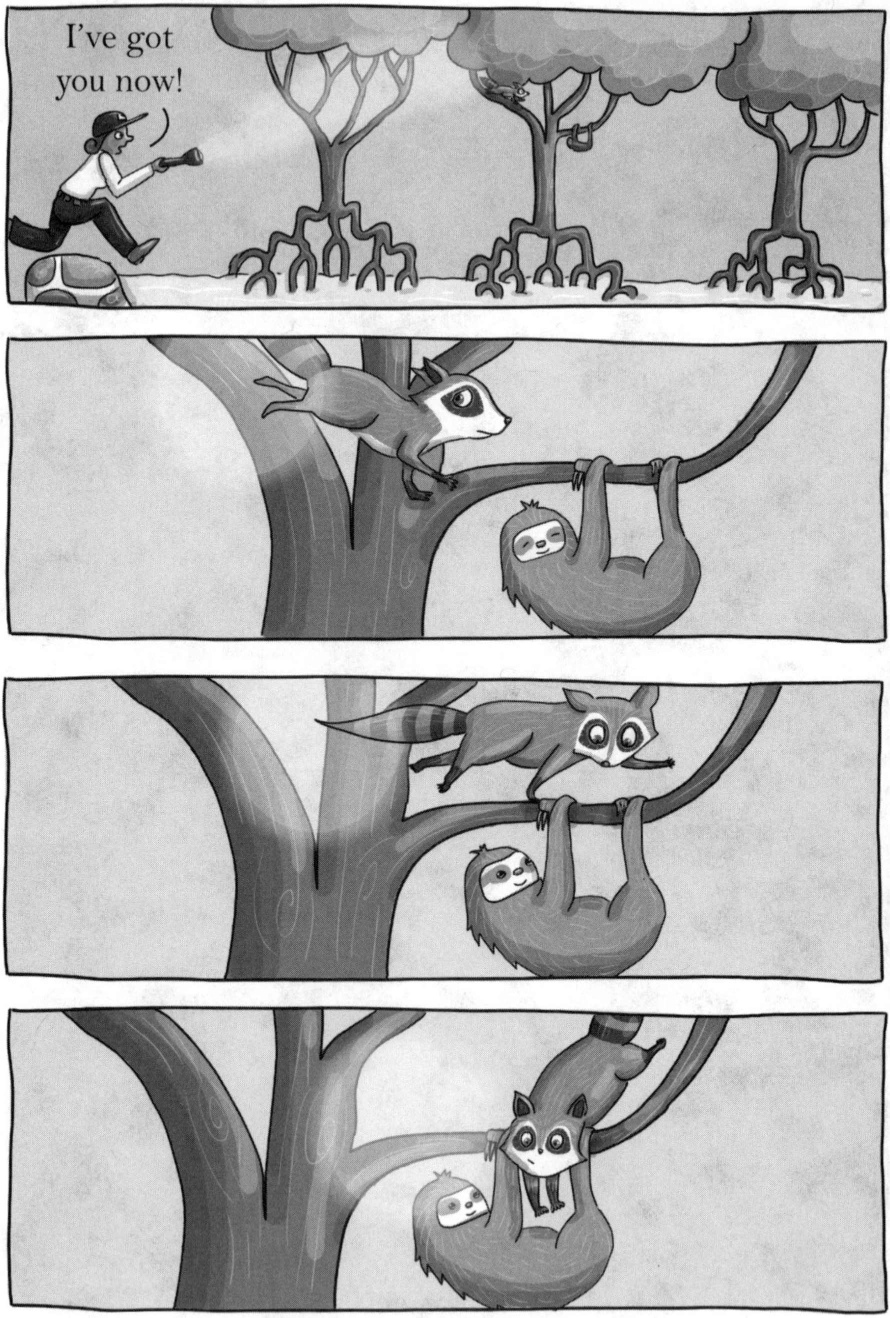
I've got you now!

AHHHHHH!!!
IT'S A MONSTER!

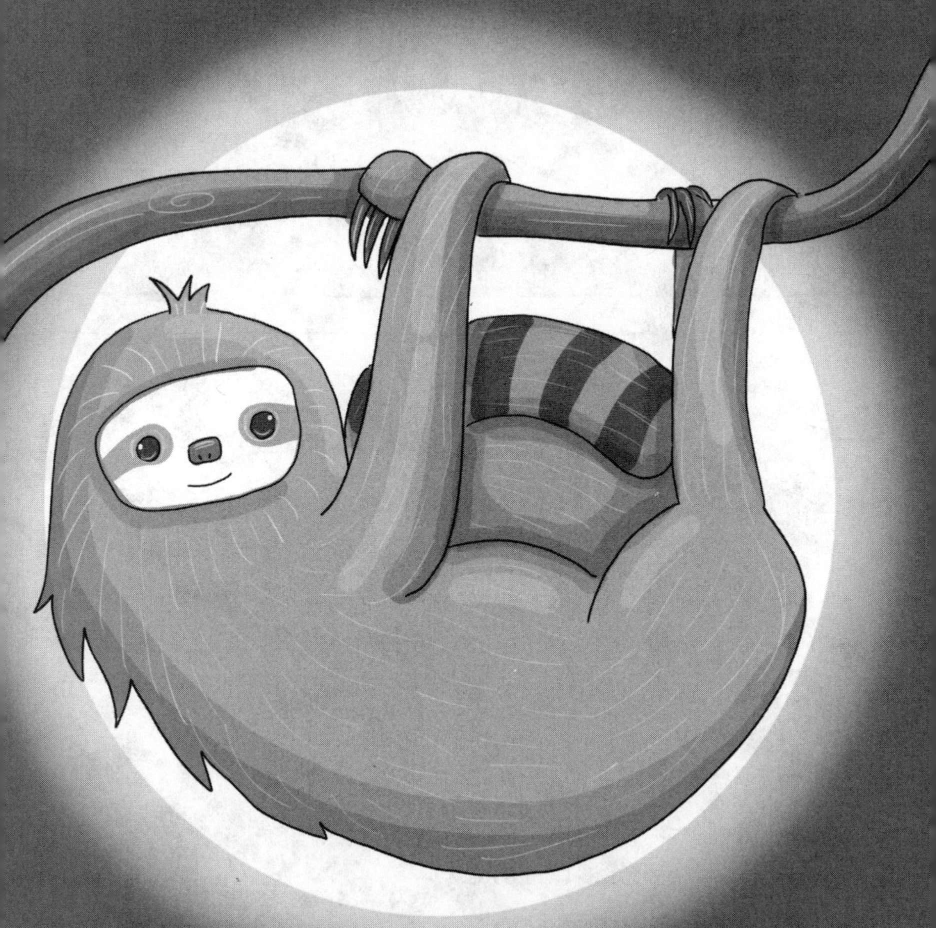

...a smiling cute monster...

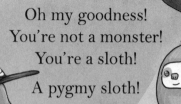

Smile!
I just need a picture
for the boss.

And I was so sure
I saw that pesky
raccoon again.

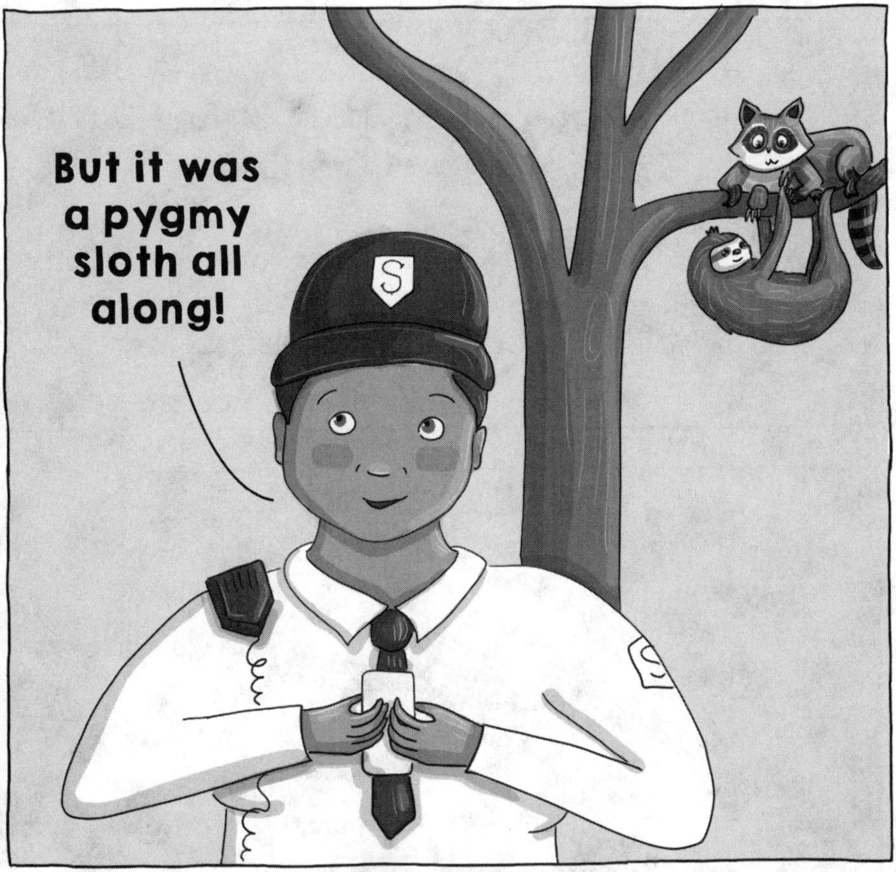
But it was a pygmy sloth all along!

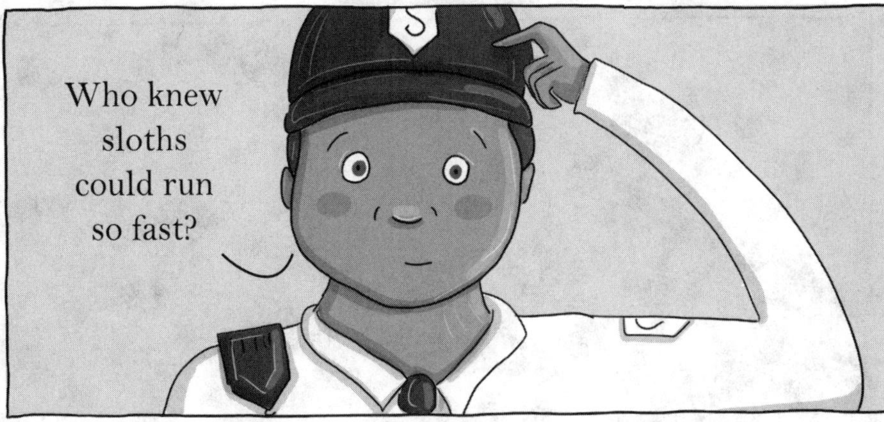
Who knew sloths could run so fast?

CHAPTER 12
A Scary-Tale Ending

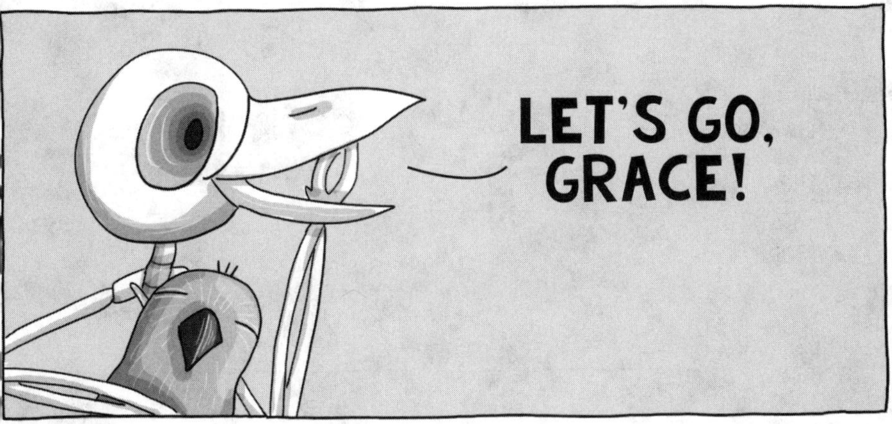
LET'S GO, GRACE!

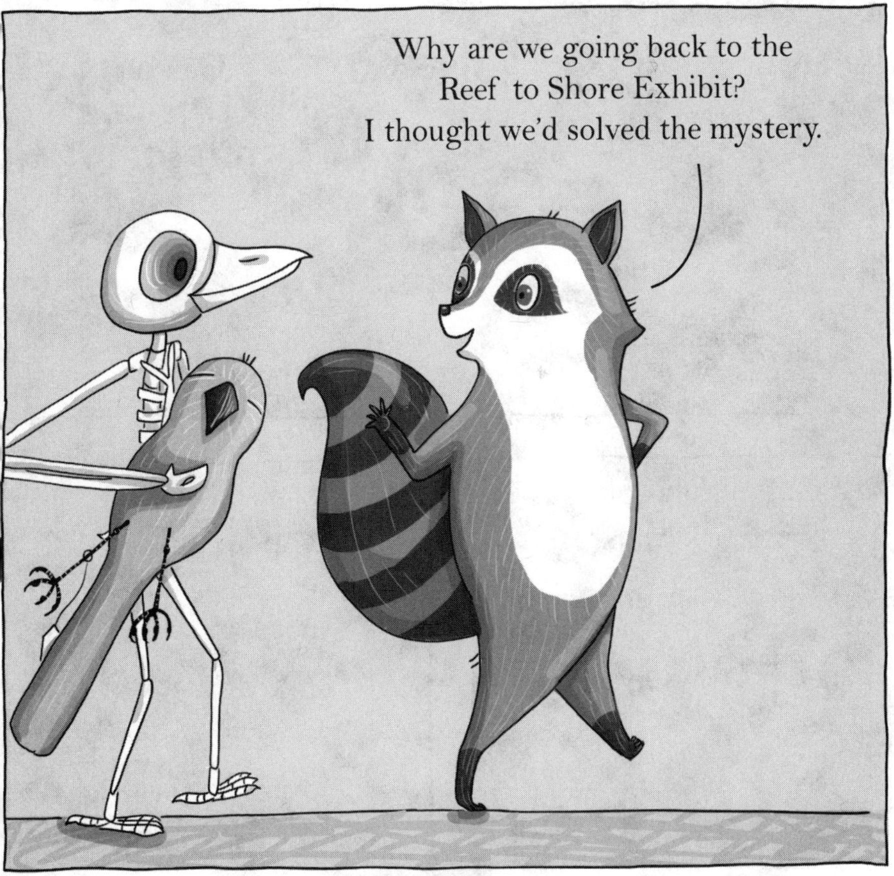
Why are we going back to the Reef to Shore Exhibit? I thought we'd solved the mystery.

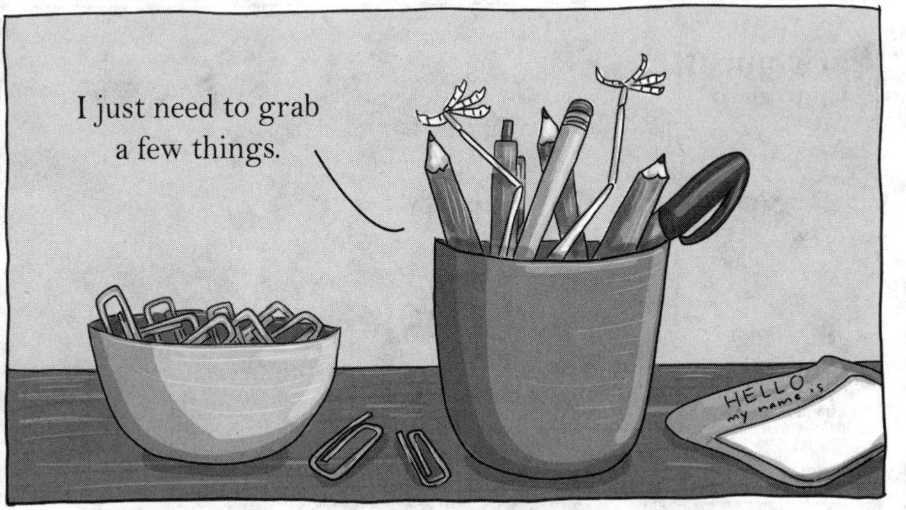
I just need to grab a few things.
HELLO my name is

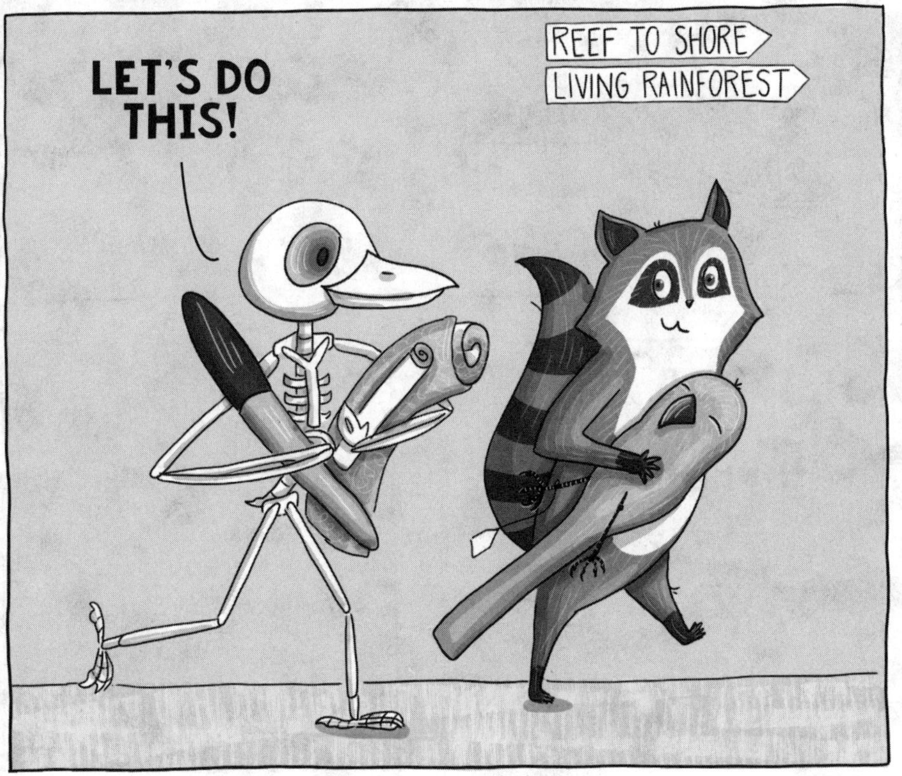
LET'S DO THIS!
REEF TO SHORE
LIVING RAINFOREST

Octopus Enrichment Program

Octopuses need mental and physical stimulation to stay healthy and happy.

Ours loves toys, games, and puzzles. What is his favorite today?

they can squeeze into tight spaces
...can survive on land for short periods
...eat a carnivorous diet of shellfish
...squirt black "ink" when scared

Algae Octopus
Abdopus aculeatus
Indian Ocean and Pacific Ocean

Hi, Nivlac.

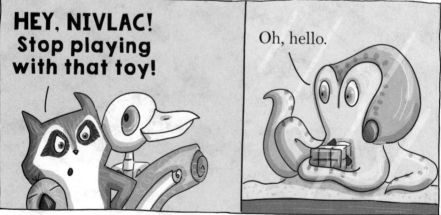

HEY, NIVLAC! Stop playing with that toy!

Oh, hello.

272

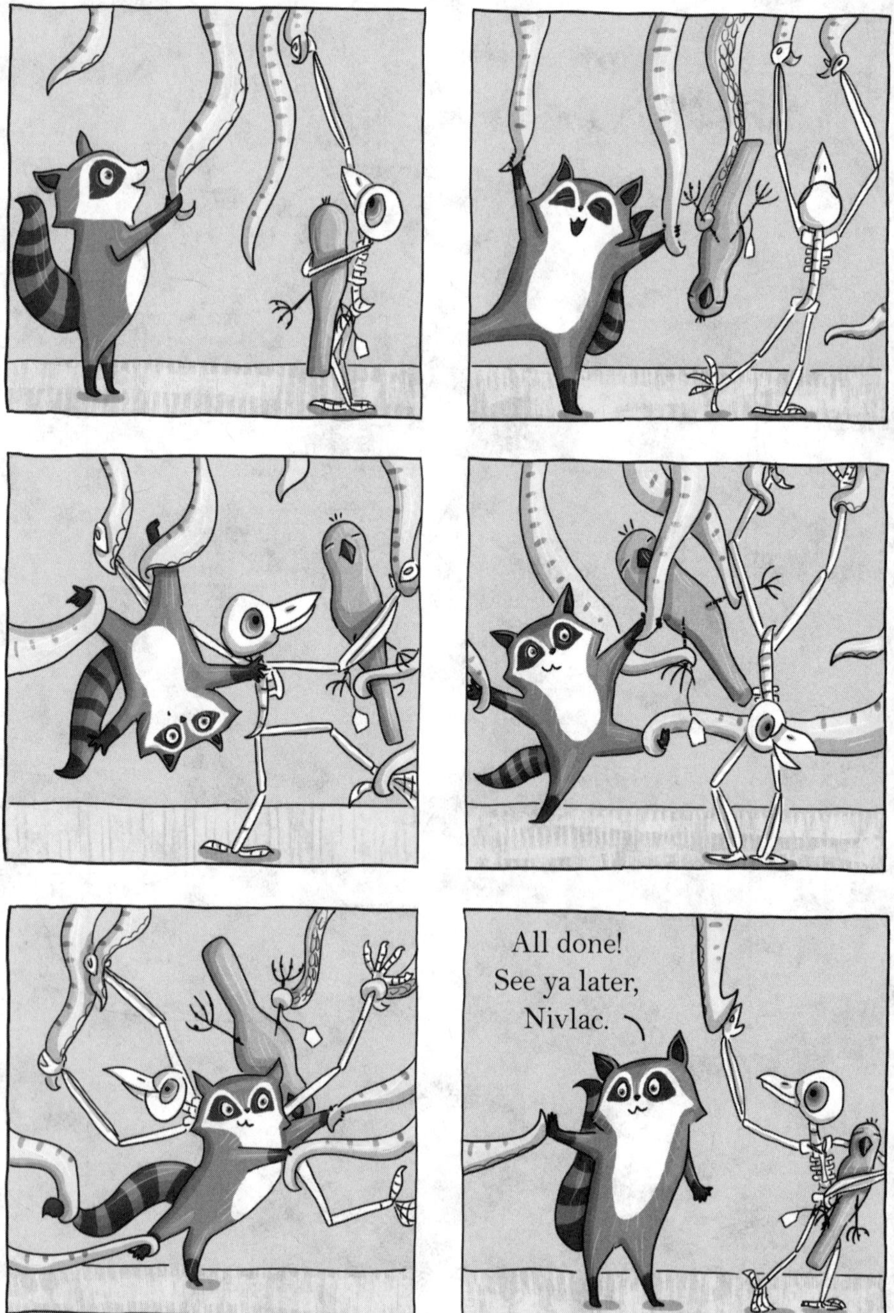
All done!
See ya later,
Nivlac.

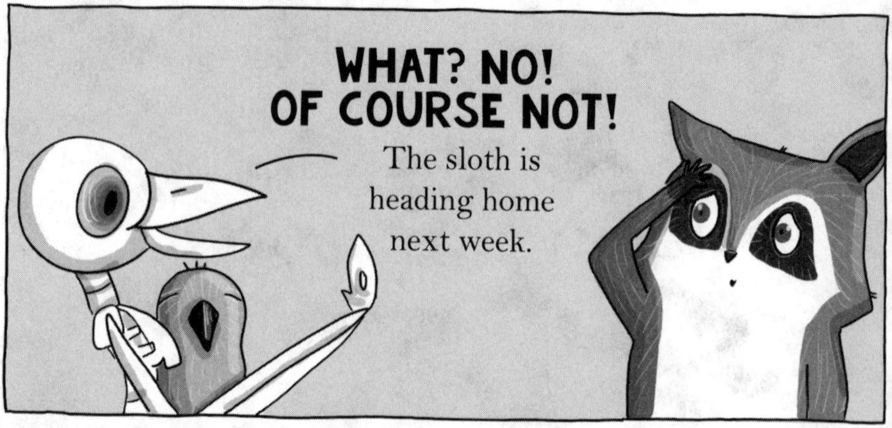
WHAT? NO!
OF COURSE NOT!
The sloth is heading home next week.

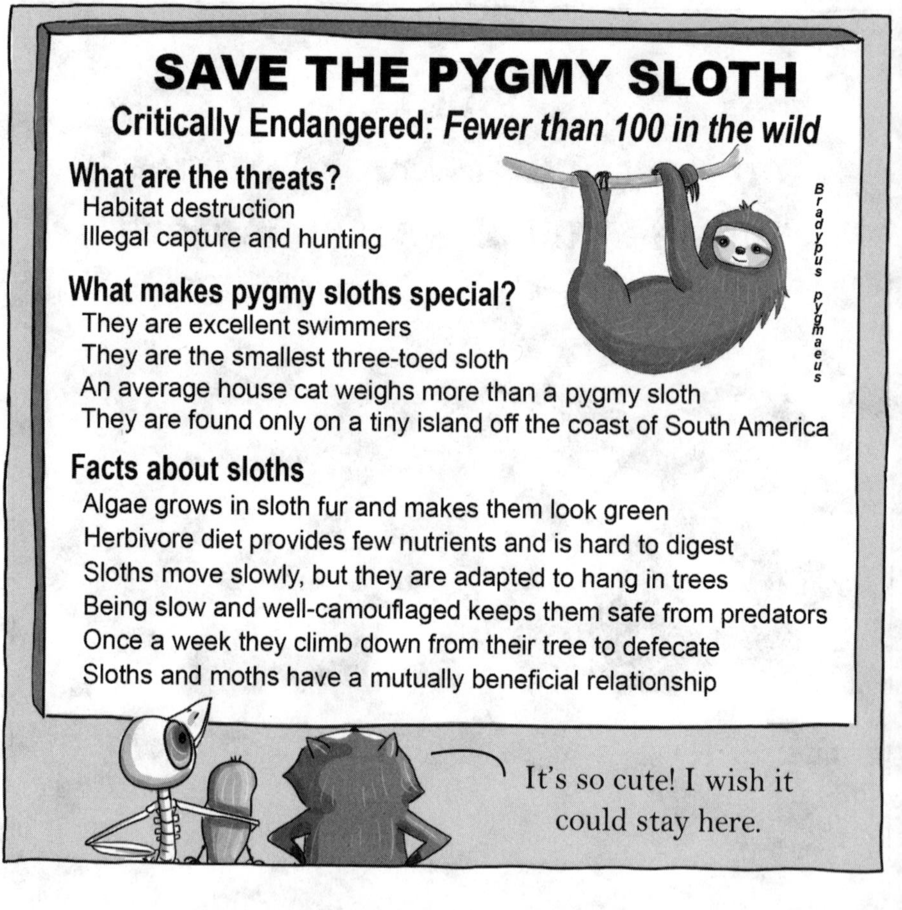
SAVE THE PYGMY SLOTH
Critically Endangered: *Fewer than 100 in the wild*
What are the threats?
Habitat destruction
Illegal capture and hunting
What makes pygmy sloths special?
They are excellent swimmers
They are the smallest three-toed sloth
An average house cat weighs more than a pygmy sloth
They are found only on a tiny island off the coast of South America
Facts about sloths
Algae grows in sloth fur and makes them look green
Herbivore diet provides few nutrients and is hard to digest
Sloths move slowly, but they are adapted to hang in trees
Being slow and well-camouflaged keeps them safe from predators
Once a week they climb down from their tree to defecate
Sloths and moths have a mutually beneficial relationship
Bradypus pygmaeus
It's so cute! I wish it could stay here.

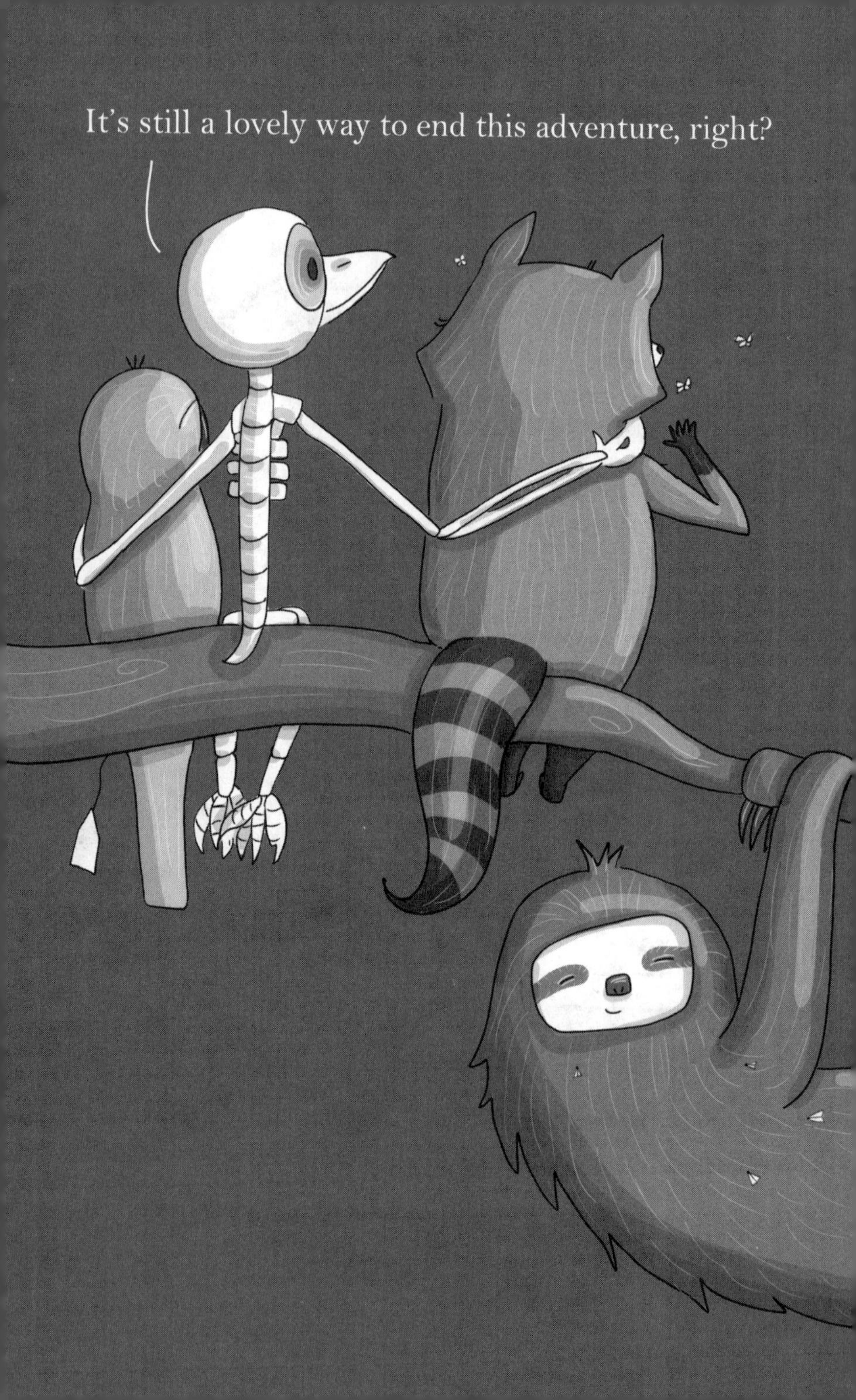
It's still a lovely way to end this adventure, right?

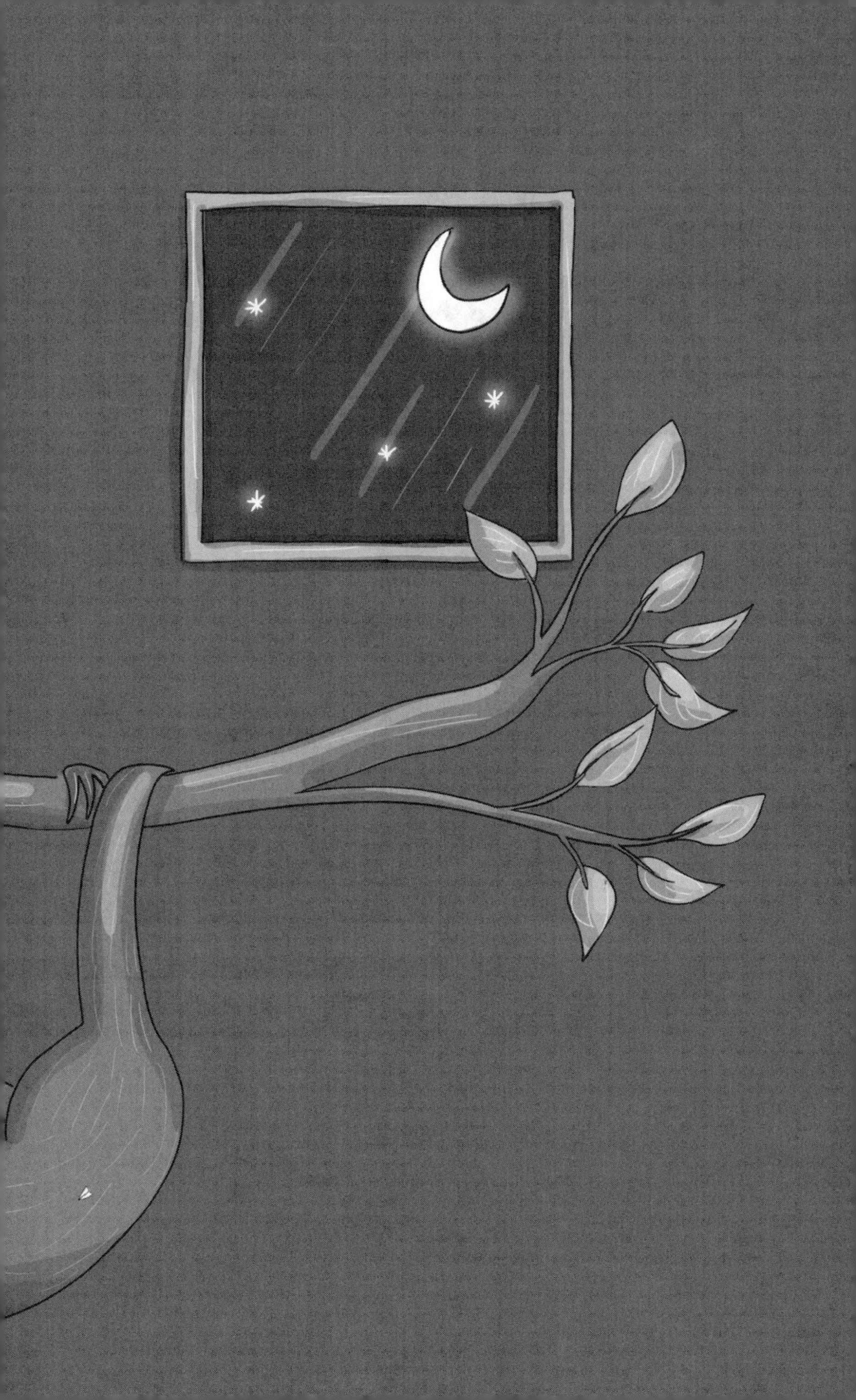

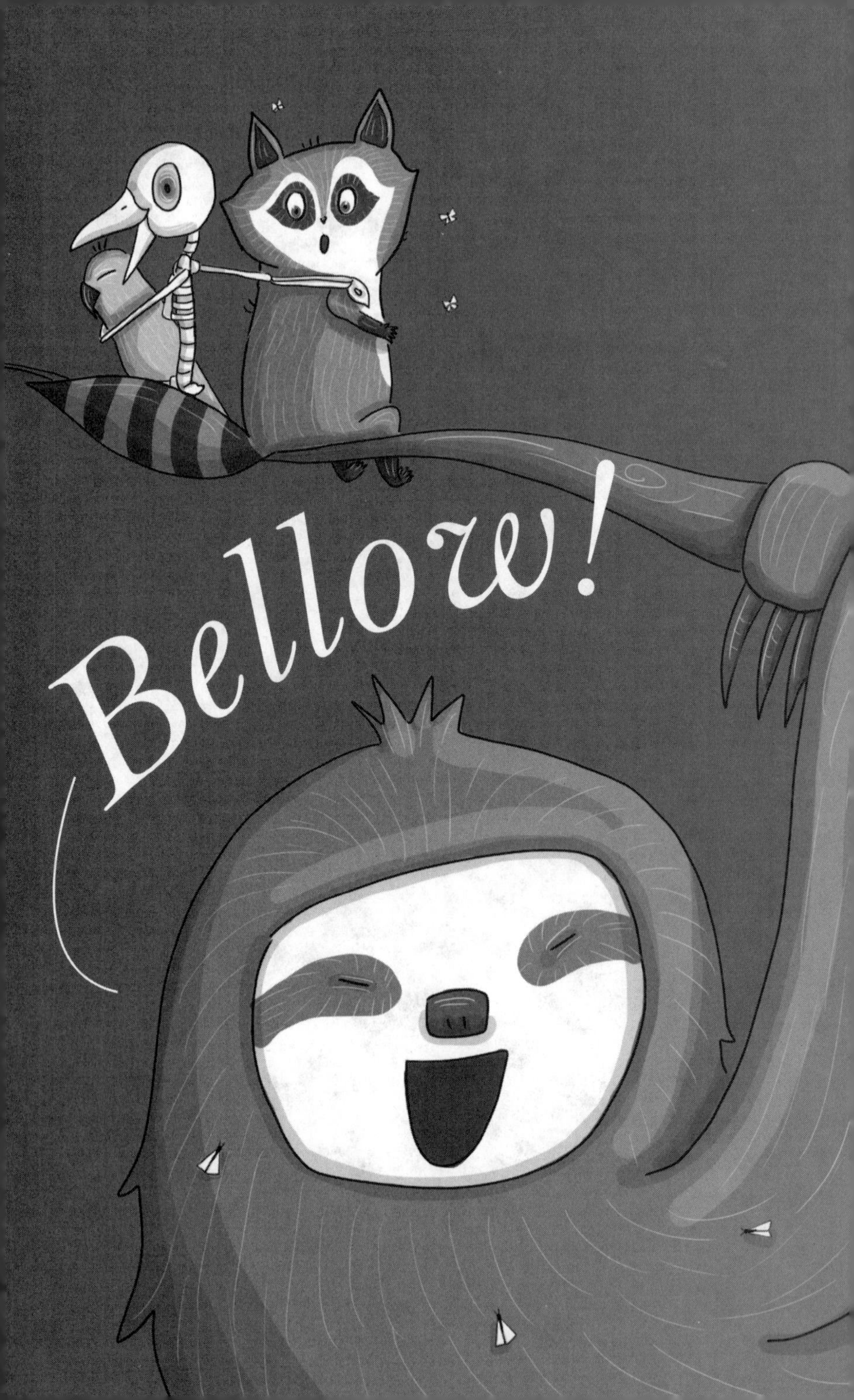
Bellow!

Etch is an imprint of Houghton Mifflin Harcourt Publishing Company.

First published by Allen & Unwin in 2019.

hmhbooks.com

The text was set in Bell MT, KG Happy Solid, and KG Summer Storm.

The Library of Congress Cataloging-in-Publication data is on file.
ISBN: 978-0-358-30933-8 hardcover
ISBN: 978-0-358-30939-0 paperback

Manufactured in the United States of America
DOC 10 9 8 7 6 5 4 3 2 1
4500818641

ACKNOWLEDGMENTS

I am grateful to all the amazing children, parents, teachers, and librarians who have written me messages, sent letters, or spoken with me at events. Your excitement helped me get through the hard parts of creating this book.

Thank you to all the booksellers for hosting me at events and selling my books—you are so important to our community and I appreciate your amazing support! Special thanks to Leesa at The Little Bookroom for her ongoing encouragement and energy . . . not just for me, but for all authors and illustrators.

Thank you to Dr. James Wood, an octopus expert who clarified a few of the finer details of octopus behavior for me. Thank you, Jodie and Sophie and the amazing team at Allen & Unwin, for creating this book with me! Thank you to Sadie and Tony for providing feedback on early (and messy) drafts of this story. Many thanks to my fellow writers and illustrators for all your wisdom and guidance, and many more to my friends for helping keep my life and family together while working on this book. And last but not least, thank you to Eric, Calvin, Tassie, and Moke for everything.